MOON CURSED

(SKY BROOKS BOOK 5)

MCKENZIE HUNTER

McKenzie Hunter

Moon Cursed

© 2016, McKenzie Hunter

McKenzieHunter@McKenzieHunter.com

ISBN: 978-1-946457-96-7

ACKNOWLEDGMENTS

~

I don't think I will ever be able to thank my family and friends enough for all their help and support throughout the process. I hope you all know I couldn't do it without you. I would like to personally thank Vanessa A. Rodriques, who helped me with the Portuguese translations. I really appreciate it.

I would like to offer a special thanks to my wonderful and helpful editor, Luann Reed Siegel, who treat each project as if it's her own.

Last, but definitely not least, I would like that thank my readers for giving me the opportunity to entertain you with my stories.

CHAPTER 1

*L*ogan sat in the chair, his gaze sweeping across the room, draped in a dark confidence that made the moment even more intense. My fingers prickled with an overwhelming need to do bodily harm to him in ways that made me a little afraid of myself. He deserved it. Every hateful and violent thought that went through my mind as I glared at him, he rightfully deserved.

He had been tasked with finding the Tre'ase that had created Maya, the spirit shade that I hosted and that was thus keeping me alive. Which he had done. But in line with most of his behavior, which seemed to be sociopathic at best, a quality he appeared oddly proud of, he'd returned with only her heart, keeping it beating with magic that was linked to his life. If we killed him, we would stop the heart and in turn kill me. Now he wanted to make a deal. I was tired of making deals with the devil.

The intense silence continued as he waited for someone to speak. The seconds became minutes, and still no one had spoken. I didn't think I was alone in being reluctant to make a deal with someone like Logan, but we didn't have a lot of choices.

"What do you feel you need and want?" Sebastian asked, although Logan didn't let that sully his mood. Logan's smug smile

1

broadened as his fingers drummed on top of the container that held the heart of the Tre'ase that had created me. He held the confidence of someone that had my life in his hands—because he did.

"Please, have a seat, we have a lot to discuss," Logan offered with pleased confidence.

"I'll stand," Sebastian said, keeping a stern gaze on him. If looks could kill, Logan would have died a thousand deaths at that time.

He shrugged. "Have it your way."

I stood, too, though I really wanted to sit. I didn't want Logan to have my life—or death—in his hands with the ability to destroy me with a simple spell.

"What do you want?" Sebastian asked, his tone rough and hard as he watched Logan intensely. This situation had quickly devolved from any hint of civility, and it was predator against predator as they assessed boundaries and looked for weaknesses. But there was a flaw; despite Logan's various weaknesses he had the upper hand and could not be divested of it.

Logan's smile blossomed, opening up to share what I was sure was a deviant and twisted wish list. "Very simple. One, I'd like these cursed marks removed from my body. They do make things difficult for me."

"Why, because they alert people that they are being magically bound to a contract and don't allow you to trick anyone into anything?" Josh offered. That was news to me, and it would have been good information to have known before I'd become involved with him. I'd assumed that they were triggered by his emotions, like that weird eye color shift thing that happened with were-animals. He hadn't taken a seat, either, but instead was switching between pacing and leaning against the counter behind Logan while intermittently sending deadly glares in his direction.

Logan smiled. "Exactly. You've noticed I'm the only one who has them. Why should I bear the marks of past mistakes that were forced on me by the dreadful witches?"

"How many did it take to invoke the curse?" Josh asked.

Logan made a face. "Thirteen."

"If these marks were given to you by thirteen witches, how are we, with one witch, going to remove them?" I asked.

Logan's attention shifted to Ethan, where it stayed for a long time before reverting to me. His tone held a cool edge. "You removed a curse done by witches before, so it stands to reason that you can do the same again. But frankly, how it is done really isn't my problem as long as it is."

Sebastian had implied that we had access to the Clostra, a book of powerful spells and the very thing we'd used in lifting the death curse witches had placed on me, accidentally lifting the ward that had kept Logan from leaving his home as well. If Logan hadn't helped with finding the Tre'ase, then we would have reversed the broken ward. We had two volumes of the set of three. Getting the third wasn't as easy as Sebastian had led Logan to believe.

The tension was so thick it was suffocating. Sebastian's eyes narrowed as they homed in on the creature that had become the pack's enemy. His jaw clenched before his lips pulled back, baring the edges of his teeth as though he was ready to strike.

Logan chuckled, placed his hand on the cylindrical jar, and smiled, a subtle reminder that he had the upper hand. The tension-filled stillness continued and he seemed to be feeding off the anger directed at him. He took his hand off the jar and stood in a dramatic gesture before clasping his hands behind him, unconcerned that he'd left the container with us.

Pacing the room, he kept his back to us and continued. "Should I go on with my second request?" No one responded. He turned and directed his attention to Sebastian and asked the question again.

Sebastian didn't speak but instead fixed Logan with the same hard stare he had given him most of the day. He took Sebastian's silence as a tacit agreement to go on.

He resumed pacing the room, a haughty smile draped over the magically modified features that disguised his actual grotesque appearance: teeth that protruded from his maw, a gruesome elongated snout that dominated his face, and horns that extended from his scalp. His usual monstrous broad build didn't lend itself to the graceful movements he was now afforded by his human form, a slim frame that moved agilely through the room. He'd changed his hair again—now it was a pale blond color with light hints of silver throughout.

But we had already stopped paying attention to him and started to concentrate on Josh. His eyes had eclipsed to a smoky color—something that happened when he called upon stronger magic. He kept doing spell after spell. I could see magic inching closer toward the jar. Then it wrapped around it like condensation before it faded away.

Each time Josh tried a spell an equal force pushed his magic away.

Logan's dark laugh filled the room as he kept his back to us. "Ah yes, did I expect anything less than the witch attempting to remove the spell? Tell me, are you having any success?" he taunted, and the glare that Josh shot in his direction indicated that he was getting to him. "I assure you, I've mastered the spell to ensure that it cannot be lifted by anyone but me. Shall I continue?"

"Go on," Sebastian urged, forcing the words out through clenched teeth.

More confident than one should have been in a room full of angry predators, Logan continued to slowly walk the length of the room. Seemingly unconcerned by our presence, he kept his back to us. He seemed to be pondering his words carefully before speaking. "Sky made a deal with me; one that she didn't fulfill. I would like her to fulfill that deal. That's my final request."

A hostile quiet overtook the room. Everyone was silent,

4

staring at Logan, who had finally turned in our direction and looked quite satisfied with himself.

In a moment of desperation, I'd sought him out in hopes that he'd remove the death spell the witches had cast on me as punishment for taking the Aufero, a protected object that had the ability to remove magic, from Marcia, the head of the Creed that governed the witches. I was still convinced it had been done in retaliation. In the process of taking it, I'd nearly drowned her, and if it hadn't been for Quell, I would have. I'd been foolish enough to consider performing a *servus vinculum* in exchange, which essentially would have bound Chris, Ethan's ex, to me. Then I could have "gifted" her to Logan. Although I hadn't agreed to it by allowing him to bind me with his magic, I'd made an implied agreement; then my guilt and conscience had caused me to change my mind. The guilt was something I dealt with on a daily basis. It was one of my darkest moments, and I refused to do anything like it.

Now he wanted us to agree to do it again. "No," I said firmly, heading for the door. "We don't have a deal."

"Ms. Brooks, I don't believe you have much of a choice," Logan said.

"Yes, I do have a choice, and it is to leave. I'm not giving you anything. You live your miserable life as it is with your goddamn marks to show that you are truly a demon and remain alone, because I refuse to give you a person to keep as a pet. And know that I will be doing everything possible to make sure that the ward is replaced and you are confined here in your home as was intended."

"I do believe you are underestimating the situation." His velvety soft voice contrasted with the harsh look he gave me.

"No, I understand the situation just fine."

He flashed me a smug grin. "Then you understand that you aren't really in a position to bargain. At this juncture, the only thing you should ask is how much time you have to deliver."

It felt like I was always dealing with compromise and watching my humanity devolve into something unrecognizable. This was one of those times I felt like the line was drawn in blood, and stepping over it would take me to a point where I couldn't return and be me, or at least happy with who I had become.

"No deal. If I have to die just so that you can continue to live this miserable life, then so be it."

I started out the door, ill prepared for the pain that shot through my heart. It felt like someone had punched through my chest, grabbed my heart, and twisted it. I dropped to my knees, panting while trying to catch my breath and diffuse the power shocking my heart, which thumped once and then stopped. Thumped again seconds later—arrhythmic, shallow. Colors flashed before me and my head swam. I couldn't pant anymore. My breaths were being siphoned off by magic and held. I struggled for every one I managed to take. The background noise was getting duller by the moment, masked by death's call. I heard Ethan scream, "Stop it!"

"I will stop when we have an agreement."

I didn't need to see it to know the tapestry on his arm was moving, the marks rolling in a slow swirl as they did when he prepared to lock someone into an agreement by which they were magically bound. I didn't want that for my pack.

"No. Don't agree," I managed to pant out as darkness drifted over me, casting its nebulous wrath.

"We agree," Sebastian said.

Magic unraveled from around me, my heart pumped a little faster, and the breathing—although labored—finally came. The heavy feeling of my body made it difficult for me to find the resolve to stand up. I lay on the floor, contemplating how fast I would have to move to get to the heart, save it, and kill Logan. But that was the problem—if I killed Logan, I might as well not have the heart, as it would be of no use to me. He had linked himself to it, so the moment he died, it would, too, and so would I. *Fuck.*

I finally came to my feet and looked around the room, feeling the wispy air of the magic that now bound my pack to their agreement with Logan. It brushed against me, sending goose bumps up my arm, and the remnants of it lingered in the air. A sick look of satisfaction marked Logan's face, and there wasn't anything I wanted more than to wipe it off. The thirst for revenge left a dank taste in my mouth. I was still thinking about it even as Sebastian and Josh walked past me and out the door. My eyes fixed on Logan, thinking of the million ways I wanted to inflict pain on him. And the thousand ways I planned to kill him.

Ethan's lips brushed against my ear when he spoke. "Come on, let's go."

As we walked to the car, anger and frustration melded together. We were screwed.

"Are we really going to do this?"

"We don't have a lot of options, Sky," Sebastian said.

"Of course we do. We don't do it."

"Do you think he was bluffing in there?" Sebastian snapped. He wore his frustration heavier than anyone else, and it marred his face.

"He was going to let you die," Ethan offered, his voice tight and strained. "What were you thinking?"

"I was thinking that I didn't want to give him the upper hand."

"He has the upper hand!"

"We don't even know where Chris is," I said. "And do you think Samuel is going to give us the third Clostra again so that we can remove a curse from a Tre'ase?"

I could see everyone's wilted frustration on their faces. This was a hard situation, and while they were probably thinking about how to solve it, I couldn't get the taste of revenge out of my mouth and thoughts of it out of my head. We'd screwed up by lifting the curse that the witches had placed on me and in turn removing an unknown number of curses. The vampires freely walked in the daytime without any aversion to the sun. We'd broken the ward that kept all the elven creatures in the dark forest and removed the ward that kept the Tre'ases restricted to their homes instead of roaming the world freely and performing countless atrocities that we didn't know about.

Ethan was right, Logan had the upper hand. And I couldn't help but wonder, what else could come from us removing his markings and giving him free rein to bind people without their knowledge? My pack made the world worse each time they tried to help me. The guilt of it was getting harder to deal with.

~

Ethan and I drove away from Logan's in tension-filled silence that continued to the point where I couldn't stand it.

"What—"

"Sky, please. Not now." He kept his eyes on the road. Platinum rolled over them each time he looked in my direction, and his frown deepened. I hated the quiet and the unpleasant discord that existed between us. When he stopped in my driveway, I got out of the car and went to the front door of the house. He exited and went around to the back. I got to the window in time to see him strip down, near the side of my house, grateful once again that I didn't live close to a neighbor and that I had compromised open lawn space for privacy when I'd purchased the home. As soon as he shifted, he ran deep into the woods, darting around the trees and receding farther into the woodland area. I thought that maybe he needed a moment alone. I certainly needed one to deal with the lingering animosity that existed between us. I also needed a minute to figure things out with Logan.

Maybe he'd be more amenable to us removing the marks even if we didn't bring him Chris. They were both terrible options, but removing the marks was the lesser of two reprehensible requests. We were faced with removing a curse that had been performed by thirteen witches. The gnawing feeling in my gut led me to believe there were more layers to that story. The spell we'd used removed the curse that had been placed on me by the Creed and made more powerful with Ethos's magic. At that time, we knew him as just a purveyor of dark magic, but we later found out he was a Faerie. His magical boost was removed by that spell. What the hell type of curse had they performed that could withstand that? If the Clostra couldn't remove it, what could?

I didn't like the Creed. They were power hungry and deceitful, but if thirteen had cursed him, that meant that they'd found his ways to be particularly dangerous. Witches were a lot of things, but unwarrantedly cautious wasn't one of them. At some point, some had felt the need to warn others that any agreements they entered into with him were sealed with magic and had consequences. Logan's marks were the only thing that allowed those dealing with him to know that they were making a magically bound deal. If we removed them, he'd be free to trick people into agreements.

The idea of tricking people bothered me to my core, but Logan's obsession with Chris bothered me even more. Of all the deals he could have made and all the things he could have bargained for, why her? He had the ability to change his appearance and appeal to any woman he would like, but he wanted her. Was it because, no matter what face he chose, Chris knew the monster behind the glamours and wanted nothing to do with it? Once, he'd taken on an appearance similar to Ethan's, one that she had rejected. I suspected in doing so, she had become his most desired prize—a forbidden fruit he was determined to get.

The most disturbing thing about him was his warped obsession with and appreciation for pain. I couldn't even imagine how he'd combine that with his possession of Chris, who had on multiple occasions said she dealt with pain well. She prided herself on her ability to do it; I considered it the result of a very troubled past.

Ethan had moved so far into the bosky area that I couldn't see him anymore. Most of my neighbors, the few that I had, didn't bother to come in my direction. David was the only one who did, and he knew what we all were. He attempted to make it seem like it wasn't a big deal, but it was, and his performance of trying to downplay how disturbed he was by it was fair at best. I didn't blame him if he showed how freaked out he was about it every time he saw me. He had every right to be. He'd been introduced to a world that was darker and deadlier than the one he knew—quite a lot to deal with. I had effectively become the weird woman in the neighborhood. Even the moms and their teen daughters who were too friendly and always had some form of food to bring over as an excuse to see Steven no longer came around, as he'd moved out.

The sharp pang still existed each time I thought about him being gone. He was the brother I'd never had, the confidant I needed, and the person I felt the most comfortable with. Even Josh, whom I considered my closest friend, didn't bring me that level of comfort. Was Ethan supposed to fulfill that role? We'd only been together for a few days and we were still getting used to each other. Anyway, the last thoughts I wanted to have about Ethan were brotherly ones. How could mercurial, abrasive, domineering Ethan ever fill Steven's role? I laughed inwardly: how in the world did I end up with a person like Ethan?

But Ethan hadn't become that way overnight. He'd been that way from the first time I'd met him, so I couldn't feign surprise— he was the exact same way he was from day one, with very little deviation from it.

I took another look outside; I didn't see Ethan. I grabbed my tablet and headed out the back door. I needed the fresh air, and I wanted to be there when Ethan finally emerged from the woods. As I moved deeper into the woodland, I closed my eyes, inhaling the crisp air fragranced by strong scents of oak and pine. It bathed my senses and was calming. The woods had become a very comforting thing to me, and at times so had my wolf.

I breathed in again before accepting the other waves of sensation that rolled over me. That odd tug, a pull that seemed to mysteriously guide me to Ethan. It had been that way since we'd performed a very strong and dangerous spell to remove the dark elf magic he'd inherited from his grandmother. It had left us with an odd connection. I ignored the fact that both of us were connected to death and darkness in a very strange way; that portentous energy might be the very thing that was the source of our mystical link. Diablerie—it was essentially what Ethan and I were. It had been given a medley of unique and beautiful names, but what it boiled down to was we were dark magic and death intertwined and interlinked.

Ethan stopped running once he sensed me, smelled me, or did whatever he seemed to do to always be able to find me. His ability to locate me predated the magic we'd shared and was something I'd always wondered about. He turned and trotted back in my direction. When he was close enough, he bumped his nose lightly into my hip—or rather my lower side. He was a massive wolf. I looked around again for neighbors. Anyone seeing a wolf would be alarmed—one that size would definitely frighten them.

He lowered his head and grabbed my pants and tugged at them. "I don't want to change."

Pulling back his lips, he snarled.

"Yeah, yeah. You're scary. Vicious. Terrifying. Carry on." I waved my hand toward the woods before taking a seat next to a tree and powering on my tablet. I had just started reading a book on it when Ethan bumped my leg with his head.

"I said no. Ethan, I don't want to change. I need to stay like this." And I did. Right now I didn't need the comfort of my wolf, I needed things to be intense and scary. Intense and scary made me think. I wanted my body to react to being in a state of high alert because I needed to figure out how to get out of this mess. My wolf was an escape—I didn't want to escape now.

He growled.

"Eek. Now you're super scary." I rolled my eyes and returned to my book. He nudged the tablet and knocked it to the ground before turning and trotting away. "Real mature. Bad wolf!" I shouted. Yelling might have eased some of my frustration, but it was pointless. It was Ethan—if I'd whispered it while sirens blared in the background, he would have heard it.

Forty-five minutes later, a naked Ethan emerged from the thicket. I stood and watched, waiting for his tense frown to relax, the menacing furrow of his brow to disappear, or the anger radiating off him to ease. It was no different than it had been in the car. Nothing had eased. The frown and anger had claimed his features and everything about him was coiled. I inhaled the fragrant oak and pine scented air again, trying to find the same comfort that it had brought before. It wasn't as soothing now, tainted by the primal force that was Ethan.

As he approached, I was reminded of the symbiotic relationship he had with his wolf. Often he gave into the primordial allure of the animal and seemed more wolf than man. The gray danced over his eyes and he stopped walking, closed his eyes, and took a deep breath. When he opened them, there wasn't much that had changed. Inches from me, he kept stepping forward, putting his hand on my waist as he walked me back until I was pressed firmly into the tree. The ragged edges of the bark pricked into my skin.

He remained silent, appraising me for a long time before he buried his head in the curve of my neck. My fingers stroked through his hair as his face moved to mine and he kissed me, gently at first and then more fervently. When he pulled away, I tried to decipher the look on his face, but there wasn't anything readable. Ethan always had difficulty controlling his emotions, but this time they were particularly unconstrained, turbulent and poorly controlled, and he was struggling. He rested his face in the curve of my neck again and inhaled my scent before burying his face in even closer. After a few minutes, he kissed me tentatively on the neck. He brushed light kisses on my cheek and journeyed over my jawline until he met my lips. He crushed his into mine as though he was seeking to expunge his emotions and seek some reprieve from them. He pulled away slightly, his tongue sliding over my lips, tasting them.

"Don't do anything like that again."

"Ethan," I responded, letting my lips brush against his as I spoke, needing the connection because I felt like something was wrong. Things were off. I pressed the palm of my hand against his face, caressing it.

He took both of my hands in his and cradled them against his chest. His gentle action was a direct contradiction to his strident voice. "No. There is nothing to discuss. Next time we are anywhere near Logan, you say nothing. You do nothing. You sit there with a smile and, if you need to, clamp your hands between your legs and don't do a damn thing. I don't care what you do, but you *will* remain silent." And with that, he pushed from the tree, turned from me and headed toward the house. He grabbed his clothes and quickly put them on while I remained against the tree, unsure how to react.

"Ethan."

He kept walking, his long stride increasing the distance between us. I yelled his name again and he ignored me and disappeared into the house. I should have waited longer before I followed him in. The inferno that had started in my chest was fighting to get out—anger running just as hot and volatile as his. The closer I got to the house, the fierier it became.

"Wait a goddamn minute," I barked as soon I entered the house. Ethan rested with his back against the kitchen counter, his arms crossed over his chest. His eyes narrowed and then settled on me.

"I am not a child. You don't just tell me to sit down and shut up. Today didn't go as expected. I can't change that. I was trying to fix the situation."

"But you didn't fix it! Instead I watched you writhe on the

ground for thirty-six minutes, trying to stay alive. No, Skylar, 'sit down and shut up' is exactly what you will do in any meetings dealing with Logan that you accompany us to. This is not a suggestion. It's not up for discussion. It's a command. As a member of the pack who is responsible for the safety of it, I have spoken. End of discussion."

I have spoken. Command. Rage pricked at my skin and started to unfurl into something that wasn't going to end well. I made an attempt to calm it, taking several deep, cleansing breaths. But it was there, blazing and ready to find a target—Ethan. This was so far from the end of the discussion—it was the beginning of a fight ignited by our discord that was going to escalate to something as uncontrollable as a forest fire. Ethan had given himself over to anger, wearing his emotions so close to the surface he'd never had sufficient control over them, and I was sure he had the desire to keep it that way. The breaths I'd taken had done little to smother my anger. It rampaged through me, and if I didn't get a handle on it, there wasn't any way it was going to end in anything but a disaster. The fact that I wanted to punch him in the mouth was evidence of it.

"Ethan." My tone softened, a wispy sound. I stepped closer to him, and caressed his cheek with my hand. The heat of his anger radiated off him. He was in a bad place. Taking several steps back, I slowly removed my clothes. He didn't look in my direction; his eyes focused on the wall across from him. I shifted to my wolf, moved toward him, and nudged his leg like he'd done mine earlier and then tugged on his pant leg. With a heavy sigh, he yanked off his clothes and I moved back, giving him room to shift. I padded back to the living room, which had a lot more open space than the kitchen, and lay in the middle of the floor. He hesitated before he moved, and then he approached slowly, each step measured and hesitant, losing the typical lithe, predaceous rhythm. Once he was within a few inches of me, he relaxed next to me. His heavy paw rested on me, and soon he'd moved until most of his body was

14

over mine. He licked my face. *Ugh, I hate when they do that. So gross.*
He made a noise and then did it again. I snuggled back into his
chest, feeling the gentle rhythm of it rising and falling against
my back.

I was the first to shift back into human, but I stayed on the
floor next to the massive wolf until he was ready to shed his
animal half. After a few more minutes, he did and rolled over on
me. His tongue explored my mouth. Then his lips lazily coursed
over mine and trailed down my body, gentle and languid. His
tongue left light, warm trails over me. He nestled between my
legs, nudging at my entrance. Then he waited to allow me to get
used to him, and I widened my legs to accommodate him. In a
slow, fluid movement, he connected, his movements gentle,
somber, languid. My nails dug into his back. His rhythm
increased; he moved more fervently, harder. His hips rolled
against mine. Kisses came harder as the fingers of one hand
entwined in my hair. His other hand curled around my thigh. His
rhythm increased as he thrust harder; I clawed at his back, kissing
him hungrily as we both found our pleasure. I clung to him for a
few more minutes, needing to remain connected to him, and the
firmness of his fingers pressing into my skin led me to believe he
needed it as much as I did.

As he rolled onto his back, he moved me with him until I was
on top of him as he relaxed into the floor. Long fingers glided
languidly over me.

"Ethan."

"Hmm." He looked at me through small slits in his eyes.

"If you ever command me to do anything like that again, you
won't like what happens next." My tone was as relaxed as I felt. I
snuggled in closer, and his chest vibrated against my face as he
chuckled.

With a casually amused voice, he asked, "What exactly will
that be?"

"Probably something like you screaming you can't believe I

kicked you in the balls," I offered, lifting my head so that my eyes could meet his, steely blue with just a hint of gunmetal.

"It was an order. In the pack, I'm over you. I have an obligation to keep you safe. Yes, I will order you to do things, and your only response should be 'yes.' You're welcome to add 'sir' to it if you'd be inclined."

Yes, jackass. How about that? "That's not going to work for me." I sat up, grabbed the throw off the sofa and wrapped it around me. He sat up too, gave the cover a look, and tugged at it until one of my breasts was exposed. He started to touch me, and I slapped his hand away, pulled the throw up, and wrapped it tighter around me.

"I'm serious. You were angry. I get it. Things didn't go as planned," I said. Anger peaked in him, and with great effort he extinguished it.

"I watched you almost die, don't ask me to be okay with that or the fact that you might do it again, because it's not going to happen."

Things with Ethan were new. I doubted I was the first person in the pack that he'd slept with, but I was probably the only one with whom it lasted more than just a night. This was a relationship. A relationship with Ethan was going to be hard, and we just added fuel to the dysfunction by being in a pack together. It was a delicate and volatile situation. I wished I could say that Ethan was above exploiting his position as Beta to get his way in our relationship, but I knew that wasn't true.

As if he read my thoughts or saw the concern and trepidation on my face, he said in a low, rough voice. "Sky, this is new for me, too. You"—he stopped abruptly and blew out a breath—"challenge me in ways that I'm not used to. I don't know how to deal with you—with this."

"Telling me I need to sit down and shut up definitely isn't the way."

With a wry smile, he nodded. "I'm not backing down; you can't do anything like that again, Sky. You can't. You can't put yourself in danger—" Gray drowned his pupils and his brows furrowed together, the ragged sounds of his breathing filling the air. He rested back on the floor and I followed, burying my face in his chest as I struggled to figure out a way to deal with him. With us, things didn't seem like they were ever going to be simple.

"I know that wasn't handled well, but Logan is the last person we want to have us in his pocket. We can't remove his marks or give him Chris. We just can't. Not even to save my life. We have to figure something out."

"I know. But for now we have to at least let him think he's going to get what he wants. If we don't put up a good faith display that we are working on it, he'll try to kill you."

We settled into an uncomfortable silence. My mind kept turning over the few options that we might have, and I kept returning to the curse that had started all of this.

Cuddled up to Ethan, it was difficult to ignore the light waves of magic that came off him, so reminiscent of the magic from the Aufero that I lifted my head to look for it. But it was in the closet, where I'd placed it days ago. Controlling the magic in it came at a cost, and Maya, who was once dormant, kept trying to make a play for control. I didn't want to give her an advantage. She was magic—old, draconian, dark magic that gave rise to power, lust, and destruction. I wasn't giving her access to strong magic until I was confident I could control her and not the other way around. But the magic coming off Ethan was so similar to hers. I snuggled in closer, feeling it, touching the boundaries of it. I recalled the magic he'd used and the spell he'd performed to kill Ethos. He'd effortlessly called on magic to demolish wards so strong that most witches couldn't erect them.

"What's wrong?" he asked.

"Nothing?" He tensed at my lie but eventually relaxed. I returned my focus to the magic, trying to unravel it and get to the core of it. This wasn't witch magic; I'd had access to that too often and was intimately familiar with it. There was a tinge of dark elven magic; I remembered the dank, stygian feel of it as well. But this was something altogether different, stronger.

Ethan sat up. "I need to get going. I really need to talk to Sebastian and Josh."

I nodded and sat up, too, but kept a cautious eye on him, wishing I had more time with his magic. The light smile that played at his lips made me wonder if he knew what I was doing.

He stood, grabbed his clothes, and started to dress. Before he left, I asked, "Do you plan on showing Josh and me the spell you used on Ethos? It might be something we need in the future."

A spark of amusement worked at his lips and they kinked into a smirk. "Of course, it's easy. It was just a spell—an archaic one. I'm pretty sure our mother showed Josh before, but he wasn't always as interested in old magic as he should have been." The wayward grin remained as he started to back out of the door, then glanced out the window.

"Your other vampire is here to visit." With the same mocking smile, he went out the door.

With all his plausible answers that made sense on the surface, I couldn't help but wonder what the hell Ethan was. I was more than just a were-animal, and so was Ethan.

My other vampire?

I turned to the window to see who he was referring to, although I had a good idea of who it was before I looked. The delicate round face had vacuous opal eyes, a result of feeding often, that stared blankly at the house as if contemplating whether to knock on the door. *Please don't knock on the door.*

Sable was a special type of crazy and left me torn between fearing her and feeling sorry for her, and she was definitely on her way to getting a gold medal in weird. As a human, she'd been the surviving member of a home invasion. Her tragic life was enough to generate pity and empathy for her—until you found out that she was the person who'd tracked down the people responsible for it and killed them, their friends, and their families without remorse. Nineteen when she was tried by a jury, she was just old enough to be convicted of the multiple counts of homicide she was charged with. Of course the Seethe had fallen in love with her and her story and had to turn her. I supposed when you were a vampire, that was what you did, scour the papers and news for sociopaths and make them immortal ones.

Nearly ten minutes had passed and I was getting tired of watching her watch the house. I stepped outside. "Sable, do you need something?"

"You haven't found your human pet?" she asked, reminding me of vampire speed because she'd cleared the twenty feet between us by the time I'd asked the question.

"Kelly is still missing. Do you know of anything more you can offer to help find her?"

Distracted, she had a look on her face as though she was trying to prevent herself from inciting chaos or doing something malicious. It was obvious that those were her favorite things, and anything else was tedious. She had taken a strange liking to Gavin, the pack's resident were-panther. When she'd threatened to kill our pack's nurse—Kelly—out of jealousy, it had strained their relationship. When Kelly had gone missing, he'd ended things with Sable. Since then, she'd made an effort to help us find Kelly.

"He still thinks I had something to do with it. He will not speak to me."

Dammit. I'd asked him to speak to her. We didn't need her unrequited obsession to make her any more unstable and volatile than she already was.

"He doesn't. Gavin's distracted, he wants to find his friend."

She kept saying the word over and over. "Friend? Friend?"

I nodded, but I wasn't definite about that, either. The pack's friendship and love were hard to define and even harder to understand. What most people considered restraining-order-stalker-obsession was just them making sure you were safe. It was their version of friendship that could only be defined as *peculiar*.

"Do you know anything more, Sable? Before, you told me that other people were missing. Have you noticed more?"

"The witches have been silent. It's never good when the witches are silent." And then she was gone. Of course sticking around for more questioning was too much to ask.

Thank you, Sable. Here I was missing my daily dose of crazy.

She was right, the witches had been silent since my last encounter with them. I'd gotten Ethos killed and ruined their chances of getting the Aufero back or possessing the Clostra, much less using any of the spells in the latter. I was somewhat surprised that they hadn't tried to retaliate, but after their fight with Josh, the Creed, which consisted of the most powerful witches in the country, was now down to two members. Perhaps they were busy trying to find suitable replacements, or nursing their battered pride.

CHAPTER 2

The size of the pack's retreat was always overwhelming and seemed unnecessary to me. I understood why we had the infirmary. It came in handy—a lot. But the sheer size of the place was staggering, especially when you were searching for a kitten. When Josh called me to ask me to meet him in the library, he'd assured me Gavin was at the house. Gavin and Dr. Jeremy had taken the lead on looking for Kelly while the others were split between dealing with the pack's ongoing business and Logan.

I caught a glimpse of him as he moved around the corner. His sleek physique embodied the panther he housed. His sinewy body and lissome movements made him difficult to track; he was also an excellent hunter, which was something I was always aware of when I dealt with him. I continued down the hall. "Here, kitty kitty. I have something for you. Come out, come out wherever you are." I glanced into the rooms I passed.

"Don't call me kitty," his rough voice commanded from behind me. I spun around. His dark eyes narrowed on me. "Skylar, what do you want?"

I smiled, large and cloying, hoping he would respond similarly. He didn't.

Ignoring his dour look, I reached in my bag and pulled out my little gift. I stepped closer, clipped a red key hook with a bell at the end to the belt loop of his jeans and tapped it. It jingled. "Now you don't have to keep scaring the hell out of people with your skulking." My smile broadened and I gave the bell another playful jingle. He wasn't amused. At. All.

The deeply seated scowl wasn't going anywhere. I ignored it and asked, "About Sable—"

"I've spoken to her already. I will not keep giving her the 'we're done' conversation. Whether or not she accepts it is her problem and hers alone."

That was a different issue, and I just didn't have the time to delve into it now let alone repair it. Fixing it wasn't an option, and I personally liked the idea that he was no longer dealing with her. Eventually, when she lost interest in him, she would lose it in me, too, and I would stop getting her odd visits whenever it suited her.

"Okay. But she thinks you aren't speaking to her because you believe she had something to do with Kelly being missing. I don't think she does."

His shoulders sagged. I concluded that he realized that, too, and was misdirecting his frustration to Sable.

"Sable believes the witches have been too silent. I'm not sure if they have anything to do with things, but maybe we should find out what they've been up to."

His long fingers stroked over his lips as he considered it. "They *have* been quiet," he acknowledged. Then he turned and started to walk away, because normal conversations with him only happened by accident. When he was done, there wasn't a goodbye or some tautology like "it was nice talking to you." Nope, His Weirdness just walked away. This time when he walked away, the bell jingled. He made an irritated sound, turned around, and dropped the now-crushed bell and keychain loop at my feet.

"And that's why you can't have nice things," I teased. "You

won't be getting any more gifts from me if that's how you're going to behave."

Gavin's dark chuckle drifted down the hall.

The witches, the manimal that had died in my neighbor's home with chemicals in his body that were synthetic versions of those found in were-animals, the feral man that Winter and I had seen in the forest—they all seemed to be linked somehow. But I had a hard time attributing it to the witches. Those things didn't seem like anything they would be involved in. They seemed like something the Makellos, the self-professed elven elite who lived in Elysian, would have their hands in since they had a penchant for experimenting and making odd, eerie animals.

After my conversation with Gavin, I went to the library. We were putting on a heck of an act like we were trying to help Logan, so much so that Ethan, Josh, and I were in the library looking over spells to remove his curse. I hoped it was just an act. It didn't feel or look like one. Books, notepads, cups of coffee that we'd filled several times, and a laptop were tossed about on the table. Josh and I kept using the laptop to look up things.

Josh looked disconcerted and glanced over at his brother, who was standing behind me, looking over my shoulder at the book I was reading, translating the Latin words before I could pull out my phone to Google them. I was wondering how Josh had found time since the last time I'd seen him to get more tattoos. Now he had a full sleeve of them on both arms, easily visible from under his t-shirt.

He slid a book across the table to Ethan. "This would go faster if you had your own book. Sky's done this before—many times. Even before you decided you wanted to start helping. So if you plan to help—then help."

Ethan glared at him and then the book, dismissing them both.

As with anything between the brothers, Josh accepted the implied challenge. "Have a seat, brother." He flicked his finger, and a chair that was against a wall pushed into the back of Ethan's legs; another swift movement of his finger and Ethan was given a magical nudge into it.

Most people could always count on their sibling rivalry to be a source of entertainment. This contest involved one of the strongest shapeshifters in the country, Beta of the most powerful pack in the world, and his brother, one of the most talented and strongest witches alive. Sibling dynamics weren't enough. Each had to subtly demonstrate his dominance over the other's perceived defiance.

After a few minutes of perusing the book in his hand, Josh asked Ethan, "Have you had any luck getting a lead on Chris?"

Ethan relaxed back in the chair and then shook his head.

"How long has she been gone?" Josh asked.

"I'm not sure. I wonder what the hell Demetrius did to her to make her leave and go underground."

"Are we really going to do this? You're going to find Chris to give her to Logan like she's property?" I snapped angrily.

"Sky, don't do this," Ethan said in a low voice.

"Don't do what? Have ethics that get in the way of what you're thinking about doing?"

"Sky, this isn't a black-or-white situation. It's not about morals, it's about survival."

"I understand what you're saying, I just don't agree with it. I thought we were going to present the illusion that we were looking and not actually look for her." I figured we needed to focus on the lesser of the two evils. "Why don't we work on a way to remove his marks first?"

Josh looked at Ethan, aggrieved. "You didn't tell her?"

"Tell me what?" I asked, my attention jumping between the two of them.

"Don't you think you should tell her? I didn't agree to this. We've done some crappy things before, but this is low. Very low. His obsession should not be our obligation," Josh said in a low drawl.

"You know I don't want to do this. We don't have a lot of options," Ethan shot back.

They kept going back and forth, but they didn't answer my question. "You all are looking for Chris to give her to that monster? Are you insane? She escaped from one, only to be handed over to another." I stood, glaring at both of them, finding them equally culpable.

Josh might not have agreed with it, but he had sat idly by and let the decision be made to do so. Perhaps I was being unfair to him, but everything I thought and felt was clouded by a haze of anger, regret, and apprehension. I felt stifled by the lack of options and my guilt was making things even harder. They were doing these horrid things to save me. That burden was becoming increasingly hard to handle, and the gnawing feeling of not knowing why my life was so important to the pack bothered me. They had made more than enough deals with people and incurred costly debts, all for me. What about me was so important that they made deals with the unscrupulous and allied themselves with those that they hated? And now this.

I turned to Ethan. "How can you do this to her? You know she's hiding from Demetrius because of what he did to her."

I didn't have details, but the Master of the Northern Seethe had approached me about using our resources to find her. When questioned about why she was missing, he'd admitted that he'd punished her. Demetrius prided himself on breaking people and took great pleasure in taming "the wild ones." And if anyone ever fit that description, it was Chris. Unrestricted by any defined codes of ethics, she seemed to adhere to her own, which differed from the norm. She allied with whoever could help her cause, and for the right price, there wasn't any job she wasn't willing to do. And the very reasons Demetrius saw fit to "break" her were the same things that drew him to her. Ethan still denied she was the vampire's lover, but since Demetrius had a polyamorous relationship with Michaela, the Seethe's Mistress, I didn't know why he was so sure of that.

"I know, Sky. I have no intention of handing her off to him, but if we need more time, well—"

"Well what, Ethan?" Revulsion crawled along my spine, the suffocating feeling of something heavy overburdening me, the nauseating sensation of bile creeping up the back of my throat. Plain and simple—I was disgusted. Disgusted with my pack. I realized there were unsavory things that we had to engage in, but this was one I would dig my heels in on and refuse to accept.

Ethan leaned in, and I forced myself not to withdraw my hand when he touched it. "Sky, I give you my word, we will not be giving Chris to Logan." There seemed to be an implied "unless," and I didn't like that at all.

"You have to promise me that under no circumstance will you do this. I'll concede to removing his marks, but we can't give him a person. We can't devolve into monsters."

Ethan made a face, a combination of amused and bewildered. His smile possessed the same conceit, confidence, and danger that I'd become too familiar with. Gunmetal rolled over his eyes as they narrowed on me. I tried unsuccessfully to hold them. "Concede? Sky, I do believe you have misunderstood your position in this pack. We consider your desires, but Sebastian and I make the decisions. You don't *concede* anything."

Then you both better decide not to do it. I really hoped I'd kept that in my head. Something invoked a primal nature in animals, that primordial need to subjugate those that challenged an Alpha's dominance. And although Ethan was the Beta in Midwest Pack, it was common knowledge that the strength of the pack was that we essentially had two Alphas. Ethan took on the role of

26

Beta, but he was far from it. In any other pack, he would have been the Alpha.

Taking on a submissive role seemed like it should have been easy. I was in a submissive position to Ethan and Sebastian, but the intimacy that Ethan and I had obscured that role. I was with him; we were two people having a disagreement about an issue. It was up to both of us to come up with a solution. But in the pack, if there was a problem, it was up to the five ranking members, led by Sebastian, to come up with a solution and make it right. It was the rules—I hated the rules.

We lived in a world of intangible rules and tenets blurred in so many shades of gray that it was no longer decipherable, but there remained one thing that was well defined—pack rules and dynamics. Even if the world erupted in chaos and everything was reduced to rubble, the pack rules would stand among the ruins. Many things the pack did toed very obscure lines between right and wrong. Deeming something *ethical* or *unethical* was dependent on whether it helped or hurt the pack. The boundaries between what they considered acceptable and unacceptable behavior were as tenuous; their rules were the only constant. Guidelines that they lived and died by.

I'd learned that the hard way when I'd tried to convince Ethan not to challenge Sebastian after the Alpha had been gravely injured. The pack rules required him to do so if he didn't feel that Sebastian could lead. He would have to challenge him if he didn't step down. Ethan had been prepared to kill his friend because of pack rules. It still left an acrid taste in my mouth and had given me an even stronger disdain for the pack's amoral system I'd bound myself to.

I lowered my head, hating the feel and taste of submission. When I looked up, Ethan was frowning. He leaned in and kissed me on the cheek. "I promise you, I will do everything to come up with something you can live with. Okay?"

I nodded.

"At what point should I be offended that I didn't get any kisses and promises? I said something very similar to you this morning, and not once did you cuddle me, and I damn sure didn't get any gentleness or sweet kisses. I'm starting to feel like you like Sky a little more than me," Josh said in exaggerated offense.

Ethan laughed. "As if there's a contest." He stood and slid the book he was holding onto the table and started out the door. "I definitely like her more than you." He closed the door behind him, barely escaping the books that Josh had lobbed in his direction. Ethan's laughter floated down the hallway, but it was his promise that had lifted my spirit. He'd promised me, something he'd never done before.

We returned to looking over the various books that were stacked on the table. "I don't think we're going to find anything that will work," I admitted, scanning over the small stack of books that we had gone through without success. "The spell we did with the Clostra removed everyone's curses, why didn't it remove his markings?"

Josh made a face, and although he hadn't resigned himself to defeat, he seemed pessimistic, which wasn't like him. "A very unique and powerful spell must have been done to make them," he said. Then he absently thumbed through a book. "What type of witches could do that?"

"That's the same thing I was thinking. I feel like there's something missing in the story."

Josh nodded. "If it was just a spell done by the witches, I'm not sure I want to get on their bad side by removing it."

I wholeheartedly agreed. Which brought up another problem. The witches had been fractured for a long time. There were many who didn't affiliate with the Creed, and most of them were powerful. Marcia had been known to find a way to punish those who were stronger than her for minor infractions. I couldn't help but imagine there was a small but powerful group of disgruntled witches out there. I just hoped they weren't as bitter and closed-minded as Samuel.

I had been in the library with Josh for several hours, looking at spells with the hope that we would stumble on something even if it could only help us understand why Logan's marks remained, when I glanced out the door and saw Steven's reddish curls disappearing around the corner. I immediately jumped up and darted out of the room to follow him. He kept walking even after I'd called his name. He'd been behaving funny and I wasn't sure why. He didn't answer or return my calls, and his text replies were simple one- or two-word responses and an occasional emoticon.

He was just about to get in his car when I caught the edge of the door. "You didn't hear me calling you?"

He didn't answer. Steven was too sweet to openly admit he was ignoring me and would rather not answer than ever tell me a lie. "Are you angry with me? Did I do something wrong?"

"No, Sky, of course not." But he wouldn't make eye contact. I waited until he looked up and searched the wide, gentle eyes that always concealed the skilled predator that lurked behind them.

"Then why have you been avoiding me?" He had a secret or something he was hiding. His eyes were cast down and shielded by a long veil of lashes.

Since I'd been badly injured a couple of days ago in the battle against Ethos, it had been weird between us. It had to be odd seeing me with that much power, capable of doing magic dark and unavailable to witches, mages, or faes. And the fact that I was the host to a dark power, a Faerie, was probably giving him pause. But I hadn't changed. I was the same person . . . or was I? Maybe the person I'd turned into wasn't someone he wanted to be around.

"I have to go." He pulled at the door.

"Steven?"

"I really need to go," he repeated in a hollow voice.

I continued to stand in the driveway long after he'd driven away, feeling the weight of my ever-changing life. Just when I had gotten used to my bond with Steven, my magical mentorship with Josh, a unique friendship with Winter, and the odd dysfunctional, adversarial dealings that I had with Ethan, things changed.

CHAPTER 3

*A*fter several hours of looking at spells, I'd been spent and needed to take a break. I'd stayed at Ethan's that night, although he hadn't come home. I'd tried to think about anything other than the fact that he was probably out looking for Chris. The next morning I was up, dressed, and speeding down the street in one of Ethan's ridiculously priced indulgences. I'd put a lot of effort in trying to shame him for them, and all I'd received was a look of derision for thinking they were unnecessary purchases. When I'd walked past all of them, the delinquent in me had wanted to put a palm print on the newly washed Bugatti, especially after I'd looked up the cost. I'd settled on the Vanquish. Each time I found myself behind the wheel of one of the ostentatious vehicles, I felt like a total and complete hypocrite. I fought the urge to take back all the merciless taunting I'd directed at Ethan. I understood his fascination with and appreciation for them. The soft, plush leather, and driving them was like floating through the streets, which wouldn't be an acceptable excuse to give the police, so I had to keep reminding myself to slow down.

I was driving distracted, my thoughts split between everything that was going on and Steven. The witches engrossed most of my attention. They were quiet. I fixated on that because it had been my experience that within their placidity was a waiting storm.

After hours of driving, I realized I needed to talk it through and went to Winter's home.

"What's wrong?" Winter asked as soon as she opened the door.

I shook my head. "Nothing, just needed to talk."

"Do we need to talk about how the phone works? It's quite simple, you know." Winter didn't like unexpected visits. I suspected no one really did, but Winter, unlike most, wouldn't let you in and would give you a lecture about the beauty of using the phone. I surmised I wasn't going to gain entry today as she kept the door open just enough for part of her face and body to be seen.

"Do you think Steven's having problems?" I tried to keep my voice level, but distress caused it to waver more than I would have liked.

She sighed and opened the door. I stepped in and saw the redhead that she had recently started dating. Most beautiful women paled in comparison to Winter, but her new interest was one of the few who didn't. Her thick, voluminous hair was pulled back by a headband and fell far past her shoulders. Her features were similar to Winter's—narrow nose, sharply defined cheek-bones and jawline—but more delicate in appearance. While Winter was tall and sleek, her new girlfriend was shorter by at least five inches and curvier. I didn't know her name; I just called her Giggles, because the night I'd met her, that's all she'd seemed to do. Well, I could have called her Bump and Grind, that was something she'd done a lot with Winter on the dance floor. But that had seemed rude. I'd figured she'd be a short-term relation-ship, possibly just a one-night stand, because Winter hadn't offered a name. So I was definitely surprised to see her sitting on Winter's sofa.

After spending the evening with her and Winter, I was still trying to figure out how they fit. I only knew of one of Winter's past girlfriends, Abigail, an elf. The first time I'd met her, I could see why Winter liked her. She'd turned out to be a deceitful opportunist who manipulated and colluded herself into power by way of using her brother, but through all that I could see how Winter could be drawn to the intellect, challenge, and intrigue. I didn't get any of that from her new acquaintance.

"Yasmeen, do you mind if we talk later?" Winter asked.

"Of course not." She kissed Winter lightly on the lips. But she stood at the door for a moment in contemplation before leaving. Maybe she was considering something, but I suspected she was trying to figure out how the door worked.

"She didn't know how to operate the door," I pointed out once I heard her drive away.

Winter rolled her eyes and stretched out on the couch. I sat in the chair across from her. "She was just making sure she had everything," she said, dismissing my accusation without hesitation.

"You mean like the purse on her shoulder? She's very interesting."

"She is," Winter added with a smile.

"Really? Prove it," I challenged.

"What do you mean, 'prove it'?"

"What's so interesting about her? Hobbies? Job? Conversation? What's interesting about your new girlfriend?"

She made a face as she considered the question for longer than I expected and came back with a shrug. "Okay, you win. She's hot. Are you happy? I'm interested in her for a very shallow reason. So what? You and Ethan . . . why? So many whys."

I took a moment to think, about as long as it had taken her to answer my question. "I make very bad decisions. Have you been watching my life?" I grinned.

Laughing, she sat up and studied me, I assumed waiting for me to give the reason for the visit. "Steven is being cold and distant and I don't know why." I kept my voice level and devoid of any emotion.

Winter didn't respond to maudlin displays of emotion, and if I'd given her one, the conversation would have ended with her telling me to come back once I had found "my big girl undies." I needed to talk, and despite all her prickly abrasiveness, she was often very easy to talk to.

With a wry smile, she sighed into her words. "Your relationship with Steven is so sweet that it gives me and everyone else around you a sugar headache. It's annoying, and that is me being very kind with my words."

I widened my eyes. "Really? That's you being *kind*? Do you know what that word means? I'm sure you can look up the definition quickly. I can wait."

She glared and gave me a half-cocked smile. When she spoke, her voice was a high-pitched dramatization of my voice. "You're my bestie." Then she moved to the side, having a back-and-forth conversation with herself. "No, you're my bestie. I love you. I love you more, Sky. Let's cuddle and share this piece of spaghetti in celebration of our love. Here's your end. Blah." When she stopped she was the only one laughing at her performance.

"He's the brother I never had."

"I understand that. Still doesn't make it any less annoying." The smile still on her lips made its way to her hazel eyes, which sparkled with delight.

She slouched into the sofa and crossed her legs. "You're friends, and there isn't anything wrong with it. Except for being saccharine and cavity-inducing and crossing a lot of boundaries. It was fine when you were considered a much weaker pack member. Your position as submissive and unranked made your weird and boundaryless relationship work. But it's not like that anymore. He wasn't able to change you into your animal when you were injured, which means you are more dominant than him. He's probably expecting you to challenge him."

"I would never do that!"

Winter was quiet for a long time. I really didn't want to wait around for what she had to say because I was sure I knew what it was, and hearing it out loud would be worse than expecting it. "You are expected to—"

"If I feel he can't perform his position and I can do it better, I'm supposed to challenge him." I was well acquainted with that rule. The one that would have led to Ethan challenging Sebastian.

I stood, ignoring Winter's gaze as I walked around her sparsely decorated room. She had a minimalist approach to decorating that seemed to focus on her ability to survive in the event of an attack. Most of the pack decorated this way. Their homes were nothing more than bastions to protect them. A dark blue sofa and a smaller one to her right were easy to negotiate but could be moved to obstruct someone's path. The leather storage ottoman was placed with the opening facing her—it held enough weapons for her to stage a siege. A casual observer would have never observed that the various knickknacks and decorative things that were in the home were there because they could be used as weapons as needed. I'd often considered this behavior and planning excessive, until Marcia had sent someone to kill me.

The pack's questionable behaviors and alliances afforded them great power and strength but weren't without consequences—they had enemies. A lot of them. The lengths they went to in order to protect themselves weren't as excessive as I'd once thought.

I had moved away from Winter with my back to her, running my finger along a ceramic figurine on a stand when she spoke. "If you ever think you would be better at being fifth, you have an obl—"

"I won't," I snapped. I looked back at her; she'd heard the snarl, too. I didn't mean it. It had just happened.

"Skylar, I understand, no one wants to challenge people—especially those you know, who would rather die than give up their positions—but in the end it's not about you, it's about the safety of the pack—"

"Got it." I was being totally unreasonable and mean to Winter and it wasn't her fault. She was doing her job as the pack's third, reinforcing the rules and trying to explain Steven's behavior, but this was just an addition to the many changes that were happening too fast. "I'm sorry." I plopped down in the chair, let my head flop back and stared at the ceiling. "There is so much going on and things are changing too fast."

"And you are changing. You've used and have access to magic that no one else has. And you are more in touch with your animal half, you've removed dark elven magic from Ethan, and you've used magic from the Clostra to kill Ethos. Yeah, things have changed."

"It's because I have access to magic that I seem more dominant than Steven. I won't ever challenge him," I said.

She nodded and with a faint smile said, "There has to be a magic exemption rule." It was her placating me and downplaying the situation, but I didn't care. I wasn't going to challenge Steven. He was better than I would be in the position. The rules didn't bother him—he was the pack's most devout advocate.

"Things are different even with Sebastian; he's worried. Sebastian rarely worries because he always has another plan. But now he's off," Winter said.

I thought I'd been the only one to notice it. Once again that guilt emerged. Was it the situation with Logan? But it could be innumerable things. There was definitely an adversarial relationship with the Creed. We, along with the Seethe and elves, were now tasked with regulating the dark elves, and Samuel was still trying to get access to the Clostra to do a spell that would remove magic from the world and in essence kill off the were-animals. And there was Kelly. She'd been missing now for a month, and the only lead we had was a dead person who knew her and had been injected with a chemical that mimicked those present when one shifted to a were-animal.

I didn't know where to start with helping the situation, and based on the scowl on Winter's face, she didn't, either. "The longer she's gone, the less likely we are going to be able to find her," she said. "We need to find her as soon as possible."

"I know."

~

Winter and I were on the same page, and minutes later we were in her SUV, traveling along the road where we'd seen the man-animal hybrid that had run in front of our car a couple of days ago and then been pulled into a car and driven away. Too many days had passed for us to track him by scent, but we were hoping there would be something that would give us some clues. The other hybrid we'd encountered had died before we could question him.

She inched down the street, surveying the area, looking for anything suspicious. She eventually pulled to the side, and we walked farther away from the road.

"Do you smell that?" she asked. I did. I inhaled the air again. It smelled like medicine—a sedative, a recent one. Who would be using a sedative outside? I saw the footprints and the torn clothes before she did. I leaned over and breathed in deeply. Medicine, footprints, and torn clothing, a bad combination. Someone had escaped, but from where? There were trees and acres of fallow land but nothing else. Ethos had abducted me and taken me underground. Could they be held underground?

"Let's go farther into the forest," I suggested. We went to Winter's car, and she holstered a gun at her side, a knife at her ankle, and another blade at her waist. She dismissed the sharp look I gave her when I saw that there were enough weapons for me to take three knives and a nightstick and still leave a substantial number. I teased her constantly about being over-armored, but at times like this, I was happy that she had a small stash of weapons in the trunk of her SUV. No matter how many times I'd practiced, I was still safer without a gun. I wished I'd brought my sword with me—after numerous practice sessions with it, I preferred it over a knife.

We walked farther into the wooded area, scanning for anything suspicious or peculiar. For nearly half an hour, we moved deeper into the thicket. Adding to the smells, magic brushed across my skin. Unfamiliar magic. Magic had a fingerprint, and people who performed magic could identify the source.

A shot rang out and then a bullet went in the ground just a few feet in front of us. Our eyes jerked up and traveled in the direction it had come from. The shooter smiled. Her familiar dark chocolate eyes, which were once a much lighter brown when she was human, held a sparkle of amusement and menace as she moved them from the scope. She was a vampire now, and I wondered if she still needed a scope or if it was something she did because it was familiar.

Cautiously Winter stepped in her direction. Responding to my curious look, she whispered, "Believe me, if she wanted us dead, we would be."

"Are we looking for the same person?" the woman asked, jumping down from the tree, her weapon still trained on us.

"I don't know. Male, early twenties, brown hair," Winter offered.

We are?

Chris smiled. "Why does my gut tell me you're lying?"

Because she is. Straight through her teeth.

Chris never dropped her gun, keeping it on us. "You can put that away," I suggested.

But she didn't. She looked at me for a long time, then her attention slipped over to Winter. "I'm on a job."

"Okay."

There was a long, tense pause as she slowly lowered her gun. When Winter took another step, she jerked it back up and focused it on us again.

"I'm looking for a missing young man, and you?"

Winter remained silent.

"Kelly," I blurted out, and Chris dropped the gun. I knew she would. She was alive because of Kelly. Ethan had made the decision to let Chris die instead of changing her to a vampire. That was something Kelly couldn't stomach, so she'd gone against Ethan's and Sebastian's wishes and helped Demetrius change her.

"How long?"

"Almost a month."

"Fuck." She cursed several more times under her breath. "How could you let her stay missing for a month?"

"We didn't let anything happen," Winter snapped, taking a step toward Chris. I moved between them, surprised it had remained civil this long. The standoff between Winter and Chris extended past what was going on. I wasn't sure what it was rooted in; maybe each was vying for the crown of Queen Bitch and felt the other one was the only real competition. They were so much alike, it was inevitable that they would either really love or hate each other—they chose the latter.

"When was the last time she was seen?" Chris directed her question to me. I wasn't sure why I gave her the abbreviated CliffsNotes version of everything, reducing what happened with Kelly—being paralyzed by the Tod Schlaf, an elven creature used for assassinations—to just a "personal problem." A personal problem that had caused her to request a leave of absence, which the pack had granted, to give her adequate time to deal with it. I didn't tell Chris that we'd assumed she'd fled from us and that it was warranted. Nor did I tell her about Gavin being constantly on edge since Kelly had gone missing. I'd reduced Kelly's disappearance to a "leave of absence." I waited for guilt to do its thing and ping me. Nothing. Did I feel like I was protecting the pack?

But from what, a few scathing remarks? Or was it the fact that Kelly had been under our care? The pack had assumed responsibility for her, and now she was missing. It was a slight to the pack.

"Was the 'personal problem' being bitten by the Tod Schlaf?" Chris's tone was sharp.

From behind me, I heard Winter take a ragged breath. "Yes."

Now there was no longer a need to give her the abridged version. I told her about the man running out in front of us, the car that had picked him up and gotten away, and the half-wolf half-man that had ended up at my neighbor's home, looking for Sebastian and carrying Kelly's ID with him. I described the man, and Chris sucked in a breath, which as a vampire she didn't need. She exhaled it along with a string of curses.

"Was that the guy you were looking for?" I asked.

She shrugged, and then she was gone. Dropping the gun at my feet, she'd run. Unlike her creator, Demetrius, she didn't have the ability to travel. All I saw was the back of her shirt and jeans as she ran with vampire speed, nearly undetectable to the eye, just a blur.

To our right, I saw what had caused her to leave. Two members of the Seethe were standing to my right. They were the first vampires I'd had had the displeasure of meeting: Chase and Gabriella, the sadistic sybarites that were somehow vampire royalty and Michaela's favorite psycho couple. They changed their looks often, but what had stayed the same with Chase was the host of tattoos that laced up his arms. He had a piercing in his lip, another small one in his nose. Classically handsome, his dark hair was cut shorter than before, buzzed. His partner, who seemed to have different color hair each time I saw her, had settled on a midnight tint with hints of blue. Winter had once described their style as "Goth Abercrombie & Fitch," and today wasn't an exception.

The terrible duo moved closer, their keen, narrowed eyes fixed on us. I gripped the knife in my hand tighter. "Who were you talking to?"

"It's just the two of us, so who do you think?" I said dismissively. Chase moved, quickly blocking me as I started to turn away.

"Ah, yes, the pack's little poodle. I'd forgotten how sharp her tongue can be," he hissed through his teeth and then licked my face.

I swiped his leg, and when he hit the ground, I jammed my elbow into his ribs. Hard. Several cracked. In one swift move, I jammed the knife into his hand. "She has an even sharper knife." I nodded toward Winter. He groaned under his breath, calling me enough names to satisfy himself—but *poodle* wasn't one of them.

"What do you want?" I asked, hovering over him, keeping an eye on Gabriella in my peripheral vision. Winter had taken a place close to her. And with one look from her, Gabriella seemed to remember the time that Winter had taken great pleasure in breaking many of her bones into little pieces.

"Chris . . . we thought we heard her voice." Chase's voice was full of pain.

Winter answered before I could. "Like Sky said, it was just the two of us."

I ripped the knife out of Chase's hand, and seconds later he was next to Gabriella. Without another word they were gone.

We went back to our search for the manimal. When the footprints ended, we decided to continue looking around.

"Why didn't you tell them about Chris?" I asked.

She shrugged. "If she wanted them to know where she was, I suspect she would have stayed."

I'd assumed Chris had left, but she was still in town, obviously in hiding. She'd kept her whereabouts from Gabriella and Chase; I planned to keep them from Sebastian and Ethan as long as I could. Winter hadn't been at the meeting with Logan, and I hoped she had been given the full briefing on it. As the third, she should have been, but sometimes Sebastian and Ethan kept things between the two of them. I suspected this was one of those times.

We continued deeper into the wooded area, feeling the magic, which was stronger, a heavy coat of it spreading throughout the air. Strong magic, different yet similar to Josh's. I closed my eyes, allowing it to brush over my skin, inundate my senses so that I could get a better feel of it. I tried not to wince at the idea of magic. I was warier of it—even of my own—than I had ever been before due to Maya's ever-present thirst to use magic and the challenge of trying to control her from making it increasingly more ominous. But I tamped down my apprehension and fear and let the magic wash over me, feeling it, hoping to determine its fingerprint. Magic was uniquely an individual's, although there were some similarities between all magic. Magic was just magic, but each person had their own brand of it, and each sect had their own markings on magic. I could always tell what type of magic was used, whether fae, mage, witch, or elven. I was the most familiar with the magic of witches because I'd been exposed to it often, particularly that of Marcia, leader of the Creed, and of Samuel, a mercenary whose sole purpose had become creating a magicless world. His beliefs were arrant and unwavering. He blamed the evil uses of magic on the idea that magic was fundamentally bad, rather than blaming it on the ill intentions of the wielder.

The magic felt familiar, but it wasn't that of witches, which was a good thing. After Josh had tossed the medallion used to show allegiance to the witches at their feet, I wasn't looking forward to running into them. But it was inevitable that we would eventually be confronted by them.

There wasn't a familiarity to the magical fingerprint, and I didn't have enough to be specific about the wielder. I moved farther into the woods, scanning the area, and then I frowned.

"What's wrong?" Winter asked.

"Magic and medicine seem like an odd combination."

"And car fumes," she added, craning her neck and inhaling. Her eyes changed. Vertical slits overtook them and looked weird in a human face. We were nearly five miles from the road; we shouldn't have been smelling fumes from cars, but she did.

We both surveyed the area, looking for a car or even a path that could be used. A four-wheeler would have difficulty navigating around the bounty of trees that crowded the area, and negotiating it in a car would be impossible. Or had they used another entrance into the woods?

A low growl grabbed my attention. A woman, a little taller than average, stood five feet from us. Long, dirty-blond disheveled hair only gave glimpses of the amber that flooded her eyes. An odd line went through her pupils. A human body, but her feral mannerisms were lacking anything civil. Just like the man who had shown up at my neighbor's home and the man we'd nearly run over a couple of days ago. She was like them. What I could see of the skin that peeked out from her oversized button-down was normal.

"Carol." An even, chilled, and commanding voice came from behind her. I took a couple of steps back to get a better look and keep them both in my line of sight. The new woman looked like her voice. At first glance, she seemed to be in her early thirties, but her eyes had aged more than her face. The deep frown made her round features look harsh. Her dark hair was pulled into a tight bun, and her dress matched her demeanor: professional and cold. Light blue shirt, dress slacks, and flat blue shoes made her look like she belonged in an office, not in the middle of the woods, trying to subdue an animal-woman. She possessed strong magic, but I didn't sense that she was a witch. Her magic didn't feel like anything I was familiar with. It was different. She was different. Very different. She shot a cool look in our direction but quickly dismissed us as inconsequential.

The animal-woman quickly adopted a defensive pose,

growling again, as though humanity was something she had never been acquainted with.

"Carol, down." But Carol didn't comply. Instead, her fingers curled, as though she was revealing claws instead of fingernails. Her lips pulled back, revealing teeth, but Carol seemed to believe she had fangs. Animalistic, she moved in a sharp, twitchy manner, lacking the grace seen in were-animals or even natural animals. Something was very wrong with Carol. I stared at her, trying to figure out what it was. Clearly she thought she was animal, but why?

"What is she?" Winter asked, approaching while keeping equal distance from both the animal-woman and the woman permeated with magic that wasn't a witch's. I hadn't been exposed to elven or fae magic enough to be sure that what she possessed wasn't their magic or some variation of it. All I knew was that it was strong. Turbulent waves of it moved over her.

"It is best that you leave and let me handle this." Her tone was just as icy as it had been with Carol, and both Winter and I had the same idea—there wasn't any way we were going to let Carol go with her. Something about her was off, and I didn't like it. Winter lunged at her. With a wave of the woman's hand, Winter was thrown back, crashing hard into a tree. A flick of her finger, and when Winter attempted to come to her feet, her legs collapsed under her. Teeth pulled back into a snarl that countered Carol's, Winter tried to make eye contact with the magic-fueled woman. Then we saw something other than stern coolness: contempt that seemed to be rooted in more than just us trying to help Carol.

"We just need to know what is going on," Winter said softly, something that was out of character for her. The woman looked in her direction and then frowned. Winter's eyes fixed on her and held her gaze. "You don't think we should be concerned about a woman who we found in the woods who clearly needs some medical care? We can get her that care."

The look of contempt quickly flickered into annoyance and she pulled her eyes from Winter's. I could see Winter's disappointment. She usually only needed a few minutes to charm someone. Being a lesser were-snake could have its advantages, one of which was getting people to acquiesce, which could have really come in handy right then.

Winter darted toward the woman, and again a blast of magic hit her in the chest. It was enough of a distraction for me to shift mid-lunge and plow into the woman. The weight of my massive form kept her secured against the ground. She struggled under me, clawing and flicking her fingers, I assumed to try to use magic against me. I couldn't figure out if desperation and fear had made her forget that magic couldn't be used against us in animal form, or if she just didn't know.

Carol turned and started to run, and Winter went after her. I kept the magic wielder under me, baring my teeth while keeping an eye on a man who was coming at me fast. I jumped to the side in time, missing the baton that whipped in my direction. I moved back again, jumping to the side when it came at me a second time, my claws catching the back of the man's arm as he brought it up to bat at me again. I dodged it, lunged, sank my teeth into his leg, and held on as he thrashed against my torso with the baton. I pulled back flesh when I was yanked back by the tail. I whirled around, ready to give someone the same treatment, when electricity jolted through me. I growled, turned, and started to lunge at the man when he moved out of the way and positioned himself next to the woman. She wrapped her arms around him, and when I lunged at them this time, I had nothing but air. They had disappeared.

Inhaling, I tried to get a whiff of Winter's scent among the strong redolence of oak, bark, dirt, car fumes, and magic that had gotten stronger. I couldn't ignore it anymore. Even in animal form, I could sense magic and smell it. I moved slowly, trying to draw in more air, and I saw Winter just as I caught her scent. Her jeans were torn, her shirt was dirty, and her knuckles were bruised and stained with blood.

"I'm starting to hate witches as much as I hate vampires," she growled.

Since my clothes were destroyed, I stayed in animal form, and she spoke more slowly, knowing it was difficult for me to understand her. I had to concentrate more than I did in human form. She'd caught up with Carol but couldn't get to her in time before she was snatched by someone and vanished.

While Winter went to her car to get me something to put on so that I wasn't flashing the cars passing by as I emerged from the woods, I changed. "I don't think they are witches."

"Mage?"

I considered the question for a while. Josh always called mages "witch light" because they were considered the weaker of the two. There wasn't anything "light" about the magic I'd just encountered.

"I don't know if it's a mage, but who else can travel and do magic? Some vampires have the ability to travel, but they can't perform magic. Only witches can travel and perform magic." I frowned as I got in the car. Had I interpreted the magic wrong? I grabbed my phone out of my purse and called Josh, but his phone went to voice mail. I called Ethan next; he wouldn't be as good as Josh, but I was sure he could give me a second opinion. His phone went to voice mail as well.

I arrived at the pack's house in a pair of Winter's yoga pants that I wished were a tad larger, and I kept tugging on the shirt she'd given me. Winter dressed to fight at all times, never giving the opponent the opportunity to grab any of her clothing to gain the advantage. It had to be exhausting to always be in a state of high alert, waiting for a ghost to pop out at any moment to attack, but given the turn that my life had taken, it wasn't improbable that there was some hidden danger lurking in the shadows.

Several cars were in the driveway when we pulled in, ostentatious vehicles that elicited my eye roll. Winter had gotten the same one for her oversized Range Rover—on several occasions I'd threatened to volunteer her to provide rides to the local junior high soccer team because it was large enough to carry a small army. Smart comments, eye rolls, and demonstrations of disdain just bounced off her and drew comments about my "toy" car. But I didn't recognize these other cars—they had out-of-state plates.

Unfamiliar voices met us at the door, and before we could find them, a man dressed in a simple claret button-down shirt and dark jeans appeared. The color failed to brighten his appearance, which could have easily been described as gray. His sharp gray eyes stood out against his fair skin and flaxen-colored hair with hints of silver or gray. I couldn't guess his age. Another benefit of being a were-animal. We aged, but not as fast as most. I placed him in his late thirties or early forties.

"Winter." The gentleman greeted her with a warm smile.

"Cole." She moved forward and then hugged him. I gawked, waiting for her to lean over and close my mouth. Winter was about as warm and cuddly as a porcupine, and any efforts to hug her or show what she considered mushy displays of affection were met with a threat to break whatever part of you touched any part of her. I'd managed several hugs without an assault, but she'd stood tensed, making them feel as unwanted as they actually were, so it was surprising when she quickly conformed to him, leaning in and wrapping her arms around him.

Cole was the East Coast Alpha, which meant he was dangerous, but there wasn't anything very dangerous-looking about him. His movements didn't possess the same predaceousness and lethal grace most were-animals possessed, which camouflaged his lethality. You saw Ethan and Sebastian approach, and your protective instincts kicked in and prepared you for whatever they had to offer. This guy might break your neck while smiling and telling you he liked your outfit.

When he turned to me, his voice was just as warm. "And you're Skylar Brooks. I've heard great things about you."

And you're a liar, too. I really need to watch you.

I looked at his extended hand as though he was offering me a tainted apple. His smile broadened. "I don't bite"—he winked and grinned—"unless you want me to."

What the hell am I supposed to do with that? Based on the kink in his grin, I was sure he thought he was being charming, but he was treading awfully close to the creepy line.

I took his hand, and his other one covered mine as he stepped closer, barely leaving an inch of space between us. "The wolf who can perform magic. I've wanted to meet you for some time now."

Ethan can perform magic, too. Why don't you go give his hands a few weird touches?

He had over six inches on me, and he leaned down to study my eyes. "I don't see the *terait*." He sounded disappointed. I felt like he'd come specifically to see the freaky animal, and here I was in my enclosure. He still had hold of my hand, studying me with interest, and a gentle smile settled on his lips.

"Cole, we'll be meeting in Sebastian's office," Ethan said from behind me. Cole's hands slipped from mine. I looked behind me when Ethan's arms wrapped around me, pulling me into his chest before he rested his chin on my head. "It's probably a good idea for you to go in and grab a seat now."

Cole was having a harder time keeping the pleasing smile, and the spark of interest dropped completely from his eyes as they sharpened. He gave Ethan another glance before he started to back away. Neither one dropped eye contact, instead choosing to hold it until Cole finally turned around.

Ethan moved away from me. "How did you injure yourself?" he asked, kneeling down to lift my shirt and look at my bruising from being pelted by the baton. The dark blue and purple marks looked worse than they were. His hands moved appraisingly over the skin before he released my shirt and stood.

"That's why we're here," I said, but I kept looking behind him at the other people heading in the direction of Sebastian's office. My focus stayed on Joan, Steven's adoptive mother and the Alpha of the Southern Pack, until she disappeared from sight.

Sebastian called Ethan's name. He looked like he'd seen better days.

"Is it possible for us to discuss how you got the bruises later?" Ethan asked. It was obvious he wanted to know, but now he had more pressing issues.

"That's fine. We really just needed Josh," I conceded.

"He'll be in the meeting as well," Ethan offered as he started to back away. "It will need to wait. Just until later. Okay?"

"That's fine." I quickly moved forward and fell in step with him. "I'll talk to him after our meeting."

Can't blame a woman for trying. I really wanted to know what was such a big deal that the Alphas of every pack were having a meeting, and I had a feeling all I was going to get via Ethan was Sebastian's sanctioned version. In the past I could have relied on Josh to give me the unedited version, but now it seemed like he had been inducted into the secret-keeper club, and getting information from him was getting harder and harder.

Ethan flirted with a smile. He moved closer to me and lightly kissed me on the lips. "That was a good try," he said with a smirk firmly in place as he turned the corner, heading for the office.

I looked over to Winter and saw that she'd watched the exchange between us and now wore a look of anxious concern. "What the hell is going on?" she asked softly, but it seemed like she was directing the comment to herself. She chewed on her bottom lip, turning her head as if listening for other voices, hoping to gather more information from anyone outside of the office—but there weren't any. Even if we considered going to the office door, which was soundproof, we would quickly be discovered. If the others' sense of hearing was anywhere near as acute as Sebastian's and Ethan's, they would hear us.

Resignedly, I headed to the library and grabbed a couple of books, making sure to send Josh a text that I'd borrowed them. There was nothing left to do but follow Winter to her car.

CHAPTER 4

*A*fter spending a couple of hours at Winter's, analyzing everything that had transpired with Carol, the possible-mage, the man that Chris was looking for, and the Alpha meeting, I meant to head home, but what she'd said earlier about Steven thinking I would challenge him still vexed me. I needed to see him. I made nine calls and lost count of the number of text messages I sent before I finally got a response from him. Each unreturned call or ignored text was like him pushing the knife I felt like he'd plunged in my back in a little farther.

I should have known he wouldn't have chosen one of the many apartments near his school. Most were-animals enjoyed privacy and the outdoors, often sacrificing convenience for the ability to roam at our leisure. When Steven was still my roommate, during the weekends when he didn't have school or other obligations, I would always find him wandering the vast, crowded woods behind the house. His new residence, a small ranch house, would work well for him, surrounded by acres of trees that made it difficult to see his neighbors. If I couldn't see them, then they definitely couldn't see the young man with the unruly red curls and vibrant green eyes change into an oversized coyote larger than anything they would ever see in nature. To them he would be the sweet guy with the big dimples and lazy Southern drawl.

He opened the door, pushing back said unruly curls as he looked past me rather than at me. That knife hurt like hell. I waited for him to invite me in. He didn't. "What's up?"

Even his voice was different, cool and despondent, and it was getting harder to pretend that his reticence didn't bother me. I looked away and blinked several times. As much as I fought them, tears formed. I hated crying, but Steven was like a brother to me, something I had never had before, and it seemed like our relationship was going to end over something as ambiguous as the relative dominance of our animals. It was a mere fraction of who we were but controlled so much of our lives. Werewolves, were-animals, the pack, and magic were my life—I accepted it, but just then it seemed like acceptance came at a price greater than I was prepared to pay.

"Sky?"

"Forget it." I turned around and started toward my car.

"Sky, please don't go."

I turned around but stayed close to my car. "Things can't be weird between us. I can handle it with anyone else, but not with us. Things can't change between us. I won't accept it . . . I . . ."

"It's fine. We're fine." He was the worst liar in the pack, but I'd take whatever he had to offer because it was what I wanted.

He stepped aside and let me into his home. I wasn't sure he'd finished unpacking. Or at least it looked like he hadn't.

"Have a seat?"

Where? On the sofa was a pile of clothes, headphones and a bag of chips next to it. The large television on the entertainment center was surrounded by glasses, empty cups, and a plate with a partially eaten sandwich. He'd obviously had breakfast, because evidence of it was still piled in the sink. When I stood in the middle of the room looking for a place to sit, he grabbed up the pile of clothes from the sofa and tossed it on top of the pile of clothes, sheets, and whatever else was covering the love seat on the opposite side of the room. I wished his housekeeping skills could have been one of the many things that had changed in my life.

"Organized chaos." He grinned, taking a seat next to me. Relaxing back against the sofa, he offered me the chips, his favorite dill-flavored, which was bad enough, but next to him was a bottle of hot sauce. I didn't even bother considering his offering. Instead I sank back into the sofa and stared at the TV screen like I'd done so many times before. Thirty minutes had passed before we'd slipped into our place of comfort. We didn't have to speak, it was just us—comfortable and easy.

"You know I would never challenge you?" I ventured. "Even though I'm supposed to be more dominant."

He grinned. "More dominant? I couldn't change you, which means I'm not more dominant than you, but we could possibly be even. If you challenge . . ." "I'm not going to. I don't want to be a ranked pack member. I don't want to fight

anyone . . . . Well, that's a lie. I kind of want to punch Ethan, he can be a real Betahole sometimes, and then he does that thing with his face, so smug, so arrogant, and so very punchable . . . but not you. Never you."

"I know you want it to be that simple, but your relationship with the pack has changed. You care about it and the people in it and that's the way it should be. Part of caring about it is caring about the strength of it and making sure it is able to protect the members."

"I don't care about it more than you. I'm sure that's not something I'm supposed to say or feel, but it's the truth. Those are not the beliefs of a ranked pack member. And that's exactly what I would say if anyone tried to force me to challenge you."

He responded with a faint smile. He'd been changed into a were-animal after life-threatening injuries, but you'd never have known he was a changed were-animal and not a born one. The primal instincts, hierarchy, and doctrines by which the pack lived and died were ingrained in him as much as in the born were-animals. I was constantly learning and still felt like there was a disconnect. I was linked to the pack, but by a fragile tendril, and I suspected that it would always be that way.

He didn't push the issue, and once again we slipped into a comfortable silence—until I broke it by telling him everything that had transpired over the past couple of days. If he knew any of it, he certainly had a great poker face as he listened intently as though it was all new to him.

"I don't know what we're going to do about Logan," I ended.

"I don't, either," he admitted. His hand scrubbed over the light beard on his face. It didn't fit him, but it was one of the many things he did to downplay his cherub features and pretty-hand-some features. Those features were the most deceptive weapon he had. They made people underestimate him, to their detriment.

"I saw Josh yesterday, he looks like he hasn't slept in days," Steven said, frowning. "Can't you do a reversal spell the way you did when the witches cursed you?"

That's how this mess had all started. Logan was cursed, restricted to his home and from inflicting his mayhem on the world by a ward. But in lifting a death curse placed on me by the witches, we'd inadvertently lifted a still unknown number of curses. It was the reason vampires could now walk in daylight without any consequences, and so many other things had occurred because of it. I was hesitant to do any global reversal spells.

"No, we can't do anything like that, it's too risky."

He stood and started to pace the length of the room, negotiating the many things on the floor that were obstructing it. His so-called organized chaos was becoming increasingly distracting. As he paced the floor, he picked up a jacket that was in his way and tossed it near the love seat with the other pile of clothes. It hit the pile but then fell back to the floor. I walked over, picked it up, and hung it on the coatrack. "It goes here."

"Thanks, Mom."

"Your mom thinks you're a pig, too. Remember she threatened to make you sleep in the barn during your last visit."

He grinned. It wasn't forced, it was the same one he always gave when I complained about his mess.

"Do you like living here?" I asked as I continued to put away things obstructing the living room.

Then I rolled my eyes in the direction of the kitchen. It was a task that was definitely going to require more than just picking things up.

"Mom has a cleaning person coming at the end of the week."

"You need to put a little more shame in your voice when you reveal something like that," I teased.

He laughed. "Only you and my mother seem to care about it. I'm fine with my organized chaos."

"What you call 'organized chaos' is what most people call a messy house. A pigsty." He hadn't answered my question, so I repeated it. "Do you like living here?"

Considering the question for longer than I thought was necessary, he gave the room a once-over. It was nice. The large picture window in the living room gave an unobstructed view of the woods out back, which were full and lush and just several feet from the back door. It felt more like he was living in a cabin in the wilderness, and for that reason, I was sure he liked living in his new home.

"I do, but not more than living with you."

"You can come back anytime."

He made a face, a combination of a frown and a scowl. "That's not an option anymore. Not now."

"Because of the lease?"

"No, because of Ethan. You're with Ethan now. He will not allow such impropriety."

Allow? I was really getting sick of "allows" and "commands." "Ethan doesn't get to tell me who I can have as a housemate." Anger and indignation pushed the words through clenched teeth.

"If that person is in the pack, he can. Your interactions with other pack members are going to be limited." His wry smile and look of quiet resolve just fueled my frustrations. And he looked at me the way one would when they were watching a friend succumb to an inevitable failure. I hated that look.

"Ethan and I aren't like that. Our relationship isn't like that. I'm not sure how things are in other packs, but—"

"It's the same way it is in this pack with you and Ethan. The way it would be with Sebastian and any woman *he* was dating seriously. There are boundaries and restrictions. Ethan can make those decisions whether you like it or not. If you'd have seen him after we found you injured, you'd know how serious what you two have is. He spent several hours caged because he wasn't in control. Ethan is never out of control."

"Ethan's the only thing keeping you from moving back in with me?"

"Sky . . ."

"I asked a question. It's just a yes-or-no answer."

He grinned. "Yes, that's the only thing keeping it from happening."

After several moments, his lips twisted to the side—a clear sign that he was searching for the right words—and I knew I wasn't going to like what he had to say. "You think things are simple between you and Ethan and things are going to be business as usual because that's what you want. After the Ares injured you, he didn't just retaliate. It was carnage, uncontrolled. It took four of us to subdue him, and we had to lock him in the cage because he lashed out at us for stopping him. I'm pretty sure he's not going to be okay with some guy living with you."

"You're not 'some guy.'"

"To Ethan, I am." He brushed his fingers over my face, the odd thing we did as an apology—but it wasn't one. It was him asking me not to pursue this with Ethan. It bothered me. Things were starting to feel claustrophobic, and the tenuous hold I had on my old life was slipping away each day.

I sank back into the sofa. I didn't want to talk about it anymore. "Winter and I went back to the area where we found that odd-looking man, the one with the weird animal eyes."

"Did you find anything?" he asked, rubbing his beard. I hoped it bothered him and then maybe he would get rid of it.

I shook my head and told him everything except the part about Chris being there.

"What happened between you smelling the medicine and running into Chase?" Steven asked.

I hesitated before I answered. "What do you mean?"

His eyes narrowed and he gave me a dry, faint smile. "There was a slight change in your cadence. And your heart rate increased slightly. What happened between then?"

"Nothing."

With one look, he let me know that he didn't believe me. I didn't know why I even tried to lie to were-animals; it never worked. And I was fully aware that each time you met one, they were assessing you from the time you walked through the door, looking for variations in your heart rate, intonation, cadence of your voice, and respiration. In the brief moment it took for them to shake your hand, they had assessed all the things that were considered normal, your baseline, and looked for any variations in it to exploit or manipulate if necessary. Had your heart rate increased because you were scared? They wanted to know what had made you afraid. Despite being able to detect lies and seeming to be quite affronted by them, their favorite tactic was "getting people to see the reality which they wanted you to believe." It was a very eloquent way of saying they were lying and feeding you BS.

I chewed on the secret and waited for a moment, debating if I should tell Steven. He and I were very close, but his devotion to the pack extended further than anything we would ever have. I knew that if I told him, it was as good as me telling Sebastian if he decided it was information that Sebastian needed.

"I'll tell you, but it has to be between the two of us."

"Sky, you know I can't do that."

"Then I can't tell you," I said firmly.

He sucked in a ragged breath and held it for a long time before exhaling. "Sky, you can't keep secrets from the pack, you just can't."

"Even if I don't agree with their decision?"

"Especially if you don't agree with their decision. At least trust Sebastian."

I did trust Sebastian and his ability to handle every situation. But I knew that he wasn't above doing unscrupulous things when "handling things" that were particularly difficult. In fact, if it was to protect the pack and its members, his behavior and the things he was willing to do at times were abhorrent. He made deals with the devil and his relatives and would switch sides and collude with the enemy of the devil if it served his purpose. Anyone who thought they were just playing checkers with him was oblivious to the fact that he had beaten them with a few moves and had moved on to three-dimensional chess.

I couldn't help but wonder if all the Alphas were present because of the Logan situation. How was this their issue and not just the Midwest Pack's problem? "Did your mom tell you why the other Alphas were called by Sebastian?"

"Sebastian didn't call them, Cole did." He had the same concerned look on his face as Winter had had, troubled about what was big enough that all the Alphas were called.

The silence persisted as we were both drawn into our thoughts. I pondered what I knew about the East Coast Pack —nothing.

"You smelled medicine and magic and then what?" he asked. I told him everything, including seeing Chris. After I finished telling him, I said, "You can't tell anyone that we saw her. You have to promise to keep it to yourself."

He sighed heavily. "Sky, you know I can't do that."

"You have to, please." Then I went into detail about everything that took place at Logan's, including what he was requesting of us. I figured I'd generate some understanding as to why I needed him to keep the Chris sighting a secret.

With arrant disgust, he asked, "What exactly does Logan want with Chris?"

"He claimed before that he was looking for a companion, but I think there is more to it. Regardless, we shouldn't be trafficking women."

"We aren't trafficking anyone," he said dismissively. "We are dealing with a situation."

"Don't do that. Don't try to make this less repugnant than it is. I can't believe using another person as a bargaining chip is even an option." Sebastian had done some questionable things to protect this pack, and I didn't doubt that he was capable of more.

Steven frowned at the idea again. "But if you think we are the only ones looking for her on Logan's behalf, I'm pretty sure we aren't. It's probably better that we know where she is before someone else finds her."

I wanted to believe him—I really did—but we had once left a woman with Logan. Even though she'd expressed a desire to stay with him, and Josh hadn't detected a spell that would have compelled her to give that answer, I'd still wanted to take her against her will. How twisted and perverse was this situation— wanting to take someone from the clutches of a monster made me a bad person, but offering someone up to him didn't. Each time I thought about Logan, it brought to mind his self-proclaimed fascination with pain and the shroud of adoration that brightened his face when he discussed it.

Chris hadn't been the only person who'd attracted his atten- tion, so had Ethan. And I would never forget how drawn Logan was to him. I knew there was a lot about Ethan that I didn't know —and I just hoped it wasn't nearly as bad as my overactive imagination had led me to believe on numerous occasions—but Logan's fascination kept nagging at me.

"I wonder if it's all connected," I said.

"All of what?"

"Everything: Logan and his sick request, Kelly going missing, and the strange animal people that we keep finding. What if they're all connected?"

He considered it for a moment and then frowned. "I think the Kelly situation may be independent of all this. It's reasonable that she'd want to leave, after all she was—" He stopped midsentence, and his eyes flashed as if he'd had a eureka moment. "She was poisoned by the sleeper—we need another one."

I was sure he thought whatever he was thinking made sense, but it didn't. Why did we need the Tod Schlaf?

"For Logan," he clarified. "Kelly was alive but unable to move, and the same was true for Gideon. If you can put it on Logan, he will remain alive but be unable to do anything, including destroy the Tre'ase that created Maya's heart."

For a brief moment, everything didn't seem so bleak. Logan could be handled—there might be a light at the end of the dark tunnel. We could keep Logan alive while we found a way to unlink the Tre'ase that had created Maya.

~

The next morning I was up bright and early, cleaning out what would soon be Steven's room. Whether my decision to have him move back in without discussing it with Ethan was a result of my desire to remain independent or spite was still debatable. By midnight of the night before, when Ethan hadn't shown up or answered any of my texts or calls, I was feeling pretty spiteful. Was that his way of avoiding any of my questions about the meeting? He knew I wasn't going to sleep without having some answers.

When Ethan's car pulled into the driveway, I opened the door and continued with preparing the room for Steven's return and removing some of the things that I had placed in there for storage.

Ethan's brow furrowed with curiosity once he found me.

"Steven's moving back in," I informed him.

His lips pulled into a taut straight line as he stepped in the room, which, with the exception of a few things in the closet, was move-in ready.

"Foi ideia tua ou dele?" Your idea or his, he asked, slowly roaming around the room. Distracted.

I watched him cautiously as I always did when he spoke Portuguese, which he'd learned in order to speak to me. It was the language my adoptive mother had encouraged me to learn to maintain a connection with my birth mother. I'd spoken it with her as well. It had been familiar and comforting, and even though I'd learned it reluctantly as a child, I'd appreciated that we had something that connected us. Now I shared that connection with Ethan. Sometimes I wondered if he used it to disarm me and make things more palatable.

"Minha." Mine. I waited for him to say something but he remained quiet, stolid. "He's under the impression he needed your approval." We didn't speak for a long time.

I smiled. *"Bobo, certo?"* Silly, right?

My response was met with a long pause as he looked around the room before the rictus formed.

"I miss him," I admitted, and I did. I enjoyed living with Steven.

"What do you miss: having all your food eaten up, finding his books tossed about in your living room, or following him with a vacuum to ensure that your house doesn't look like a sty?" Derision was heavy in his voice, and the smirk firmly fixed on his face.

"There were other things. My life didn't consist of just that."

"Then what is it?" His interest seemed piqued more than it had ever been before. With the myriad of complex things there were about me, this was the one that held his attention the most?

But the relationship and comradery that I had with Steven wasn't easily explained or understood. He'd lost his parents when he was a child, and then his sister. He'd been brought into the pack, he wasn't of the pack. He was one of the few people that I interacted with who had found that fragile balance between being a were-animal and part of the pack. He was dedicated to the pack, but there was still a small part of him that seemed like he was on the outside looking in, the way I often felt.

He was still part of the everyday, non-supernatural world. His adaptability and the nuances of his nature were the very things that kept me grounded. He was more than just acute senses and a person who shifted into a coyote when necessary. When he was in human form, he was as human as my neighbor. Ethan didn't possess that; there wasn't a moment when, in his overwhelming presence, I forgot that he was a wolf. The primality of his animal was so blended into his very nature that he always presented as mostly were-animal and only passably human. I accepted that about him and most of the pack, but I still needed something different—Steven was different. We were different.

"He's fixated on the fact that he needs your approval. Give it to him so he'll move back."

"Sky—"

"Steven makes things"—I didn't have the right word that really expressed it—"he's comforting."

He made a face, then nodded slowly. Could that have made Ethan jealous? I wondered when his mood changed. "I'll take that into consideration." And with that he left the room.

He could consider it all he wanted. Good for him, but it wasn't his decision. As he took a seat on the sofa, his hands clasped behind his head, he seemed casually amused by me grappling with the polite way to tell him exactly what I was thinking. "Get bent" seemed like the wrong way to start off.

I took a long, calming breath. Then another. I needed several to work through all variations of telling him where to take his "consideration." With a sweet, cloying smile, I finally said, "It's good that you're thinking about it. But since it's not your decision, it really doesn't matter."

The stern look of defiance should have deterred me. I didn't want to argue with Ethan—we had more pressing issues that we needed to deal with than Steven's living arrangements—but once again I found myself on the precipice, realizing that if I allowed this to go unchallenged, things with Ethan would devolve into this relationship being totally in his control. Everything in it would be based on his whims and decisions. For a few moments, the idea that those factors had existed from the moment things had changed between us and we became "involved" made me uneasy.

"It's not your decision to make," I repeated, infusing my voice with steel, determined that this was going to be one of the battles I won. I wasn't going to allow Ethan to control what went on in my house, and for a brief moment I understood the dynamics between Ethan and Josh and the rest of their world. The pack, whether you wanted them to or not, became a huge part of your life, consuming so much of it that your life was the pack. Period. But those dynamics didn't have to exist in my personal micro-cosm. Ethan wasn't going to be the Alpha of our own little pack or whatever the hell was happening between us.

He considered me for a few moments, and I wondered if he was experiencing the same uncertainties that I was.

"But it is," he said calmly, cool and stolid as though the discussion was over.

"Ethan—"

"This discussion is over. I don't want another man living with you."

"Another man? It's Steven, not some random guy."

When he sucked in a breath, I knew that he was fighting a

dominating and aggressive response because he was unaccustomed to being challenged, especially by members of the pack. If he told Steven not to move in with me, it wouldn't be challenged. It would be what was requested. He shrugged. "As I stated before, I'll take your request under consideration."

Why did that sound like he was dismissing me? Probably because he was. Placating me with a falsehood in order to move on. *Yep, and right there is the punchable face.*

"Just call him and tell him now," I pressed.

"No." He extended his hand out to me, and I stood a few inches from him, staring at it. "We have more pressing things to deal with." As much as I hated to admit it, I knew he was right and that we needed to put the living arrangement situation aside.

I took it and let him draw me to him. I sat astride him and he smiled and leaned into me, his breath warm and breezy against my lips. "See, if Steven lived here, we couldn't do this." His hands slipped under my shirt, kneading at my skin, stroking it. I was aware of him watching my response as he moved over the previously bruised area. It was healed and just a little tender. Nothing compared to how it had felt initially.

"Of course we can. In fact, I owe him a couple of uncomfortable moments. I can't tell you the number of times I found one of his stray one-nighters in the house. At least I know your name. That's more than I can say for him and the random half-naked woman I had to have my coffee and breakfast with."

Ethan laughed and I leaned against him. "I'm sure he knew their names."

"A couple he couldn't give with certainty. He was reduced to calling them 'sweetheart' or 'hon.'"

"And yet you miss that?"

"No, I don't miss that. But I do miss him."

Ethan frowned. "What happened yesterday?"

I told him the same edited version I'd given Steven, taking care to monitor my vital responses as much as I could. I wasn't ready to tell him about Chris, yet. The situation still seemed too complicated.

His lips pressed against mine, soft, gentle, soothing. Warm breath beat lightly against my lips as he held my gaze for a long time before speaking. "Who did you see, Chris or Quell?" His tone was soft and devoid of anything readable. Was he angry? Disappointed?

At least there was disgust, which was something he exhibited often when Quell's name came up. Ethan and most of the pack referred to him as "my vampire." And in a peculiar way, he was. He was a misanthropic vampire who chose to feed from a plant rather than a human because of his disdain for them, and somehow I was the only person he would feed from.

I held Ethan's gaze and failed at keeping everything even and consistent. I steadied my breathing and the cadence in my voice and was careful with how many times I blinked. I'd never be able to control my heart rate no matter how much I tried, but I controlled as many things as I could that I knew he would monitor and assess for changes. Ethan was good, and I figured a distraction would impair his abilities. I brushed my lips against his and he pulled me closer, kissing me hungrily as his fingers moved through my hair. When he pulled away he asked again, "Who did you see, Chris or Quell?"

I shook my head. His wry frown lasted for a brief moment before it became a disappointed one. Tension remained between us, and what started out as just a few seconds of quiet turned into several long minutes of silence. The extended quiet always bothered me more than Ethan, and he could have sat there, watching me, until I recanted my statement. I wasn't ready. Continuing the story, I dropped my eyes from his and found a spot of some interest behind him. "The witch or mage or whatever was strong. Standing next to her was like standing next to Josh, but the magic was different. I haven't been around enough mages to—"

"Seventy-seven. Your heart rate has increased to seventy-seven. You're lying to me. Answer my question and then finish. Tell me everything. I know it had to be either Chris or Quell because those are the only two people you would be reluctant to tell me about. Which one was it, Sky?"

For a long time I considered ignoring the question and finishing the story, and if I were dealing with anyone else, I might have. Tenacity was one of the traits Ethan possessed in spades, and I knew he wasn't going to be put off.

"Chris," I croaked out in a tight voice.

The moment platinum began to roll over his eyes, he closed them. "You can't keep things from me, Skylar."

I held my pot-kettle comment because it would only have made things worse.

"I don't agree with her being brought into this, not even to appease him for a moment. Even if it buys us more time."

"It's a last resort. No one wants this, but so far, Josh hasn't found anything. What do you suggest we do, Sky? If you have an idea, please share it with me."

I had nothing. A way to fix this had dominated most of my thoughts, and in the end, I really had nothing. The only thing I had to offer was Steven's suggestion. He listened and then smiled. "That's a great idea."

It was a great idea that required me convincing him that it would be better handled by Winter and me. More specifically Winter. He reluctantly agreed after an unnecessary debate, and midway through that conversation, I started to feel like he just enjoyed arguing with me and was already agreeable to us doing it.

Settled as I was against him, my face pressed into his neck, his fingers gently stroking my skin were a distraction, and one I was sure that he was very aware of. "What was your meeting about?" I asked.

"Nothing, really." He wrapped his arms around me and lightly kissed me on the head.

I adjusted myself, moving back from him.

"A meeting with all the Alphas was for nothing? That's really hard to believe."

He shrugged, the hard frown eventually slipping, but he looked distracted again. "Cole called the meeting. He tends to be more inclined to overreaction than most."

Okay, then, if Cole is considered an overreactor by the king of over-reactors, then Cole has to be the drama kings of all drama kings.

"What is he overreacting about?"

Ethan nuzzled at my neck, ignoring my question. Then he kissed me, gently at first and then more commanding, drawing a moan from me. *Oh, Mr. Distraction is in rare form today.* I jerked away and stood back several inches.

"I'm not that easily distracted."

He hit me with one of his overly confident smiles. Confidence and arrogance melded together in a way that was definitively and uniquely his. There it was in all its glory, the look that made me want to inflict bodily harm upon him. *Yeah, you're super sexy. Good for you.* "Cole, being overreactive and dramatic, called a meeting for what reason?"

Conceding to the fact that I wasn't going to drop the topic, Ethan rubbed his hands over his face and then leaned forward and rested his elbows on his thighs. It took a moment for him to focus on me. I wasn't buying the "Cole was overreacting" story. I had a feeling the meeting had had something to do with me or Josh, and Ethan was doing what he always tried to do— protecting us and hiding the truth. That was where our belief systems were diametrically opposed. He protected people by keeping them in the dark while he attempted to handle it behind the scenes with them being none the wiser. I believed the darkness left the person vulnerable and unable to defend themselves.

"Cole was told that we would be cursed and the packs would fall at the hands of the wolf that wasn't anchored to this life."

"We are going to be cursed because of me. Who told him this?"

"A fae. One with foretelling gifts like Claudia's. The East Coast Pack has a good relationship with them. It was a warning."

"Why do you think it's an overreaction? It's possible."

He shook his head, but it lacked conviction. "You have control of Maya. You have this. I have no concerns. And anything a fae sees is never going to be as accurate as what Claudia knows. She isn't concerned, so I'm not."

"You've seen what I'm capable of. Maya has unlocked a lot of magic in me." I brought up the fact that when we'd removed Marcia's curse, we'd removed others. Vital ones that protected people. How did we know that we hadn't activated curses, too? The full impact of what we'd done was constantly unfolding, each discovery more ominous and devastating than the previous one. And for the record, I wasn't the only wolf "not anchored to this life"—there was Ethan. He'd been hiding something that had always existed, or something had awakened in him, too.

"You're different, too."

He dismissed my accusation with a wave of his hand. "Are we going to have this discussion again? It's really getting old."

"I don't think you're being honest. You did magic that not even Josh knew to kill something that couldn't be destroyed with a spell from the Clostra or Faerie magic. You want me to believe it was just a spell that Josh forgot to learn?"

"I never said he 'forgot' to learn. Josh wasn't always as assiduous as he is now about magic, so there are spells that I know that he doesn't."

I knew Ethan would have a logical answer for everything I tossed in his direction. It all made sense, except Josh had said the spell that Ethan had done was so strong that even a level one witch would have issues completing it, yet he'd done it with ease. Ethan, because his mother was a witch, had access to magic that most didn't. He'd often said it was weak, residual magic and that somehow upon his mother's death, it had been split unequally between him and Josh. Ethan possessed skills that his brother didn't, including being able to disarm most wards. My curiosity was unsettled. I felt that Ethan was more; he was hiding something, but I wasn't sure who he was trying to protect by doing it.

"I feel a lot of things would have to transpire for you to be a danger."

He stood, and before I could ask any more questions he gave me a quick peck on the cheek and started for the door.

"You're not staying?"

He shook his head. "I'll be back tonight."

I had to wonder: was knowing that Chris was in town the reason for his abrupt departure? Was there more about the Cole situation that he was trying to handle inconspicuously?

I stopped him before he could go out the door. "Don't look for her. She can't be part of this, Ethan." He grunted a response and exited. I shouted to the closed door, "And don't forget to let Steven know he can move in!"

The door opened again. "Steven's not moving back," he said firmly. I started to say something, but he raised his hand to quiet me. "Steven will never do anything to hurt you. He just doesn't have it in him. Like my brother, he coddles you. Which leaves me being the bad guy—"

"You're good at it."

The insult rolled over him and he smiled as though he'd accepted it as a compliment. "He's happy where he is, and that is where he will stay."

"How do you know?"

"Because Joan said he is. She has no reason to lie about it."

I nodded. He waited a few minutes, I assumed to gauge my response. Before he finally left, he said, "If he wanted to come back as well, I would be okay with it because it is what you both want. Your wants can't override his."

He closed the door behind him.

CHAPTER 5

*W*inter wasn't very happy about visiting her ex and probably never would be—Abigail's betrayal and manipulation of Winter's residual feelings for her had assured that—but for the good of the pack, she reluctantly did it.

We waited patiently at the door, near the sentinel who had let us in, but not before confiscating our weapons and anything that could be conceivably used as a weapon, including keys. As Abigail descended the spiraling stairs of her new home where she and her brother lived, which was provided to him as the new ruler of the elves, a smile overtook her face. Although she wasn't entitled to be there and had no official title, she had settled in as more of a co-leader than a counselor. She'd manipulated and colluded her brother into the position of ruler of the elves that she'd actually wanted for herself but was precluded from holding by patriarchal rules. He considered her his political surrogate and had made it known that she should be given the same respect and privileges afforded to him, and she'd settled for a position of power by association. Her soft violet-colored eyes and whimsical smile could easily have fooled someone into believing that they weren't dealing with one of the most calculating and unscrupulous people that I'd ever encountered.

Abigail's and Winter's appearances both contrasted and complemented each other. The former's skin was fair, the latter's was a sun-kissed brown. Abigail's long pale blond hair was pulled back into a neat French braid, while Winter kept her dark brown tresses in a sleek ponytail. Both of their faces had narrow, delicate angles that were envy-worthy. Winter, like me, was dressed in jeans and a simple t-shirt. Abigail had on gray slacks, a slim-fitting white shirt, and a pearl necklace and bracelet. She had slipped into her new role quite well and appeared to be enjoying the benefits of it.

At Abigail's approach, Winter stepped back, keeping her distance. Abigail, seemingly incensed by it, made an attempt to get closer. Winter stepped back farther and shot her a harsh look that dared her to do it again. The bitterness that she felt over Abigail's exploiting their former relationship had created an irreparable rift between them. The many apologies that Abigail had offered had been met with cold indifference, which to Winter was worse than hate, which was at least still rooted in some type of emotion.

"It's good to see you, Winter," Abigail said, but she maintained the distance that Winter had put between them.

"This isn't a personal visit," Winter said in an even tone. She looked around the massive home. Pale yellow walls surrounded the room, expensive-looking sculptures were placed in the corners, and art in ornate brass frames covered the walls. With the exception of the decorative stairs and art, it was minimally decorated.

"Is your brother here?" Winter asked.

Abigail shook her head. "You requested that we meet alone. He's at a meeting, I stayed behind so that we could talk." She directed us to the living room, which was definitely for short impersonal visits. The pearl-colored Chesterfield sofa that she had us sit on was as uncomfortable as it looked, clearly serving to hurry guests along on their way.

As soon as Winter sat, she asked, "How did you get the Tod Schlaf?"

Abigail tensed, scanning the immediate area before speaking. "The person that was able to acquire it for me is no longer available for such projects."

Projects? Putting your brother in a catatonic state was a project?

"And why is that?" I asked. I wished I was better at detecting lies instead of having to rely on Winter, but at least everything that she felt was revealed on her face, including her disdain for the new information.

"Unfortunately, he is no longer alive."

Yes, it was quite unfortunate, and I was willing to bet that Abigail had something to do with it. Perhaps he'd attempted to blackmail her and she'd considered him too much of a liability to keep alive.

"Well, we need one," Winter demanded.

"I'm sorry, I can't get you one. Other than visiting the dark forest to get one yourself, I'm not sure how you can get one."

"Then get us into the dark forest," Winter countered.

I didn't want to go to the dark forest. We'd had to go there to find the antidote to the poison of the sleeper that had bitten Kelly. I'd seen how damaged Sebastian had looked when he'd come out of it. The most dangerous creations were kept in there—the ones the elves had created and considered failed experiments.

"I wish that was a request that could be handled as easily as before." She sighed, and anger and frustration dulled her features as irritation forced her smile into a scowl. "The Makellos' alliance with the witches has complicated things." Fire blazed in her eyes at the Makellos' ability to circumvent their rule. There was still that spark of jealousy of the self-proclaimed elite elves, who, due to their pure lineage, lived segregated from the other elves they deemed tainted from interbreeding with humans. The elite lived in the beautiful Elysian, which in contrast contained one of the most dangerous forests known to exist, where they kept their "magical mistakes"—animals so dangerous they had to be separated and kept behind wards to keep them from escaping.

Abigail and Gideon belonged among the "elite," something that Abigail wanted, but because of Gideon's contempt for them, they were never invited.

In addition to the latent hostility between the Makellos and the Abigail/Gideon duumvirate, dissension between Liam, the head of the Makellos elves, and the were-animals had been cultivated by Marcia, the head of the Creed, when Gideon voted against the Makellos in favor of saving Ethan. I should have known that would ignite an alliance between the witches and the Makellos. Because of Gideon and Demetrius, we'd gotten Ethan out of being "contained," their florid word for genocide, by one vote from the vampires. I hadn't seen that one coming, nor had anyone else—especially Marcia.

"I can see if Liam can be reasoned with. With the witches as allies, he displays even more arrogance and confidence than before, which has made him more difficult to tolerate and compromise with."

More arrogant, is that even possible? He couldn't be any more arrogant if he tried, but if he was allied with the witches, there had to be a renewed confidence and the power to back it up.

One of the agreements made between Abigail and Sebastian after we helped her with her brother was that she would incite a civil war between the different elves and in turn allow Gideon, who the were-animals had a shadow alliance with, to rule. This was proposed under the assumption that, based on the difference in numbers between the elves and the Makellos elves, Gideon would be the victor. But since the witches were now involved, that wasn't necessarily the case anymore, and Abigail wouldn't risk her position on a war she was confident they could win.

Abigail offered another apology but assured us that she would work on trying to get us into the forest. Winter didn't seem convinced, but I was. Despite Abigail's power-hungry ways, she seemed to be determined to obtain Winter's forgiveness. But I wasn't sure about her motives—was it sincere remorse, or putting herself in a position to exploit the relationship and Winter again?

~

Three days crept by and we weren't any better off. We weren't any closer to finding Kelly or uncovering anything about that strange magic I had encountered or the rabid girl that we had seen. After the Alphas had returned home, Ethan spent most of his time away, and I concluded he was looking for Chris, although he would never admit it to me.

The lack of progress made something like Abigail convincing Liam to allow us into the dark forest seem like a bigger victory than it was. Sure, why not go into a forest where the odds of your getting out were even worse than the already dismal chances of your getting in? But we were desperate and had limited options.

When Liam finally called to agree to a time, it was a good thing he couldn't see the look of pure derision and disdain on Sebastian's face. Perhaps Sebastian had thought the situation was going to be handled more amicably and didn't mind Winter and me being in the office. It started out casual, cordial—*yeah, sure, why wouldn't it be?*—two men of power who couldn't stand each other, all in a day's work. *Quelle surprise* when it slowly devolved into poorly veiled threats and outright insults.

"I helped you contain those creatures when your wards broke. I assumed you would be more amenable to repaying the favor. I'm not asking to use your people as an escort. I think we are more than capable of negotiating Elysian on our own. I am just requesting entrance into it. Why do you feel this is a situation in which I owe you another favor? As far as I'm concerned, the many resources we used to clean up that mess more than satisfy the debt I incurred the last time we went there, and in fact leave you with an arrearage."

Of course, Sebastian didn't point out that the ward had fallen because of the spell that I had performed. But Liam didn't have a problem bringing it up.

"You have no proof that breaking the ward was our doing, and until you have that proof, I will invite you to not accuse us of anything."

Did he just say that with a straight face?

"I understand that Marcia may have made you feel emboldened; she has a way of making even those that don't have a chance in hell feel as though she is their savior. The Creed, formerly the most powerful witches in the country, is down to just two. We did that. I don't think this thing needs to be handled by force. I understand you are doing me a favor. I will reluctantly incur that debt because we have no other choice; however, I will remember this egregious lack of gratitude for our previous assistance."

Liam's voice was pitched lower, and I had to strain to hear him. "It is my understanding that you have the Aufero in your possession. I would like it. For that, you will have full access to Elysian and the forest."

"No, it is best in our care, and I will caution you from taking your commands from Marcia. Do you understand what that object is capable of? As power hungry as Marcia has proven to be, you do not want her to have the ability to divest someone of their magic so easily. What will you do when she turns on you—don't be so naïve as to believe she won't once you've served your purpose."

I couldn't believe that Marcia was still after the Aufero. Had she taken up her former obsession once again now that the others had ruled against killing Ethan for being a dark elf? Or was this a way to get back at Josh?

We were probably overly cautious, but it seemed warranted. Liam's agreeing to our visiting Elysian was something that had been initiated by Abigail, and we all had the right to be apprehensive. Where had she gotten the leverage?

Hours after Sebastian's conversation with Liam, Sebastian, Ethan, Winter, Josh, Steven, and I were trekking through Elysian behind different guides than those we'd had the last time we'd visited. Before we'd been met by Liam, his stout look of contempt at our presence, and his military. This time he didn't bother with any of that. Guides met us in front of the entrance to say the incantation that opened the doors to it. They were identical twins—amber eyes with flecks of red and fiery red hair that was so long it caused them to keep raking it back out of their faces. At the same time. Each time. When the coltish men asked us to follow them, it was in unison. And when they weren't doing that, they were finishing each other's sentences. The elves had the patent on creepy twins—fraternal but androgynous twins Abigail and Gideon, and now these guys, were prime examples. The odd looks that Josh, Ethan, Sebastian, and Winter gave them made it apparent that I wasn't the only one wondering if they weren't one of the elves' odd creations that belonged in the dark forest, too. If they weren't, the animals that they'd brought definitely were. Nothing as majestic as the creatures provided to us before, which had been a beautiful and enchanting blend of okapi and horse.

These monstrosities were a vile combination of many things. The long necks of giraffes were topped by horse faces. The brawny appendages of horses had been replaced by thick, powerful feline legs made for sprinting. Top them all off with horse tails, and there you had it. On our previous visit, we'd been treated as invited guests welcomed to enjoy the beauty of Elysian. Now it was very evident that we were unwanted interlopers.

Ethan looked at the guides with caution as they forced us in a single-file line, putting Ethan and me in front. Answering the curiosity on Ethan's face, they said together, "I sense magic, it will help keep the rift open longer."

The last time we'd come to the dark forest, Sebastian and Gideon had been the only ones to enter, and it kept trying to break open to retrieve Ethan. He struggled, fighting as it attempted to claim him, and it wasn't until he shifted to his wolf that it quieted. I figured that it was because he possessed dark elven magic, but the opening was different than before. The edges of the wall formed little vines that looked like fingers, stretching out to receive us—to receive Ethan. They brushed against him.

I touched his arm. "It's fine," he whispered.

Is it? Magical walls forming fingers to touch someone is far from fine.

Despite my apprehension, Ethan stepped in first. I hesitated, making sure that Winter, Sebastian, and Steven were close. Josh stood a couple of feet away. He was going to stay behind in Elysian; we'd decided it was a good idea because of how upset and angry it had made our guide team. They took a few minutes from looking down at us to show their disdain. Josh was left behind in the event things didn't go as planned. He was the anchor on the outside who could help get us out. Or so we hoped.

The slip in the divide closed before anyone else could come through after me. Had we been set up? I plunged my sword into it, and it closed around it. I pulled the blade out and looked back at Ethan; spastic rolls of platinum consumed his eyes, and his teeth were clenched, hard.

After taking several calming breaths, he looked around the area. "Dark forest" was a misnomer—it wasn't much different than what was on the other side of the ward. Florets of greenery stretched over us; small man-made ponds were spread throughout the vast area. The plants were the oddest thing: they looked like flowering trees. Their stems were wide as tree trunks. Instead of green, they were variations of brown and hues of yellow. Like the plant Quell used to feed from, Hidacus, they moved as though they had life in them, a gentle beat at the nodes, between the stem and the internode. I stepped closer, and the beat increased. The metallic smell of blood inundated that air, covering the exotic scents of small buds of flowers that lingered throughout the space. Ethan turned his head to listen. I didn't hear anything, but whatever he heard made his face falter into a grimace.

"Stay close," he said as he started to walk farther. I thought the best plan was to get the hell out of there, but we might as well get what we had come for and then worry about getting out. I prepared myself for the worst of the various odd animals that I'd seen in Elysian and the horrible things I'd seen out of it—the monstrous way that Logan looked; Thaddeus, the Tre'ase that Chris had introduced us to; or even Ethos in his original form— and yet nothing looked like the mutated thing before us. Curved horns extended from a wolflike creature's head. Large teeth made it difficult for it to close its mouth. The long, lean, sinewy body ensured that it would be quick. A kick from the stout legs and cloven feet would definitely cause injury.

"There are more," Ethan said as I focused on the one directly in front of us. I wondered if this was just the first defense to getting farther into the forest. The last time we'd visited it, we'd been told the antidote for the sleeper's poison could be found on the "vilest creature," which in this place could be anything. I assumed the same would be true for finding a Tod Schlaf. How did we decide what was "vile" in this place? Sebastian had returned from the forest with talon marks on his shoulder. I looked up; a creature that flew would normally have talons, but in Elysian, it could very well be a mutated bunny rabbit.

The animals started to approach, slowly at first, studying us as intensely as we studied them. They were moving carefully, as if we were prey and they were just determining how to take us down. The strategic planning of a predator was something I was quite familiar with. I'd been around it more times than I wished.

"Do you think the horns are poisonous?" I asked.

In this forest I wasn't putting anything past the creatures. Sleepers looked like insects, and I wouldn't have suspected them to be as deadly as they were. The creepy-crawly that possessed the antidote looked like a wide leech. I had no idea what to expect. The mutated wolves attacked, speeding toward us, teeth bared, inhuman growls filling the air. Ethan waited, maintaining a defensive stance. I couldn't do it—my fight reflexes were in full effect. I didn't like being cornered. Three of them pounded toward me. One leapt, and I lowered my body to the ground, injuring the creature with a sweeping half arc of my sword that took it to the ground. I turned in time to dodge out of the way of the horns that were trying to impale me. It quickly retreated and advanced again. I spun around, bringing my sword down over them, cutting them off—one less weapon to worry about. It stumbled back, made a screeching sound, and attacked again, baring its teeth. I shoved the sword into the open mouth, and it made a gargling sound and dropped to the ground. Its mouth had closed around the blade, so I pressed my foot into its face to give me leverage to pull it out. Fast-approaching paws pounded to my right and dirt kicked up as another animal's powerful legs pushed him at speeds unlike anything a typical wolf could produce.

Magic. I raised my hand, feeling it unfurl in me, and shot it out, trying to push the animal away. Nothing. I turned and yanked at the embedded sword again, making hard jerks as I tried to dislodge it. Thankfully the dead thing's teeth were clenched around steel and not me.

I pulled out the sword in time and readied to take out the other creature. Ethan grabbed it in a midair lunge, quickly stopping it.

We advanced farther, the sky darkening and quickly eclipsing into darkness. It took a moment for my eyes to adjust to the changes. "Dark forest" wasn't a misnomer at all. Trees crowded the path, making navigation harder. Breathy sounds filled the area, and deep growls were so constant that they became nothing more than white noise. Ethan didn't seem to be as anxious as me as we moved through the dim, portentous area, a space dominated by hisses, labored breathing, and predaceous movement of unknown animals that the elves had thought were a good idea to create.

"Why are they allowed to do this?" I asked.

Ethan's low voice mirrored mine. "I've wondered the same thing. It has never been an issue, so we never got involved." It didn't affect the pack, so it wasn't their concern, but a couple of months ago, the elves' problem creatures had spilled into our lives. Animals of unknown destruction and devastation shouldn't be able to be created for amusement. It was something that should have been addressed.

"I don't think they should be allowed to do this. Not anymore."

He stopped walking, his eyes narrowed on me. "But if they weren't allowed, then what would be our option to stop Logan?"

I hated the nebulous concept of necessary evil and indiscernible lines between right and wrong.

"Let's just get what we need and get out of here."

Yeah, that's easy, seeing that we were pretty much thrust in here by ourselves. I wondered if he considered it suspicious that the elves only wanted the two of us in the dark forest. Did they believe we belonged here with the other mutated creatures? A mistake, but not of their doing?

A distinctive whoosh sounded in the air, slicing through the various noises that consumed the area. It was a taloned creature, and not a damn bunny, either. Calling it a dragon wouldn't have been a stretch. A reptilian creature, with daggerlike teeth and talons in place of hands. I couldn't imagine anything being more dangerous than this thing—here was what Sebastian had gone up against to get the sleeper antidote. I extended my sword, preparing to engage. The winged creature grimaced, drawing back its lips. Then odd fiery orange-and-red eyes fixed on Ethan, and at that moment it began to choke with a gargling sound and fell to the ground in front of us.

Its breathing sped up and the choking sound increased as Ethan approached it and began to search its scaly body for sleepers. I saw several of the leechlike antidote carriers and a number of the Tod Schlaf. Ethan selected one of the latter and placed it in a jar that he'd pulled out of the small bag he carried. When the dragon-thing finally went quiet, so did everything else. All the mutated animals that lurked in the darkness retreated, something scaring them into silence, and that something wasn't me. It was the same person that the dark forest had tried to claim the last time we'd visited Elysian—Ethan.

I couldn't help but stare at the subdued animal that had dropped at just a look at Ethan. My attention quickly fixed on my companion. "What happened to it?"

He shrugged and tugged my arm, guiding me to the front of the forest. Handing me his bag, he took my hand and urged me toward the opening where we'd entered. The ward barring exit stretched, thinning to a diaphanous curtain that allowed us to see the figures of the people on the other side, but it held. I pressed into it and it rebounded back, pushing me into Ethan. I pushed it again, and magic twitched at my fingers pressing into the barrier, but not enough to open it. Silence prevailed, more ominous than before. The magic I'd been holding back before surged through, and I pressed my hand to the ward. It ripped and I slipped through; as soon as I did, it sealed on Ethan's wrist. I clasped it tightly, shifting my weight and trying to tug him through. He wasn't putting any effort into assisting, and moments later he slipped back. The barrier closed completely, thicker and stronger than before. I handed Ethan's bag to Sebastian.

Josh's eyes went black and hard as he called upon stronger waves of magic to blast against the ward, which wavered and bulged in but never gave. I no longer considered this place a heaven of magical beauty and unique creations. It was fucking hell.

The guides started to back away on their odd animals, warning, "It's time to escort you all out."

They said it in a steely tone of indifference that only made me angrier. Josh glared at them, baring his teeth, before returning his attention to the ward. The more magic he directed at it, the stronger the magical wall became. The weight of his failure quickly coursed over his face. He leaned into it and sighed.

"We have to go. Please let us escort you out." The guides' tone was gentler, a hint of unspoken condolence.

Sebastian shook his head. "We're not leaving without him. Give us another opening."

"We were instructed to arrange one entrance and one exit. It takes a great amount of magic to open the ward, leaving us weakened. We will not make ourselves vulnerable for the likes of you," one of the guides began to assert, with his brother finishing the sentence. Their amber eyes became stony and cool, as had Liam's when he dealt with us.

The anger that I had tamped down the first time they spoke reasserted itself and roiled through me like a wave as the desire to control it seemed to slowly decrease. I took a step forward, clenching the sword tighter, before Sebastian stepped in front of me. "Then we are going to have a problem, because I'm not leaving without him. If you think reopening it will leave you vulnerable, then you have no idea what I plan to do with you all if we don't get Ethan back."

They urged their animals back and then whipped around and trotted away. Who knew what they planned to do—their intentions were getting harder to read as they scurried away—but soon the animals were coaxed into a full-out run until they were no longer in sight.

Sweat glistened around Josh's brow when he finally dropped to the ground, the ward as strong as it had been before, with no signs of faltering or giving. He closed his eyes, then inhaled a ragged breath before speaking. "I don't know if I can get him out." There was the crux of it—they'd allowed us in to get the sleeper in exchange for Ethan, someone that the forest had wanted to claim long ago.

I placed my hand on Josh's shoulder, regretting leaving the Aufero at home, because I'd thought the borrowed magic from Josh was enough and I hadn't wanted to provoke Maya. I had also had no idea if I would be able to control magic in the dark forest or in Elysian, and I hadn't wanted to risk it. Now I didn't care. I wanted unconstrained, reckless, turbulent, and destructive magic.

Winter pushed up from the tree where she had been painfully silent the entire time. Every once in a while, her placid look and the tight lines of her lips faltered into a frown. The last time, it took more effort to remove it, and she washed her hands over her face several times and turned away to scan the area.

Blade in both hands, she advanced toward us and the thunderous sound that came up behind us. Liam moved toward us first, his animal a midnight horse with lava-colored eyes that possessed the same level of heat as magma. Its curved horns twisted and looked as dangerous and ostentatious as the crew of people behind them. The first animals had been there for transportation; now the Makellos had animals equipped for battle.

Swaddled in his trademark arrogance, Liam exuded a haughtiness and contempt that were as refined as the green suit he wore.

As if he needed anything else to make him more confident, he'd brought along a small army that outnumbered us five to one.

"Sebastian, you have been asked to leave. We've been more than generous by allowing you all to come here. The forest is not some playground." He regarded Sebastian idly before he continued. "Even your kind aren't a match for that which we hold in there. Your arrogance is your failure—that is your burden, not mine. You will be given the courtesy once more to leave of your own volition." He looked back over his shoulder, and a new set of odd twins, this time male/female, presented us with animals to use to get us across the area quickly and out of their territory.

Without giving him the courtesy of an answer, Sebastian was the first to shift, fur puncturing through the skin of his hands, the transition slower than I'd ever seen—a display of immeasurable control and a nonverbal challenge. He was about to drop to the ground when a scaly slim body shot past us. A six-foot-long snake slinked around, its ventral scales expanded. Winter's head darted and several of the soldiers dropped from their animals and hit the ground, paralyzed by the venom from her fangs. In were-animals, the state only remained for ten minutes or so, but we didn't know how long the effects would last on others. Winter rarely donned her animal form; this was the first time since we'd met that she'd used it for battle. Her sinuous movements were faster than I expected as she moved through the area, powerful strikes knocking the soldiers off their mounts. She continued the rampage, retreating back only when someone advanced toward Sebastian.

We'd seen Sebastian in fights before. He was a force to reckon with, and it was easy to consider him indestructible and undefeatable. Winter was trying to protect him, and it didn't go unnoticed. Since his near-fatal injury weeks ago, she had been cautious around him, protective. Several bullets had hit his chest and body, and as he'd fallen to the ground, the illusion of his indestructibility had been shattered in one sweeping act. He was like us, capable of falling and being wounded, and Winter seemed to have taken it harder than anyone else. Her loyalty wasn't misplaced: he'd fought and annihilated an entire pack to save a young Winter's life. The massive snake had now wiped out half the Makellos army, most on the ground, frozen in a state of confusion and fear. The others had been tossed a distance away when her tail coiled around them and displaced them.

I was left speculating upon which form Winter was the most dangerous in. Arrows whizzed through the air toward her, and

Sebastian reached up and plucked the first one from the air. The second hit her, but it looked superficial because Sebastian had grasped the end of it and only the tip had punctured her skin.

"Change back," he ordered her as he pulled out the arrow. She quickly shifted back to human form. One of the benefits of being a lesser were-animal and a snake was that her shift didn't destroy her clothes in the process.

Sebastian's low, rough tone was laden with threat, and so was the snarl on his face as he forced words through his teeth. He looked at the men Winter had disabled in just a few minutes and then directed his attention to Liam. "That was just one of us. It's your decision—do you really want to do this? Next time, I won't stop anyone. The casualties of this will be your burden alone."

Liam's grimace gave way to a tight frown; he took a few moments to survey the results of just minutes of Winter's assault upon his army. The level of abhorrence he had for us was going to be the downfall of his people. Conceit and stubbornness were as much a part of him as his magic. I thought he didn't know what to think of Sebastian's calm countenance, which I'd quickly discovered was the serene moment before the tumultuous storm. It was something that needed to be experienced only once.

Liam raised his hand to his people, but the way it was positioned, I couldn't tell if it was going to tell them to retreat or attack. Before he could specify, a burst of magic hit us all, pounding against our backs like shrapnel—hard, dark, deadly. I turned, and Ethan stood in front of an opening that gaped larger than the one that had allowed us entrance. It wasn't until one of the elven-created creatures stepped through the opening that the elves reacted. They moved toward it, trying to counter the strong magic that forced the opening. It was nothing like theirs, and the difference was tangible.

There were small tears in Ethan's shirt, and his hands were stained with blood, but he didn't seem injured. His eyes were slowly being taken over by specks of black, similar to the way Josh's eyes looked when he called on more magic.

He gave me a faint smile as he moved closer to me, and I made every effort not to stare at his eyes. He stopped for a moment, leaning against a tree, his head pressed back against it. He'd taken a similar posture when he'd been fighting to keep from being pulled into the dark forest during our first visit. Now he was fighting off something entirely different—magic. I took several steps back to give him space as he attempted to ward off whatever it was. The elves who had broken away from the others were trying to contain the animals that had escaped and replace the shattered ward. The male/female twins mounted their animals and made impatient sounds, preparing to escort us out.

Ethan took a few more controlled breaths, and when he opened his eyes, they had returned to their natural color but somehow weren't the same. The coal color had retreated, but its presence lay just below the surface.

The elves ushered us out, and their parting words made it very clear that this was the last time we would be allowed into Elysian under any circumstances. Sebastian and Josh split their attention between Winter, who winced each time she moved her arm where the arrow had hit it. Blood stained the area. "You shouldn't have done that. I hadn't given an order to," Sebastian said, his tone firm but gentle.

Winter started to speak but stopped, chewing on her bottom lip. Words didn't need to be spoken: she wore her emotion and fear for Sebastian over the gentle lines of her face. He seemed to be having as difficult of a time determining how to deal with her break in protocol and the reasons she'd done it. Steven got into his car, but Sebastian stopped Winter as she started to get in the passenger side.

"You ride with me. We need to talk." She nodded but had difficulty making eye contact with him as she followed him. Although most times it seemed difficult for me to hold eye contact with

Ethan, today I didn't have any problems. I scrutinized him, the way he looked and the peculiar ominous magic that had settled over him.

After I'd slipped into the passenger side of Ethan's car, next to Josh, who offered to drive, Ethan handed me four small containers before getting into the backseat. I held them up. "What are these?"

"The antidote for the sleeper." I glanced at the creepy-crawly little leeches like the one that we had used to cure Kelly. We had been so focused on finding a sleeper to use on Logan that we hadn't considered the antidote, although I doubted that was something anyone was really concerned about.

"We have them all now. If anyone wants to use one, they will have to go through us. We need to give them to Dr. Jeremy," he said coolly.

"Is this why you allowed yourself to be pulled back in?"

He nodded, keeping his eyes on the road, but I was determined not to see the reality in which he wished me to believe. I'd felt the magic, seen his eyes, and witnessed the response of the dark forest animals to him.

"Why do some creatures and Tre'ase respond to you the way they do?"

With a quick shrug, he dismissed my question.

"We removed the dark elven magic," I said.

"I know, I was there."

"But you still have magic. I felt it and saw it."

"My mother was a witch, remember?"

"I'm very familiar with witch magic. Your magic was distinctively different from anything I've felt on Josh or any witch. Darker, deadlier."

His tone was level and cool. "All magic can be considered dark and deadly, Sky. Please don't find a problem where there isn't one."

CHAPTER 6

he drive home from Elysian was riddled with uncomfortable glances and quiet. Ethan worked hard to pretend things were normal, but I wasn't going to let it go. While Josh drove, he kept casting curious looks at his brother, who was resting in the backseat. When Ethan's eyes opened, they locked on his brother's in the rearview mirror. I studied their interaction, still certain that their communication came from more than a sibling connection. A look spoke volumes more than it should have, and whatever Ethan conveyed to Josh assuaged his curiosity enough that he didn't ask questions. Josh drove to his home, and when he got out of the car, Ethan did, too, and then moved into the driver's seat. Curiosity drove me, and I had a hard time managing it but convinced myself to wait. Waiting lasted a total of six minutes, and that seemed too long. "Ethan."

He sighed heavily, preparing for incoming questions. Good, because I had plenty.

Preemptively he said, "I can do magic. This isn't a secret. Just like Josh, when I need to, I can use more. You saw it's not readily available to me. It tires me as well. I responded differently in there, too. I have no answers as to why."

I really wanted to believe him. I knew Ethan's life was a myriad of secrets, and I'd really thought I could just accept and live with the fact that it was going to be that way with him. But what I'd seen today in Elysian and the dark forest was something I wasn't sure I could just live with. Would he ever feel the need to share what he kept from me?

I was about to ask, when he pulled up to my driveway and I saw the peculiar man resting against my door. His look had changed, but his amethyst eyes were the same. Logan enjoyed the ability to manipulate his appearance more than others. The form he'd held the longest was very similar to Ethan's— chestnut-colored hair, defined features, and a tall, muscular build. Logan had traded that shell for a more classically handsome appearance with a square jaw, wide brow, and darker brown hair that looked as if he'd used too much product to attain the style. His eyes, which I'd once found kind and intriguing, were pits of menace and nefarious intent.

His lips pulled back in a tight smile that he directed at me as I got out of the car. When Ethan got out, Logan's attention focused solely on him, eyes narrowed with interest as he pushed himself up from the door and stood up even taller. The ever-present intrigue and wanton interest were there as he approached us, never taking his eyes off of Ethan.

Lips parted, he was in a place of mesmerized awe, and the seconds slowly became uncomfortable minutes as he held his hands at his side, fingers twitching with desire to touch Ethan. The being who'd been around from the very beginning, when were-animals' appearances were more beast than human and Winter's kind were snakes that used their tails like legs, stared at Ethan as if he were the most remarkable thing he'd ever seen.

Logan, who found wonder and amusement in pain, was strangely captivated by death and darkness—and Ethan.

Giving in to his curiosity, he started to touch Ethan. One of

Ethan's hands grabbed him by the wrist, the other by the throat. The threat came out as a coarse rumble. "Don't touch me."

And just as I sensed it, so did Logan—he fixated on Ethan's eyes, where stygian magic lay just below the surface. There wasn't any denying that what Ethan possessed was more than witch magic, and I wasn't sure what about the forest drew it out, but it was there, strong and commanding.

"Why are you here?" Ethan growled, his hands still placed on Logan, who was so enchanted that he was having a hard time focusing. It wasn't until I spoke that he bothered to pull his eyes off Ethan.

"I wouldn't expect such rudeness, from either of you. This courtesy is a friendly reminder that you have a job you need to complete and something you need to return to me."

It made me nauseous that he had reduced Chris to an inanimate object to be returned to him—as if she was just loaned apparel that he wanted back.

Ethan released him, dropping him to the ground and walking past him toward the door, not caring whether he'd gotten his footing or landed on the ground. I didn't really care, either. Ethan kept his back to us as he spoke.

"We never agreed to a time. You'll get everything when we are able to deliver it. We told you we would do it, and we will, we just need time."

"Time is one thing I have plenty of, but do you?"

Ethan snapped around, baring his teeth, and Logan was dealing with a fiery and very pissed-off wolf.

He was clearly pleased with himself and smiled as he slowly backed away, happy that he had sufficiently goaded Ethan. I fixated on his last words before he left as I slid past Ethan to open the door. Why didn't we have time?

Ignoring my inquiring look, Ethan went straight to the shower. He must have sensed that I only had one more question when I'd declined his invitation to join him. When he came out, he stood next to me.

"I'm sleeping with a stranger. What are you hiding?" I asked.

He sighed. "You are making something that isn't into a big deal."

"If it's not a big deal, then you have nothing to hide. I saw you in the forest and the way that creature responded to you. And the way you were after you broke through the ward to get out. Something is off, and you can't just tell me that it's residual magic like I'm a fool. If you're keeping it from me to protect me, I can handle it. If it's something that is confidential, you know you can trust me. I just can't continue to live in the dark. I can't be with you—"

He moved closer, pressing his lips against my face, and when he spoke, his breath wisped against my ear. Languid, gifted fingers caressed my skin. Distractions—that's all they were, and Ethan deserved an award for his ability to do it. His intense carnal sexuality made it hard to deny him, but I wasn't going to let him reduce me to some empty-headed paramour and our relationship to nothing more than inanities and heated rumbles in bed. I wanted more. We needed to be more. I attempted to step away, but his fingers pressed into my skin and he pulled me closer.

Grasping my hand in his, he brought it to his lips and kissed it. *Nope.*

I jerked away and took several steps back until we had a few feet between us.

"What are you?" The question seemed so absurd coming from me. How many times had he asked me a similar question?

"Sky," he pleaded.

It was a gentle entreaty, and I felt light-headed. I attempted to take in a breath that wouldn't easily come. The air was thick, I was unable to breathe, and my heart slowed to a crawl. I succumbed to the darkness and felt Ethan's arms around me before I could hit the floor.

~

I awoke cradled against Ethan's chest; I was hyperaware of his scent and various other ones around me. His paced breathing and gentle sighs became just other sounds that I was aware of. He pressed his lips lightly against my forehead and pulled me closer to him. "Are you okay?"

"I can't breathe," I choked.

"What?" he asked, panicked.

I squirmed under him. "You're squeezing me too tight. I can't breathe!" He relaxed back, but when I attempted to stand, he tugged a little more and held tighter. He just couldn't go with the flow of things.

"I need to stand. Please." I really just wanted to tell him to get off of me, but his emotions were as raw and turbulent as those I picked up from Sebastian, who was standing just a few feet from me. When I finally stood, I saw Winter to my right, Steven just a few feet from her, and Gavin settled into the corner . . . being . . . well, Gavin-y.

Closing my eyes, I tried to recollect everything that had happened moments before I'd collapsed, and then my eyes flew in Ethan's direction and narrowed on him. It was similar to what he'd done to me several months ago when he'd taken on the abilities of a dark elf after his grandmother had died and passed on the benefits and flaws of the magic. Its energy couldn't be destroyed with death but was passed through lineage. Since his mother was deceased, it went to the eldest grandchild, Ethan.

Our eyes connected, and it was as if the others didn't exist—at least that was how it felt to me; he seemed very aware of everyone else's presence. He finally spoke, answering the nonverbal question I was sure he recognized in the accusatory look I gave him.

"Logan decided to make a point. We aren't moving fast enough."

Silence consumed the room, and the tension in it heightened. I had a short list of people I just really wanted dead. Michaela, the Seethe's Mistress, was on the top of it; rather, she had been on the top of it. Now Logan had that spot. Marcia and Michaela were below him, and between the two of them whoever took second and third position really depended on the day and how I was feeling.

Making a point. He was so far up the list, he was on a separate page with his name only.

Ethan looked angry. Sebastian wore his concern like a weight, and if he was allowing it to be seen, it was bothering him. He was usually stoic in dealing with most things; you were likely to see anger from him but nothing more. He protected the pack by dealing with more things than could be imagined, becoming the guardian of our secrets and all the things stowed away in the closet, an illusionist who made people see the pack and the things that went on in it the way he wanted them perceived, not the way they actually were. In the end, he was always steps ahead of people with his Machiavellian insight, making things fall the way he needed them to. But now, he didn't seem to have an answer or a pretty and tidy plan for how to fix this—which said a lot about the situation. *Pretty* and *tidy* meant something totally different for him. *Pretty* didn't have to mean leaving no scars, bloodshed, or trails of bodies. *Tidy* only meant he was okay with whatever happened.

He took in another ragged breath and spoke in a stiff voice. "He'll need something done in good faith. Josh hasn't found a spell to remove his markings, and—"

The words didn't have to be spoken; we knew what he was going to say. Chris—we had to find Chris. I pressed my lips firmly together, afraid of what I would let slip. I didn't want her involved, and I felt strongly about it. We had two options: try to remove the marks, or offer up Chris. Neither option was good, but Chris was the best one. She'd be in a position to put the sleeper on him and give us more time to unlink him from the

Tre'ase who'd created Maya and take possession of its heart. I swallowed all the feelings of unease that kept coming up. These were necessary evils, I tried to tell myself, and the more I tried to convince myself of it, the worse it became.

"Why can't we try to put the sleeper on him?" I asked.

"Do you really think we can do that without him doing something to Kalese, Maya's creator? This isn't something I want either, Sky, but it is what needs to be done." The curt way Sebastian answered told me there wouldn't be any more questions and answers. He'd established this as the best plan, but the nagging question remained: why did they want me alive? This question had plagued me and extended further than me being part of the pack. My life had been important to them before I became a member.

"Why is my life so important to you all?" I asked, my gaze bouncing between Ethan and Sebastian, the guardian of the secrets and the keeper of the skeletons that flooded the pack's closet. What bone was threatening to peek out that my life was helping keep hidden, or what secret was going to be revealed if I no longer existed?

"You are part of this pack. It is my job to keep you safe," Sebastian said simply. Then he directed his attention to Gavin, who had long since lost interest in anything that was going on in the room.

"You need to find Chris." Gavin was the best hunter they had. If he was sent out, you were going to be found. Ethan was good; Gavin was the best. The question of what condition you would be in after he'd found you was always the issue.

"We need her retrieved unscathed," Sebastian emphasized, and gave the same instruction over and over. Gavin listened, his dark eyes blank as he looked at the pack leader. His long dark hair kept forming a curtain over his face, and dark brown eyes peeked from beneath it. Every so often he brushed it away, allowing us to see his sharp, defined features and his tawny-colored skin. His almond-shaped, expressionless dark eyes didn't give anything away, which had to make it hard to be on the receiving end of any interaction with him. You didn't know what you were dealing with.

"No," he said softly.

Sebastian's eyebrows furrowed. "No?"

"I'm busy. We still need to find Kelly, it's been thirty-four days." When he brushed his hair from his face, it made me think of her as well—she'd threatened to take scissors to his unruly strands if he didn't cut them, or as least bind them together. Usually he'd tie it back, sometimes in a messy short ponytail. I missed Kelly's spray bottle as well. The innumerable times she'd pulled it out of her bag and spritzed him with it while calling him a "bad kitty" were laughable. I felt the ache, more so as the facade broke and I saw sorrow flash over Gavin's face for a few seconds. If I'd seen it, Sebastian had to have as well.

Sebastian washed a hand over his face. "Okay, you look for Kelly. Ethan, you find Chris."

Now *I* was the one having problems. I would have been a fool not to be concerned about the history Ethan had with Chris. Most people didn't understand why their complicated interaction and tumultuous relationship had ever existed or continued. The heated fights and arguments were infamous. I certainly couldn't understand what there was between them, and I didn't think anyone other than Ethan and Chris could.

"I have information. It's flimsy at best, but I have a hard time thinking this is all coincidental." I repeated what had happened with the woman, us seeing the possible mage, and the building with the ward.

"A witch and a scientist?" Sebastian asked, frowning.

I didn't like the sound of it, either. "I don't think it was a witch, definitely someone who has magic, a great deal of it, but it didn't feel or smell"—*dammit, I really need to stop smelling things*—"like Josh's or any witch magic that I've encountered. I think it was a mage."

We didn't have enough to go on, but Sebastian sent Winter, Gavin, and Steven to check out the area where we'd seen the feral woman, Carol, and Ethan was tasked with finding his ex-girlfriend.

I guessed my job was not to die, feel guilt over everything that was going on, or obsess over Ethan and Chris.

CHAPTER 7

J'd heard constantly about Chris being good at her job, to the point that when her name was mentioned, I unconsciously added the part about her job efficiency. She was also good at hiding, which she was doing quite effectively. Three days after the incident with Logan, we still hadn't found her. Ethan's trademark way of handling things had become his disadvantage, while becoming Chris's advantage. "Do what I ask or I will hurt you" wasn't well received by most.

By day four, he was reduced to enlisting Claudia. He wasn't happy with me when I pointed out he had to get help from his godmother. On the surface, Claudia was just a dealer of expensive artwork, and that kind, cultured persona had served her well. There was a lot more to the soft-spoken woman who had connections in the otherworld that made her a force to be reckoned with. Her involvement in the conclave called by Marcia had led to Ethan's life being saved by her voting on behalf of the faes, which from my understanding she wasn't, but claimed allegiance to them. She was something else, more than the patron of the arts that I knew. She was an empath and, like me, a Moura Encantada, responsible for the care of one of the protected objects. Hers was the Vitae, the very thing that was keeping Josh alive, since he'd been cursed to die on his eighteenth birthday because of a forbidden spell his mother had done for Claudia. The fact that Claudia had saved him by hiding the Vitae in his body was a secret that Ethan had shared with me, something I unwillingly had to keep from Josh.

Claudia's ability to find people remained astounding, although she'd proven to be quite skilled at it on many occasions. After Ethan had made a call to her less than three hours before, he, Sebastian, Josh, and Winter waited in my home for her. At eight on the dot, the doorbell rang, and Claudia, who was always pleasant, greeted us with a smile, a very angry Chris in tow.

She nodded respectfully in Sebastian's direction. "I do apologize for the meeting being here rather than your office, but I believed this would be more acceptable for Chris." With the same genial smile that belied the power and connections she had to possess to have made this happen, Claudia addressed Chris. "I appreciate you for accepting my invitation to this meeting."

Chris glared at her and remained silent. Ethan thanked Claudia, and he and Josh, who were always polite in her presence, gave her two air-kisses before she departed. After taking hold of Josh's arm with her gloved hand, she noticed more body art on it and frowned.

"No more," he promised. Ethan had tried to get him to stop almost ten tattoos ago. I wasn't sure what type of superpower she had, but it was on the list of things I hoped to acquire. Again, Sebastian thanked Claudia for her help.

Once she'd left, Chris looked around the room like someone who had been strongly coerced rather than invited.

I didn't speak because I wasn't in agreement with all this. I knew what it meant for me—for the pack—and I knew it was important to meet Logan's demands. Even if Chris was okay with it, I still wasn't, but I doubted she knew the full extent of the situation.

"What do you want?" she asked in a hard, rough voice. She definitely hadn't accepted the invitation willingly.

"We need to hire you," Sebastian said evasively.

"This is new. You had me tracked down to hire me. What job can I do for you all that you can't do yourself?" she asked suspiciously, crossing her arms and resting back against the wall.

I really wanted to stand right next to her with my arms crossed and watch them explain what they needed her for. I couldn't wait to see what creative spin they were going to put on it to make it appealing.

"Logan wants you, and we want you to go with him," Ethan blurted out. *Oh, no spin at all. Just the despicable truth. I guess that's one way to handle it.*

She raised a brow and frowned. "Wants me for what?"

Go ahead. I'm dying to hear this one.

"I have no idea. Just another admirer? Nevertheless, he would like you to visit him for a while, and we want to pay you to do it."

Hearing it out loud was worse than actually thinking it.

"You're paying me to spend several nights with a man who wants me. Sweetie, that's not my job, that's the oldest profession and I have no interest in it." She pushed up from the wall and started to leave.

"Chris, wait," Josh said. But she didn't, so before she could get to the door, he started telling her everything, from us asking Logan to find the Tre'ase who created Maya, to him killing Kalese and linking himself to her heart, and how he'd threatened to destroy it if we didn't do what he wanted. She didn't seem terribly moved, and I wasn't sure I blamed her, but when she spoke her tone had lost its edge.

"Bambi dies if I don't go?"

Josh nodded.

"Okay." Then she looked at me. "I owe her, so I'll do it."

I didn't want the debt she felt she'd accumulated when I hadn't turned her over to Logan before to be repaid this way. The irony of the situation didn't escape me: she was repaying her debt to me by agreeing to go to the very person I was going to give her to. It made me feel unsettled. I'd been so sure she was going to tell us to go to hell that I would have been okay with that. I was about to voice my objection and demand that we find another way to fix things when someone knocked at the door. Chris moved fast and was nearly across the room away from the door by the time I reached it. Based on her reaction, I knew who it was before I opened it—Demetrius.

I was going to ignore the knocking, but it persisted. "Skylar, I know she is in there. Please open the door."

I looked back in Chris's direction, but her blank expression didn't give me any feedback. After a few moments of her being tense and still, she nodded her head and said, "Let him in" in a small voice.

When I hesitated, she repeated herself, louder, stronger. Now she sounded like herself.

I cracked the door. This was going to happen if she was okay with it, but if the Master of the Seethe was going to come into my home, he had to offer something, too. Quell.

"Okay, you can come in, but on one condition—"

Ethan interrupted with the invocation to drop the ward that was preventing Demetrius's entrance and opened the door. He wrapped an arm around my waist as he urged me back. I jerked away, whipped around, and bared my teeth, fighting the urge to use them. I wanted to rip into him, and the smug smirk wasn't helping. He leaned into me, speaking into my hair. "We'll discuss it later."

Definitely.

I sidestepped him, too angry to respond without making a scene. He remained close enough to make Demetrius leave if things started to go poorly. Chris maintained her distance but held eye contact with her creator.

"You need to come back." Demetrius's accent was thick, something he was able to mask unless his anger was heightened.

"I'm not coming back."

He exposed his teeth like weapons. "You didn't get what you wanted—so what? The south was never going to be yours even if you had successfully killed Alexander. Your little stunt warranted your punishment. You have no one to blame but yourself. Accept it and your position in the Seethe. I've been tolerant of your tantrums—I won't be any longer. You have two days to return on your own. After that you will be brought back, and it will not be with care. Do you understand me?"

Chris's movements were faster than even my eyes could process as she soared through the air, moving so quickly she seemed airborne. Grabbing a knife out of the butcher block, she slammed Demetrius into the wall and pressed the blade to his throat. "I'm not coming back. Not to you. You locked me in a fucking box like I was an animal. For what, because of Alexander? You can't . . . I don't like . . . you can't lock me . . ." Her voice quivered, and the knife bit deeper into his skin, blood streaming down it. She pressed harder. More blood. "You can't lock me in boxes!" she spat out through clenched teeth.

I looked over at Ethan, then Sebastian, Winter, and finally Josh, and not one of them made an effort to move. *We're just going to let this happen? Allow Chris to murder the Master of the Northern Seethe in front of us while we watch like we're at the movies? No one's going to move?*

Forget stopping it—they looked bored and inconvenienced.

"You disobeyed me, did you expect something different?" Demetrius said in a low, cool voice, seemingly unaffected by the threat and the knife held at his throat.

Really? This seems like a good time to goad her? Part of me wanted to let it happen, too.

She pressed harder; he winced and then smiled, his hand reaching up to touch hers. I thought he would have tried to remove the knife, since that's what most sane people who don't have adoration for pain and violence would do. But I was dealing with Demetrius, and his Seethe seemed to have a masochistic tendency that still left me bewildered.

His thumb lightly stroked her finger, gently, lovingly. He smiled, his adulation of her and this particular moment apparent. That was what you did when you were a person like Demetrius—developed a crush on the person holding a knife to your throat. "I've missed you."

The feeling wasn't mutual. Chris's hands were trembling, and I realized she didn't have as much control as she would have liked. We didn't have time for the Seethe and their revenge for Chris killing him and us letting her do it.

"Chris," I said softly. The same mild, soothing voice I had to use with were-animals on the brink of losing control. It was like handling a bomb—she needed to be dealt with quickly and gently. First I moved Demetrius's hand from hers, and then I covered her hand with mine. She relaxed, allowing me to guide the knife from her.

"Demetrius, please leave." He hesitated before again looking at Chris, who had put some much-needed distance between them.

Frozen, he remained with his attention fixed on her. I wasn't sure if his feelings for her were genuine or just the obsessiveness of a man who was used to people bowing to his every whim and desire. Was Chris someone he wanted, loved, or the wild one he'd like to break?

"Demetrius, Sky asked you to leave. Honor her request or I'll make you," Ethan said. I was still too angry to look in his direction.

After several moments of contemplation, Demetrius left. Several more had passed, and I began to ask Chris where she was going as she started out the door. "I said I will help and I will, but I have to feed."

"I assure you if you leave, you will not be able to come back. Demetrius will make certain of that."

She grinned. "You give Demetrius and his Seethe too much credit. I stayed in business because he's not nearly as good at hunting as he'd have you to believe. I'll be fine."

"You can use me," I offered before she could leave. Amusement made its way to her eyes and brightened them, although they were now an odd cross between crimson and black opal, very different from her brown human eyes. Long mascara-coated eyelashes and thick lines of liner drew attention to them. Her laughter filled the air. "Bambi, I would love to take you up on that offer, but if Quell is any example of what happens when a vampire tastes Bambi blood, then I'll have to pass. Fawning over the cute brunette in the Midwest Pack is really not on my to-do list."

I thought we had a moment and then you do this. Fine, starve.

"I'll do it," Josh offered.

Chris stepped away from the door and examined him, looking over his arms. She shook her head. "Ink. I can't stand the taste of it."

Finding a spot on Josh that wasn't inked was a task. He had two full sleeves that ended at his wrists, and even a small one on his hand. I knew that some vampires fed from the saphenous vein, the one running down the inner thigh, but I wasn't sure if that was available because he was quickly running out of visible skin to ink. He tilted his head, exposing his neck while backing into the couch and then taking a seat.

Chris approached him slowly, the offer more tempting than she appeared to want to let on, but I could see the thirst in her face, in the way her eyes widened and the pupils pulsed at the sight of the proffered vein. The terait, the orange quarter ring around the pupils of the vampire's eyes that indicated they were hungry, was more pronounced now.

I'd fed Quell a number of times, but nothing we did looked remotely like what happened between Josh and Chris. She crawled on him, her legs astride his. When she spoke, her voice was low, for his ears only, and it would have been if they were anywhere else other than in a room full of were-animals.

"Have you done this before?"

"Yes."

"Neck?"

"No."

"Okay, I'll be gentle." There was a hint of humor in her voice, but it didn't help temper her intensity. Furtive glances from everyone went in Ethan's direction, but he maintained the inscrutable look on his face. As she moved in closer to his brother, her face nestled into his neck, her fingers curling into his hair as she pulled him closer to her. Then he made a sound—I would have liked to say it was a groan, but I'd heard people groan and that wasn't it. It was something more carnal and laden with pleasure. Eyes flew in Ethan's direction as Josh rested back on the sofa, exposing more of his neck. His hands rested at his sides but soon slinked up, kneading into her skin, an act that seemed more intimate than anything that had ever happened between me and Quell. I caught Ethan looking at me and wondered if he was thinking about me and Quell or Josh and Chris.

The feeding between Chris and Josh had reduced us to voyeurs watching something that was undeniably intimate and bordered on erotic. I was glad that I wasn't the only one in the room who was uncomfortable. She finally pulled away, examining the puncture marks on his neck before slowly laving over them to close them.

Josh's arms were still resting on her hips when she finished, and she smiled and looked down at his lap and then smiled. His wayward grin was accented by streaks of red that ran along the bridge of his nose and cheeks. It was a moment before he stood, and it didn't take a genius to figure out why.

Chris's face had brightened from recently feeding, and her tongue slid over her lips, removing all rivulets of blood. She made her way to her bag across the room, pulled out a pen and a pad of paper and scribbled something on it. "This is my fee. It's high, and you're going to be a little pissed. Get over it and wire the money to the account below."

It didn't just piss Sebastian off, he stared at it for several minutes before thrusting the paper back at her. "No."

She blew out an exaggerated breath, making her lips ripple. "How many times must I tell you all—we aren't going to haggle. I said I'd do it to save Bambi; I didn't say I was going to do it for free. But if you need time to pretend you don't need me, I'll be around. Apparently, Claudia knows how to find me."

Glaring at Chris throughout the entire process, Sebastian took out his phone and, after a few moments, nodded in her direction.

After she checked her phone to confirm delivery, she asked, "So I visit him and what? There has to be more than that. Do you have a plan?"

Sebastian gave her a small nod and then said, "We have possession of a Tod Schlaf."

Without needing more explanation, she smiled. "So, I'm assuming since you all don't want me out and about, I'm staying with Josh?"

Josh shrugged, indifferent.

"Josh? Hell, no," Ethan snapped. He was noticeably angry about the arrangement, and I could feel everyone's stares on me.

"Why not?" Josh asked.

"If Demetrius does decide to come and get Chris I don't want you put in danger."

I frowned at the answer because it was as thin as his voice. Josh had on many occasions proven his ability to stand up against vampires.

"I'll be fine. I have a ward that I will set up, and I'm sure Chris and I can handle ourselves if they try."

Ethan's stern look persisted, and as usual sibling rivalry reared its head, with Josh consistently trying to retain control that Ethan tried to take away. The brothers' pack of two seemed to face daily challenges to determine who was going to be the Alpha.

"We'll be fine," Chris said as she started for the door with Josh close behind. Graphite rolled over Ethan's stormy blue eyes, and I could feel the tension radiating off him.

Even once Sebastian started to speak, he stayed focused on the door.

~

I hadn't thought sleep would come easy when Ethan and I went to bed, and it didn't. We hadn't spoken after everyone had left, and each time I considered talking about Chris, it sparked jealousy and anger. I didn't like feeling that way.

After several attempts to sleep, a problem that Ethan didn't have, I stared at the screen of the television and had no idea what I was watching because I had turned the volume down.

"You can't sleep?" Ethan asked, leaning against the wall. *No, I'm considering dressing up like a superhero and going out to fight crime.* I barely glanced in his direction because when I did, I thought about how he'd fought to keep Chris away from Josh—that bothered me. How difficult it had been for him not to show emotions as Josh had fed Chris—that bothered me. And the influx of all the new emotions I was feeling and having a difficult time controlling —that bothered me, too. The warning signs were there, and I'd ignored them and let things happen between Ethan and me that I was probably going to regret.

"What's wrong?"

"Nothing," I responded stiffly.

The irritated growl reverberated in his chest. "You know I hate when you lie to me. Don't do it."

"Do I have to worry? About Chris? Do I have to worry about her and you together? I saw the way you responded to her feeding from Josh. Is her being a vampire the only thing that's keeping you from her? Eventually, that won't bother you so much."

He rested against the wall in silent contemplation, rubbing his hand over the shadow on his face that had been there for a couple of days—seemingly, he'd decided to grow a beard. "Chris was easier to be with," he started.

"Nice to hear, you plan on putting that on my Valentine's card? Or do you have something even more insensitive?"

"Do you have more or are you going to let me finish?"

I clenched my teeth together because I had plenty more to say, but none of it was going to help the situation. The uncomfortable moment lingered for longer than I'd wished, and although I refused to meet them, I could feel his eyes on me. In a low, somnolent voice he called my name, and I looked in his direction. "Can I finish?"

My head barely moved into the nod. I wasn't sure why I was nervous to hear the rest.

"Most people didn't understand my relationship with Chris."

Most? Every time it's described, it's compared to a natural disaster that caused insurmountable devastation. Yeah, most people don't understand your relationship with Chris and consider it an event of mass destruction.

Instead of sharing that, I simply nodded for him to continue. "It was easy with her, contrary to what others thought. Our relationship didn't extend any further than the walls, more specifically the bedroom. When we were there, we were together. I knew what she was capable of and likewise she of me. Our loyalties and expectations like everything else ended when we went out the door. I'm not saying it was a functional relationship—it was riddled with dysfunction—but it worked for us. What you and I have is complicated and extends further than this bedroom, this house. I've accepted everything about it and about you. I didn't enter into anything naïvely or blindly. I knew what I was signing on to when I decided to be with you." He took a moment and bit the corner of his lip, the way his brother did when he was uncomfortable. "It's worth the trade-off. All of it."

He walked over and sat next to me, and I leaned into him. He kissed me on top of my head. "Sky, I don't want to keep having this conversation."

"We've never discussed Chris before," I pointed out. I felt like Josh at the moment, trying to establish my position in our little pack or whatever it was. Ethan was so used to answering to one person only, Sebastian, and because of his dominance level and the understanding that he would be the Alpha in any other pack, their interaction was that of two Alphas as opposed to that of a Beta and an Alpha.

"We have had this conversation. I told you once, you don't have anything to worry about. You don't. Okay?"

I nodded.

"Now we need to discuss Quell."

Thoughts of Chris had caused me to forget that. I pushed up from him. "Why did you intervene with Demetrius? I was just—"

"I know what you were just going to do, and I won't allow it."

There goes that word allow *again.* I really needed to get him a thesaurus or a book on the power of words. I sucked in a sharp breath. "*Allow?* Do you want to rephrase that?"

"Okay." He grinned. "I'm not going to let Quell come back. That's not up for debate. He's fine. He settled into a nice house, and from my understanding, he has a donor and she's safe with him."

I made a face. "What?"

"He found a donor, a brunette with curly hair and similar features to yours. Her eyes are blue instead of green." He studied me. I didn't say anything. Ethan had once asked if I was in love with Quell, and I wasn't able to answer him because I didn't know. I had feelings for him and perhaps it was love, not romantic, but I had a connection with him—I always felt that we were each other's anchor. He was there ensuring that I didn't get submerged into this world and forget my humanity. And because he was a person who had lost all faith in humanity, I represented that hope for redemption. It was a heavy burden, but part of me needed the accountability. And now he was gone. I missed him as much as I missed Steven sometimes.

"How is he doing?"

Ethan's tone was cool, brusque, and so was the smile he attempted. "I find it oddly convenient that he was unable to survive without you, yet he seems to be doing just fine now without you. I can't help but wonder if it was an excuse he used to have access to you because he knew you would be there if he needed you."

"He's not like that."

I didn't try to read his stolid expression. It was obvious he'd already come to his own conclusion.

He stood up and extended his hand to me to help me up. "I pose that same question to you. Do I have to worry about Quell?"

I shook my head.

"I need to hear it," he said softly.

"No. You don't have to worry about Quell."

CHAPTER 8

*O*f the many bad ideas I'd had, this ranked in the top five. The decision had been made, Chris paid, and the process started, but it didn't stop me from slipping out of bed at three in the morning and driving to Josh's home. I wondered how long it would be before Ethan noticed I was missing. Who was I kidding —he'd probably heard me the moment my feet had touched the floor. As I knocked on Josh's door, part of me expected Ethan to drive up. I exhaled a sigh of relief when he didn't.

The situation had been handled and wrapped up in a pretty little disturbing and sordid package. I was supposed to be okay and be acquiescent. I just couldn't do it. It settled too hard on me, and it was more than guilt. We had dived too deep into the swamp and there wasn't any way to come out smelling like anything other than filth. At what point was a necessary evil just pure evil? No matter how blurred we perceived them to be, there were still boundaries, definitive lines between questionable and pure egregious acts against humanity. Giving Chris to Logan even if she'd agreed to it had taken the pack and our plan across the line between necessary and reprehensible.

Perhaps it was my guilt-clouded mind that had made me feel

that way, but I didn't care. Josh answered his door, and I wasn't sure if he'd been asleep or not because he looked the same way whether it was midday or the wee hours of the morning. Instead of wrinkled relaxed jeans, he had on a pair of boxers and no shirt, once again not very different from what I was used to. Unless he was outside in public, he held to that beloved tenet of the pack, the fewer clothes the better. The boxers were just a courtesy to whoever was knocking on the door, because he was content with answering it as naked as the day he was born.

But he didn't look like he had been asleep. He managed the pack's club, a job that often required him to be out late. As they did with most of our lives, pack issues made his attendance at a job a problem; today he probably hadn't gone because he'd been dealing with Chris. As I gave him a sweeping look, I was reminded of the ribald little show he and Chris had put on earlier.

Drinking at the city's "it" spot and dancing with whatever hot socialite he'd picked for the night was really taking creative license with the word *work*. But somehow the pack had qualified it as such.

He rubbed his hand over his mussed hair, widening the door. "What's up?" he asked. The scent of alcohol wafted off his breath, and I inhaled the pot-drenched air coming from behind the door. I made a face and he grinned.

"You didn't invite me to the party," I teased. Walking in, I scanned his home. It was very different from the high-rise condo in the city he had had before; after too many mishaps, he'd been asked to find other living arrangements. His house fit him. It was as eclectic and unique as he was. In the heart of suburbia, the three-bedroom Art Moderne ranch with unique lined architecture definitely stood out among the more traditional homes.

It no longer had the frat house look inside anymore, which meant either Ethan's designer or Claudia had paid a visit. Metal art covered the cranberry-colored walls. A large-screen TV covered a greater part of one wall. I was sure the decorative rug hadn't had stains on it when it was first placed in the house. Espresso-colored furniture had replaced his well-used post-college pieces. But while you could take Josh out of the frat house, you couldn't take the frat house out of Josh, and ignoring the cluttered space was difficult. The tall bookcase was nearly empty, and it looked like most of the books that had once occupied it were stacked on the sofa. Papers with scribbling on them were scattered on the love seat and another table in the corner. There were two tumblers on the kitchen table and an open bottle of wine on the coffee table. Josh rarely drank wine, so it had to be Chris's. Another flash of her feeding from him popped into my head.

Chris's scent inundated the room and fanned off him as well. But she wasn't in it. "I would like to speak with Chris, where is she?"

Again, fingers fidgeted with his hair. I noticed the red mark on his neck, on the opposite side of the previous one. He flushed when I focused on it before looking back at him.

"Just a minute, I'll go get her." He started toward the back of his house, and I moved in farther, watching him go down the hall. To the right was his room, to the left a guest room. Vampires didn't sleep. Quell often said they rested but they didn't need to do it. I assumed that they were like everyone else and just needed a break. Josh went into his room to get her.

At least Chris was dressed—well, sort of, in a pair of micro shorts and a tank top that was just as flimsy as the shorts. With a disapproving frown, I scrutinized her attire and then went back to Josh. My eyes narrowed on him and he flushed even more, having a difficult time holding eye contact with me. I had no idea what was going on. Had sibling rivalry been reduced to this?

"Give it a rest, Bambi," she said, moving past Josh. "I'm not sleeping with my ex's brother. We were just talking."

She might not have been sleeping with him, but there was definitely something going on between them. Steven had once accused me of being drawn to Quell feeding from me, which I'd considered an absurd accusation at the time, but it was the very thing that drew people to become part of the Seethe's garden. They agreed to be used by the vampires as food or whatever else was required of them. Some did it with the hope of one day being changed and others because of the euphoria it offered. I couldn't get past the pain to find pleasure in it; but Josh, whose body was a multitude of tattoos and piercings, was a tribute to an appreciation of, or at the very least a lack of aversion to pain.

If that was the case, I wasn't sure how to address it, either. Even if I wanted to, I wasn't going to be able to, because after Chris had sat on the counter in front of me, Josh took that as his cue to leave.

"So what do you need, Bam—"

She bit off the rest of the words when I glared at her. I didn't need her insults—I was trying to save her life. "Do you understand what Ethan and Sebastian are asking of you?"

"Of course, I was there, remember?"

Her eyes were just as dark and weighted as the wry smile she gave me. "Bambi, I'm okay with it, but you seem to have a problem with it."

I didn't want to admit it, especially under her judgmental gaze. The whole thing was dangerous, and in the end she could be sacrificing her life for something that wasn't guaranteed. I could feel her eyes on me, and they were so intense it felt like she knew it all before I could confirm or rebut it.

With a lazy smile, she asked, "Do you think my life is worth more than yours?"

I shook my head. "But I don't think that someone should sacrifice their life for something that is uncertain."

"You don't know that until we actually try it," she offered. She fidgeted with her hand. When she finally spoke again, it was in a whisper. "If things were reversed you would do it for me. Whether you deny it or not, I know it. I don't understand you. I really don't get you." She sighed and hopped off the counter. "And

I doubt I ever will. But you had an opportunity to hurt me—and I've given you more than enough reasons to want to—and you didn't." She shrugged. "I guess this is me repaying the favor. I hate debt."

"You've already repaid me."

With a half-grin, she brushed off the comment. When she moved closer to me as the grin faded, I watched her with caution. Chewing her words, she made a face as though they were rancid, and when she finally let them fall from her lips, they were so soft I really had to focus to hear them. It was as if she wanted them for her ears only.

"I guess," she started out slowly, "of the people I know, I would be disappointed if you came this far and died. Honestly, when I first met you I really didn't expect you to survive the year. You've survived, quite surprisingly, especially for someone like you. Impressive."

"Thank you?" I was sure there was a compliment interwoven in her little speech.

"Bambi, if you're going to be killed, I think you've proven you deserve a death better than one at the hands of"—she scowled —"Logan." She said his name with the disgust of someone who had just taken a whiff of soured milk. "I'd like to make sure that doesn't happen." She backed up toward the hallway, refusing to look at me. I heard a door shut and fought the urge to see which was closed, the guest bedroom's or Josh's.

When I slipped back into bed, Ethan asked, "Did you get the closure you needed?"

I didn't answer. Maybe he was talking in his sleep.

He turned, his lips kinked into a knowing smirk. I just wanted to wipe off his haughty smile. "You're more predictable than I even imagined," he said.

The insults were coming fast and hard tonight. "I know why we're doing it, but don't ask me to be okay with it."

He studied me for a moment and the smirk fell, giving way to a gentle, sympathetic smile. Just when I was starting to feel inured and prepared for everything, this Logan business had thrown things off course. Those thoughts stayed with me.

∾

Less than forty-eight hours after we'd delivered Chris to an elated Logan, my conscience and my stomach were still unsettled. Everyone else seemed to have left whatever apprehensive feelings they had at the door. Filtering out the disdain each time I looked at anyone was getting harder. I focused on the end result: Chris had the sleeper with her. All she had to do was place it on him, and this part of it would be over.

Brushing thoughts of Chris aside, as I sat in the living room of the pack's home, I refocused my attention on Gavin, who was talking and pacing. He directed his question to Josh. "What do you think?" They'd gone back to the place where we had seen the feral woman.

"The ward is strong. I felt a lot of strong magic, too."

"Then it has to be the witches," Gavin surmised. He was just searching, in need of a lead. With so many possibilities, he seemed desperate to narrow it down.

"I didn't feel witch magic when I was there," I said.

"I didn't, either," Josh said before turning to address me and Winter. "There isn't any activity in there, either. We were there for several hours, and nothing."

"Not even in the location we told you about?" I asked.

Josh shook his head. "Seeing you must have made them more cautious. I didn't break the ward because it would have alerted whoever erected it. But I suspect there is a house deeper in the forest." Strong wards made with blood were directly connected to the person who created them, and if they were broken, the creator felt physical pain. I'd seen it happen to Josh, when the one around the pack's home was compromised.

"Do you know who owns the property?" Sebastian asked from a chair across the room, keeping a watchful eye on Gavin. He was frustrated, which was to be expected, but he wasn't of any use if he allowed it to dictate his actions. "If we have that information, we might be able to find out if it's the witches or someone affiliated with them. We don't want to go in blindly." Deep creases formed on Sebastian's forehead, which happened often when he discussed the witches. They had become a thorn in the pack's side, and Sebastian's tolerance for them was running considerably low.

Gavin shrugged. "The geek's working on finding out."

"His name is Matthew," I offered. Gavin dismissed the young man in the same manner he had when we'd taken the guy in with other members of the recently acquired Worgen pack once Sebastian had decided he would no longer allow small packs in the area. They weren't excited about joining, but the merge was quite easy, and since they were given jobs within the pack, they seemed to like it and assimilated well, or as well as they could. There was no way to put a lovely spin on it: they were weird. Yes, you could call them *unique* or *eclectic*, but you wouldn't be doing those words justice. They took weird to an Olympic level. And even Sebastian gave in to the disdain when he heard them speaking to one another in a language that we later identified as Klingon. But they were better with computers than anyone we already had. And Dr. Jeremy seemed to enjoy them because anything he could think of for the infirmary they could build, which had quickly earned them the status of being as valuable as he was.

While everyone had made an effort to make them feel welcome, or as welcome as the pack was capable of, they weren't going to get a welcome basket or a reassuring handshake, just a somewhat friendly nod or a grunt of acknowledgment. Which worked for them because they weren't really friendly, either. The small pack of twenty could easily have existed separately as lone were-animals.

"If there is a house or something behind the ward, you can't be sure that Kelly is in there. We can't just go in without more information," Sebastian told Gavin in a calm voice because Gavin was becoming increasingly agitated and was being controlled by impulse, not logic.

"We should go in just because there's something terribly wrong going on," Winter suggested with the same look of disgust she'd had after we'd seen the feral woman. "If Kelly is in there, we really need to get her out."

Sebastian sighed heavily, his fingers steepled as he considered the situation. It was a problematic one, because whatever was going on, it needed to be addressed. However, if we became involved in something else that wasn't a pack priority, like finding Kelly, resources would be spread thin. Depending on whether or not our involvement caused an onslaught of other problems, it might not be something that even needed to be addressed at the moment. I understood Sebastian's and Ethan's pragmatic thinking even though I didn't always agree with it.

When Sebastian's phone rang, he looked at it, and there was just a glimpse of a frown before it faltered and he became professionally stoic. "Chris?"

It wasn't Chris on the other line. "I am not amused," Logan said. Cold, harsh anger edged his words. Ethan winced at his voice as it came over the speaker because it was an indicator that Chris had failed. Then Logan hung up.

Josh, Ethan, Winter, Sebastian, and I entered Logan's home without waiting for an invitation once we knocked. He looked up from the floor, his anger palpable as magic coursed through the air, forming thick, stifling clouds in the house. He was having a difficult time holding his human form, and seeing the massive

117

misshapen jaw peeking through, horns that appeared and disappeared, and the misshapen face that fought to hold on to its attractive human features made it very difficult to focus on what I needed to—Chris. She was on the ground with a stake through her heart. Several half-empty blood packs were scattered throughout the room. It looked like he was bringing her back from reversion only to send her back into it. I didn't know what it felt like for vampires, but I'd seen Quell's and Michaela's tortured appearances when they went through it.

"Step away from her," Sebastian's icy voice demanded.

"No. She is mine. This deceitful little bitch will not get away with her treachery, and neither shall you. The curse of the lunar eclipse will happen and I will have my vengeance as I watch all of your kind expire in the very way the Faeries saw fit for such treacherous animals to die. You will be put down."

I had no idea what he was talking about, and even Sebastian and Ethan looked stunned by the ramblings of this madman. His eyes were fiery with anger.

A strike of Josh's magic hit him, sending him soaring into the air. Logan's eyes glowed, the variegated marks on his arms coiled and wrapped around them, his lips moved fervently, and then he stomped his foot on the ground. Magic rose from it, thick waves of it. A tsunami sent us all crashing to the ground. The marks glowed, and we were readying for another onslaught of magic when the sofa smashed into him. He was sent hurling across the room and slammed into the wall on the opposite side of it. Blood spilled from his nose and cuts on his head and hand.

"Careful," Ethan urged, watching as control slipped from his brother's grasp. "Josh?" Ethan's tone was sharper and more commanding as he tried to force his brother back into a controlled state. Josh took a slow breath as he kept Logan fastened to the wall. Logan was relaxed, too relaxed, his eyes illuminated and drifting from bright lilac to black. The magic felt dark as it slowly moved around him, and the smell of necrosis seeped into the room. Something pierced my skin, causing pain so intense bile crept into my throat. We all doubled over. Blood rolled down my cheeks. I choked on the pain, and although he'd said he wouldn't kill us, allowing fate to have its way with us instead, it felt as though he was trying.

Ethan forced himself to stand with a growl and lobbed the kitchen table at Logan. It exploded midair, but the Tre'ase was distracted and missed the large serpent that had darted in his direction. She struck, and he clung to the wall, trying to keep himself from succumbing to her venom. Incantations fell from his lips and weak magic pulsed off of him, soon becoming diluted brushes of it that stained the air before he collapsed to the ground.

Josh ran over to Chris. Reversion had taken over half her body, and she no longer had the use of her hands. She grimaced in pain as she attempted to move them. He grabbed a blood pack and put it to her lips, but she was too weak to open it. I ripped open another pack with my teeth and handed it to him. The bit of blood that seeped into my mouth was a reminder that part of me craved it. I shivered, trying to shrug off the feeling I often staved off with bloody rare meat. The metallic flavor of it and the desire to taste it again lingered on my palate. I turned away from Josh and licked the remainder from my lips.

Three packs later, she was whole but still hungry, and it was evident in the way she looked at Josh and buried her face into his neck as he helped her up. "Later," he whispered. I wasn't sure what was going on with Chris and Josh, but they were wading in very complicated and distorted waters.

"The Tod Schlaf is in his bedroom," Chris offered as she pulled herself up to stand. Sebastian quickly went there and returned a few minutes later with it carefully grasped between his hands. We placed it on Logan and waited for a couple of hours to see if he would awake. No one wanted to travel with him until they knew he wouldn't wake up.

≈

Dr. Jeremy frowned the moment Sebastian walked into the infirmary with Logan draped over his shoulder, followed by Chris, who moved slowly, even compared to human movement. I wondered how long Logan had tortured her, sending her into reversion, saving her, only to do it again. My stomach felt queasy remembering his disturbing adoration of pain and obsession with death. Had he done it for punishment or his own pleasure? I swallowed the bile that crept up in my throat. I felt queasy because we'd had a hand in this. No, not a hand. We had done this. I had done this.

"What happens now?" Dr. Jeremy asked Josh, after Ethan, Sebastian, and Winter had left. When it came to magic, that was Josh's job.

"We find a way to unlink him from Kalese." Josh looked over at Chris, who was crouched in a corner, scanning the area, her nostrils flaring, smelling the blood of donors that she couldn't use —with the exception of Josh and me. She screwed her eyes closed and kept inhaling deeply. When she looked up again, her eyes fastened on my neck. The aversion she had to feeding from me seemed to have disappeared.

When she shifted to a standing position, I changed my stance, preparing for whatever might happen. She was too unfocused and distracted, which made her more dangerous than usual.

"I can get you blood," Dr. Jeremy offered, stepping into her line of sight, aware that he wasn't a viable source of food.

"She's fine," Josh said softly, approaching her with the foolish confidence of a person willing to move toward a strong vampire in the throes of bloodlust.

Her eyes zoned in on his neck, and when he was within reach, she grabbed him, pulling him to her. He jerked his hand and magically bound her to the wall. When he spoke, it was low and soothing. "Slow, okay?"

She nodded.

It didn't really matter whether it was bloodlust or hunger; Dr. Jeremy and I found a lot of things in the infirmary that became a little more interesting than watching them after he released her from the wall. Her fingers entwined in his hair, she pulled him to her, her lips brushing against his neck, and when she bit him, he moaned. I felt like a voyeur, watching something that was far too provocative and lascivious to be considered a meal.

Dr. Jeremy eventually pulled his eyes from the microscope that had garnered a great deal of his attention as he tried to distract himself from looking at them. He considered them for a long time, the bonding that had surpassed a simple feeding. He stepped out and returned with two blood packs, which he wedged between the pair, keeping them there until they became enough of an annoyance that Chris unlatched from Josh's neck.

She took them and quickly sank her fangs into each, draining them within seconds. Josh watched. I waited for him to move, and for a moment I suspected he was going to take them from her and offer himself again. So did Jeremy.

"Josh, you should probably figure out a way to unlink Logan from the heart quickly, just in case the sleeper doesn't have the same effect on him as it had on Gideon and Kelly," he urged, nudging him toward the door.

Josh hesitated, his gaze fixed on Chris. I moved closer to him and touched his arm. "Come on, I'll help you."

We'd been in the library for nearly twenty minutes, and I kept splitting my attention between the book in front of me and Josh's neck, which bore the marks of Chris's fangs and was blush red.

He worked hard at avoiding eye contact, and that just made me even more suspicious about his interaction with Chris.

"I have three spells that I think might work. You can go through your book, but you probably won't find anything in there. Those are weaker spells. It will have to be something strong. Look for spells that have words like *transfer, soul,* and *capture.*"

Oh, I see we're going to pretend that thing with you and Chris didn't happen. Okay.

"But we don't want to do that. We want to reverse it."

He nodded. "We will reverse it." Then he hesitated. "Reversing spells are darker. *You* may have to do it and then you'll have to link Kalese's heart to you."

He had to notice my terrified look and realize I didn't want to be linked to another strong magical being.

"It's not the same as hosting Maya. Kalese is your life source, she's the source of both of your lives. You can't live without Maya, and Maya can't live without Kalese." That explanation made it a thousand times worse, but once again, with limited options, I couldn't really say no.

I liked magic, and I had mastered dark magic—or rather I'd prevented it from mastering me—but the darkness lingered each time I used it. Each time it opened me up to more, and I easily saw how people could succumb to its allure. Forbidden and different, it tapped into a side of me that was raw, inhibited, and unencumbered by morals, rationality, and reason—there was a certain freedom in it. As I waded in the liberation of it, so did Maya, pushing the boundaries of her existence, waiting to be given free rein over a body that she seemed to want to claim as her own. Once I'd thought she was a benign spirit; now I knew she was much more. I didn't want to keep giving her opportunities because I wasn't sure when she would come out the victor.

"There isn't anything going on between us," Josh said, looking up from his notepad once he caught me staring at him again.

A doubtful moue quickly formed on my face. "Are you sure you two don't have *something* going on?"

His lips quirked into a smile as his brows rose. "Well, Sky"—then he did air quotes—"the 'something' you are talking about is a very purposeful act. I'm usually pretty active and quite involved during those times, so I can assure you that nothing is going on between Chris and me."

They might not be sleeping together, but there was something going on.

"Are you trying to make your brother jealous?" I kept my eyes on the book. He remained silent until I looked up.

He considered me and the question for a long time—so long that I wondered if he was speculating about it as well. "No," he finally said. I felt like he was being honest. There weren't very many secrets between me and Josh, but since he'd joined Ethan and Sebastian as a keeper of the pack's skeletons, he'd seemed more comfortable with lies of omission and keeping things from me. He might not have been trying to make his brother jealous, and he definitely didn't have the same aversion I had to feeding vampires.

Magic was ambiguous no matter how much you knew about it because there wasn't a master key to it. Tre'ase magic was different from witch magic, and each spell was like looking at a lock and choosing a huge bunch of keys, hoping one was close enough to unlock it. As Ethan, Sebastian, Josh, and I stood next to Logan, who was immobile, we felt the abstruse nature of magic more profoundly than ever. Because he was unable to use magic to maintain his human form, we were faced with the actual monster that we'd dealt with. That Chris had dealt with. The demon that we'd made a fuliginous deal with.

"I don't like it," Ethan finally said, looking over at his brother. "You are going to play with Sky's life each time to 'see' if it works."

He was right. We'd had two failures already, and discovering whether or not an attempt had worked was the hardest part. They had to take him to the brink of death, and in turn me, too. I wasn't in a rush to keep doing it. There was a laundry list of things I would have preferred to be doing.

Josh sighed heavily, rolling his eyes from his brother to get another look at Logan and the heart that Logan had magically linked to himself, pulsing inside its jar as though it was still in a body. My survival was housed in that jar, which didn't exactly inspire confidence in me. At my request, we'd tried other spells, ones that Josh could do, and they had failed. Josh was right about the spell we needed to use. My ability to convert natural magic to dark magic had led him to believe that I would be able to mimic Logan's magic to unlink it.

He swiped my hand with the knife, then Logan's, and finally his, and we joined hands and said the invocation to link us. I said a separate one to link me to Logan. I felt the strong influx of gritty, ancient magic and tried to detect the nuances that made it different from dark magic and natural magic. Logan's magic had parallels to dark magic, but it was different, too, in its ancientness. It awakened something in Maya, a familiarity, an affinity, a connection.

I tightened my hand around Josh's, and he gave it a reassuring squeeze as I laced our magic around Logan's magic, mimicking it as closely as I could before performing the unlinking spell. The words flowed as they had before but became increasingly stronger, poorly controlled. More words, unfamiliar to me, spilled from my lips, in the same rhythm as my own which I had practiced for hours before doing the spell. Dual spells occurred at the same time as Maya rode my words as if they were her own. It was different: a combination of dark magic, natural magic, and ancient magic. The temperature in the room dropped, and frost coated my words as I spoke them. I kept going, trying to get mine out, hoping to prevent the others from passing. A brisk wind battered at my skin. I increased the pace of speaking to prevent the other spell, to no avail. When the spell ended, I opened my eyes, and Ethan, Sebastian, and Dr. Jeremy were on the ground. Logan wasn't just still, he wasn't breathing—dead.

Josh snatched his hand from mine and went to his brother to check his pulse, nodding when he found one. He checked the others, and they were all alive as well. It took me a moment to realize that I was, too. Logan was dead, but the heart still beat in the jar, and I was alive. The room had returned to its normal temperature, but goose bumps covered my arms; they had nothing to do with the temperature and everything to do with the spell that I had become an unwilling executor of. I quickly walked over to Dr. Jeremy's desk, grabbed a piece of paper and scribbled everything I remembered about the other spell, which wasn't much. Spoken in a language I was unfamiliar with and that I suspected predated any language that I possibly could be familiar with. Just minutes after I'd transcribed everything I could remember, everyone had regained consciousness.

"What the hell was that?" was the first thing out of Sebastian's mouth as he stood. "What language was that?"

"Faerie, their original language. It's old, very old," Ethan supplied.

All eyes turned to Ethan, but he didn't offer anything more. I wasn't sure if he had more. What we knew was that during an unlinking spell, Maya had performed one of her own, but we didn't know if my spell or hers had killed Logan. If hers wasn't the deadly one, what was the spell for? If it had been her spell that killed him, why did she want him dead? Had she been doing it to protect me—to protect us?

CHAPTER 9

$\mathcal{T}$he next day I sat in the library, looking over the words I'd written out. I'd spent nearly an hour looking at them and the many books in front of me and had the same amount of information—nothing.

Logan was dead, I was alive. That should have been cause for elation, but it wasn't. The ancient magic that I'd felt and used was a heavy shawl that I couldn't shrug off. Had it been an act of benevolence to kill Logan, or was there more? I stared at the paper where I'd jotted down a hurried transcription after the incident, and it didn't make any more sense to me today than it had yesterday. Faerie language was ancient, but it couldn't be completely unrecognizable. All languages were derived from another, so I just had to figure out which language was the root of Faerie.

I didn't know of any faes that could help. Logan had once called them diminutive and pathetic descendants, spurious offspring of their powerful antecessors. As a result of interbreeding with humans, they were no longer a force to be reckoned with, as they had once been. Faeries were the closest things to gods in history of supernaturals. Their preference was to mate with other Faeries; witches were a close second to preserve their strength, power, and the stranglehold that they had over the supernatural world. They were feared more than revered, and that had eventually led to their fall. For years, they had been hunted and killed, and even the children weren't exempt for fear of another takeover. That continued to bother me—infanticide that doomed a person before they had ever been given a chance to prove themselves. It was a safety measure the witches had adopted as well, and it didn't sit well with me.

If it were up to the witches, Ethan would have been killed because of his magical ability, and now I wondered if that was why he was hiding whatever it was, beyond the dark fae ancestry I knew of.

The books that I had pulled out were of no use, and I found that searching Google didn't seem to be of any help, either.

"It must be very important," said a newly familiar voice. Cole was leaning against the door frame, a cup of coffee in hand. A smile flitted across his lips as he regarded me with intrigue. He wasn't in claret today but instead wore a white button-down that made his eyes look more silver. He appeared more relaxed and comfortable in the jeans he had on today than in what he'd had on before. His gaze swept over the books and scattered papers on the table.

I shrugged. "Research."

"Well, it sure has your attention. I've been at the door for over six minutes and you didn't notice." The part about him just standing at the door watching me without making his presence known was creepy enough; imagining the number of faces he must have seen and the sounds of frustration he must have heard added to my embarrassment. I was sure he'd heard a couple of choice words and variations of *fuck* as well.

"That had to be interesting," I said, feeling warmth creep up my cheeks and over the bridge of my nose.

That coaxed a grin from him. "To say the least. It was

fascinating."

"You're back, why?"

"Another meeting. I will probably stay for a couple of days until it is resolved." He was about to say something when he stopped and looked over his shoulder, and the gentle smile that had settled on him vanished. A few moments later, Josh and Ethan moved past him.

"What are you doing here?" Josh asked. I turned the paper toward him, and he looked at the scribblings and frowned before he went to the bookcase. He scanned some of the titles and pulled a few off the shelf.

"These should be of more help than the ones you have." The depth of his knowledge never ceased to amaze me. It was so easy to be distracted by the body art, eclectic shirts, and wayward smile that just didn't seem interested in much. The white t-shirt with *Bazinga* scrawled across it didn't help. I laughed and gave his slouch hat a pointed look. When he didn't immediately catch my derision, I made a face.

"Really?" He glanced at my hair. I'd come into the library with a ponytail, and somehow in my frustration, I'd fidgeted with it, taking it down and putting it back up while trying to focus on my task and not my hair. I was sure it was a pile of disarray.

"It's not that bad," Ethan said, and then he leaned forward and kissed me. A gentle, sensual, commanding kiss that would have easily led to more if there weren't other people in the room. When he pulled away, I panted softly against his lips.

"Okay, I guess this is my new hairstyle?" I joked.

He laughed and glanced at the door where Cole had been. Probably made uncomfortable by the display, he'd excused himself.

Josh rested against the wall, his arms crossed over his chest, his face branded with an amused scowl as he studied his brother. "Next time, why don't you just whip it out and pee on her leg to mark your territory?" He pushed himself up from the wall, grabbed a piece of paper and a marker off the small desk in the corner, and wrote something on it. "Let me help you out, brother. Here, Sky, why don't you carry this? Better yet, pin it on the front of your shirt so my brother doesn't have to mark you with his lips anytime another man's around. It will save us time."

Ethan looked at the paper and then glared at his brother, who based on the half-cocked grin was quite amused with himself. A mischievous glint sparked in his eyes. On the paper in big letters was written, "Ethan's. Don't Touch."

Ethan rolled his eyes dismissively and frowned.

"Should I make another, bigger so they can see it at least ten feet away? I'll make sure she has one that she can pin to her back as well. We want to warn the locals." Josh's lips tightened as he suppressed his laughter when a growl of irritation radiated in his brother's chest. Wolfy was not amused.

Ethan glanced at his watch. "We have a meeting," he said, ushering his brother out the door rather roughly.

"No need to manhandle me, I'm just trying to be helpful."

Josh winked at me as he went out the door but twisted to avoid his brother. Then he poked his head in again. "Don't forget to put on the sign," he said loud enough for Ethan to hear.

"No one thinks you're funny," Ethan snapped from down the hall. Josh laughed and followed him, his laughter drifting.

I held the katana, becoming familiar with the weight and the blade. I swung it in a figure eight to get my arm warmed up and then switched arms. Sebastian always pushed being proficient with both arms. He was, and he often preferred using two weapons at the same time. Show-off. Slicing the blade through the air was more therapeutic than I'd thought it would be. I'd spent an hour going over the books Josh had given me and still hadn't been able to figure out anything from the other spell. Part of me wanted to talk to Maya. The idea that I had been conned into keeping her made me feel foolish most of the time, but the more I thought about it, the more I realized her offer not to share my life with me was a hollow proposition. It wasn't her choice. She couldn't just pack up her bags and leave, and death wasn't really an option. A spirit shade didn't die when the host did, it died when the Tre'ase that had created it did.

Practicing in the gym was my only option, because trying to hear anything at the door of Sebastian's office was absolutely pointless. Apparently, I now had the reputation of being "nosy." The moment they knew I was near the door, I could expect either Ethan or Sebastian to poke their head out to ask me if I needed anything. *Sure, I need to be part of the meeting. Can you help me out?*

Nothing good could be happening when all the Alphas in the country were having another meeting—secrecy wasn't an option, in my opinion. I realized that they carried the burden of whatever befell their respective packs and had the responsibility to keep them safe. In return, they expected loyalty and allegiance to the pack and for no one to question the man behind the machine.

In theory, it worked. Members didn't question the manner in which an Alpha achieved something, they just knew that it would be handled. My only experience with pack life was of Sebastian as Alpha, and the man behind this machine was more than gifted at navigating the politics of the otherworld. The gradations between making someone an enemy or an ally were things he'd mastered, and yet I wanted to know what went on. I wondered if I was the only one who felt that way or if others were better at hiding it. Maybe they just didn't get caught as many times as I'd been, trying to pull the curtain back to get a glance at the people who were helping the machine to run.

I lunged, thrusting into my imaginary opponent, and retreated. The sword whipped through the air, making injury-inflicting strikes. I went over the many sessions I'd had with Sebastian, trying to recreate my losses and changing the final scene when I hit the floor and had a blade at my throat or some vital part of my body. I moved, shifting my weight, jumping back, and wielding my weapon with the expertise that he demanded, each time hearing his stern voice giving instruction on how to defeat him, and yet I still couldn't. I made a half-turn, a defensive move to avoid being hit, and then delivered one that should be fatal.

I stopped midexecution when I saw Cole standing at the door, a smile feathered across his face. Once again, I found myself under his watchful and assessing gaze.

His approach was slow, the agile movement of a cautious and efficient predator. Through the years, I'd learned to assess their strengths and deceptions; that way, becoming prey was less likely. I returned his smile.

"Sebastian or Winter?" he asked as his eyes moved over the length of the blade. "Who trained you, Sebastian or Winter?"

"Sebastian."

"Ah, then you must be quite skilled."

I knew there was some skill to sword use, but I still couldn't help but revert back to my initial belief: swing it and hit something soft, and your opponent's day got a lot worse. "It's a sword, just swing and hit. There's bound to be some damage."

He chuckled lightly. "True. But what I saw wasn't just mindless novitiate techniques. I see why it's your weapon of choice." I didn't correct him by telling him my weapon of choice was a knife. I was better with one, but fighting with a sword did have its advantages, one being it allowed distance to use not only the sword itself, but also weaponless combat moves like kicks, punches, and strikes if necessary.

He moved over to the wall of swords, going over them until he came to another katana, which he picked up.

"Come on, let's play."

If that's how he played, he, too, like most of the were-animals, had failed Social Skills 101 and was in desperate need of remedial classes.

"Show me what you got," he demanded, approaching me.

"You don't want to warm up or take a few practice swings?"

He shook his head. "Now you have the advantage. Let's see what you can do, Skylar." My name rolled off his tongue in a low purr.

We circled each other as I tried to determine which was his dominant side, where he was most vulnerable, and which direction to lunge. He didn't seem to give me the same regard. Amusement sparked at his lips and eyes as he watched me studying him for an advantage.

He kept the katana at his side casually, while I held mine in a defensive stance, preparing to move in. I advanced, swinging in an arc. He blocked it quickly and turned. Once he was facing me again, I struck again. He blocked, but the amused look fell from his face as he assumed a defensive position. He moved, striking fast and sharp. I blocked, turned, and my elbow went into his back, a quick jab. I knew he felt it.

"Impressive. I was hoping you would take that one. It was an open move. Good." He stepped back, and there was a gentle lilt to his voice. "I suppose I don't need to go easy on you."

Parry. Strike. Turns. Retreats. For several minutes the room rang with the clank of metal against metal. Sharp jabs, drops to the floor as one of us attempted to swipe the other's leg and bring them to the ground. The smile that was frozen on his lips taunted me as warmth pricked at my skin. I could feel the perspiration, and he didn't seem to be working very hard. It was like practicing with Sebastian, who I suspected made errors to build my confidence, allowing me to land blows or at least get the advantage.

When he rested his sword at his side, my only goal was to get just one blow in. I advanced, strike after strike, and he blocked. With a quick change of hands and a half-arc swing, he knocked the sword out of my hand. Both of our eyes followed the sword as it fell just a few feet away.

"Nevertheless, you are quite impressive, Skylar. Sebastian's prodigy has definitely earned the high regard in which he holds her."

Really? The man who just called me a nosy, obstinate child less than an hour ago holds me in high regard? Prove it.

After replacing the sword on the wall, he turned to me and nodded. "It has been my pleasure getting to know you."

If that was how he got to know people, he, like most of the were-animals, was in desperate need of a refresher on social norms and contracts. Attacking someone with a sharp weapon wasn't a greeting.

Cole barely acknowledged Ethan, who was standing at the door, his face threatening a scowl that he was trying hard to fight. When he addressed Cole, his voice was cool, even, and rough. "I'm glad you've decided to stay to offer your assistance. It's kind of you. But, there are certain things that are off-limits to you, and we should discuss it later."

I stood between them as they subtly tested the boundaries of their dominance for no other reason than they were two Alphas who had a difficult time occupying the same space without challenging each other.

Cole smile flickered and fell just for a moment into a tense line until he mastered it and forced another less genial one that bared the edges of his teeth.

"Of course. I am your guest, and I realize there are boundaries. I have them as well in our home, and I look forward to hearing what yours are." Then he turned his attention to me. "Thank you, Sky. It was fun playing with you." And he started up the stairs, walking past Ethan, who kept his eyes narrowed on him and the scowl he'd denied himself now locked firmly in place.

Ethan watched me carefully before walking past me to grab the sword that I'd lost during the sparring match. He was quiet as he replaced it on the wall.

"Sebastian has chosen to be your instructor with the use of this type of weapon. It's best that you continue with Sebastian or me and no others." When he turned, the scowl had been replaced by a noncommittal smile.

I wasn't acquiescent by nature and bucked against commands without reason. "Is that anyone, other Alphas, or just Cole?"

He moved closer to me, leaning down until his mouth was near my ear, and I could feel his lips moving into a smile. "For now, all listed. We'll revisit the terms later."

I stepped back, increasing the distance between us. Commands just didn't work for me. Commands from Ethan were even harder. I, too, found myself testing boundaries, not as an Alpha but in trying to find where my position was in what seemed like our pack, our union or whatever it was. And I had a burgeoning understanding of the ongoing conflict between Josh and Ethan. Josh was essentially in the Midwest Pack but often given special considerations because he wasn't a were-animal but a blood ally. However, there were rules he had to abide by, one being that he had to respect his brother's role as Beta of the pack, which was something that he seemed to have a difficult time with. I was experiencing the same thing, but I managed to tamp it down as much as I could. I stepped back and frowned.

"You know you'll get further with me if you don't command me to do things and make them seem more like requests than commands."

A brow lifted and the wolfish grin settled over his features. "Fine. Sky, I request that you follow my commands."

You're not the boss of me. If it wasn't such a juvenile rebuttal, I would have said it out loud. I started to say something, and seconds later, he was next to me, pressing his fingers against my lips. He really hadn't learned his lesson. I couldn't count the number of times I'd bitten him for doing that, and I was considering doing it again when he removed them.

"Please," he blew out, rolling his eyes.

"Doesn't really sound like you mean it," I offered and looked at the finger that seemed to be inching close to my lips again.

"You're pushing it."

I bit back the grin. He started up the stairs but turned back, looking over the room, unsettled. Did my sparring with Cole really bother him that much?

"I wasn't practicing with him. He asked to spar, so I did."

"Just follow my request."

Using *request* in lieu of *command* was that same thing.

"How was your meeting?" I needed to change the subject and migrate away from dealing with Ethan and his commands, or strongly worded requests.

With a dour smile, he shrugged. "It was okay. Let's discuss it tonight at dinner." And with that I followed him up the stairs. If dinner was when he wanted to discuss it, then that was exactly when he planned to discuss it. A lesson I'd learned from my first dealings with him.

When I opened the door, Ethan didn't say anything at first, instead giving my attire a long, lingering look. Loose brunette waves flowed over my curve-hugging single-strap dress just a few shades of green darker than my eyes. I'd paired it with a pair of pewter-colored shoes that reminded me of Ethan's eyes, which was why I had chosen them over black. Ethan preferred business casual over jeans any day, and he looked amazing in tailored suits. The navy-blue suit picked up the hints of blue in his pupils that were usually drowned out by the gray of his wolf.

"You look . . ." He stepped back and gave me a long look again. "Beautiful. Absolutely." Then he kissed me, pressing his lips firmly against mine, and his arms wrapped around me. As the kiss deepened, I started to question whether dinner was going to happen when he pulled away and took my hand and led me out of the house.

Although the restaurant was large, it seemed private and intimate. The room was dimly lit by recessed lights from above and small candles that decorated the tables, and whatever light managed to peek through the curtained windows from the city lights. Even the waitstaff seemed to move effortlessly through the restaurant, speaking in hushed voices and managing to blend with the music, becoming nothing more than white noise and quick tranquil sounds in the background. Despite all that, we were still ushered to the back of the restaurant, to a private section. I was aware that from the time we'd left the house, Ethan had kept his hands pressed against me. In the car, his hand caressed my leg the entire time.

The private area of the restaurant boasted a simple elegance. The tuxedo-style tablecloth matched the seats. Chandeliers hung from the ceiling and only offered a hint of light, just enough to keep the place from being completely dark. Instead of being accented with traditional art, the walls had a textured finish of hues of gray and white. Light music hummed in the background.

Ethan ordered wine. As we sipped on it, the conversation didn't evolve into anything more than mundane topics. I ordered my food similar to the way Ethan ordered his: steak—his rare, mine medium rare—potatoes and vegetables.

"Make hers rare as well," he said before the waiter left. And then he grinned. "And bring her a slice of red velvet cake with her salad, please."

"I wanted my steak medium rare."

Shaking his head, he quickly pointed his finger at his eye, and I knew it was his way of telling me that he could see my terait, the thing that vampires got when they were having bloodlust. Most people would have ignored the flick of orange in my eyes and considered it nothing more than an optical abnormality, but it seemed to bother Ethan. A lot. Light orange circled my pupil, a reminder that l was never just a werewolf. Perhaps I denied it too much; even when hints of it peeked through, I ignored it. Ethan was acutely aware of its existence, often noticing it before I did.

Even when it was obscured by my green eyes, he still spotted it. Most of the time, I found myself looking in the mirror for several minutes, trying to get a glimpse of it when he pointed it out. Without fail, I eventually saw it.

"Whoever started that rumor about me and dessert needs to stop," I quipped.

"Is it a rumor if it's true?" he asked, his brows raised, then he smiled. The conversation remained mundane until the server dropped off the salads and my cake. Ethan pushed his salad in my direction and I moved both his and mine to the side and grabbed my fork and started on the cake. I ignored his haughty knowing smirk and busied myself with shoving a forkful of cake in my mouth, taking in the decadent flavors of cocoa sweetness and cream cheese.

"Tell me what happened yesterday with the spell. Be specific."

Between bites I went into explicit detail, happy to share the burden with someone else. I told him everything, and he listened patiently as I walked him through an overly detailed description, but I wasn't sure why I did. Maybe I felt like telling him would lift the heaviness that I'd been carrying and absolve me of the guilt that I might have somehow been an accomplice, again, to a spell that might have grave consequences. There was something disturbing about Logan's death and my life being in a small jar in Dr. Jeremy's lab.

Ethan's concern-laden gaze remained on me as I stabbed my fork into the cake and moaned.

"Should I be worried?"

"About what?" I asked, putting another forkful in my mouth.

"About the cake. I think you're cheating on me with it," he teased.

"Oh, I'm so cheating on you with it." I laughed.

"And here you wanted me to think you weren't a 'dessert first' type of woman." He leaned back in his chair. I figured at some point I'd get used to Ethan's appearance. The defined jaw, hewn features, intense eyes and intangible ways, added to his primal allure, and intoxicating beauty. I still found myself staring and had to pull my eyes from him.

He wasn't at all unaware of it and grinned at my effort not to stare.

"Back to what happened. Have you found anything that resembled the spell?"

His next question mimicked the one I'd had when it happened. "How did you know it was Faerie language?"

"Isn't that what we established Maya is, and Ethos? It only makes sense that's what she speaks," he offered.

It answered some questions but left so many unanswered. She had been killed as a child; how did she learn the language? I didn't know how old she was or how many bodies she had inhabited before she'd been hosted by my mother. How many powerful supernaturals had she lived her life through, picking up spell after spell, learning dark and forbidden magic, and using languages that were no longer spoken, therefore making them difficult to translate and spells in them even harder to stop?

"If it is, and we can't translate it, then what?" I inquired.

"I don't know."

"Do you ever wonder what became of the other Faeries?" I asked. The deadliest and most powerful ones' whereabouts were unknown. It seemed like that was something we should have made an effort to find out. Someone who was strong and able to in e magic that ancient, dark, and powerful was someone whose location we really needed to have a fix on. Who were their hosts, and did they have the ability to control the powerful beings within them, unlike me? Or had they just become nothing more than shells for the spirit shades, unwilling stewards to their cause?

Ethan considered the question and frowned. "I don't know." Something lingered behind his words.

"You don't know, or you can't tell me?" I asked.

The same indecipherable look remained on his face, and I

tried to read through the lull, find a hint of which answer was right. He leaned forward with his fork and picked up some cake, turning it toward my mouth. I hesitated.

"Skylar."

I kept my lips pressed firmly together, which only made him grin at the defiant response. Challenges didn't bother Ethan as much as they amused him when it came to me. Probably he and I both knew, between the two of us, hands down he was the most indomitable, but we were at a stalemate. Several seconds passed and he stayed positioned with the fork turned toward me. Even when the server arrived with our food, Ethan remained across the table, waiting for me to take his offering. Sensing the waiter's impatience, I glared at Ethan and took the food off the fork. He sat back and grinned.

Halfway through dinner, when he finally seemed over his ill-gained victory, I asked, "What was the meeting about?"

"We'll discuss it when we get to your house."

I studied him for a moment, trying to figure out whether this was a delay tactic.

As we continued to eat, I shot furtive glances in his direction.

"Sky, I do wish I could be an open book for you, but I can't," he admitted softly.

"You said we would discuss it," I reminded him sternly. "I refuse to be in the dark about this."

"And you won't be." He looked around the room, and I wasn't sure why there was a need for more privacy—there wasn't another person within fifty feet. "But as I said, we'll talk about it at home."

Once in the house, Ethan put down the cake he'd gotten from the restaurant, clasped my hand, and led me to the bedroom.

I dug my heels in. He wasn't going to use this as a distraction tactic. "Ethan—"

"I'm about to show you what the meeting was about." He led me into the bedroom. He turned on the lights, a faint smile barely curving his lips, and slowly unzipped my dress and removed it. His touch was featherlight as his fingers trailed over me, cruising gently over my shoulders, my breast, and then he kneeled down and looked at my stomach. He kissed me gently there and then stood. His touch was gentle but clinically attentive. "Ethan?"

"Just let me finish," he said in an even, low voice.

Then he moved around me, just as focused, searching my body. Periodically I felt his warm lips against my skin.

When he finished, he sighed in relief. "You aren't marked," he said. He looked away, and confusion and relief seemed to have equal play on his features as he allowed his stolid mask to drop.

"Marked? What are you talking about?" My tone was rough enough to pull him out of his distraction. He removed his shirt and turned. In the middle of his left shoulder blade was a crescent moon that hadn't been there before.

"Most of us have them. All the Alphas and ranked were-animals, with the exception of Steven and a few others." Then he named several other weres that I didn't know.

I hesitated asking the question because I knew the answer, and hearing it out loud seemed like it would make it worse. "When did you get it?"

"Yesterday. Cole noticed it and called Sebastian, and we spent most of the meeting trying to get a tally of who has it and who doesn't."

"What does it mean?"

He sat on the bed and rubbed his hand over the light stubble forming on his cheek and jawline. After being quiet for several minutes, he spoke, his voice gruff and weary as if he'd been over this a million times and was begrudgingly conceding. "We all believe it was just a tale. You know, one of the many tales of our being cursed, which never turn out to be anything but embellished retellings of things that never happen. I can't even count the number of exegeses there are about our origins and whether it was a curse on humans or animals. Our existence has been attributed to everything from a nefarious spell performed by Faeries to a curse for the wrongdoing of a spirit wolf. No one knows how, but we've always been immune to magic. Our ability to change without the call of the moon or Mercury rising, transits of Saturn"—he stopped briefly—"or an eclipse"—the last added Winter, who from what I knew was unique, although they continued to perpetuate the notion that she wasn't the only one for her sake—"is new."

He was taking time with his words, and I didn't think it had anything to do with him withholding information. "Immunity to magic has always given us an advantage and has unsettled most." Pushing himself to his feet, he started to pace the length of the room like an anxious caged animal, captured and confined by a situation that he had no idea how to escape.

Inhaling a deep breath, he exhaled and continued. "No one knows how we got these marks. It could be the result of something that happened to the vampires and the Tre'ases, a curse or spell of some kind." He gave me a look, and I knew he was referring to the spell that had removed the curses that had bound them by wards and daylight.

I continued to stand listening to him, chills running up my arms.

"This is a curse or the removal of one?" I asked.

Studying me, he approached slowly, feeling my unease. He leaned down and kissed me softly on the lips. Any other time it would have been welcome, but it did nothing to comfort me now. The quiet lingered longer, and I waited for him to continue. "It's a curse." And he said something in a language that I wasn't familiar with. An ancient language similar to the one I'd spoken with Maya's influence. I studied him as much as he'd studied me.

"How do you know that?"

"Did you finish reading the book I gave you about the Faeries?"

Skimming it probably didn't count. I wanted to, but the tales of senseless murders, abuse, infanticide, and torture made it a hard read. There were stories of the many things that they had done for their own entertainment, spells that did horrible things to people. I understood why people had come together and wanted them dead.

"Before we became this"—his hands swept over his body—"we were weaponry against them and a big reason why they were defeated."

I recalled Logan saying that once upon a time, we weren't "pretty little things" but monsters. Creatures that had walked on two legs but had been undoubtedly more animal than human, more monstrous than typical animals. When we'd changed to our animal form, it hadn't been much different than the beasts we'd presented daily. Based on Logan's description, we'd behaved like those creatures as well, savagely. I could see why the Faeries had considered us competition.

"In an effort to keep us from being used as weaponry, they attempted everything, trying to find a combination that could do magic against us. Nothing worked. It wasn't just their cruelty that led to their demise; their unyielding efforts to try spells to kill us off caused others to come together to defeat them. Apparently one curse was said to work, although it is questionable. Josh read one account that said it's tied to the lunar eclipse. It was the symbolic death of our total immunity. We bear the curse of the lunar. Once that curse is performed again, it is true death."

I didn't know what to say, and neither did Ethan. A lunar eclipse would happen in twenty days. Yesterday the curse had taken place. Maya had fulfilled the Faeries' final wish to get rid of the were-animals—or those who were descendants of the were-animals that had existed when they ruled.

This was the clusterfuck of all clusterfucks.

CHAPTER 10

*E*veryone was preoccupied with trying to find out more about the curse of the lunar, but I hated that after the night Ethan had told me about it, he'd gone MIA. And so had Josh. I'd never felt more in the dark. Responses to my questions were reduced to single-word comments via text. I wasn't supposed to question the men behind the machine, but I didn't operate that way and didn't know how to with something as serious as this, something that I had inadvertently been the trigger of.

It had been refreshing when Claudia had asked me to lunch, and I'd quickly accepted, hoping that she might be able to provide more insight. A part of me also craved the maternal comfort that she exuded. It wouldn't change anything, but I needed something to quell the feeling.

Claudia's warm smile met me as I walked through the door, and my attire garnered an appreciative nod. I'd traded my jeans for a pair of black slacks and heels and a beige silk shirt. I'd even managed to tame my curls and pull them back into a long French braid. I wouldn't have her brushing back my hair and telling me how pretty I was—Claudia's sweet way of telling me to handle my hair.

No matter how much effort I put into dressing, I doubted I could ever look as refined and elegant as Claudia, who was dressed in a pearl-colored suit and lilac shirt. The light gloves that she wore never looked out of place on her. They enriched her style, while on anyone else they would have looked odd, pretentious.

Her melodic South African voice greeted me. "Ah, Skylar, I'm so glad you decided to accept my invitation."

She was probably indeed pleased that I hadn't turned her down because it would have been an absolute first. I knew Claudia was a gallery owner, but behind the gentle eyes, dulcet voice, and refined demeanor was someone with great connections and more power and secrets than even the pack, and I had no idea what she was. She'd helped save Ethan a couple of days ago, when it had been discovered he was a dark elf, which carried a death penalty. Representing the faes, her vote, Gideon's, and Demetrius's had been the ones that had saved Ethan. How did a peddler of expensive art have such connections? And I couldn't forget the reverence with which Demetrius had treated her.

Guiding me by the elbow, she led me to her office. "Where are we having lunch?" I asked.

"Here, of course."

Translation: I thought we could talk, and we would need some privacy.

She directed me to the small table that already had two covered plates on it. I uncovered mine to find roasted duck, pota-toes, and vegetables. She gave me a half-smile as if she was apolo-gizing for the meal. I wasn't sure why, but I assumed she felt I wanted something different—were-animals' favorite, rare steak.

Once seated, she slid a chocolate mousse in my direction. "It is my understanding you enjoy your dessert first, please don't let me stop you." I *was* a "dessert first" type of woman, but with Claudia, it seemed totally wrong to do.

I slid it over. "I'll eat it later." We ate, engaging in the most banal casual conversation, which I suspected was a prelude to more. After all, this was the woman who had once asked me if Sebastian could kill Ethan for the safety of the pack. She was an enigma, and her line of questioning often fell in with that.

"I understand your human is missing." She liked to attribute ownership of people to others. When she'd first met me, she'd asked Ethan and Josh whose I was.

"Yes, Kelly is missing."

She lifted her eyes to meet mine. "How is Sebastian handling your Kelly being missing?"

I couldn't help but smile; I wasn't sure if Claudia would be exempt from getting sprayed with a water bottle by Kelly for wording it like that. Once, Kelly and Sebastian had been at a stalemate and had a peculiar stare-off as she held the water bottle, ready to spritz him for what she deemed bad behavior. In the end, she'd mumbled under her breath about him being a bad wolf and walked away. Thinking about her made me realize how much we missed her. The gnawing guilt came back. Why hadn't we looked for her sooner? Why had we given her so much alone time? We should have at least checked on her. Anxiety about something bad happening to her coursed through me.

"He feels guilt, like the rest of us. We should have protected her."

She nodded slowly. "I do believe the best was always done to ensure that she was protected. This, too, will be handled if Sebastian doesn't become too consumed with guilt and his perceived failure to rise above it. I do enjoy the changes I've seen in him; you and your human have softened him." The curt displeasure in her tone contradicted her words.

"He's still capable of leading. He's just more considerate," I pointed out.

"I've never doubted his effectiveness to lead and never will. He is a skilled and astute Alpha. I think it's the kindness that you see in him that has made you willing to accept things so well. I am glad you continue to think so highly of him despite the situation. It is a great sacrifice on your part, and you must trust him and care for the pack a great deal to offer such a gift."

What that hell was she talking about? "What gift? Despite what situation?"

She paled, and for the second time since I'd met her, the genteel facade dropped. She was having difficulty hiding the red streak of anger that fell over her features, and it spread, racing up her cheeks.

"I do apologize, I've misspoken. Please continue with your meal." She excused herself from the table and walked over to her desk, where she picked up the phone and dialed a number.

"Yes, hello, Sebastian. I'm having a lovely lunch with Skylar and do believe I've misspoken. Perhaps I was wrong, but have you not had the discussion with Skylar about the lunar curse and the way to stop it?" I couldn't hear him on the other end, but Claudia strained to keep the smile on her face.

"Well, of course this isn't my pack and it is indeed yours, but I have an obligation to protect what is mine, and that is contingent on you doing your job as the Alpha of the pack and the Elite. There are others involved. Although I appreciate your fondness for Skylar, it is a disservice for her not to be informed of all things. We will be here for a while, please join us. I do think such information should come from you, but I will be more than willing to tell her. If you aren't here by the end of our lunch, it will be my duty to do so."

She didn't give him a chance to respond; she simply smiled.

For thirty-five minutes, Claudia and I had lunch while engaging in the most frivolous and trite conversation imaginable. Each time I broached the topic, she simply smiled and reminded me that Sebastian would be joining us soon. Which only led to my imagination running rampant. My curiosity about Claudia was no longer just a gnawing interest—it had become a need. I needed to know who the woman was who Ethan and Josh considered godmother, who with one call could literally command Sebastian to join us for a meeting.

"Besides being an empath, a Moura, and an impresario, what else are you?" I asked, softening my voice until it lacked the urgency I actually felt, and yet it still seemed like I was being rude to her. How did she do that to people? It was a simple question and something I had the right to know, but the small grimace that settled on her face made me feel like I had asked her the most intrusive personal question imaginable.

"Nothing more. Why, have I given you a reason to think otherwise?"

I nodded. *I've hopped on the train to Rudeville, might as well keep traveling.* "People who are feared by most seem to be apprehensive around you. Marcia considers herself and the witches superior to most and often refuses to cooperate, yet somehow you were able to get her to allow her assistant to help us when Kelly was injured. And the situation with Ethan—what would give you the right to represent the fae on something so important? It seems like you are more than what you present yourself to be."

She nodded slowly, the grimace blossoming into a genteel smile, but her eyes were still shadowed and it was apparent she wasn't accustomed to being asked such things.

"I do believe your understanding of this world has made you cynical. You had a rough introduction, and your first encounter was with Demetrius and Sebastian. What they possess in strength and power they lack in diplomacy. It is a flaw that they both have. I find that when there is mutual respect, then negotiations can be easier. I've made many sacrifices to acquire debts that have worked in my favor. You, from the outside, look to be no more than what you are, but from my understanding, it was because of you that the vote went in Ethan's favor—I don't believe I ever thanked you for that."

Damn, she's good. She'd said a whole lot of nothing. There wasn't any way I planned to leave this lunch without knowing more about her than I had when I'd walked in. "Do you mind me asking what sacrifices you have made and how Marcia became indebted to you? Before, you said that she didn't like you. I find it hard to believe that a person like her would ever allow herself to be indebted to you. So how did it happen?"

The smile didn't falter. "Your assumption is the debt was from Marcia; it wasn't. Her assistant, Bernard, had an obligation he had to fulfill."

"Are you a fae?"

"No."

"But they accept you as one of them."

"I have similar gifts."

It was like pulling teeth, and when she stood, feeling like I was about to lose my opportunity, I blurted, "What are you? I want the truth, no more convoluted answers." Watching her eyes narrow and the frown slip into a smile, I knew I'd violated some unspoken rule, but at the moment I didn't really care. I wanted answers. The truth.

"You're right, my introduction into this world was challenging, and you've been one of the people who have made the transition easier. I'm tired of being in the dark." Before she could give me the line she had given me before about how sometimes the darkness was where we were safest, I continued. "Being in the dark doesn't make me feel safe. It makes me feel uncomfortable and more frightened than I need to be. In the last month, I've found out that the shade that I am hosting is a Faerie. I'm one of the few people in the world who can read the Clostra, and I can manipulate magic in ways that no one else can. I don't think being in the dark is a good thing for someone like me."

She considered me for a long time. "Dark elves were sentenced to death because of their ability to cause death with a simple touch, something that most of them could not control. They were considered the worst of the otherworld, because very few know that people like me exist. I am a Messor." She shrugged, as if her reveal was inconsequential, but you didn't tell someone that you were a Reaper like you told them you liked peanut butter instead of jam on your toast.

I hoped my Latin was off and what she was telling me was incorrect. I looked at her gloved hands and was glad that she wasn't a shapeshifter with the ability to detect my emotions and changes in my physiology because my heart was racing. I could feel it. I took several sips of water because my mouth was becoming increasingly dry. I saw why Demetrius looked upon her with aversion and fear. She had earned it.

"So you're death?"

She sighed softly, and I concluded that more often than not, she had to explain what she was, and I needed an explanation right now. What I was imaging might be more nefarious than what she was. Messor also meant harvester. Maybe she was the garden-growing diva.

"I can use the energy from death to perform magic."

Nah, that's about as bad as her telling me she's the Grim Reaper. I ushered a plaintive smile onto my face, where it remained. She might not have been able to recognize or sense the distress, but Sebastian did, and the moment he walked into the office, his eyes flew to me, where they settled and stayed. After a long moment of consideration, he turned to face her.

"It was not your place to tell her anything," he snapped.

"I didn't tell her any of your information, I told her mine." Her tone was more gentle than usual, as though she was trying to soothe the agitated predator before her, but she was just as dangerous and predatory as he was. "Sebastian, I respect your position and your role in the pack; however, when it comes to Josh and Ethan, there aren't any boundaries. And if you have any boundaries present when it comes to them, please know that I will have no problem crossing them."

The gentle smile might have belied her words with anyone else, but that didn't do it for Sebastian. He bared his teeth, taking her gloved hand in his and kissing it. He showed a level of reverence that led me to believe that there might be more to being a Messor.

"Claudia, we've always been on the same side with mutual interest, and I hope this will continue. You are someone that I hold in deep regard, and not just because of your relationship with Ethan and Josh, but because you have earned it. However, when it comes to my pack, boundaries are not optional. It's good that while you deserve to be feared and revered, were-animals are immune to your magic as well."

He slipped past her, and they both kept the fake smiles plastered on their faces. There wasn't anything more uncomfortable than predators out-polite-ing each other while issuing thinly veiled threats.

Sebastian took a seat on the chair across from the small table that we were sitting at and crossed his arms. He was focusing more on the art on the walls and around the room than on me, but from the intensity of his face, I knew he was weeding through the thoughts in his head. His hands washed over his face several times before he sighed. Holding his gaze was hard, but I did.

"I didn't hide this from you out of cruelty but to keep you from needlessly worrying, and I still feel we are at a juncture where it isn't a cause for worry."

"Seventeen days, I assure you it is time to worry," Claudia interjected. "Worry and take action. This can't be handled without the urgency it deserves."

He glared at her, and when he looked at me, his amber eyes were soft, saddened. "We've been trying to find a way to reverse the curse. We've asked around, Josh has researched it, and for now there is only one way. To end the curse at the source."

His nice way of saying the curse ended when the source of the curse did.

"That's not an option we're considering," Josh said as he walked in. Like Ethan always did, he stopped, taking Claudia's hand and giving an air-kiss on each side of her cheek before coming farther into the room. His hair was disheveled—not the typical artfully careless way it usually looked—and I suspected he'd been running his fingers nervously through it.

Sebastian continued. "Josh has been working to find another option, and he's close." It was Sebastian's confidence in the face of potential defeat that made him a good leader. Even if it was a certain form of hubris, any other time it would have helped. Now it didn't. They would work tirelessly to find an alternative, but if the sacrifice of one life to save many was a choice, he would have to make it, no matter how hard it was. I thought of the jar stored in the pack's home that was linked to my life and mine to it. There was a macabre irony that in her effort to kill off the were-animals, Maya might have guaranteed her death.

CHAPTER 11

Josh's house looked like an office supply retailer had decided to set up shop there. I counted six dry-erase boards on stands, three with spells on them. Books were stacked on the sofas, side table, and small desk near the bookcase. He had his laptop open and a headset tossed to the side. I assumed he'd been calling his good friend, London, who was better at magic than he was. She wasn't stronger, but having completed her magic studies, she was better at spells from an academic standpoint.

When I walked in, he gave me a wry smile as I went to each board and studied it and then glanced over the various books he had opened. I tried not to let my confidence wane, but I wanted to direct a lunar curse undo. Josh was talented, and anything he came up with would be the best, but my fear was that his best wasn't going to be good enough.

His room had been converted to a mini library, with a significant number of books from the pack's collection now there in his home. I wondered if the change of location had something to do with Cole and Ethan's persistent desire to keep him away from me.

Hours later, after Josh and I had winnowed the spells down to those that he appeared to have strong confidence in, we received a call from Gavin to meet him. Josh hesitated and I understood why; at this point we had only seventeen days until the lunar eclipse. As he contemplated leaving, I said, "Kelly doesn't stop being our responsibility. If we can help her, we need to."

It didn't take much convincing. I knew he probably felt that way, too, but he was torn between obligations, like we all were.

We arrived near the same place Winter and I had seen the feral woman, Carol. Then we moved deeper into the wooded area. The magic that came off it was more intense, and the wards several feet from the home were strong. Gavin had started to watch the place daily, finding a pattern, and it was worse than I'd suspected.

I stood next to Ethan, Gavin, Josh, and Winter, and we watched as two feral-looking people, one male and one female, were taken outside by men in military-like uniforms and the woman we'd seen before who had the peculiar magic. She scanned and slowly walked the area. We were hidden in the thicket of trees, trying to figure out what the hell was going on. Gavin reported that the first two days, several vans had come in but he couldn't see what they were carrying. Magic and science made a horrible combination.

I wondered what they were creating, were-animals or the opposite—people who behaved like were-animals and had all their attributes—strength, keen and enhanced senses—without changing. Why would anyone want something like this? Was it for business or pleasure? Both were disturbing, but the former made sense.

We were concerned, very concerned, but we had to make sure Kelly was in there.

"It's a mage," Josh finally said after studying the woman for several minutes. He seemed to have the same look of incredulity as I'd had when I'd realized that she was one. A diet-witch she wasn't.

There wasn't anything light or weak about her or the three other people who had joined her, one man and two other women. Ethan and Gavin leaned in each time they spoke, trying to understand what they were saying. The creep factor was really strong when I realized Gavin, Ethan, and Winter could hear them from nearly thirty feet away. I concentrated on listening, too, instead of gawking at them like someone had given me a private viewing at the freak show. I strained. I heard nothing. I leaned in more; the mage's voice was light as it carried in the air, but I could only hear faint sounds and not enough to distinguish what she was saying.

Gavin moved first, approaching the guarded compound. We were just inches away when the diet-witch smiled, and with a nod of her head, the ward fell, the gate opened, and four more man-animals approached us, their appearance human except for the eyes, which were like those of the man who had ended up at my neighbor's home and the woman Winter and I had seen a couple of days ago. They had the eyes of an animal, and just as I suspected, the strength and speed of a were-animal.

The first one lunged at us, and Gavin charged him, meeting him midair. Gavin landed a single blow and the guy went skidding back and stayed down. He was still breathing, sharp, ragged breaths. They looked strong, normal, but they were fragile. That fragility was why, when we'd attempted to save the one that had escaped to my neighbor David's home, he hadn't survived.

The others looked as though they were ruled more by primal urges to attack than the desire to survive, something it was doubtful they would do if they were attacked themselves. Another one ran toward Winter. The mage whipped her hand in the air, and the were-human was pulled back. They all winced in pain and moved, following her as she eased them back like animals on leashes. It irritated me, and I could see the same fire blazing in Josh as he fought the urge to counter.

When she jerked the person again, he couldn't resist. He countered. Magic thrashed her in the chest, and she stumbled back. She tried to return it, but Josh erected a thick pellucid wall. Her magic hit against it, battering it until it faltered. Several more unyielding hits against it and it fell. His bullet-like force of magic hit her hard enough to send her back, making her go airborne for a moment before she crashed into the ground. Her eyes blazed with anger.

She attempted to strike back, but with ease, his magic kissed the air, sending it back at her. She crashed back to the ground with a harder thud than before.

Coming to her feet, she said, "Josh, you are as talented as you are rumored to be."

"Well, now you have me at a disadvantage. I don't know who you are."

"If you don't leave, you can call me your worst nightmare."

"Fine. Nightmare. Is that Ms.?" he asked in a playful, flirty voice. "Nah, it doesn't matter. Bad girls are only fun for a day or two. Let's get the niceties out of the way. I'm not sure what you're doing, but stop."

Possessing the confidence of someone who shouldn't when faced with four were-animals and a kickass witch, she smiled. "Is that an order?"

"You can take it any way you want."

The blast of magic from behind us happened fast, hitting us with thrashing force before we could turn. I slammed into a large oak tree so hard my head bounced off it. Various colors of magic danced through the air, lingering. The magical fingerprint that gave the wielder away. Strong magic, and Josh sensed it, too. He erected a protective field around those of us who were left standing before scanning the area to look for them.

I knew it had to be only a matter of time before Marcia and the Creed made an appearance. A retaliatory endeavor to get back at Josh, who was now their enemy.

Another hit of magic, the protective field bulged, and then a ripple. Waves of magic hit until it shattered. From the right, a wolf ran toward him. With a reflexive reaction, Josh extended his hand, pushing the animal, and it moved back, far. Magic hit Josh in his back; he tumbled forward and lost his footing, slamming to the ground. The wolf plowed toward him. It lunged. Ethan slammed into it and rolled over onto it. The wolf clamped down on Ethan's arm. Ethan's fist drilled into its temple, trying to get it to release. He maneuvered to the side and wrenched the wolf's head to the right.

Winter went to the right; I headed left, looking for the source of the magic. Residual magic moved through the air; the finger-print still lingered, and so did the scent. *Crap—that again.* They were gone. I went back to where Ethan, Gavin, Winter, and Josh stood over the fallen wolf, whose body had started to change, half man and half wolf. It was a were-animal, because upon death, when in animal form, our bodies attempt to revert back to their human state. We were immune to magic in animal form; why wasn't this one?

As we walked back to the car, the quietness was uncomfortable. We were faced with the ongoing question of a were-animal that wasn't immune to magic in animal form and a mage who had magic as strong as a witch. There were too many things that just didn't add up.

~

Perched on the table in the living room of the pack's home, Josh was gnawing at his fingernails again, which meant he was nervous. It was a reason for us to be concerned as well. If Ethan was equally concerned, I couldn't tell—he was his usual stoic self. Sebastian's emotions had placed a scowl on his face.

"You're sure it was a were-animal?" Sebastian asked Josh.

He nodded.

"And you were able to use magic against it."

Josh nodded again.

We'd been over this several times, and this had just been added to the ever-growing list of things that the pack and Sebastian had to deal with.

"Were-animals are being used as well as humans," Sebastian speculated quietly. "We have to get in there."

It seemed like a great plan, breaking the ward and seeing if we could get into the compound. Entering might not be the problem —getting out would probably be a harder task, especially if they had found a way to use magic against us in any form.

Sebastian and Ethan looked at each other, and it didn't matter that their faces didn't display it—I knew how they had pragmatically dissected the situation. If they were certain Kelly was in there, it was worth the risk going in. But they weren't ready to address anything else until they had dealt with the most pressing issue—the curse. There were so many things about that setup in the woods that bothered me and had gnawed at me since we'd left. Why didn't they keep the man-animals in the compound and exercise them there, or do whatever they were doing with them? It seemed that they didn't want them isolated. They were introducing them to the world, observing something. Were they trying to determine if they would run if out? If they could survive on their own? Checking their senses? There were so many things that seemed off, and I couldn't make any sense of them. Even more troubling was the were-animal who wasn't immune to magic in animal form. How were they linked?

Life and timeframes had been reduced to nothing but how many days and hours it was from the curse, and now we were expecting it to become reality. Assuming that it was just an elaborate tale could lead to many lives being lost. And yet, we couldn't focus everything on the curse if Kelly was out there possibly undergoing the same things that Carol had—being reduced to an animal used for experimental purposes.

Josh stood in front of one of the dry-erase boards in his home, staring at the same board that had garnered a great deal of his attention for nearly half an hour. I divided my attention between it and the stress balls he was playing with. Small metal globes floated through the air and performed a choreographed dance around his hands as he paced the floor. His cerulean-colored eyes were as intense as the furrow of his brow.

I'd tried two simple spells, which were unsuccessful but not unexpectedly so. Now we were looking at spells that would require dark magic and Faerie magic—Maya's magic. That was going to be a more difficult task. I would not only have to control the magic and mimic it, but also force her into compliance. Lately she wasn't amenable; it was a challenge subduing her daily.

I couldn't deny my adoration for magic, but some days it was more; it felt like I was staving off an addiction. Most of the time, I found myself riding the turbulent wave as it forcibly flowed through my body, beseeching to be used. Denial of the need was getting harder. The taste of it lingered on my palate, but I wasn't ready to use it again, reminding myself of the damage that magic had already caused.

"If magic can be used against were-animals, it will change things," Josh admitted, looking away from the board. His face displayed both intrigue and aversion. The witch in him was clearly drawn to the supreme power that they would have. Immunity to magic was one of the best defenses we had and gave us an advantage. Josh had a devotion to the pack that extended further than just his relationship with his brother. He was as much a part of the pack as I was.

I nodded. "Which is why I think Marcia is involved. It seems to be the very thing that bothers her the most. I definitely can see her doing whatever she could to nullify that immunity. The issue is, how? I'm sure she's tried to do this before, what's different now?"

"Science," he offered with a sigh. We both looked at his board, where the extent of the overlap between science and magic was displayed.

"But it still takes money. That type of discretion isn't free, nor are the talent and equipment you would need to execute it," Chris noted as she walked through to the kitchen. She grabbed a bagel and moved around with familiarity until she found a knife and some Nutella, which she smeared on the bagel.

I stared, and my brows rose with curiosity.

She smiled. "It's a habit. I like bagels."

If only that was what I was actually concerned about. I was speculating on at what point I'd get to ask her why she was still in Josh's home and when exactly she planned to leave. The even more pressing question was why she had on only one of his t-shirts and a pair of shorts. Her presence and his scent wafting off her made ignoring the light bruising on his neck more difficult.

I yanked my eyes from her because if I didn't, eventually keeping my thoughts to myself was going to become more difficult.

"Marcia is definitely involved, you all really rub her the wrong way."

I was sure we'd aggravated her even more after circumventing her attempt to kill Ethan and hold the Midwest Pack accountable for their violation of the agreement to "contain" dark elves. In the end, though, she had had a minor victory. We were then tasked with being responsible for all dark elves. Another weight on our shoulders, and something we needed to address.

Chris sauntered into the living room, taking advantage of the opportunity to peruse the massive extensive library of magic books that Josh had, some of which were on loan from the pack's library. I made a note that she looked at the ones in English and the few we had that were in Spanish. Demetrius was Italian, something I'd figured out on the rare occasions he'd become angered—his nearly imperceptible accent was more pronounced then. With the similarities between the two languages, I wondered if it helped her or if in fact she spoke both of them. Known for her knowledge of and connections in the otherworld, I figured she would consider being multilingual a strategic advantage.

Feeling Josh's eyes on her, she turned. "I made a promise, and I will honor it. You've more than earned it. Anything I learn from being here will never be repeated or used against the pack."

There was a time I would not have believed her, and I was having difficulty not seeing her as the enemy, which was how I was first introduced to her. Gray lines bothered me; ill-defined roles were problematic sometimes. Right now, Chris was an ally, but next week that role could change. Although I wasn't sure what ethics she held to, she seemed to honor her debts seriously. Kelly had helped save her life, and I was confident Chris would therefore do what she could to help.

She'd been staring at Josh's board but finally gave up. I didn't blame her. It was headache-inducing. Magic was more than waving a hand and saying "hocus-pocus."

"I don't think it's just Marcia involved," she finally said. "The witches have capital, but not enough to hire guards for the home, pay scientists, and bring in were-animals. You know they wouldn't dare even think about using one of Sebastian's wereanimals. If in fact they have Kelly, it isn't Marcia's doing. Not hers alone."

Then she took a seat next to Josh, who still had the stress balls dancing around him. It was apparent that neither one gave a crap about personal space. I listened to her while shooting Josh "what the hell" looks that he either missed or ignored, because he didn't move. And when she took a sip from the glass of scotch he'd been nursing for the past hour, I treated her to the same look.

She grinned. "I think if I can feed from someone, it might be okay for me to drink from their glass."

Josh chuckled, but when my eyes narrowed on him, he quickly stopped. Sitting up straighter, he shifted his weight and put a little space between them.

Chris took over Josh's drink, speaking between sips. "Marcia is vengeful and cruel, but she is also calculating. She wouldn't risk Kelly without anything to gain from it. And there are many people they could have taken instead of someone who is a friend of your pack. It's an amateur move. She wouldn't have taken her. So if Kelly is involved, Marcia didn't do it."

"Then who?" Josh asked.

Drink in hand, she stood and paced, talking low enough to be heard but working it out for herself. "The person has to have a lot of money to buy secrecy and pay the witches for their part." She paused for a moment.

I added, "Unless they are bartering with the witches. The were-animals' immunity to magic has always been something that has bothered them. The were-animal in the forest wasn't immune to Josh's magic. It wouldn't surprise me if that was part of the deal. Now who would want were-animals that don't shift?"

"Do you know who owns the property?" Chris inquired.

Josh grimaced. "It was like going through a financial maze, but we do—it's DXB Realty."

Chris stopped pacing and stared blankly at the wall. "That asshole," she mumbled.

"Who is DXB?" Josh asked.

"He likes to be called X, such a fucking cliché, but he's a mage by the name of Dexter, and if you think the ones you've met are lightweight, then his skills would be considered laughable. What he lacks in skill and manners, he more than makes up for in money. His real business is a string of restaurants and stores, and he has a casino, I believe. What he likes to do is gamble, a lot, on fights. Bare-knuckles-to-the-death stuff. He's a real piece of work." She paused for a long moment. "That would explain why he is trying to make superhumans for his entertainment, or maybe he needs to win."

"But what about those were-animals' nullified resistance to magic?" I asked.

"That's no one other than Marcia. Dexter needed strong magic. You think Marcia wouldn't loan out hers in an effort to stop the were-animals' immunity to magic?" Josh's voice was tight. I glanced in his direction. He was tense and angry, and magic radiated off him like sparks off a live wire. Marcia had been trying to turn all sects against the were-animals for years. It wasn't beyond the scope of belief that she was going for a power grab and was allying herself with anyone she thought could take down the were-animals.

But I didn't want to lose focus. We needed to get Kelly first and deal with the other things later. "We don't need him to shut his operation down, do we? Just go in there and get Kelly if she's there," I said.

Chris shrugged. "Sky, you will not be able to do that. And believe me, this will not be the last person snatched. If X is behind this, you need to shut him down. Period."

"Can you arrange a meeting?"

"Better yet, I can tell you exactly where to find him. But I'd take a fae who can compel him to truth. He has a rather casual relationship with it. And he's an asshole just because he can be."

Faes' ability to compel was a nice trick, but not necessarily the subtlest way of getting people to tell the truth. They did it with a kiss, and from what I'd seen, it could be evaded. Ethan had done it —with much effort and he'd nearly injured himself, but he'd definitely done it.

"I'll take Ethan, it'll be just as good," Josh offered.

Chris scoffed. "Ethan and Dexter in the same room? This is going to be interesting."

Once we were out of the house on the way to Josh's car, I made a note that Chris seemed to have clothes, which made wearing Josh's a choice and not a necessity.

What the hell is going on with them?

We'd almost made it to the car when a small cadre of vampires approached us, Gabriella and Chase leading them. It had been a few days since I'd seen them, and once again their looks had changed. I figured their life had to be quite boring if they spent so much of it changing their hair and overall style whenever the whim hit them. Today they were going for something dark and dangerous-looking. Their hair was jet-black with a hint of indigo highlights, their clothing all black. Black and silver makeup covered Gabriella's eyes, and Chase's looked like he had done something to darken them. Behind them I could see four other vampires.

Chris turned, giving them an appraising look. She, too, had thick lines of makeup that darkened her black-opal-colored eyes, which were giving them a hard stare. "I'm not going back. Tell Demetrius to stop. I'm done."

"That's not up to you," Gabriella barked back. "You don't get to be turned by Demetrius no less and betray him like this. You *will* come."

Chris took several steps forward. "I would like to see you make me."

Gabriella charged Chris, and Chris's fist slammed into her chest with force. She hit the ground with a thud. Chris was on her, thrashing Gabriella's head into the ground. She rolled away in time to miss an attack from the back from another vampire. She jabbed her elbow into his nose, he stumbled back, and she retrieved the stake that she had secured in the back of her jeans and shoved it into his chest. He dropped to the ground, reversion slowly inching up his legs.

One of the other vampires' fist caught her on the face. She responded with a heeled foot striking into his. After her spin kick forced him to the ground, like the other vampire, his fate was secured with a stake through the heart.

Chase advanced, and I struck the heel of my hand into his chin. His head jerked back with force. I delivered a quick ankle swipe, and he collapsed to the ground. My foot landed on his forearm and I twisted his hand until I heard it snap. He wailed curses. I moved toward one of the staked vampires to retrieve a stake when Gabriella lunged at me, knocking me to the ground.

"That's enough." Josh waved his hand, and forceful magic battered against me as it sent Gabriella back. Chris and I moved closer to him, and when Gabriella regained her feet, her attack was stopped by the protective field Josh had erected around us. Her fist pounded against it, and each time was met with a stronger force that shoved her back.

Josh sighed heavily. "I can do this all day, Gabriella." He looked bored, making it obvious that this was just a minimal trick he had at his disposal. Glaring, she backed away, helping Chase up, and they left seconds later.

Once we were finally in the car, Chris said, "After this meeting, I'm leaving."

"What if we need more information?" I asked. If this was a good lead, it was because of her. She was resourceful and a fountain of information. I didn't necessarily want her in Josh's home, though, and whatever was happening between them was going to be disastrous at best.

Hiding emotions was something Josh was absolutely terrible at, and disappointment showed on his face. He only provided an unconvincing "okay."

"If you need me, I'm sure Claudia can find me." Chris was even worse at hiding her irritation over that.

Ethan was waiting for us next to Winter when we arrived at our destination, and quickly fell in step with us as we made our way to a bar. Chris had described it as a little dive where the mages usually hung out. Judging from the outside, calling it a "dive" was insulting to that type of bar. The name of the place that was scrawled over the door had discolored letters. The wood door had been battered and nicked. The blemished brick building was off-white, and I couldn't determine if it was weathered or in desperate need of a thorough cleaning.

This is where Mr. Moneybags hangs out?

The moment we walked in, I could tell there were wielders of magic in it. Light magic inundated the room, as well as the strong magic coming off of Josh. I looked around; the outside was just a ploy to deter people from coming in. All eyes were on us, interlopers that weren't welcome. But the attention quickly went to Josh. There was an array of expressions marking the faces of the onlookers. Everything from amazed and awestricken to balefully resentful were exhibited.

The place was vastly different inside. A large oval-shaped bar with a glass counter was placed in the middle of the room. Cyclic lights wavered underneath it and made the stainless-steel supports glow. Decorative silver lights hung from the ceiling. Stainless-steel pedestal tables with glass tops and round white lights created circular waves around it. In the corners were unique box-shaped pieces of contemporary furniture.

The bartenders, who had to be mages, made an elaborate show of making drinks. They might not be as strong as the witches, but what they lacked in strength, they made up for in showmanship. I stopped near the bar for a moment, remembering my favorite childhood movie, *Fantasia*, as olives danced in the air and dropped into martini glasses, orange peels whirled about before landing in a glass, and cherries twisted and bounced before plopping into a drink.

"What the hell is going on with Josh and Chris?" Winter hissed in a low tone in my ear, pulling me from being distracted by the show, once Ethan, Chris, and Josh had gotten some distance from us.

"I don't know. He says nothing, but—" I sighed, cutting off the rest.

"I can smell her all over him. And she is still staying with him, why?"

"Your guess is as good as mine; we can't talk about it now. But she's leaving."

"Good, she needs to."

We rushed ahead to catch up with them. The club was a lot larger than it looked from the outside, and when we went through a second set of doors, we entered a room with several pool tables, a large sofa, and a foosball table and darts on the other side of the room. A less ostentatious bar. Homage to the vintage look was seen throughout the vast room. A jukebox in the corner, which I was sure played CDs, a rotary phone on the wooden bar, a vintage Harley in the corner. It might not have been as modern-flashy as the front of the bar, but the accoutrements indicated money unnecessarily spent for show even in the corners of the room, although in here, the bartender wasn't making a presentation out of giving people their drinks.

"Dexter," Chris said toward three people playing pool in the nearly empty room.

He grinned, leaning on his pool cue. "X," he corrected her. He gave all of us a passing look before he settled on Winter. "I'm X, and you are?"

I didn't have to look to know that Winter was giving him a cool glare of disinterest and probably rolling her eyes so hard it gave her a headache.

"I'm with them," she said flatly.

"I'd still like a name."

"Winter."

"What's in a name? You don't have to be so cold, baby." He took a few steps toward her.

Ugh, I hate this guy already.

When Winter moved back a few steps, he quickly closed the distance.

Damn, he's going to end up with that stick shoved up his hindquarters before we can even talk to him.

Winter gave him a warning look and another opportunity to move. Chris stepped over, blocking his advance. "I can assure you that is a bad idea unless you really feel like visiting the ER tonight."

He chuckled, a deep melodious sound, before taking a few steps back. He tossed one more look in Winter's direction before resting on the edge of the pool table. He was needlessly arrogant. Pecan-colored narrow eyes. The beard was a poor attempt to sharpen and define his rounded face. He had just two or three inches on my five-eight frame. Dressed in a simple gray button-down and jeans, he wore a Bulgari watch that looked out of place with his casual appearance. He paid very little attention to Josh or Ethan, leveling dismissive glances in their direction, while his attention focused either on Winter, me, or Chris. With a half-smile still on his lips, he turned to Chris. "What can X do for you?"

Ugh, he is a douchebag.

"I have it on good authority that you own a couple of properties that we are interested in," Ethan answered.

"And those properties are?" He'd turned his back to us and started racking the balls. Sometime during introductions and him gawking at Winter, his friends had left.

"The ones you have over near Camby Lane, in the woods, protected by a ward that a mage couldn't even begin to erect," Josh spat out with annoyance clearly displayed on his face.

"Josh—it is Josh, isn't it?" For a brief moment, his forced middling smile turned to a scowl as he gave Josh a long, roving look before returning to the table. He took a shot to break the balls. "I've been made aware of your feelings toward us. 'Diet-witches' and 'half-witches' are what you all usually call us, right?"

"I prefer diet-witch. Half-witch gives you all far too much credit."

"And yet I have a ward that you can't seem to break. So I guess you aren't the witch that you are rumored to be."

Then X shot Chris a look before saying to her, "I will remember you brought them into my house."

"I wasn't aware that you lived here. Hard times?"

"If I own it, I consider it my house."

"My apologies" was her lackluster response as she shrugged off his poorly veiled threat. "They are looking for their friend, and I've been trying to find someone for the past few weeks. I think you might be able to help us."

He continued to play, hitting the balls and barely acknowledging our presence. Ethan clenched his hands into fists, and it seemed to take a great deal of effort to keep them at his side.

Chris noticed it, too. "Let's not be coy. What the hell are you doing in that house?"

He chuckled and stood. "I thought you said you didn't want to be coy? Let's not be. Let me guess." He finally directed his attention to Ethan. "I should be honored that you'd deign to come off your little high horse to come visit. Apparently I have something of yours."

"It's not a something, it's a person," I snapped. I really hated this guy.

He brushed me off with a shrug and a condescending look before returning to the table. Ethan stepped forward and tossed the table aside. "We need your attention."

Mr. Douchebag X cut his eyes at Chris. "Thanks for bringing this into my house." His voice was drenched with arrogance and entitlement, and my tolerance for him was starting to match Ethan's. "There isn't a need to play games. We will finish our little experiments and you'll get her back"—he smiled—"new and improved."

"Unless she dies, like the rest," I pointed out.

"There's that. I've had some losses, but things have improved. I hope she's not one of the casualties of this. I can see why you are fond of her. She's kind of cute, quite the fighter. They had a hard time keeping her. She nearly escaped twice. Please know, I had no idea who she was until I was informed of it." He waved his hand dismissively. "My bad. I'll make sure—"

Ethan held him off the ground by his throat. His face became increasingly red as he fought to breathe, and his fingers clawed at Ethan's hand before he remembered he could do magic. A flash came off his fingers, pushing Ethan back, but it wasn't anything but a light shove that he was able to withstand. X's face became ruddy and patchy.

"They will kill her," he rasped out. Ethan dropped him. X's legs folded under him and he fell to the ground. "If anything happens to me, they've been instructed to get rid of all evidence. If anything happens to me, it is your doing."

Josh reacted, sending him back until he hit the wall and was held there. "What are you doing with the people there?"

"I guess what you lack in brains, you make up for in magic. A human with were-animal senses is an asset. Like here in my club, as guards. But they also have human fragility and are able to be controlled with magic. I'm sure Chris has already told you how I like to spend my leisure time. Can you imagine the show?" He reeked of the very conceit that allowed him to feel he could do anything he wanted without consequences; he'd probably gotten away with it for many years.

Josh kept him secured against the wall. We knew most of what he was bragging about, and his wards were too strong to be mere mage magic. It wasn't too hard to piece the rest together. We started to leave when Mr. Douche X continued to talk—he'd said too much, and there wasn't much more we needed to hear from him. As we walked out the door, Josh released his magic, and once again, the mage hit the floor with a powerful thud. He cried out and I heard a snap—I really wanted it to be his leg. But I kept myself from looking back because I wasn't confident that if it wasn't his leg, I wouldn't go back to complete the job.

CHAPTER 12

*A*fter our meeting with Dexter, Ethan went back to the retreat. I wanted to go, but I needed to practice my magic with the Aufero, because it seemed as if I was going to have to use it to help Josh bring down the ward around the compound where the mage was holding the strange were-animals and for the spells to remove the lunar curse. The ward was going to be the easier of the tasks without a doubt.

For the past ten minutes, the Aufero had been in the corner, where it was getting a well-deserved time-out. Simple spells like protective fields and some wards worked fine, but the stronger I made them, the darker the results. The final protective field that I'd made, which I'd attempted to expand to protect others without moving it, had had me writhing on the ground gasping for breath as all the oxygen was drawn from it.

I changed direction, worked on defensive magic. Three balls of magic levitated just above my hand, moving just as the metal stress balls had with Josh earlier in a synchronized pattern of beauty, until their teal color phased into black and heated like coals. I moved my hands just in time—instead of burns on my hand, I had three scorch marks in my carpet.

Exhausted, I plopped down on the sofa to rest before I started again. Using Josh's magic wasn't difficult because I didn't have to manipulate it as much. The magic in the Aufero was both natural and dark, and I had to work around the difference, manipulating it and changing it to get the results I needed. I was convincing myself to take another fifteen minutes before starting when someone rang the bell. I looked at the clock: it was close to eleven, and I knew it couldn't be anyone else other than my neighbor. The full moon was just a few days away and I hadn't received his monthly basket. It had been weird the first time—he'd called it a celebratory gift. He knew so much about this world—and I'd seen the way he looked at me sometimes—I thought of it more as a condolence offering. But each month, I was gifted with a large basket, mostly of chocolates, with an assortment of wines and cheeses or specialty popcorn. It was never apples. David knew me too well; it was rather hard to keep smiling when someone handed me a basket of so-called exotic apples. Unless they were dipped in caramel or chocolate, they were just apples—unimpressive. I'd come to anticipate my treats and enjoy them, so I jumped up to answer the door.

When I looked out the peephole, David was slumped and Demetrius was holding him by the throat. I snatched open the door.

"He is alive for now, Sky, but whether he remains that way is up to you. We need to talk. If the conversation goes well, he will stay that way."

"Talk," I said through clenched teeth. My fists were balled so tightly at my side my nails were digging into my skin.

"Invite me in."

I looked at David's ashen appearance and didn't see any bite marks. That was a good sign.

I dropped the ward, and Demetrius stepped over the threshold and released David. I grabbed my friend before he could slip to the floor and carried him to the sofa. Demetrius's handprint had left a red band around his neck, and his breathing was slow, but at least he was breathing.

"I didn't hurt your fragile little friend, but if this conversation doesn't go well, believe me, I will."

My breath caught in my throat and I assessed the situation. Demetrius rested casually against the wall, his midnight eyes as cold and crisp as the black shirt and slacks that he wore. Never before had he reminded me of the Prince of Darkness, the way most people described him, yet it was very fitting at the moment.

"What do you want?"

"Let's not play this game. Chris. She's at your witch's house. She should be with me. You will make that happen." He snarled, "She is mine, give her back to me!"

For all their sophistication, expensive clothing, and self-indulgence, it was obvious that vampires were nothing more than slaves to their ids, seeking whatever would satisfy their primal cravings at that very moment and ignoring any consequences. Their acts of violence were nothing more than the tantrums of a child. Waah, give me what I want or everyone dies. Waah, he has my toy and I want it back. Waah, she won't play with me anymore.

"If she was yours, then wouldn't you have her? I've dealt with her on many occasions, including earlier, and she doesn't seem like the type of woman that wants to be owned. Well, that's the impression I got when she was kicking the asses of the vampires you sent to claim her."

"I've muzzled Michaela, but not for long. If you choose to disobey me, then there will be consequences. I will give her free rein, and you do *not* want that."

"Do you even think about the words that you say before you actually let them come out of your mouth? Or is thinking before speaking beneath you? Perhaps the sounds of words in your head are just as annoying as they are coming out of your mouth?"

A dark grin lifted the corners of his lips into a snarl as his eyes narrowed on me with ire that he was ready to act on. "Sky, do you not understand your position? Quell is gone because of you. Michaela's very unhappy about that, and the only thing that is standing between her retaliating in the only way that she knows how is me. Contrary to what your hubris has led you to believe, your fate is entirely in my hands. Give me back what is mine!" His voice was drenched with the air of privilege that was notoriously the vampires' brand, and it annoyed the hell out of me.

And I'm supposed to be the arrogant one.

"I'll entertain you. Fine. I'm not going to lift a finger to get Chris back for you. When she's ready, she'll come back, and if she doesn't, which will probably be the case, you'll live with it. Poor you, now you only have just your partner to be with. You don't have your mistress. Life must be *so* hard for you. Why don't you write about it in your journal?"

"How arrogant you and your pack have become. You are still just wild animals, barely domesticated enough to be entertaining. The pack forgets it takes days to make a were-animal and still many don't survive; those who do require some training to be of any use." Then he looked in David's direction. "He could be part of my Seethe in twenty-four hours. When he wakes, he will be strong, fast, and a viable adversary. You all train and have to work at being a fraction of what we are at rebirth. Remember that."

I listen to his haughty soliloquy, waiting patiently and hoping that was the end.

"Chris and I have had disagreements before. I've long tolerated her tantrums and rebellion, but it is time for her to come back to me."

"I'm sorry you're getting bored with your mate and your mistress doesn't care to be bothered. Kind of sucks to be you."

"Do you really want to challenge me?" he said. His dark eyes clouded with anger, and he bared his fangs.

"You bore me. It's the same song and dance every time, and frankly you and Michaela need new material."

He lunged. I sliced my hand through the air, and he smacked

into the wall hard. Feeling the magic that I had denied for several days pulse through me, dark, deadly, and raw, I didn't deny or fight the darkness that took over. I willingly accepted it as it washed over me. I took out the sword that I kept in the umbrella stand, an idea I had borrowed from Chris and Winter, and plunged it into his stomach.

"Unlike whatever strange crap goes on between you and Chris, this is neither foreplay nor a bizarre display of affection. Understand, this is me getting ready to kill you."

I didn't care about retaliation from the Seethe, or unspoken rules about not killing its Master, or the so-called debts we owed him for siding with us *once*. He and Michaela were pains in the ass. The only thing that had stopped me from killing Michaela was that it would hurt Quell, but he was gone because they had sent him away. When it came to the vampires, I had absolutely no more care to give.

And then Maya peeked through. I could taste, feel, and smell her presence, but I couldn't give her credit for any of the ominous thoughts and feelings that I felt. I embraced Maya with a comfort that should have bothered me, but it didn't. Demetrius gritted his teeth and bared his fangs, reconciled to the pain. I jammed the sword deeper in. Then I ripped it out. He slumped down, his head drooping and obscuring his neck. I grabbed him by his hair, yanked his head up and tossed him back. I then secured him against the wall with magic, in a perfect position to behead him.

"Bye, Demetrius." Just as I drew back the sword, a bloodcurdling scream rang through the air. A slim, pale body lunged at me. Dark hair and limestone-colored skin were just a blur as it soared through the air. All I saw was hair and nails that clawed at my face and ripped at my hair. Michaela was a wild, savage creature reduced to barbaric retaliatory tactics as she pounded at me. Her legs wrapped around my waist, and shrieks rang in the air. I tried to pull her off me while keeping Demetrius secured against the wall. Her nails raked over my face, and I closed my eyes to protect them when I felt the magic slip. With a thud, Demetrius was released from his spot on the wall.

I grabbed a handful of her hair and tossed her over my shoulder. I grabbed the sword that had fallen at my feet and swung it in an under arc. She rolled, and I missed her by just inches; I lunged forward, determined it wouldn't happen again. Demetrius pulled me back, his arm wrapping around me, restricting my arms to my side.

"Good-bye to you, Skylar." Sharp fangs sank into my neck, pain seared through me, and blood squirted from the puncture wound. I pounded my fist into his head, but he wouldn't release me. It wasn't until I pressed my thumbs into his eyes that he moved. He jerked back. Through the fuzzy vision and lethargy, I whispered a spell; both Michaela and Demetrius were thrown across the room. I cast another and waved them away, tossing them out of the front entrance as they took the door with them. The last thing I was able to do was erect the ward before I dropped to the floor, holding my blood-soaked hand against my neck to keep pressure against it.

David's voice was off at a distance. I fell on the hard wooden floor. "Keep your eyes open," David commanded.

I tried to keep them open as they fluttered. David's panicked voice remained in the background.

"What am I going to do with you?" Dr. Jeremy asked when I opened my eyes.

"Help me kill Demetrius and Michaela," I offered, my voice hoarse and rough. "And can this be done like yesterday?"

He chuckled, but I could see the concern as he used his finger to turn my head. When his fingers ran over my neck, I winced. "Sorry, but it was a bad bite. Don't play with vampires for a while. Okay?"

I tried to sit up, but he stopped me. "I'm not sure what type of freaky BDSM things go on in your life that you consider this playing, and I really don't want to know," I said.

Dr. Jeremy rolled his eyes and pressed me back into the bed when I tried to sit up.

"Is she okay?" I heard David's voice but I couldn't see him. Minutes later he was hovering over me, his usually vibrant peachy skin blanched and his eyes red, with noticeable blood vessels in them as though he had been crying.

"I'm so glad you're okay. I thought I did the wrong thing."

"How did I get here?"

"I called Sebastian. I wanted to call an ambulance, but I was afraid of"—he leaned in to whisper—"your condition being found out."

"You don't have to whisper. Everyone here has the condition, too."

"Oh, twinkie, I forgot." *Damn.* I sent up a silent wish that if I died, he wouldn't be the one to order my tombstone. I could only imagine what it would read: "Here lies cupcake, snickerdoodle. She was a wonderful buttercup and my special little kitten when she wasn't being my poodle-puff. When I wasn't calling her ridiculous names, my partner and I were doting on her and thinking of more ridiculous names to call her. Between stints of name-calling, we liked to ogle the guys at her house. May she rest in marshmallow Heaven."

Sebastian's smile held a level of tolerance and understanding as he watched David from across the room.

"That was a pretty nasty bite," Sebastian said, now hovering over me, too.

"It didn't feel good, either," I said.

At least Sebastian managed to remain a lot calmer than Ethan. I could see him walking on the delicate edge of losing it. He kept closing his eyes, taking slow breaths, and balling and opening his hands, the incipient stage of his anger apparent. He worked hard to control it, and the effort was noticeable.

"Is he okay?" David whispered.

"He's a little angry," I said, dropping my voice a little lower, hoping he'd get the hint before he said something he shouldn't.

"He's an intense one, isn't he?" he whispered, or he used what he thought was a whisper. In any other room, it would have been one, but even Dr. Jeremy, who had taken a seat at his desk, looked over at Ethan.

"His bark is bigger than his bite," I assured him. It was a total lie, but I felt like David needed to hear it. He had been thrust into this world, and everything about it revolved around death and violence—I needed it to be more to him. Despite the evil look Dr. Jeremy shot in my direction, I sat up.

The hard look of pent-up violence remained on Ethan's face, and it was starting to make David uncomfortable. Winter walked in and looked at Ethan and then David. She ushered a dulcet smile onto her face, and David immediately noticed it because it was something he always commented on. He referred to her as the Dark Swan and often said she was so beautiful, but her resting angry face always made her look dark and cruel.

Her smile welcomed him. "David, why don't I show you around? Trent should be here in a few minutes."

If his partner, Trent, was being brought to the retreat, they must have figured he was in danger as well.

I forced my voice to be sprightlier than I felt. I wanted to sleep and put ice on my neck to keep it from throbbing. But I also wanted Ethan to stop padding through the room like he was ready to pounce on anyone who dared to get his hackles up.

"Ethan."

He turned to look at me. I smiled; one look at him, and I knew he wasn't going to return it. "I'm okay," I said.

"He's a fucking coward. He and Michaela were gone," he growled. That might have been a good thing. This wasn't going to end well, but we needed to address the curse and Kelly first before dealing with them.

When he was close enough to me, I rested my head against his shoulder. "They probably need to nurse their wounds. I wasn't very gentle when I tossed them out, and Demetrius will not be looking out his right eye anytime soon." That seemed to offer some comfort, but not much.

As soon as David and Winter were out of earshot, Ethan asked, "What happened?" His tone matched the look on his face: he was having a very difficult time finding a calm place.

I didn't have to ask—Sebastian and Dr. Jeremy took the cue and stepped out.

He touched the bandages on my neck. I had no idea how many hours had passed and if it had been enough time for the punctures to have healed. If they still looked bad, it wasn't going to help the situation. He removed the bandages and examined my neck, and then relaxed a little bit. "It's not that bad now. There was a lot of blood." He paused for a moment and looked at it again, lightly tracing the area. "Why did you let him in?"

"He had David and threatened to kill him if I didn't."

He nodded and appeared to understand, but I knew that he didn't. But he was aware enough of how I felt about David and Trent not to say what I was sure was the first thing that came to his mind, which was probably that I still shouldn't have let him in. Michaela had dropped a dead body in the middle of my living room floor, a woman that Quell had befriended, just to get back at me. She was someone that he'd fed from and liked, and Michaela, out of jealousy and the delusion that she was being replaced, had killed her.

"Chris?" he asked.

I nodded. "He expected me to return her to him as though she's property." I couldn't relax the frown on my face at the way he'd made her seem like a shirt that he needed returned.

A long stretch of time passed, and Ethan finally relaxed. "She's gone. Josh seems concerned about that."

The knowledge of her being gone noticeably eased him. I couldn't help but wonder what about her presence in his brother's house bothered him the most. Was it because she had settled in with Josh or that he needed her far away so that he wouldn't think about her? I knew he'd said that I didn't have anything to worry about, but jealousy kept rearing up in me. I was riddled with questions about what had drawn them together; nothing about their relationship had been the foundation of anything good, and a litany of things about them seemed to have guaranteed that it would have failed the moment they'd met. Her dedication to her job and his to the pack were the main ingredients in a recipe for destruction, and yet they had been together for years. I'd lied to myself long enough, thinking it didn't cause me some concern that whatever was going on with Chris and Josh might be rekindling whatever it was that had drawn her and Ethan together. I winced at the thought.

"What's the matter?" he asked.

"My neck is bothering me. Maybe I need to lie down for a little while." I lay back down on the bed, rolled to my side, and caressed the pillow, considering the most torturous way to kill Demetrius and Michaela and vowing to do it as soon as I could. Ethan stood over me for a moment. I closed my eyes, but I knew he was there —his scent, his presence, the odd prickle of magic that came off him that was stronger these days. And if those things weren't a giveaway, his body blocked out some of the light that filtered through my lids.

The bed depressed, and the warmth of his body brushed against my back. He kissed my ear and then whispered, "If you are going to make lying your thing, at least get better at it."

I didn't sleep, but we stayed there quiet—something that I hadn't realized I'd needed so much. "What happens with Demetrius?"

"I'm going to take care of it."

"It's not wise to do anything right now. Let's get Kelly back and remove the curse from the others and deal with everything else later."

The crisp, heavy breath he exhaled showed that he agreed with me. No one was opposed to an altercation with the vampires, but their interference was too much right now.

The hour I'd taken to sleep was enough. The search for David and Trent wasn't daunting, just annoying. I was surprised not to find him in the absurdly large and even more absurdly decorated entertainment room, with a movie theater–sized TV, pool table, smaller TVs with game consoles, a small bar, and pretty much anything that could be distracting. I figured it was something they would desperately need. Instead they were in the gym. David's face was a mixture of aversion and disgust, and Winter held a sword in her hand. She was still wearing her forced genteel, cloying smile, and it seemed to be taking more effort to hold it. *Taking one for the team.*

The sweet smile made what she was saying all the more disturbing. Well, at least for David. His partner seemed oddly intrigued. "I'm going to loan you this. One swing, it will take the head clean off."

What the—

"Josh will ward your home with a blood ward. It's pretty hard to get past one. In fact, nearly impossible. But it's good to always be prepared. It will not stop humans. If you didn't invite humans, they might be part of the vampires' garden and will do anything for them. If you didn't invite them over, they don't belong. It's a threat. Take their heads off, too. Same with a witch or anyone else who comes through the door."

No wonder David looked disgusted: the Dark Swan's way of

introducing him to defending himself in the otherworld was promoting a felony. "This is sharp—really sharp. Don't engage. Swinging a sword is an easier way to protect yourself than staking a vamp in the heart."

Oh, but when I say using a sword is easy, all you have to do is swing and hit something soft, I'm *the silly one.*

"Winter, are you sure you want to instruct them to cut off heads and ask questions later?"

That brightened her hazel eyes the same way that participating in and discussing violence always did. "I'm positive. If a vampire comes in your home, cut its head off. That's a lesson *you* need to learn as well. No talking or reasoning with them. You cross the threshold, you lose your head. Easy enough rule to follow."

David's look was just disgust at how casually Winter discussed and accepted violence. I fondly remembered that look because it was the one that I'd given them all before, when I'd considered them monsters. So much had changed in the last few years, but the most drastically changed thing was me—I couldn't deny it, I wallowed in the sewage of violence and toed the line between ethical and unethical behavior. What I wanted to do to Demetrius and Michaela would make someone think I was devoid of humanity. I didn't look at Winter as a monster but as a person who had seen what I had, if not more.

I inched closer to David, and his gaze moved from me to Winter and back again. "Hey."

"Hi."

"You don't need to chop anyone's head off. Josh's ward will hold. But it's not a bad idea to take the sword just in case. I'll be across the street, okay?"

He didn't look like he felt any better, but at least I hadn't cosigned the chopping off someone's head rhetoric that Winter was proposing.

I was okay, he'd been given a sword, and Josh was going to put a ward up on his house—that seemed like more than he wanted to discuss or know about. When I offered to take him home, he agreed quickly and nearly knocked me over getting out the door. But he didn't make it out before Sebastian had given him the details of who was going to be guarding him until this matter was under control. As he'd received Winter's sword and head lecture, I knew he had an idea of what was meant about the situation being taken care of, because he chewed his lips and looked pallid.

As Sebastian spoke to him, reassuring him of his safety, he looked in my direction, and I tried not to show the guilt that I felt. Just a couple of years ago, David had approached while I'd been on my morning jog, unaware that it would be the catalyst that removed his life from normal. Now he was having the "how did things get so fucked up?" moment and couldn't seem to shake the look. His hair, which was always assiduously styled, was messy from his fingers running through it. I hadn't seen him in jeans, let alone a rumpled shirt or pants, and now his clothes were disheveled and had bloodstains. His gray eyes were dull and reflected the day he'd had.

Trent seemed to be handling it a little better, but I was sure the flask that he kept bringing to his lips when he didn't think anyone was looking was the true reason for his newfound bravery. His tall, lanky form hugged the wall. In his state of alcoholic bliss, vampire head chopping, blood wards, and sentinels weren't going to bring him down, and he had a big simper to prove it. I had a feeling he planned to be in this state for a while.

CHAPTER 13

It took longer to reassure David and Trent that they were safe in their own home. After seeing the sentries that Sebastian had provided and the small arsenal of weapons Winter had left with them, their fear of a cadre of vampires bursting through the door to attack lessened. Once Josh had erected the blood ward, even Trent had put aside the sword he'd been carrying around since we'd arrived in the house. That lifted my concern that he was more likely to hurt himself or David than anyone else, and since he'd adopted Winter's strike-first-ask-questions-later rule, I was afraid for anyone who got within striking distance. David just smiled at his partner, who paced in front of the door, a glass of red wine in hand, periodically looking at the sword he'd placed against the wall.

By the second hour, they were noticeably relaxed and we felt comfortable leaving them. Which needed to, because we needed to get Kelly.

I stood next to Josh in front of a ward erected nearly a hundred yards from the house. His magic was alive in me—familiar,

184

natural magic. Nothing that I had to manipulate or wonder if it was going to try to take over. We whispered the incantation as the others waited. We had no idea what to expect, and we'd surveyed the area so much that anyone worth anything had to know that we were coming. Sebastian looked directly into the cameras that surrounded the place. They had Kelly, and that was all we needed to know. *Please let her still be here.*

The ward fell, and we cleared the space between it and the house quickly. Steven and Gavin in animal form were swift as they moved past me. A few others, too. It was rare that this many had been called, and we also had the benefit of three other Alphas, who had remained in the city. Joan moved slower in her jaguar form, scanning the area. Cole, as I'd suspected, was a wolf, light gray in color but as massive as Sebastian. He stalked the area, moving as though he'd been given permission to hunt, and whether he had been or not, he was ready to.

The large shatterproof glass windows of the massive three-story brick Colonial-style home were covered with dark curtains. The doors were metal, thick, with keypads and several locks. The house was equipped to withstand most forms of trespassing. There were two cameras placed near the door in plain sight and three more at the corners. I wondered how many there were that we couldn't see. It didn't matter, though; being seen wasn't going to deter us.

Shatterproof glass didn't mean unbreakable by magic, and there weren't too many locks that could withstand a powerful witch. Josh blasted open the door; those in animal form went in first. Strong magic and the same tinge of medicine met us at the entrance, along with dirt, oil, and other foul odors. There were two visible staircases: the one in front of us led up, and I assumed the other set led to the basement. I followed Ethan and half of the group up the front stairs, and the others followed Sebastian downstairs. Gavin ran past us, then he let out a loud and commanding roar. We followed—he must have Kelly's scent, and at this point he couldn't care less who knew we were there.

We passed several doors, each one with a keypad lock. Sterile white walls gave the home an institutional feel. The various scents became overwhelming and interlaced with the putrid smells of decay and death. The sneer on Ethan's face and growls from Cole told me that they smelled the foul miasma, too.

That familiar imprint of Marcia's magic wafted through the air. She had performed magic here recently, and so had others. It still lingered, its existence brushing over my skin. The combination of mage and witch magic felt rough as it moved over me.

The farther we walked down the long hall, the stronger and more turbulent the magic became. Hostile. Aggressive. Violent. I heard before I felt the impact of Marcia's magic, just before a blast slammed me into the wall. I returned the favor, sending a wave of it toward her. She crashed into the armed group of men behind her. I sent another surge that hit a protective field instead of her. She moved in step with the men, ensorcelled in the magical bubble, her eyes fixed on me. I prepared myself, knowing she would have to drop it if they planned to use their weapons. I needed her to drop it. Blasting the borrowed magic, which was substantially weaker, I battered it. It dropped but it was too late.

One shot, a dart, went into Steven, another into Gavin. Ethan grabbed another guy before he could take his shot, disarming him and taking the darts from him. I laced the magic around Marcia and shoved; she tumbled back. Darkness flooded her eyes, her lips moved quickly, and magic thrashed through the air.

Those standing behind the protective field that Josh erected were safe, but Steven had been smashed into the ground, and Gavin had been hit hard enough that his solid-muscled form smashed into the banister, breaking it. He fell to the lower floor. I heard him pounding back up the stairs and breathed a sigh of relief. Kelly had to be on this floor; he was coming for her. He bared his teeth at Marcia before lunging at her. Seconds before he could make contact, her magic tossed him back. I realized the darts they'd shot them with nullified were-animals' immunity to magic. This was why she'd been silent. This was what she'd been working on with X. Gavin pulled his lips back, baring teeth, growling as his animal felt the brunt of her magic for the first time.

I heard more footsteps from behind Josh. Magic just as strong and powerful as Marcia's swept through the air. More men with the same weapons focused on their targets—any of us in animal form. Behind the men were the magic-enhanced mages, who indiscriminately whipped people out of their way. As they approached Josh, self-assurance and arrogance lifted their lips into deviant smiles. Josh had his back to me, and I couldn't see his face, just the looks of fear that wiped away the mages' grins. Magic curled around him like a viper around a tree and felt just as deadly. Stronger than anything I'd ever felt off Josh. More powerful than it should have been since he'd shared his magic. But it wasn't different—it was dark, violent, and totally unhinged and out of control.

Seeing the fate of the mages, who were toppled over, only one of them breathing, Marcia vanished.

Josh, on a path of destruction, went through the house, clearing anyone that wasn't part of the pack. The house filled with the sounds of screams, glass shattering, and objects being tossed. The metallic odor of freshly spilled blood quickly overpowered the other scents in the air. I held my breath and tried to get a handle on everything. Gavin, in human form, carried a body wrapped in a sheet; Kelly's pallid face peeked out from it. More weres in human form came out of the rooms, either holding someone or guiding the ones able to walk. I counted at least twelve. I gathered all the darts like those that had been shot into the were-animals, some of the weapons, and everything I figured could be of use. I gave it all to one of the were-animals directing people out.

Ethan, Winter, and I split up, going through the house to make sure we had gotten everyone out. I found an addition to the house that had been converted to a lab. Inside it, I found several cages. The rotting smell of death and decomposing flesh couldn't be hidden by all the floral scents and plug-in room fresheners in the world. The smell of old and new blood inundated the air, and I ignored the bodies on the other side of the room. Dr. Jeremy's bloodstained hands loaded up things from the desk, papers, and smaller equipment into a bag he'd procured. I gathered up vials with the unknown substances.

He grabbed a laptop and started out, then stopped to take another look at the room: beds with straps on them, electric cattle prods, chains. I knew guilt would fester in him, and there wasn't anything I could do about it. Anger and frustration overtook his features, making his gentle, regal appearance hard and menacing. His gaze shifted to the bodies discarded throughout the room, and it was hard to ignore the lust for violence that flickered in his eyes, a wish that he could do it all again—more savagely, to savor the revenge and retribution. The longer he looked at the room, the tenser I became, the way anyone would when faced with an unknown animal. At the moment, I wasn't familiar with the violent, bloodthirsty beast next to me.

The warm smile, kind eyes, and paternal smile that had defined Dr. Jeremy as the gentle doctor for the pack had faded to all predator. After a few more moments, I urged him to move. He did so reluctantly, with the same graceful strides as the tiger he changed into, and he seemed just as dangerous. I wanted to say something, but I wasn't sure if anything I had to offer was going to help. We had Kelly, but we now knew that for all the days she was here, she had been experimented on and subjected to the unthinkable. All the signs of violence that filled the hallways, the blood and gore that flashed past me as I walked out of the house, didn't bother me as much.

Moving down the hall, I did another quick sweep of the rooms that we passed. I needed to be the calm one because Dr. Jeremy was gone. It became harder to do so as I looked into the window-less rooms, some with cages and others with beds with restraints. They all were as sterile and plain-looking as the walls. I could sense the hopelessness that anyone had to feel being there for days, weeks, and maybe even months. I had no sympathy to give to any of the people who had been killed. Even if they were just coming to do their jobs—at what point did this stop seeming inhumane to someone? I thought about Quell, who was always questioning the humanity that he didn't believe existed in people anymore. He'd become misanthropic for a reason, and I was feeling that way, too.

The thirst for more violence was building in me. I had to get the hell out of there. When I was a few feet from the door, a weak dust of magic hit against my back. I turned to find X, flanked by two other men, approaching us, his hand illuminated by magic that looked more impressive than it actually was. He shot one at Dr. Jeremy, who stumbled back and dropped the items in his hands. X directed his men to retrieve them.

He hit me, and I stumbled, but not enough to fall. A burst from the mage to his right hit the wall. Sliding to the floor, I assumed a position on my hands and knees, preparing to shift to my wolf when a massive tiger lunged over me, mouth open, and grabbed one of the men's neck. He was dead by the time he hit the ground. X started to back away as Dr. Jeremy turned his attention to the other mage with him. X was at a full run when Jeremy's claws slashed across his companion.

I shifted, chasing after X as he ran down the hall. I increased my speed, pounding after him so fast that I skidded into the closed door. I thrashed against it, trying to open it, but it was solid and reinforced, clearly made not to be broken down. No matter how I tried, I couldn't open it using my paws, so I shifted to human, opened it, and then shifted back to wolf, racing after him.

He was nearly thirty feet away. I moved fast, racing to get to him before he could get to the awaiting car.

As I gained on him, he pulled out the same type of gun that had been used on Gavin to nullify his immunity to magic in animal form. He shot; I skittered to the side, barely avoiding the dart as it went into the ground just a few feet away. I was able to dodge three more shots while gaining ground on him. I had just a few more feet. I jumped at him and felt a sharp pain as a hard object slammed into my ribs. I howled and whipped around to the attacker. It was one of the witches, holding the tire iron that she'd just used on me.

She hit again and I accepted the blows until I could get hold of her arm. I buried my teeth into the offending hand as she wailed in pain, blood spurting over my face and blurring my vision until I couldn't see the blow from her other hand coming. She slammed into the side of my head. My grip on her arm loosened enough for her to disappear. When I turned back to the street, X was gone.

When I turned to the house, Dr. Jeremy was back in human form, naked and carrying the papers and computer. We found the others ushering everyone who could walk into the SUVs and carrying the people we'd found who couldn't. Josh's face was hardened into a disgusted frown that became more intense as the minutes went by. He waved his fingers in Dr. Jeremy's direction and clothing slowly wrapped around him, covering his nudity. Once I saw him do that, I changed, and the moment I did, he covered me. Like Dr. Jeremy, I was in a simple t-shirt and jeans.

In the car with Ethan, Sebastian, and Josh, I informed them about X attacking us and trying to retrieve the computer.

"The witches worked with Dexter just so they could create something that would make you all vulnerable to their magic," Josh said, disgust lying heavily on his words and distorting his features. He closed his eyes and shook his head, and I knew he was doing the same thing I had been working on—trying to get the images of the people and the rooms out of my head.

"It looks that way," Ethan said. He was speaking softly, very softly, in the manner one would use to calm a volatile animal or person.

"They don't even care about the witches anymore, or anyone. It's just about power, and they will do anything to achieve it." Josh was angry and we could feel it. It felt like a sandstorm in the SUV as his magic drifted chaotically about, wild, uncontrolled. Before anyone could say anything to calm him, he was gone.

∼

The pack's retreat was in a state of disorder. We had recovered fifteen people, including Kelly, and they all needed to be examined. The shifters that had been injected with the serum that nullified their immunity to magic waited outside at Sebastian's command. They looked scared at the very idea that they could be subjected to magic in animal form. Dr. Jeremy was confident as he informed them they wouldn't stay that way. I really hoped he was right. We had taken the computer, the records, and a lot of things from the building, but I didn't know what information X and Marcia had and if they could recreate what we'd taken.

Cole and Joan helped Dr. Jeremy, assisting him as he triaged everyone to get an idea of what needed to be done. Worried eyes followed him around the room as he went to each one, checking their vitals. When he drew blood, the fear that they displayed made anger well in me again.

"I feel violent," Cole admitted, taking a position next to me at the entrance of the infirmary, his gaze following mine as I looked at everyone in the room.

"Yeah," I said softly. It was hard not to. "And X is still out there." I let my mind wander, because if the image of his smug, entitled face popped up, I wasn't sure if I would have the control necessary to be of any use.

"You handle yourself very well," Cole said, and again I found myself under his watchful gaze. He smiled. "The pack is very lucky to have you."

"We are happy to have your help and Joan's." I used that opportunity to look away, but I could still feel him looking at me. He was about to say something when Ethan's arms slinked between us as he pulled me back into him. "We have to go get Josh." Once I was a couple of steps from Cole, Ethan slipped his hand in mine, and we followed Sebastian and Winter out the door.

I didn't need to ask where we had to go retrieve him from. I'd seen his face and felt the draconian magic that came off him, only overshadowed by his anger. It wasn't a matter of where he was, but the condition the place and the people would be in once we got there.

Ethan drove with Sebastian behind him, but there wasn't a sense of urgency. We knew we were already too late. Marcia and the Creed had crossed the line one time too many. They had destroyed the tenuous lines of civility that existed between them and us and attacked his pack and his brother more times than Josh could tolerate without it being checked. They'd incited a war, expecting him to be acquiescent and concede. They were wrong.

We pulled up to the store that was a front for their office. The portentous smell of death and blood inundated my senses the moment we opened the door. Remembering the anger on his face when he'd left and knowing that it had been expunged through his retaliation against the witches, I hesitated. Having had my fill of dead bodies, blood, and violence, I readied myself for what I might see. Splatters of blood trailed to the doorway.

As we made our way to the room where the witches often met, the energy of Josh's anger filled it just as much as magic did. Thick and suffocating. Sebastian, who was ahead of us, stopped and waited for Ethan to catch up. Waiting at the threshold, this man who had a disturbingly high tolerance for violence and the macabre frowned at the vision before him.

Sebastian moved aside when Ethan approached, moving

slowly with an uneasiness. Residual magic and blood flooded the air. Josh's body was tension-filled and stiff, and when he finally turned once Ethan called his name, he didn't look like his charismatic, quirky, easygoing self. Unremorseful coal-black eyes watched us with caution as we walked into the room with blood-stained walls, crumpled bodies, shattered glass from the mirrored wall that had been destroyed, and splintered and broken furniture.

"Hey," Ethan said in a low, gentle tone as he closed the distance between them. Josh's labored, sharp breaths were an indicator that he was still trying to deal with his anger. He struggled to gather some semblance of control.

Josh's small smile surfaced quickly, and when Ethan was just inches from him, he reached for him, cradling his head and pulling him toward him. Ethan rested his head against his younger brother, who was so far gone that control wasn't easily in his grasp. "You kind of made a mess of things, huh?" Ethan said softly.

Josh nodded once and sucked in a breath.

Ethan looked around the room. "It's okay. We'll fix it."

Josh nodded. But there really wasn't anything to fix, just to clean up. A lot of cleanup, and damage control regarding what had happened.

Ethan and Josh rested with their heads against each other, finding a familiar sibling comfort that we could never understand or offer. Josh finally moved away, quickly appraised the area, and then said, "I guess I should clean up."

But his words were drowned out by the clicking of heels against the floor.

"Nah, we got this," replied a female voice from behind us. We turned and faced a crew of eight, all dressed in black with the exception of one. Half of them carried crossbows and looked skilled in their use and unafraid of using them. I gave a passing look to all the unfamiliar faces, and my eyes landed on one that I knew—London. A longtime friend of Josh's who'd helped us on multiple occasions. Now she was aligned with this group of witches, which offered some comfort since she'd made an effort to stay away from Marcia and the others.

The only witch that stood out other than London was the woman who headed the group. All the others were dressed in black, and she had on all white. The pants were fitted and molded to her body, and her flouncy shirt moved with her as she strolled through the room, her heels clicking a beat.

"Well, they weren't wrong when they said you were powerful." The attractive stranger acknowledged Josh with a forced smile. She looked around the room, but her face remained indecipherable as she regarded the mess. Walking slowly throughout the room, she used magic to pluck the bloodstains from the floor before making them vanish. Then she moved to the bodies lying in various positions. She looked over in Josh's direction, and then back at them.

"Please, handle this until we can have a proper burial," she instructed the three people to her right. Moments later, their fingers moved, and magic that they handled with the skill of musicians strummed over the room. Vibrant colors twisted and wound around their fingers. Synchronized, they performed an invocation. The bodies disappeared. Strong natural magic was a dense blanket in the air.

The new witch continued to clean up the place, waving her hand over the furniture, flicks of magic dancing and curling over her fingers, a pastel rainbow of colors as she drew up the fractured furniture and reassembled it like new.

The others joined in, controlled power twirling throughout the room. For several moments, she and the other witches worked in silence as they cleaned up the place.

"Josh, you can relax, no one here plans to hurt you," she said. But her words didn't cause any of the tension to ease. As she walked throughout the room, making a performance of cleaning up, delicate long fingers danced through the air as though she was playing a piano. Being the maestro and director of the magical presentation, she would occasionally give orders. Finally the room was clean—not pristine, as I was sure it had been before Josh's wrath had taken hold of it, but it looked as though violence had never taken place there.

Giving the room a sweeping look, she said, "Good, I work better in a clean workspace." Full lips spread into a pleasant smile as her gaze landed on each of us, assessing in the same manner we were assessing her. I wondered if she recognized the fragility of the situation—it could easily become a disaster, one that we didn't need at this time. The gentle rounded features didn't diminish my apprehension. Far too often, the wolf was hiding in the clothing of the most docile-looking sheep.

She made her way to Sebastian, studying him, and he gave her a similar appraising look. The taut line of his grimace relaxed and beveled into a charismatic smile.

"You're Sebastian, and your reputation definitely proceeds you."

Interest sparked and I knew exactly what it had to be. The rumors painted him as a glorious monster, and it was off-putting for most to find the beautiful package that it came in. "I'm Ariel. I will be taking Marcia's place." Then she pulled her attention from Sebastian to Josh. "I figured it would only be a matter of time before this happened. Months ago I decided I was going to have to initiate a coup, but it worked itself out, *didn't it?* Civil wars are such ugly things, and it can be quite difficult to garner loyalty from those who are on the losing side. But Marcia and her antics made it quite difficult for most to be willing to pledge their loyalty to her. Her power-lust was her undoing, and the weak minds of the others in the Creed who became complicit deserved their fate."

"You coming in with your magical show, albeit impressive, might not be enough to gain their loyalty and convince them of your qualification to be the new leader of the Creed," Josh offered.

"Well, if the Creed is to be made up of the most powerful witches in the country, you are looking at them. Yes, despite Marcia's many attempts to make sure we didn't exist, we managed to survive." The anger that anyone must have felt knowing they had become a target just because they were powerful showed in her grimace. "Your choice not to finish magic training was made out of youthful ignorance"—she smiled—"or defiance; it was a good one. That is where they observed us, and ones they considered a threat became targets. Between the ages of ten and eighteen, I do believe I had more attempts on my life than I had candles on my birthday cakes."

She waved her hand in the direction of the seven other witches that accompanied her. "We all are bonded by more than magic—we survived the Creed. Foolish Marcia—instead of cultivating our skills and making the witches stronger, she chose to weaken us for fear of not being the great and almighty witch. Deluded woman."

Josh looked over the faces of witches whose magic rivaled his, who wouldn't consider him an adversary but possibly an ally. He looked relieved, but when he spoke it was with cautious intrigue. "There are eight of you. The Creed consists of five." As he spoke, his attention fixed on London. I'd always wondered about their friendship. He said they were friends and sometimes lovers. On more than one occasion, it had been apparent that "sometimes" wasn't entirely accurate. "Sometimes" didn't cause you to look at anyone the way they looked at each other. And the matching tattoos that they had were reminders that the bond they shared had existed since they were children and had grown over the years. He returned the half-smile she gave him and then redirected his attention to Ariel.

"There isn't a rule about that. There weren't always five; at one time there were more, as many as nine. The more people that are involved, the harder one person must work to control and corrupt. That's not to say it is true with all things." The gentle smile continued as she refocused her attention on Sebastian. "It has worked for you. And the were-animals."

Sebastian nodded. "We do things differently than most."

"So I hear. I will say, for someone with such a terrible bark, it is my understanding the bite is just as bad, too. I personally do not want to be on the other side of that bite," she said softly, but she had closed the space between them. If he wanted their lips to touch, he simply had to lean forward.

"It's not always that bad," he teased.

I looked around: I seemed to be the only one feeling uncomfortable with this so-called business meeting. It seemed to have moved past the confines of a meeting.

"And it shouldn't be. The witches and the were-animals were not always enemies, and I hope we can return to that." She stepped back a few feet to look at all of us.

"Marcia and I had an alliance at one time, which she broke. Please forgive me if I'm not running to form one with the witches again. As you said before, power-lust can become a problem, and I'm not convinced you are exempt from it," Sebastian cautioned.

"Of course, but please let me prove my desire to make this happen." She fished in her pocket and pulled out a vial. "This is what Marcia had made to destroy your immunity to magic. I'm sure your doctor, if the rumors are as correct about him as they are about you, can find an antidote. He'll have Josh's help, and I will offer my assistance if necessary."

She extended her hand to give it to Sebastian. His hands covered hers and lingered over it for a long moment as he kept his gaze rooted on her. She was flushed when he released it, and with effort she pulled her eyes from his. He grinned and looked down at the vial, inspecting it, and then he brought it to his nose to smell it. He nodded and handed it back to her.

"We already have it. And I doubt this is all that you have, or that you haven't figured out how to duplicate it. This is of no use to me."

It was the first time her veil of confidence dropped and she looked flustered. If I saw it, there wasn't any doubt that Sebastian and Ethan had as well. But they didn't let it show on their faces and let her flounder for something to offer. Even with all the tales, no one was ever truly prepared for Sebastian.

"I suspect your offering isn't just goodwill; what is it that you want?" I was sure she wondered how he knew, and I wished I could tell her the countless things that Sebastian had probably been assessing about her the moment she'd walked through the door. Something as simple as her blinking one too many times had given him the upper hand.

It's off-putting to me, too.

Moments passed as she struggled for the confidence and control that she had had at the very beginning. One little wrench slipped into the cogs of her spiel and she was thrown off. After a few more moments, she mastered it, standing up a little taller and smiling. Sebastian watched her; amused. "Go on. What do you want?"

"The Aufero is in your possession."

"You're not getting that back," I blurted and then snapped my mouth shut.

A gentle curve caressed her lips. "Skylar Brooks, right?" I nodded. "Once again, I must admit that the person who has often been referred to as the Midwestern Pack's doe-eyed assassin is not nearly as vicious and savage as I expected."

Assassin. Doe-eyed? What? I don't like those names at all.

"Don't be cross over the name. I'm sure it is an embellishment, just as I am sure the story of how you viciously attacked Marcia has been altered."

I tried to hold her gaze but couldn't. It wasn't an embellished story. It was the truth, but I wasn't sure why or how I'd gotten the "doe-eyed" title.

"I'm quite confident that if you did savagely attack her, she undoubtedly deserved it. And I think it is unfair and probably a misnomer to call you a killer. But if you are the one that killed Ethos, then you, too, are far more than what meets the eye, and your bite is quite impressive as well."

Ethan helped.

"Ariel, what would you like us to do for you?" Sebastian reminded her.

"The magic that was stolen from the witches using it. I need to make an attempt to gain their trust and loyalty. If my first act is to return that to them, I think that will be a step in the right direction."

Sebastian took a long time considering her request. So long that Ariel and the others started to look worried. He'd promised Samuel that he would allow him to return the magic. Although Samuel had disappeared, I assumed he would still honor his promise. I was wrong.

"Consider it done." I assumed making a deal with a person who wanted an alliance was better than keeping a deal with someone whose sole purpose in life was to end magic and possibly destroy the were-animals because of his nonsensical belief that magic was inherently evil and needed to be vanquished. "But I will need a favor from you and your witches."

"And what is that?"

"I don't know yet."

"I don't make open-ended bargains."

"Not until now," he said with a half-grin.

She started to speak, but he silenced her with a look as amber rolled over his eyes along with the wolfish grin he gave her. It wasn't a threat, but a display of the predator she was making the deal with. One that she didn't want to renege on. "Do we have a deal?"

He extended his hand out to her, but she didn't take it. "As I said before, I do not make open-ended bargains."

Sebastian's tone was playfully dark as it dropped to a low rumble. "Then, Ariel, you should have brought a better bargain to the table." He started backing out and signaled for us to follow. He turned his back to her, and just before he exited, he looked over his shoulder. "I trust that when you are ready to make that deal, you know how to find me."

Just in case you haven't figured it out, Ariel, he's stubborn and you lost.

I expected to see anger when I glanced back, or at the very least disappointment, but her look of smug amusement mirrored Sebastian's.

As we started out the front door of the store, I heard footsteps behind us. We all turned to find London walking swiftly to catch up with us.

"Josh." She said his name. He turned, and as it was whenever he dealt with her, he relaxed.

"What?" Despite his seeming more relaxed, his tone was cool, distant.

"We should talk."

He nodded, and she walked with us to the car. London was petite. At five-eight, I had nearly six inches on her. Josh was six feet. She still had the waves of pastel-colored hair, and her gentle round face, cherubic features, and docile eyes that made it look like you were staring into the face of a deer made it easy to forget she was a powerful witch, and even more so since now she was a part of the Creed. We tried to give them some space, but even several feet away, we could hear their conversation.

After a few minutes of talking, they started to hold hands; it was casual and normal for them. They possessed an intimacy that transcended anything that could be explained. Their relationship was odd, bound by a strength forged when they were children, and had evolved into something complex in their adulthood. Josh said they were "sometimes lovers," which after being around them I realized might not be as infrequent as he'd led me to believe. And as he watched her with a look of pain and betrayal, it was obvious there was something between them far more than "sometimes lovers." But I'd assumed that when I'd noticed that they had body art so similar that it couldn't be a coincidence. His ragged breathing was hard to ignore, and so was his look of disappointment.

"Do you trust her?" Josh asked.

"With my life," she said without hesitation. London was cautiously cynical, and her support of Ariel spoke volumes. "This was a long time coming. But for years, Marcia somehow held on to some of the witches' loyalty. The more desperate she became for power, the easier it was to see that she didn't have our interests at heart. We've been planning for years to do this."

"Why didn't you tell me?"

"Because I was sworn to secrecy. Josh, your—" She stopped abruptly, and I knew what she was about to say: his involvement with the pack made him a liability. It was always a source of problems because his allegiance would always be questioned. People didn't understand that it wasn't to the pack; it was to Ethan. The same was true regarding Ethan. If he had to choose between the pack and his brother, there wasn't a member in it who couldn't predict his choice. It caused complication, even within the pack. "Your affiliation with the pack makes things complicated," she admitted diplomatically, and it was evident that she was going to be good at her role as a newly inducted member of the Creed.

There wasn't a lot more information she could have provided. Nothing that we hadn't already figured out. Now the Creed was made up of the most powerful and talented witches in the country —with the exception of Josh. They had been forced into hiding due to multiple attempts on their lives by the previous sitting group. Their power and freethinking made them untrustworthy and a liability.

I wasn't sure how Josh felt about the way things had been handled, but his tone held a palpable relief when he spoke to London. "Thank you for telling me." He leaned down and pressed his lips to her forehead, and although it was a chaste act, there was an implied intimacy between them that made it seem like we shouldn't be listening in on their conversation.

"Of course," she said. As if she realized we were all still standing there, she gave us a weak smile and then said to Josh, "We'll talk about it more tonight. Okay?"

He nodded.

Okay, I hope he can get more information about Ariel from their "talk."

CHAPTER 14

"They were given three different formulas," Dr. Jeremy said the moment we walked into the pack's house. He bit into his lip as if he was trying to bite back the words or maintain control. For a moment, I was treated to a glimpse of the man I'd seen back at the compound who had meted out his revenge on the people who'd hurt Kelly. "Some of them are getting sick. Fevers, blood pressures that I can't get down."

Sebastian listened, unusually calm, which was needed to try to help Jeremy, whose agitation was escalating with each word. "Okay. What can we do?"

He looked in Josh's and Ethan's direction and then toward the stairs, and they followed, going up them, I assumed, to check on the other evacuees from the house.

"We need to change them to true were-animals. That might be the only option, and we need to do it quickly, before they are too sick to even tolerate that." His voice was low and disheartened. "They aren't true were-animals and don't have our ability to fight things off. If we change them now before they get too sick, they will adopt our immunity."

Sebastian sucked in a shallow breath and looked at Joan and Cole, standing behind Jeremy. They all had the same look of being just reduced to a thousand fucks because that was the situation. Take people who had been abducted, subjected to barbaric treatment, and experimented on, rescue them, and have them undergo a painful transition to being a were-animal.

Washing his hand over his face, Sebastian considered the situation. Then he looked at Joan and Cole. "I will need your help. There are twelve."

"That's a lot of new weres to have at once," Cole said, concerned. I remembered Demetrius's comments about having to control newly changed were-animals. Were they really as savage as he'd depicted, or was that an exaggeration to add to his theatrics?

"Are you sure this will help them?" Sebastian still maintained a gentle visage as he dealt with Dr. Jeremy.

He sighed into his answer as he shook his head, desolate. "We don't have another option."

Sebastian looked past Dr. Jeremy toward the open door, which led to the rescued, who'd been divided after being triaged. Sebastian's tone changed, kind but stern. "Gavin, you will be responsible for Kelly."

I looked around, because clearly Sebastian was suffering from stress-induced hallucinations. As soon as he spoke, Gavin came into sight from the hallway adjacent to us.

The were-animals' keen sense of hearing wasn't something I had forgotten about, but it still seemed weird to have a conversation with a person who wasn't in the room.

Stilled, Gavin held Sebastian's gaze for as long as he could and then dropped his head, backing out of the room and refusing to consent. Sebastian's nostrils flared as he battled the impulse to handle the situation with Gavin with force. After a few minutes, he'd resolved the anger, but amber pulsed in his eyes with a steady beat. When he finally relaxed his clenched hands, he looked at me and then the door Gavin had left out of. Sebastian looked at the door again and then me. And back at the door.

After a few moments, I said, "I got this," heading in the direction that Gavin had gone. *I guess that's my new job, kitty wrangler.*

I looked around the vast area and didn't see him. I inhaled, but the smell of the forest commanded the air. I knew he was near being broody and sulky; that was what he did.

No matter how many times I was presented with pack property, I was always overwhelmed by the crowd of oversized trees that nearly obscured any path. The thickets of grass were so green that they didn't seem real. At any given time of day, you would find a were-animal in his animal form, enjoying the freedom of running without being seen. It was the closest thing we had to being in the wilderness—providing miles and miles of woodland.

"Here, kitty, kitty," I said in a low voice, knowing he could hear me.

"I said not to call me that!"

I followed the voice and looked a couple of feet away. He was perched languidly on the top branch of a massive tree, legs dangling off it.

That's it, Gavin, be weirder. You definitely have a patent on it.

"Can we talk?"

"Yeah." Since he didn't move, I figured he meant up there. Of course—because talking standing in front of the tree was just too easy. I jumped up on the closest branch and pulled myself up, climbing from branch to branch. Every once in a while Gavin laughed when I lost my footing and had to catch myself and pull myself up.

When I was close enough, I found a branch close to him and cradled my butt into the groove between it and the trunk. "Nice day for a climb," I joked.

Nothing.

"I'm not going to do it," he said firmly as soon as I was settled.

"So you're going to let her die."

"If I'm the one to do it, she's going to die anyway. I've tried before—I can't do it."

I nodded slowly. "Does Sebastian know this?"

He shrugged.

"Don't you think it's something you should tell him? He won't push you to do it if you don't think you can. Talk to him. And talk to Kelly, too. If it has to be done, I think she will want it to be you. And if you choose not to do it, she deserves the courtesy of your telling her why. She'll understand. But if you don't tell her anything, she's going to feel like you abandoned her. That's the last thing she needs right now. Okay?"

He didn't say anything; he slid off the branch, leaping from one branch to another with light, graceful movements that made the task of climbing down that massive tree look a lot easier than it was. *You're welcome. Anytime. Always a pleasure having these weird conversations with you.*

I hugged the tree closer, inhaling the relaxing scent of oak that came from it. I still thought Gavin was odd as hell, and whatever brooding contest he was in, he was winning the hell out of it, but I totally understood why he had chosen the tree as his place of solace. I closed my eyes and rested my head against the trunk.

"Why are you up there?" Ethan asked.

"Gavin."

As though that was answer enough, he nodded. He stepped back, leapt up to the first branch, and moved from branch to branch a lot quicker than I had. Clearly this wasn't his first time.

"He does this a lot?"

He chuckled. "They all do. Cat," he said with derision. "But he does it more often than most." He smiled at me as I relaxed back into the large trunk, reluctant to let my legs dangle the way that Gavin had for fear of falling.

"He doesn't want to change Kelly. He's afraid that he won't be able to do it successfully. How hard is it?" I didn't think it was as easy as changing someone to a vampire, which was probably one of the reasons it was usually a last resort. The subsequent change that the body had to go through was brutal. Steven was the only person I knew in the pack who was a changed were-animal.

"I figured he wouldn't. He had an incident last year and took it hard. He lives in Clayton Park."

"He enjoys the thrill of living in a questionable area."

Ethan laughed. "Probably, but crime in his neighborhood has definitely decreased since he moved there. He could have moved anywhere in the city for what he paid for renovations, but it's where he wanted to live. There was an incident, and two people he considered friends were injured, badly. He tried to change them both and it didn't work."

Gavin had wanted me dead from the moment he'd met me and voiced it often. Over the past few months, if he still felt that way, at least he'd been courteous enough not to say it. I couldn't help but feel sorry for him.

Ethan sighed. "One of us can change her, it's fine. The next best choice will be Dr. Jeremy. But it would be best for this pack, for Gavin, if he does."

Answering the confused look on my face, he continued. "When you change someone, a bond, a special connection is formed. Similar to that of a recently changed vampire and his sire." He frowned at the idea of comparing anything to do with were-animals to vampires.

My brows rose. "Are you sure about that? Because I distinctly remember Chris trying to cut Demetrius's head off with a kitchen knife. Or am I missing the special bond thing?"

"But she didn't."

"Because I stopped her!"

"She let you stop her. It's the sire bond that allowed her to show restraint."

"Oh, my fault, I didn't realize *not* cutting someone's head off with a kitchen knife is a show of endearment. I'm going to go drop that from the dysfunctional category."

"It's Chris," he said gently. I tried not to make it an issue. I hated that when he spoke of her it made me jealous. I wondered how long it would take for it not to.

"Can you imagine Gavin if Kelly is changed? I don't want to force him to do it, but they both need it. He needs to have a successful change, and I think she needs it to be him." Then he gave me the same expectant look Sebastian had given me earlier.

Am I the Gavin whisperer? How did I get that job and where do I submit my resignation? I frowned at the thought. "You want me to talk to him, again?"

He nodded. "He responds well to you. He likes you."

"You're using both of those words wrong."

He leaned in with a grace of movement that for a few minutes made me forget that we were in a tree, balancing on its limbs, and kissed me on the cheek.

"I have to go; are you staying up here?"

I shook my head. Although I wanted to, I figured Dr. Jeremy would need my help. Like Gavin, Ethan made springing from branches look a lot easier than it actually was, or perhaps he didn't care as much about the chances of stumbling and crashing to the ground. It wasn't an acceptable option for me.

"I can't. I have to go talk to a weird panther who's probably skulking in the shadows somewhere, being . . . well . . . Gavin-y."

Ethan laughed. "See, you have a way with him. I just call him a pain in my ass."

But I didn't have to talk to him. Sebastian seemed to have beat me to it. His face was relaxed, which I knew took some effort. Sebastian gave orders—that was his way. Either you did it or he made you wish you had. I suspected his change in handling things had more to do with Kelly than it did with Gavin. Sebastian had also developed a fondness for her. It could have been because of how much Dr. Jeremy seemed to care for her; Sebastian went to great lengths to keep Dr. Jeremy happy. He was instrumental in the success of the pack and its low mortality rate.

Gavin wouldn't look at Sebastian; as he spoke to him, his face was cemented into a scowl that grew deeper with every passing moment. He had finished listening before he decided he was finished pretending to do it as well. He started to walk away, and I could sense the annoyance rising in Sebastian. Once again, Gavin had tested Sebastian's limited patience and the depths of his mercy, and it was only a matter of time before it escalated to something that wasn't going to help anyone. Sebastian looked in my direction, and I let him know I would handle it.

But could anyone ever really handle Gavin? The very person who was the best at it was the one who needed him.

Here we go again. One of the few times that Gavin was easy to find was when he was in panther form, moving throughout the wood, easily recognized among the hues of brown and green of the grass and trees. When I called his name, he walked away faster.

"Stop. Now."

I couldn't believe that worked.

He turned and trotted toward me. It was hard to stay still when you saw a panther charging in your direction, but I did and steeled my eyes on him. When he was just a foot or so away, I knelt down and spoke slowly.

I started to touch his fur, I couldn't help it. Next to Dr. Jeremy, he was one of the more mesmeric animals. His midnight coat that shimmered under the moonlight provided a beautiful backdrop for his emotive yellow eyes. He batted my hand back. Another attempt was met with the same response.

"I know you are afraid that you will hurt Kelly, but she's going to die if you don't try to change her. You and I both know if someone else does it, they will make that connection with her. The very one that you deserve"—after all, she's already been subjected to your crazy love, and no one else will have you—"so it will be hard for you. It's not like doing it before; you have us here and we will help you through this."

He dropped his head in contemplation. "I'll be in there if you want, and so will Dr. Jeremy. You can do this, Gavin. I know you can, for her. Weeks you looked for her because you needed to help her. You can't stop now. Okay?"

His head was still lowered, so I didn't know whether or not I was getting through to him. He leaned forward against my hand, brushing his head against it, and when I reached to rub his fur, he let me. Standing there for several moments, I enjoyed something that wasn't likely to ever happen again. He padded away, switching back to human form just a few feet from his clothes.

Once again I was looking at a man's naked butt. "You couldn't wait until you were closer to your clothes?"

"It's an ass, you haven't seen one before?" He yanked on his pants, keeping his back to me. At least I wasn't going to get a full-frontal view. I had seen enough of that, too.

"This pack really *is* lucky to have you." Cole's voice came from the right.

"I've been lucky to have them as well," I said.

"I'm sure, but I feel like the scales might be tipped in their favor." He fell in step with me as I walked toward the house.

"You're too kind. Ask Sebastian, the scales aren't in their favor. This pack has helped me a lot."

"You are very modest, aren't you?" He sped ahead to get the door, where he stood in the entrance.

I shook my head. "Not at all." I was faintly aware that he kept decreasing the distance between us.

"I hope that you recognize what an asset you are to them."

"I'm sure they do." I slipped past him and went into the house.

By the time I had made my way to the infirmary, Gavin was next to Kelly's bed. Her eyes were closed. Sebastian stood next to Gavin, looking concerned as he spoke. Gavin nodded absently, keeping his focus on Kelly. Sebastian regained Gavin's attention briefly, but it slipped back in her direction. Giving him a reassuring pat on his shoulder, Sebastian left the room. Gavin leaned over and kissed Kelly on the forehead and then he shifted again.

"What happens during a change?" I asked once Sebastian had taken a place next to me. His forehead was pressed up against the observation window next to mine.

"It's just a bite, but you have to release the enzyme to cause the change. That's the tricky part."

Sebastian was watching so intently I didn't want to keep peppering him with questions, but I had a ton. How was were-animal saliva different from regular saliva? Did it taste bad? How did you know it was in your system?

Sebastian tensed, pressing his head into the window as he held his breath. I did, too, but I had no idea what I was looking for. Was there something that indicated that it had occurred? But when he relaxed and stepped back, I assumed he had seen all he needed to. All I saw was a huge gash in Kelly's arm, then blood, quite a bit. But it coagulated and stopped.

"It's going to be a while before you see anything. But I'm certain it worked."

"What's a while?"

"Anywhere from four to six hours," he said.

Gavin had taken a spot next to her bed and plopped down, ready to wait it out. And I had every intention of doing it, too. Not just out of curiosity—I needed to make sure she was going to be alright. We all seemed to bear the guilt of her injuries although they weren't in our control. Anger and frustration simmered in me again even though all involved had been taken care of, except that pesky little Dexter, who would be hiding if he had any sense. Part of me hoped he was arrogant enough not to.

I hoped it was a good sign that it didn't take four hours but closer to three and a half. Perspiration ran down her face and glistened on her forehead. Her body twitched for a moment and then it convulsed. She lurched up screaming—the loud, shrill sound rang throughout the room, and I understood why Sebastian had left. It was torturous to watch, but the frown on Dr. Jeremy's face had relaxed, so I assumed things were going as expected. She collapsed back on the bed. She wasn't moving, but since Jeremy didn't look alarmed, I stayed calm.

Now what?

Seeing someone change for the first time was something I'd rather not see again. I distinctly remembered my mother's look of helpless horror the first time I'd changed, and the pain of it was so raw that thinking about it made my skin throb. The same look that my mother had had was now on Gavin's face as Kelly went through her first change. The crunching sound of bones breaking was the hardest, but the whining noise that the ligaments made as they stretched to accommodate the new form was a close second. And fur didn't just ease out like a blossoming flower: it punctured through the skin. No one could stop it all from happening no matter how much they willed it, but it looked as if Gavin was willing it with all that he had. The violent convulsing just before those changes started had thrown her off the bed onto the floor. Gavin sat next to her, helpless to do anything but watch. When it was over, a panther, with a slightly smaller frame than his own animal, was lying next to him, asleep.

It was the first time Dr. Jeremy had had color in his face since we'd rescued her, and he relaxed back in his chair. It was more than obvious an immeasurable weight had been lifted off of him. It was difficult to bask in the moment of success as screams and whimpers took over the home. Eleven more changes were occurring in succession. The torturous screams that resounded made it seem more like a house of horrors than a retreat.

Three hours later, the silence was the most pleasant thing imaginable. No more wails of pain, sounds of the first change. Just somnolent quiet and the realization that we had twelve new were-animals we would have to deal with. Well, that Sebastian, Ethan, and Dr. Jeremy had to deal with.

CHAPTER 15

The next day we had moved back to the library. Moving things back and forth to Josh's house was becoming an unnecessary hassle. The days were dwindling, and we were back up to four potential spells.

I looked up at Josh, who was at the dry-erase board again, the one next to the desktop computer that had several open windows on it. He'd been in there for a while. I couldn't sit down, not yet. I was reduced to the same person I'd been years ago, fearful of magic. It didn't help things that Josh seemed distracted while working on the spells. Several times he stared off, and it took me calling his name for him to refocus.

"Chris left?"

"Mm-hmm," he said, keeping his eyes on the board. His demeanor remained the same. That didn't seem to be the issue bothering him, and what probably was couldn't be broached tactfully. I couldn't ask him if he was having second thoughts about annihilating the remaining members of the Creed, including Marcia, and coincidentally preventing a civil war among the witches and giving way to new leadership. That act surpassed any of the orchestrated moves that Sebastian had initiated.

"What do you think of Ariel?" I asked, easing my way into the conversation.

He slowly turned, crossing his arms over his chest as he gave the question a long consideration. A question that I suspected he'd been pondering since meeting her. "I don't know," he concluded. "London came over last night." There was a slight relief in his voice. "It will be good to have someone new in the position, but I'm not convinced it will be easy to resist corruption once in that position. I'm hopeful for London's sake—and for mine. But if London trusts her, then I do. It will be a nice change not to have to worry about the witches all the time."

Truth rang in his words, but Josh had to split his allegiance between sects that were at odds with each other. It had to be a relief to have the potential of a veritable relationship with the witches and not deal with the strain and complication of dual alliances. I knew there had to have been a sense of loss, as if he'd been exiled, when his bond with the witches had been severed.

He turned back to the board. "I wish London would have clued me in on some of it. I'm getting a little tired of being the last person to find out things that I should know."

I was hit with the same twinge of guilt that always reared its head when he said things like that. I hated that I knew about the curse on him and had been sworn to secrecy. I started to disclose it but instead pressed my lips together and dealt with it, feeling the strain of split loyalties as well.

Josh called my name, and when I turned, he was standing, holding up an open palm that had been recently cut. Blood was just starting to well. I hesitated.

"Sky." It wasn't a request. Once I had moved close enough, I took the knife he held and sliced over my hand. Face-to-face, we linked fingers, and I closed my eyes. His breath wisped across my face as he chanted. I became ever more aware of how close we were. There was always an unavoidable intimacy between us when we shared magic. Before, it had never bothered me—I liked the magical bond that we had, the special connection. But with Ethan in the picture, it felt too intimate and the connection malapropos. All thoughts vanished as Josh's magic coursed through me, the gentle ocean breeze, the calming nature of it, and as he relinquished it to me, I gathered it. But I knew this wasn't the purpose of the exercise.

I had mastered his magic. It was comfortable because it was easy, and if it became too difficult to control, I knew that Josh was there to take over. It was when I switched it over, where he had no control and it became something dark, reckless, and deadly, that it was difficult. Now it was my responsibility to subjugate it and control it rather than allow it to control me. I had to dominate it. Each time it felt different; unlike Josh's magic, dark magic seemed to have many threads, depths, and dimensions to it.

It drowned me and I crawled out from the depths of the bleakness. It wasn't working. I was wading through it, trying to control its mercurial ways without success. The dormant power-hungry monster awoke, drawn to the darkness and the stygian magic. She sought to control it. I heard her chants off at a distance become louder and louder. I tuned them out, working harder to gather the magic under my command. I was aware of things vibrating around me, bumping into one another, and the stuffiness of the room and how Josh's breathing became sharp gasps as he struggled to take them. They wouldn't distract me—I had one goal, not to change natural magic to dark, but to use dark magic in the same manner I used natural magic. I opened my eyes for a moment to look at the state of the room and closed them again. *Concentrate.* Instead of destroying those things, I slowly reshelved the books and placed broken pieces from shattered drinking glasses into the garbage.

I kept my eyes closed and leaned into Josh. "Don't be afraid." I touched his chest. His heart was dragging at a sluggish beat, and his breathing was now just choked gasps. If I stopped the dark magic, things would return to normal. I wanted to do that with the magic—so I did. Josh's heart started to beat faster, accelerating at a low rate.

When I opened my eyes, he was a little red but still had the afterglow he always did when he dealt with strong dangerous magic. Josh seemed as drawn to deadly magic as the were-animals were to violence.

"Well, that was interesting." I followed the voice to the door where Cole stood. He stepped over the threshold and looked around the room and then inhaled. I could smell magic. Eventually Cole's eyes landed on me and his lips kinked into an amused smile. "Skylar, you are far more interesting even than I initially thought. That was a very impressive show. Is it always like this around here?" He slipped into a seat next to me.

Josh shrugged. "It depends. Did you need something, Cole?" His voice was cool and despondent, different than it was with anyone else. Josh had never met a stranger, and most people were drawn to him to the point that I'd started to think it was an innate attraction to magic, that desire to be close to it.

Shrugging off Josh's ungenial response, Cole kept his smile. "We contract out for magical services; we aren't so lucky to have a witch as part of our pack, so I rarely get a peek behind the curtain." Once again, his gaze slipped in my direction. "Very interesting."

Josh was fighting the emergence of a scowl, and I wasn't sure why he wasn't fond of Cole. I was used to the strained interaction of dominant were-animals—they were always testing the boundaries—but this was different. I'd been around Josh long enough that I knew when he distrusted someone, and that wasn't it. I would have picked up on that with Sebastian as well, but Sebastian didn't hide it; he was quite vocal about his feelings. Cole definitely wouldn't have been invited to stay at the retreat if he couldn't be trusted.

Josh eventually plastered on a fake cordial smile and said in an even tone, "There really isn't a lot to see now. Just boring research, but when the fun happens, I'll make sure to invite you for the show."

"I would like that." Cole came to his feet with the predaceous grace that was a subtle reminder that he was a were-animal and the overwhelming confidence that showed he was an Alpha. It was as though he was reminding Josh as well. The tension-ridden silence was uncomfortable, and Cole's gaze remained fixed on Josh, which wasn't a good thing. If there was such a thing as an Alpha witch, Josh would definitely be one, and this was brewing into something that I didn't like.

"Josh, which one should I try first?" I asked, picking up two of the books on the table. It took a moment before he dragged his eyes from Cole's. Then he pointed to the one on the left, and I opened it. Once again, I was the object of Cole's attention.

I gave him a smile, which he returned. "Thank you, but as you know, we have our work ahead of us, so we really need to get to it."

"Of course. If there is anything I can do to help you with it, don't be afraid to ask."

Josh was about to respond, and I was willing to bet it would be something that would rekindle the odd stare-off, when I shot him a sharp look.

"What the hell was that, Josh?"

He frowned. "He seemed very nosy."

"Aren't most Alphas? Do you blame him for being curious? After all, his life is on the line, too."

"If he was only curious about the magic, that wouldn't be a problem. He seems really curious about you."

"Yes, because I'm the only thing standing between him and a death sentence. I'd be curious, too."

Josh didn't seem convinced, and I wasn't entirely convinced of it, either.

CHAPTER 16

"*A*re you ready?" Josh asked in a low voice, standing just inches from me.

Of course I wasn't ready to try his bootlegged spell that he'd concocted from several other spells. But I had to—it seemed like the most reliable. It was the one he was convinced would work. From the look on my face, he gleaned I was apprehensive. I closed my eyes for just a moment, drawing from the confidence that Josh had in the face of uncanny adversity and possibly failure. As usual it emboldened me. Made the mountain I was about to climb nothing more than a steep step that I could navigate with ease.

I didn't want to perform strong magic with an audience, but all the Alphas were present. The indelible mark on them had become their death sentence, and I was the key to removing it. I was giving up control of my body and volition to someone who wanted to take over. But the options were limited.

I'd practiced it so many times, I knew the spell and everything that it would entail. It had to be pure Faerie and dark magic, so I couldn't even be anchored to Josh or have the privilege of something comforting and safe. I looked around the room again, but my gaze still went back to Josh because he was the one I trusted for reassurance. I had this.

The knife slipped over my hand, blood rose to the surface, and I started the incantation, watching as the light in the room was eclipsed to darkness and all the people, sounds, and things around me disappeared. Completely swaddled in darkness, I kept going, breathing the words out. First they felt foreign, and slowly they unfolded into a familiar language, her language.

I saw the world before it was the way we knew it. Things that were mutated versions of what we called were-animals, more beasts than men in the basic sense. Wild, vicious animals that spoke. The world that Logan described, before were-animals became "pretty little things." I tried to ignore the other things around me, the witches performing strong magic, vampires that looked nothing like the ones I'd met—hairless creatures, garnet eyes, all fangs, inhumane pale monsters that were the walking embodiment of nightmares.

I couldn't ignore the violence. Were-animals were complete savages, roaming through the streets, and even the vampires moved away from them. The witches cowered in fear. I kept saying the incantation, pleading for a quick escape and respite from the violence and blood, the pleasure felt in carnal cruelty. I kept going. Again the world became black, the images gone, unfamiliar faces appearing and disappearing—except for the bronze man that Josh had warned me of, that very man who had taken on Ethan's image when we'd gone to the in-between, and was still in Ethan's image. *Never let him touch you*, that was the one instruction Josh had given me. I tried to move. My feet were planted on the ground; the smell of death whispered in the room, and magic soon claimed it. Dark magic. Strong magic. Deadly magic.

The bronze man shifted to a wolf, then a panther, and continued with various other animals. I kept going. What would happen if I stopped—what was supposed to happen? Was he supposed to stop shifting? That was when I realized I wasn't adequately prepared for this. The words didn't come anymore no matter how I willed them. I choked on them. No, it wasn't the words. Someone was trying to claim the spell and me with it—Maya, her language off in the distance with another spell to counter mine.

The bronze figure continued to shift, his language matching Maya's, clouding my head, animals forming, peeling away, and being discarded. Visions of the animals and their horrid acts against humanity filled my thoughts. I heard cries of pain, felt despair as vivid as my own. I owned the sorrow, and it claimed me as its own. I tried to shrug it off, but nothing happened. I was forced to live through it, to see and feel our acts. To truly know what we were until I hated us. Hated us as much as others did. Until I wanted us cursed and dead, too.

The bleak emptiness of death and dark magic compounded and increased with each animal cast off. It was exactly what was going to happen to the pack. Once considered savages and monsters, they were cursed, and Maya and the man before me weren't going to change it. I screamed; the bloodcurdling sound shattered the magic, along with that vision and parts of me, too. I felt torn between the two worlds as I clawed my way away from it. Maya spat my name as if it were a curse. No longer the person who saved her, I had become her enemy that was working to contain her. I needed to contain her.

Still bound by magic, I tried to shed the tenebrific cloak, but I couldn't. I opened my eyes to an image just as disturbing. They were all on the floor, spasming, gasping for breath. My head spun as I tried to find a way to stop it. Nothing. Through blurry vision, I tried to make out the faces in the room. Another cut on my hand, then someone grasped it, and words floated, and it all stopped. Josh, his magic a cleansing wash, neutralized it. It wasn't gone, but it had become a dense obscurity of gray, and Maya was quiet. I lay on the floor as voices skated over me; at first, they seemed like they were off in the distance, and then finally they were closer, in the same room.

Once the pain had ceased, after a few moments they came back to themselves, getting to their feet. Sebastian was the first to lift his shirt—the mark was still there. The others revealed that theirs were there, too. How many more days did we have?

"Sky, are you okay?" Ethan was cautious as he approached, concerned.

I nodded absently.

"Are you sure?" Josh asked. He frowned.

No. I wasn't sure at all. I thought I was fine. I felt fine, or as fine as I could be based on the circumstances, but everyone kept looking at me. I rubbed my hand over my face, needing to make sure it wasn't beastly or I hadn't sprouted horns, because they were looking at me as though some variation of that weirdness had occurred.

Josh stepped closer and entwined his fingers with mine. He whispered the words he usually did when he loaned me magic. I felt it, stronger than it had ever been, a direct contrast to what I had subjected myself to before. Strong natural magic overtook whatever was lurking behind. I'd been so deeply submerged in it, I'd lost the sense of what it was. I didn't want that type of magic to become my norm, where I couldn't distinguish between the two and was unprepared to deal with each differently.

"Better?" he inquired. I nodded. Physically I was better, but looking at Ethan, all I saw was the bronze man who was death, shifting to all the other animals and discarding them. The others around me were the carnivorous savages that destroyed everything in their paths, that caused others to cower in fear, that warranted death; they were condemned, too. I swallowed the sickness that was threatening to surface.

"I need some air." I backed out of the room. I heard Ethan call me, but I ignored him and continued shedding my clothes.

I was naked by the time I crossed the threshold of the back door and had shifted mid-jog without breaking stride. I kept running, around the trees, leaping over branches, ignoring the low ones that I missed and that scratched against my face. My paws pounded against the loose dirt, kicking it up. I ran faster, my lungs opening up as I pulled in air, hoping it would cleanse me of the memories. The aromatic smell of the trees, the crisp air, the grainy smell of the sparse grass washed over me. I ran faster, dirt becoming smoke that I ran through. Each time my paws hit the ground, I propelled myself farther, pushed myself faster, pounded the ground harder, trying to escape the memories—but they couldn't be evaded. I wasn't sure how long I ran and what I was running for, but when I finally stopped, I wasn't sure how to feel. But at least things were muddled enough that I could have some reprieve.

I plopped down in a little spot in the bosk and waited, once again unsure of what to do next, how to feel, what to think.

"Sky." Ethan's voice was soft and plaintive. I looked up but eventually settled back into a resting position. I didn't want to talk, either.

"Sky, look at me," he commanded. I looked up, holding his gaze as he knelt next to me. "You've been gone for three hours. Change."

Nope.

When I didn't make an effort to do so, he reached out to touch me. I snapped at him. He jerked his hand back as gray rolled over his eyes and they narrowed on me. "Sky. Change. Now."

I howled, a mournful sound, and buried my head in my paws. I didn't want to change—not yet. I needed a reprieve from it all, and the moment I changed, it would all come back.

"Okay." He lowered himself to the ground and sat next to me, resting back on his arms. I slid up and put my head on his lap and fell asleep.

When I awoke, he was in the same position. It was dusk, and he still had the concerned look on his face that he'd had when I'd refused to change. I slipped out of my animal shell, a place that offered me more comfort than my human one. He took off his shirt and handed it to me. I slipped it on. Then he took my hand, locking his fingers with mine as we started back toward the house.

"You are going to have to tell me what happened. That's not negotiable," he said.

I told him everything in more detail than I would have wished, as though he could absolve me of the memories. When I told him about the person who resembled him but felt like death, shifting to several animals and discarding them as a feeling of death ensorcelled him, I turned to face him.

"Ethan, what are you? Don't tell me you're just a wolf. It all just seems so wrong. *You* seem wrong sometimes."

"Sky, I'm not sure why that happened or why your mind has chosen to—"

I released his hand. "Ethan, don't."

His lips pressed into a tight line. Whatever secrets he had, whatever it was that he felt he needed to protect me from, it wasn't going to be disclosed, and I was tired of it. I snatched up my clothes, which someone had folded and thoughtfully placed closer to the woods, only taking my eyes off him to put on my shirt before tossing his at him.

"I think I've done enough to earn the pack's trust, your trust. I can't be in the dark, struggling for some glimpse of clarity, only to be blindsided when you all need me. I'm not going to do this, Ethan."

"It's complicated."

"It always is," I said, walking back to the house, thankful that he hadn't followed me.

I'd gone straight to my room. It felt like my room, anyway, since I always ended up in it—the one where I'd first met the pack—out of so many rooms to choose from in the massive house. Initially, they'd been strangers trying to save my life for some unknown reason, and for years that seemed to be the M.O., but now I knew the reason. If the curse was correct, I was the key to ending it. Honesty be damned. Screw transparency. You saw whatever screwed-up, illusionist reality they created on a foundation of lies of omission with the goal of allowing people to see the reality they wished them to believe.

When someone knocked on the door, I continued to look out the large window, past the crowded forest, transfixed by the light illumination of the moon that pulled at me. I now found comfort in my wolf, and magic was an intricate part of my very existence. Things had changed so much since the first time I'd awakened in this very room three years ago.

"Skylar." I turned to look around. Cole entered carrying a bottle and two glasses. "I figured you could use this."

I didn't say anything and returned to looking out the window. I didn't want him to go away. Okay, he could leave—I didn't want the full bottle of vodka to leave. He could scuttle back to whatever Alphas-only den of secret meetings he had come from.

When he took up a position next to me and handed me a glass, I took it and gulped it down. *Oh, that's right, I don't drink vodka for the same reason I don't drink gasoline.* But it didn't bother me too much, and dulling my senses seemed like a pretty good life plan.

"You've had a rough day."

What gave it away? "Yeah," I said into the glass.

"Sebastian is very confident in your ability and Josh's to fix this."

I could feel his penetrating gaze on me—looking for affirmation. Needing it. I needed it, too. I nodded and turned to face him. "Yeah, it's not going to be easy. Things like this never are, but we seem to manage." And that was the truth; most of the time I thought it was more luck than skill, and at some point, luck had to run out.

He smiled. "Based on what I saw today, you are truly an asset to this pack." He raised his glass to me and took another sip while closing the distance between us. The fingers of his free hand brushed lightly against my hand. "The witch and the magical wolf seem to be a very good team. And very good for this pack."

Taking a couple of steps toward the window, he looked out, appreciating the same beauty that we all did when we looked at the moonlit landscape—the freedom to be able to easily roam in peace. It was a comfortable sanctuary.

"I often found myself envious of the power and prestige afforded to this pack. After all, technically it has two Alphas, and that lends to its strength as a unit." He turned and looked at me, his eyes leisurely scanning me from head to toe. "In the short time I've been here, I've noticed that the pack is cloaked in secrecy, but I trust Sebastian, so I'm sure there is a good reason."

Again, I found myself under the gaze of a watchful Alpha.

A whisper of a smile lifted his lips. "The secrets would bother me, too. But you can find comfort that they keep them from us as well. There's always something more to the Midwest Pack, but it's just another day, another secret. I get it, I'm not part of this pack. It doesn't bother me, but you seem to be having a hard time with it."

I shrugged it off. It didn't surprise me that he could sense it, that he knew it. My thoughts went to the primitive were-animals I had seen earlier and how they must have used their skills to hunt and terrorize. I took another long draw from my glass. Placing his hand over my hand that was holding the glass, he showed a gentle understanding that I really needed. Something was off and I wanted to be able to fix it, to understand it, but I couldn't.

"It's okay to feel this way. I only saw what you went through, and it bothered me to see it happening to you. I hated being a helpless observer. But no one could do anything about it. I'm sorry." The little space that remained between us, he'd closed in a single step and I was aware of his hand over mine, his kind silver eyes, the gentle knowing smile, and his breezy breath against my lips. I stayed still as he moved closer, wishing the alarm to move would ring, or at least ring a little louder so that I wouldn't ignore it.

He leaned in to kiss me. Shocked into a response, I moved back. "No. I'm with Ethan."

He smirked. "Are you? I've seen you together. He's the director and author of the little drama that you consider a relationship. It's awfully one-sided and appears to be only what he wants it to be. I presume your relationship is of his own creation. It happened when he wanted it to, not when you did, and he only gives enough for you to perform for him."

I brushed off his words, but his observations stayed with me.

"I think you deserve better than Ethan." Although he maintained the distance I had placed between us, his overwhelming presence made it seem like he was just inches from me. Too close. I averted my eyes from his.

"That's how he is, I knew from the beginning. We make it work." My tone was cool, a warning to drop the subject.

"No, *you* make it work. You will eventually grow tired of it." I was sure he wanted me to do it rather quickly.

I finished what was left in the glass, set it on the nightstand and started to leave. "You might be right, but I still want him. And if I no longer do, I'm not going to betray him. I'll just end it."

The smile was still there, and so was the taunting, devilish sparkle in his eyes. "You know where I am, and if you ever want to come and see how things are done in the East, feel free to come visit me. While I'm here, my door is always open, if you want to talk."

Talk? Is that what they're calling it these days?

He raised his glass to me and then finished it off. I was down the stairs in seconds, rushing through the house, looking for someone to take me home. There were several lights still on: one in the library—I suspected Josh was still in there—Sebastian's office, and the clinic. I hoped Kelly was in there. She'd settled back into her role as the pack's nurse rather quickly. She was still the same, except that she seemed to enjoy changing to her animal half a lot. It was a little quirk of hers. I started walking aimlessly, and for some reason I ended up at Sebastian's door instead of in the clinic.

"Will you take me home?" I said to his back. He was in his chair, staring at his odd collection of books. My interest always went to the books of poetry that he had. I smiled, envisioning the ferocious beasts from earlier sitting down and enjoying beautiful words.

He turned. "Of course." Grabbing his keys off his desk, he followed behind me.

I knew Sebastian would give me the silence I needed. I wouldn't have to relive the moment in the library again. For most of the drive, we sat in a comfortable quiet, or as comfortable as it could be between us.

"I guess knowing where we evolved from is a lot different than experiencing it." His tone was bleak and remorseful.

"It wasn't that bad."

"Yes, it was. I was there."

He regarded me for a long time, concerned. "Why are you doing this?" he inquired.

"What?" I asked. "I don't have a choice," I added before he could answer.

He pulled the car over. His hands rubbed over his face in frustration. It hadn't been a trying couple of days for just me. If Josh and I couldn't remove the curse, I still lived—Sebastian didn't.

"You could have left. You could leave now and vow never to put yourself through such things. Josh does it because he and

Ethan will do anything for each other. But you—I'm trying to understand the why with you."

"Because you need me to, and I can't stand idly by and watch people I care about die because I can't tolerate a little discomfort," I offered. "I wish you all would have told me. Maybe I could have done things differently."

"Like what? Hole yourself up in your house, afraid that anything you did could be the catalyst for a curse that no one believed was real? I know you believe it's an act of cruelty to withhold information from you, but I don't see it that way. Some things are best hidden, not out of mistrust of you but out of self-preservation. We don't keep things from you because we don't trust you. What would it have helped, telling you, if the information was incorrect? If we would have told you, it would have changed things for you. Just like if we—"

He stopped. I was positive he knew Ethan had informed me about the situation with Josh. He was so bound by his vow of secrecy he seemed unable to repeat the secret to someone who already knew. "You would have worried. In the back of your mind, you would live your life thinking about it—that's who you are. You would have sacrificed and resisted using magic, and you never would have been able to kill Ethos." Technically, I hadn't killed Ethos, Ethan had. I was positive Sebastian was aware of that now. "Now, Mouras are safe because of it. No more sentence of death. That's because of you.

"I'm glad you consider this an obligation and you can't walk away." Sebastian hesitated before leaning forward and gently putting his hand on top of my head. I knew it was his way of showing affection, but I felt like he was petting me. "It's what makes you uniquely Skylar."

"I think if anyone else in the pack had the ability to do it, they would."

He nodded. "I have no doubts about that. But everyone in the pack *is* the pack." He pulled back into the street, keeping his eyes straight ahead. "It feels like you are in the pack."

I understood what he was saying. I had a hard time internalizing everything about it. For years, I'd resisted my animal half because it had made feel like a freak, an outsider, too different. Despite that fact, I knew I was on so many levels. The pack was an extension of the disconnect, that difference. Whether or not you knew why, when in the presence of a were-animal, you felt the difference. The more entangled you became with the pack, the more of yourself you gave until you *were* the pack. I wasn't sure if I was there, or if I would ever be.

Sleeping was nightmare-riddled, so at nearly three o'clock in the morning I'd given up. Staring at some images that flashed in front of me on the television, I didn't care that I didn't find them remotely interesting. Someone knocked lightly at the door. I didn't bother looking out the peephole. I could feel him on the other side. Ethan stood just outside my door in a pair of loose-fitting jeans. It looked like he'd just grabbed clothes and put them on without giving much thought to it, which wasn't like him.

"I couldn't sleep, either," he said quietly.

No other words were exchanged. Hands linked, we went to the bedroom and got into bed. Resting against his chest, I snuggled in closer and found sleep immediately.

CHAPTER 17

The next day I expected to find Josh in the library with a new spell to try. It was doubtful he'd slept at all, given that he had the daunting task of trying to find another spell. We'd exhausted everything else; I refused to think of the alternative. It wasn't an alternative for either of us—or was it? I shoved the idea aside. There sat the Aufero on the table, illuminated a vibrant orange, pulsing with magic—strong magic. The allure of it was too tempting.

I moved to the corner away from it and pulled a couple more books off the shelf I'd been through too many times. There wasn't anything new in them. I scooted them closer to the middle of the table and took out the Clostra. Since Joan's return, we now had two of them, but they weren't any good without the third one. And since my cousin and I were the only ones who could read them, they weren't any good to anyone else, either.

"Good morning, Sky," Cole greeted as he walked into the library and took a seat next to me.

"Hi," I said coolly. I didn't want to be rude, but I didn't want a repeat of yesterday's conversation. Pulling one of the books from the center of the table, he started to peruse it. With a limpid smile, he asked, "You can read this?"

"Not all. I'm better than I was, but I still have to use Google Translate a lot or ask Josh or Ethan for help."

"Ethan speaks Latin?"

I nodded.

"Very fortuitous for the pack. But his mother was a witch, it's to be expected." He moistened his lips, still looking over the pages. "I shouldn't have said what I did, yesterday."

"It's okay. I understand how things between us might look to others. It can be complicated at times."

"You misunderstand. I'm sorry it was said at an inopportune time, but I meant it."

I didn't want to talk about my relationship with Ethan, nor did I care to hear any more insight regarding it. "The book next to it is in English."

He picked it up, turning over a few of the pages. "You can do spells like these?"

Barely nodding into my answer, I narrowed my eyes on him. "Are you trying to poach me?"

His eyes flew up and his brows rose. "Poach?" He grinned.

"Yes, *poach*. I'm not leaving this pack. It would be advantageous for you to have a witch in your pack, but I'm not interested in leaving this one."

"If I was even considering such a thing, Sebastian would have to agree to the transfer, and I'm sure he wouldn't."

He went back to the Latin book; I figured the mystique of the foreign words was more interesting to him. Taking out his phone, he swiped over a couple of things and then began typing, I guessed translating.

"I do believe your modesty may be your most appealing attribute. There are far more interesting things about you than your magic. It's unfortunate that Ethan . . . the others"—he seemed to add that as an afterthought—"haven't done a better job making you see that."

I let the quiet moment settle between us, reading over the Clostra, I leaned over, letting my hair fall over my face. I was startled when he moved closer, brushing it away and tucking it behind my ear. "Better. I may need your assistance with this one."

He moved the book over and slid his chair even closer.

"There isn't anything in that book that will help."

"Perhaps you're right, but Josh isn't here yet, so you can't work. Will you at least entertain my curiosity?" he asked softly.

I started to read it, explaining what the spell did. I could feel his attention and fascination. I finished and moved the book back closer to him.

"We hire out," he admitted. "This is my first time being so close to the process." He pointed to another. I didn't feel like giving a magic lesson to someone who would never be able to use it, but I didn't want to tell him to just go away.

"I really need to finish going through this," I said.

He looked over at the Clostra, and the words disappeared from the page, as they did for anyone but me and my cousin. "This place is a world of wonder." He looked around the room, at the various books. He stood to go over to one shelf, taking some books off to look at and then reshelving them. "I haven't heard Latin spoken often, but to my untrained ears, you speak it quite beautifully, for a novice."

"And you can learn Latin, too. Why don't you take the book and go study somewhere?" Ethan said sharply from the doorway.

When Cole gave him a dismissive glance, Ethan responded with a sharp look. Once again I found myself between them, the boundaries being tested. It was worse than in the gym when I'd been sparring with Cole.

Ethan's eyes narrowed, steel gray flooding them. He moved to enter the room, but before he could, Josh slipped in and quickly moved in front of his brother with two coffees in hand, putting a barrier between him and Cole. He handed one to me and the other to his brother.

"It probably needs to be warmed up a little," he said to Ethan, an easy look on his face as he tried to get him to focus on the cup instead of the target that he'd zoned in on. His gaze was unwavering; Josh was unable to redirect him.

Coffee in hand, I slipped past Josh and placed my hand on Ethan's stomach, feeling the grooves of his abs that were tauter than usual because his whole body was rigid. "We should warm it up."

I nudged him back. He didn't budge. I made another effort. I lifted to my toes and gave him a light kiss on his lips. When he looked down at me, I lifted the cup. "I'm about to become caffeine-less Sky. No one likes her. Right, Josh?"

"Why do you think I brought it? I can barely stand her, and since we have work that needs to be done, please get her some warm coffee," Josh joked as I nudged Ethan again. With hesitation, he backed out of the room.

I looked back over my shoulder to give Josh a thankful look and got a glimpse of Cole, who was still looking at me, rubbing his fingers absently over his lips.

The luxury of time was no longer ours. Josh and I worked for several hours on another spell, one that we'd rejected because it was stronger and darker than the one before, but we were in a desperate situation. Once again, we were in the library, Joan in one corner, the West Coast Alpha in the other, Cole on one side of Sebastian and Ethan on the opposite side.

Ethan's arms were folded over his chest. He stepped back until he rested against the only bare wall in the room, dividing his attention between his blank looks at me and glares at Cole. The palpable tension between them was making me uncomfortable and making it even more difficult to concentrate on the spell. Josh was usually perceptive, but he was too involved with the magic or the spell to pay attention to anything else. After my third failed attempt to say the spell all at once, something had to be done. The incantation had to be done that way, a single invocation of a plea for assistance without a break or pause, a magical song that had to have the notes and beats right, or it wouldn't work. And that was always the problem with stronger spells—they required far more precision than strength.

Sebastian's gaze bounced between Ethan and Cole. "I need the room," he said, looking at everyone around him.

There was just a brief moment of refusal from both of them, but in the end, Sebastian the Elite Alpha gave a look—a scary look as amber rolled over his eyes. Without shifting, the wolf just peeked through, vicious and feral. Cole was the first to leave. Defiance marked Ethan's glare and response. It was rare that he did that, and on those infrequent occasions it had always been because of Josh and his desire to protect him and prevent him from doing dangerous things. Rarely was the fuse of discord lit, but for a brief moment, it was, and it didn't revolve around Josh.

"I won't ask again," Sebastian said. With a scowl, Ethan pushed from the wall and walked out of the room.

As the last words fell from my lips once again, I was treated to another dark world, similar to the one before, but with the stronger spell, I felt things more intensely. I clutched the edge of the table, absorbing the feeling of despair, the violence, the bile that crept up my throat over the devastation that the creatures left in their wake. The same thing, as if it was just a loop, but this time, when I saw the bronze man, I didn't run.

I stood, keeping a distance from him, waiting for him to speak. He didn't say anything. Massive claws formed around his hand,

and he slashed them across my stomach; I jumped back, but not in time. Pain seared through me. Pulling magic from the Aufero, I found its darkest source, and it took everything I had to control it, teetering on the line before I found myself submerged in it.

I heard people gasping around me, but I cast the spell. Words that I'd only heard spoken by Ethos, the purveyor of dark magic, and Maya flowed from me as naturally as my own. Blood streamed from my stomach, warmth fell over it, and the words continued. I still don't know what drove me to continue, but I did, knowing that the words were not my own and the spell I was casting was something foreign to me. I was compelled to do it. The desire to perform it at that moment felt stronger than the need to breathe, to exist.

The bronze figure's eyes changed to a deep gray and he fell, shifting into a wolf. Frozen in place, he stared at me before dropping his head in submission. Something changed between us; there wasn't fear, or darkness, but a sameness. A synergetic existence that felt almost comfortable. I hesitated before I reached out to touch his bowed head.

Josh's voice rang through the darkness, and strong magic beat against me like a windstorm. Josh's voice came closer. More voices came out of the abyss. The blasting wind stopped. I heard Sebastian telling me to come back. I focused on the wolf, and just as I leaned in to touch him, I was jerked back violently.

The spell ended. Josh was pressed against the wall, the room was a mess, and Sebastian was bent over on the floor.

I was in the library on my back. I covered my eyes at the bright light, opening them enough to see Sebastian's and Josh's hazy figures over me.

"You're hurt," Josh said, his eyes just as dark as the place he'd pulled me from. The cleansing breaths he took weren't enough. Magic reverberated and hummed off him. He took several steps from me and then rested back against a bookcase.

After a few minutes, he had come to a reasonable calm, and tepid blue eyes were staring back at me. "What the hell were you doing, Sky? You were pulling magic from everywhere. We weren't connected, so I don't know how you did it."

My heart was still pounding so hard I couldn't focus on Sebastian talking to me. For a few moments, I forced myself to drown it all out, reducing it to just white noise as I tried to make sense of it all. No matter how I framed and dissected the events, I had no clue what had happened.

"Did it work?" I asked, focusing on Sebastian once he took up a position in front of me.

He lifted his shirt to display the visible mark and frowned, his tone heavy with disappointment. "Nope. Still there."

The others came in and displayed theirs as well.

I didn't have to turn, I sensed his presence. "Ethan, what about you?" I asked, spinning on my butt to look at him.

"Sky, you're bleeding."

My body had become numb as it thrummed with magic. I was too intent on trying to bring it to a calm to focus on anything else. I looked down, where the claws had raked over my stomach. Blood soaked my shirt.

I repeated my question, my tone more forceful.

He didn't lift his shirt to check. "It's gone." His voice had fallen to a light whisper for my ears only, but in a room of were-animals that wasn't possible. The only person who might have missed it was Josh, but his look, forged from suspicion, doubt, and mistrust, suggested otherwise.

He held my gaze in silence, and then the questions came, and I didn't know which one to ask to get the answers I wanted. I decided to just ask whichever one came to mind when Dr. Jeremy rushed in, panicked. I knew he'd seen worse, but you wouldn't have known it by the way his eyes widened and he rushed me to the clinic.

"Am I going to make it? Do I need to say good-bye to my loved ones?" I teased.

He grumbled, "Not if you keep giving me lip." Then he frowned. "You've been hanging around Winter too much—you sound just like her."

"Probably because we've noticed you have a flair for over-reaction."

"Well, excuse me, back in my day a gut wound was kind of a big deal. But I'm old-school." He directed me to an exam table. I walked, only aware of the wound because of my shirt, which was sodden.

Once he had me on the table, my skin exposed, I realized that maybe he wasn't overreacting. The cuts were deeper than I'd thought, but minutes later they started to heal, faster than my usual healing process, and within minutes, it was as though they were never there.

"I don't say this often—I've never seen anything like that. Skylar, you, my dear, are quite the anomaly."

"That she is," Cole said from the doorway. Before he could walk in, Ethan pushed past him, looking concerned. When he looked at my stomach, his brow furrowed.

"What the fuck?"

"Yeah, I'm right there with you," Dr. Jeremy admitted. But it didn't stop him from quickly going into mother hen mode and directing Kelly to help him.

Kelly was tasked with assessing me, and as she took my vitals in the same automated way she had before, I studied her as much as she studied me. A sweet, inviting smile was her mask and she wore it with ease, but I knew I wasn't the only one concerned by the keen way Dr. Jeremy watched her from across the room. Was she really adapting to her new life, or was she putting on a very believable act?

"How is she?" Cole asked. Ethan shot him a cold, sharp look but didn't respond. When he stepped in, the gray pulsed like a heartbeat along his pupils, and his hands clenched tight enough to cause the muscles of his forearms to bulge.

Cole was equally reactive, taking a defensive stance. When their eyes locked on each other, Kelly slipped in between them. She easily eased into a docile role that forced them into the need to protect her from harm and made them unlikely to attack each other with her in the middle. Even though she was a were-animal, there was something so delectably human about her, and I wondered how long it would take before she shed it, if in fact she ever did. It was intertwined into her very existence, from her unassuming, wise walnut-colored eyes, to her delicate features, even to the thick coiled hair that lent her a more youthful appearance.

It made her tenacity and her smart-mouth behavior easily forgotten. Lacking in strength, she resorted to another way of handling situations, and it worked on most people—with the exception of Sebastian. He saw past the act of innocence when she stepped over the line that she toed very closely. When she crossed it, she quickly slipped into her submissive mode, making an attack against her undesirable—preying on the innocent, cowardly.

"She's doing fine, but we really need to check her out more. When magic is involved, you can never be too sure." It was a true statement. "I'm not sure if we are going to keep her. Cole, do you mind stepping out and coming back?" When he started to look in my direction, she spoke again, directing his attention back to her. "You can do something to help me help her. Why don't you tell me everything that happened?"

She guided him out of the room, and reluctantly he let her. Taking a page from Kelly's playbook, Dr. Jeremy intervened, asking Ethan questions about the removal of his mark, but he didn't offer anything of use, simply that he'd felt the magic, and once the crashing and the magic had stopped, he'd looked and the mark was gone. I had a feeling he knew before he'd looked and was connected to the magic more than he was admitting.

I didn't make an effort to hide what I was thinking, and I was sure it was displayed heavily on my face. When he turned from Dr. Jeremy to approach me, if he'd mistaken the look for anything else, there wasn't going to be any mistaking my words. "There is a reason that you were the only one who was fixed—are you going to tell me?"

He started to open his mouth, and I stopped him, raising my hand and giving him a quelling look. "I don't want an excuse, or a reality in which you want me to believe. I want the truth, Ethan. Nothing else."

As he focused on the wall for several moments in considera-tion, his tension and indecisiveness were evident.

"Ethan, I can't deal with the secrets. It's not fair to me . . . and if there is still an us, I can't continue without you being honest and open."

He exhaled a long breath. "I know," he said heavily. I could see the internal battle that threatened to consume him, and for a moment I felt a twinge of guilt. His secrets were an armor of protection for him, his brother, and this pack. But they were obstacles between us. I'd had become an open book to him, every-thing about me displayed clearly to him, but he was a tapestry of lies of omission, convoluted distraction, and stories manipulated to serve his purposes. Behind the nobility of the intent, there were still the lies and manipulation.

He stepped closer to me and pressed his forehead against mine, the internal battle so intense I could feel it. He kissed my forehead, then said, "I can't. If that is something you can't live with, I'm sorry. You have my answer; now you need to make that choice."

He turned, heading in the opposite direction from the one Kelly had taken Cole in. Minutes later, she walked in and stopped, inhaling the air, and then she made a face and looked off into space, distracted.

"What's wrong?"

"Gavin's here."

"Is that a bad thing?"

She shook her head. She hadn't adopted the fluidity of movement seen in most were-animals, nor did I see hints of her animal in her eyes or her mannerisms. It was indeed a separate part of her, but it had only been a couple of days.

She looked in Dr. Jeremy's direction, and for a few minutes he just stared; she smiled. As if they had their own language and nonverbal way of communicating, he stood and excused himself, but I couldn't ignore the troubled look that was profoundly displayed on his features when he looked at her. Guilt was an odd emotion that distorted the facts and outcomes in an unusual manner. It forced people to take responsibility and bear the burden of things that were beyond their control, and ignore any streams of good that might come from a situation. Kelly was alive, that was a good thing. He focused on the other things, and I believed no matter what I said, what cogent and logical argument I delivered, he would wear that burden like a scarlet letter.

"Everything's different. A lot. I can hear the conversations down the hall. I can smell the scent of blood, and I feel things deeply. A lot."

I was born a werewolf, so those things had developed as I grew, and I had always accepted that I was a freak of nature with heightened senses. I could imagine how much one had to adjust to the changes.

"You'll get used to it. It'll become your norm."

She made a face. "And Gavin?"

"What about him?"

"I can sense him and his scent . . . he smells . . ." She chewed on her bottom lip. "Delicious."

That wasn't any of the things that went through my head when I thought of Gavin's scent. Spiced oak: yes. Musky earth: yes. But not in a million years did I smell him and think "delicious." The wanton look on her face didn't indicate if *delicious* meant she wanted him on a plate with potatoes and a side salad or if she wanted him in her bed so she could do naughty things to him.

She continued leaning in as a light blush rose over her cheeks and she cast her eyes to the floor. "I've been avoiding him, because when he's around—" When she looked up, I didn't have to guess anymore. She looked the way I felt when Ethan emerged from the woods naked, exuding a primal allure that made me want to ravage him, not the way I looked at the basket of Swiss chocolates David gave me as my full moon gift. She didn't want him on a plate with a side of anything. Not by a long stretch. *How in the hell did I get in this conversation?*

"That's understandable. I don't think you should avoid him. I think the feelings are mutual."

She relaxed into her smile, and I knew that whatever she wanted to do was probably going to be explored really soon, and I needed to get out of the house quickly. Very quickly, because I'd walked in on enough romps from people sparring and it going a little too far. I'd sparred with plenty of people, and not once after punching them in the face had the urge to rip off their clothes and ravage them become an option, but for most of them, it was foreplay and a prelude to carnal activities that blurred the lines between eroticism and violence. I found myself a voyeur far too often, confused and mesmerized.

When Gavin came to the door and rested casually against it, one look at Kelly and I knew that if I didn't get out of there soon, I was going to become an unwilling observer to them going at it like animals in heat.

"Hi," he said.

She smiled. And responded. The pheromone-drenched room was getting to me. I briefly wondered what Gavin did to women. First Sable, now Kelly.

I slipped past them as they slowly approached each other; I hoped to get to the door and out before the "delicious" happened, but I wasn't totally confident they cared whether I was there or not. I stood at the door and inhaled, trying to determine Cole's location. I wanted to avoid him about as much as I wanted to avoid what was clearly about to happen between Kelly and Gavin.

"Who are you looking for?" Kelly asked.

I looked over my shoulder and wondered if she could tell I wasn't looking for anyone but rather trying to avoid someone.

"Cole. Which room is he staying in?"

Her brow furrowed. "He's staying at a hotel. He decided that was best once he issued a challenge for the Beta position this morning."

I whipped around. "What?"

She stepped away from Gavin, who had settled into her, oblivious to my presence. Apparently she smelled delicious, too, because he kept his face cradled in her neck and she had to nudge him away.

"You didn't know," she said softly.

I swallowed, afraid to ask the question because I knew the answer, but there was a part of me that wanted to believe otherwise. "Did he accept or is he going to step down?"

Kelly stood in front of me, her words laced with sympathy and compassion. "Sky—" She stopped and sighed as if she was hesitant to say it out loud as well. I started out the door, and she grabbed my arm. "Cole agreed to wait until after we find a way to reverse the curse. He's not unreasonable."

She seemed reluctant to say I should try to talk him out of it. Perhaps there was a rule about trying to discourage it, but I didn't care—I was about to break it. It was common knowledge that Ethan would be an Alpha in any other pack, but that didn't offer any comfort. He was going up against another Alpha, and I'd seen Cole fighting when we'd rescued Kelly. He was a terror, a skilled and merciless fighter. A dichotomy of the human mask he wore, and it was indeed a facade, concealing the ruthless warrior I'd seen. My mouth was dry, and controlling the panic was getting harder to deal with. Another issue compounded by the existing ones.

Kelly gave me the name of the hotel he was staying at; it was close to the city. I wondered if he'd chosen to move out or had been strongly urged to do so. Did he consider it in poor taste to stay here when everyone knew that he was out looking at property to move into?

CHAPTER 18

You need to make that choice. Ethan's last words to me at the pack's retreat stayed with me. I rolled over and pressed my face into him. When he'd shown up the night before, I should have sent him away. I'd wanted to, but I'd needed to sleep beside him.

I cuddled in next to him, my face resting against his bare chest. I kissed him, my tongue slipping out to taste him. Moving up, I rested my face in his neck, inhaling his masculine musk. I inhaled again, my teeth grazing over his skin. My tongue laved over him, tasting. He groaned, exposing his neck to me, and pulled me closer. I nibbled at first, then bit down. Hard. Drawing blood. He cursed and pushed me away. My gaze was fixed on his neck, the hunger throbbing in me, the enticing aroma of blood appealing to my palate. I moved in again, and he pushed me away harder. Rolling away, he ended up on his hands and knees, fixing me with a hard stare.

"I'm hungry," I admitted.

"Clearly," he said in a rough voice, studying my eyes. He eased away and headed for the bathroom and brushed his teeth and washed his face. He kept a watchful eye on me as he moved out of the bathroom and slipped out of the room. I screwed my eyes closed. *What the hell?* I was hungry, and Ethan smelled good in a way he normally didn't—appetizing. Maybe I had lost more blood than I'd thought when the bronze man cut me. I wanted that to be the case.

When I smelled fresh meat in the air, I inhaled, letting the scent of raw flesh wash over me. I went into the bathroom to brush my teeth. I didn't need to look in the mirror—the taste for blood was an indicator of what I would see: a terait, an orange ring around the pupils that vampires got when they were experiencing bloodlust. It was a constant reminder of how I had come into this world. It was never this bad. I wasn't sure that nearly raw meat would be enough.

Ethan slid the plate with two steaks that had barely touched heat, just a hint of brown and the rest red and succulent, in my direction the moment I entered the kitchen. He cut a piece and put it in my mouth. He cut another. I waited impatiently, fighting the urge to grab the entire steak and shove it in my mouth. His platinum eyes flattened with concern as he cut up several more pieces and kept them coming, faster. Sensing that it wasn't fast enough, he moved the plate closer to me and handed me the utensils.

I devoured the second steak, feeling sated. I looked up at Ethan, who was looking at me with apprehension. Kelly's words came back to haunt me, but I wasn't convinced my "delicious" was the same as hers. Each time I looked up from my plate, I found him staring at me—at the corners of my eyes. The terait was probably still there, because the hunger was.

"Have you ever tried to feed from someone?" he asked.

"Why would I? I'm not a vampire."

He moved closer and traced his finger over my lips and with a faint smile said, "You're not quite a wolf, either. Now are you?"

Hey, kettle, stop calling the pot out, why don't you?

"Neither are you," I pointed out.

He made a face. I thought it was at the comment until the doorbell rang and the brackets of his frown increased and steel gray flooded his eyes.

I opened the door to find Cole standing there with two cups of coffee, a smile flashing across his face as his silver eyes shone with amusement. "Things can get ugly if you don't have your coffee, right?"

"What are you doing here?" My tone was more cutting than I expected. I opened the door wider so he could see Ethan, but I had a strong inkling he didn't care. He hadn't become Alpha by not being strong, a good predator with heightened senses, so I was sure if he hadn't heard or smelled him, the sports car parked in my driveway had to be a giveaway.

The bristling coolness of contempt became palpable. I could feel Ethan's eyes on me. Cole glanced in Ethan's direction and then breezily disregarded him with a flit of his eyes as he redirected his attention to me.

I wished feelings were more amicable so that we could discuss the challenge. But once a challenge was issued, could things truly be cordial? I quickly dismissed the idea that anything other than poorly veiled discord was going to exist between them.

"Just checking on you. Your wound looked severe yesterday, but Kelly said you'd left. I wasn't sure if you were released or you went against medical advice. You didn't seem very concerned about it, but I think you should have been."

"I'm fine. Thank you."

"May I come in?"

I hesitated, and rightfully so—this could end very badly—and before I could decline, Ethan spoke. "Yeah, you can come in."

Cole walked in, then offered me one of the cups in his hands. "I didn't know exactly what you like, but I smelled peppermint in the coffee Josh brought for you, and white chocolate, so I took a guess. Peppermint white mocha, is that your drink?"

I nodded before taking it. He took a sip out of his. "I got regular chocolate, just in case."

He watched as I took a couple of sips and then turned in Ethan's direction. "Good morning, I didn't expect to see you here."

"Obviously." I didn't have to look back to see how hard Ethan's jaw was clenched or that he was barely keeping it together; it was in his sharp response. Cole simply smiled at that reply.

For a few moments there was just silence. Long, heavy, uncomfortable silence that I wanted to end. I felt the warmth of Ethan as he stepped closer to me. He wrapped his arms around me, pulling me back to him. I could feel the rigid muscles of his chest, tightly coiled, against my back. "Mine."

I knew I was supposed to be flattered, and that part of me that didn't think claiming people like property was egregious didn't mind, but that part of me that had a problem with a person planting a flag in me like they were claiming land had a hard time being so complimented. I ignored the latter person and leaned back into Ethan.

"Of course she's yours, pretty much like all the others." Then he turned to the door and before he exited said, "But if she really were yours, she would bear your mark—she doesn't. Why don't you go ahead and add the little disclaimer 'for now' and save her the trouble and heartache?"

Cole looked over his shoulder at me before closing the door behind him. Ethan's lips covered mine in a heated kiss, his tongue exploring mine with increasing intensity. He walked me back closer to the counter. Swiping his free hand across it, he knocked everything onto the floor. Then he cupped my butt and lifted me onto the counter. My shirt rode up as he nestled between my legs, and heat rushed through me as he pulled away enough to tug off my underwear and then his. He rested against me, seeking entrance. With a breathy mewl, I yielded to him. He was unbridled pleasure—intense, passionate, and overpowering.

His hips swiveled in a slow and persistent rhythm, his lips

dragging lightly over the skin of my neck. His tongue peeked out periodically to taste me. Arousal strummed through me, and I moved, meeting his thrusts with need. Commanding hands splayed over my thighs, his fingers curling into my skin, and the rhythm of his movements increased. He kissed me again, his emotions riding him hard as he crushed his lips against mine. My nails clawed into his back, and I tightened my legs around him, pulling him closer to me. His raw sexual energy dominated me as he thrust at a frenetic pace and dug his fingers roughly into my skin. We moved with carnal ferocity as we sought our pleasure. Then he relaxed into me, his face buried in the valley of my neck. He licked at the pulse there. Warmth blanketed over me as he secured me close to him, with a need to be enclosed within me. As his breathing slowed, his kisses became more languid. I could feel his apprehension as his lips slowly coursed down to my shoulder, and I hoped he could feel mine.

His teeth grazed against my skin. I tensed as he whispered, "Mine." His teeth pressed even harder. I swallowed, apprehension increasing. Marked—a bite from your mate that couldn't always be seen but was sensed by others, sealing the commitment to be mated. It seemed too soon, and there were still so many things about him that were unanswered. How could I do this with someone who had secrets he refused to disclose? It had only been a couple of weeks for us. It wasn't like I could wake up as if it was a drunken mistake and look at him and say, "My bad, let's get this annulled."

He pressed a little harder—controlled, tentative. Waiting for my consent. A long moment passed, and I couldn't bring myself to give it.

"Ethan," I said, softly.

"I know." Placing a delicate kiss along the area, he rested his head against my chest. I stroked his hair.

Things should have been better after sex. Eventually he moved away, his gaze vacant, his tone flat. "Is it Quell?"

I shook my head.

His voice tightened with disappointment. "Are you interested in Cole?"

I shook my head. "It's you. I don't want to do it because of you." The deep breath I took and held on to was supposed to be cleansing, but it made me feel light-headed. This was about to be one of those "talks" that ultimately ended with people going their separate ways. I watched him, waiting for him to say something, too afraid to be the one who spoke first and a little afraid of what would be said if I did.

He moved away from me, closer to the wall. At that moment I realized how fragile we were—our relationship was. But I bit the bullet and did it. "I've proven myself to be trustworthy. Everything there is to know about me, you know, and most of the time you know before I do. I've accepted that when it comes to you I will never have all of you, including the secrets you have. I've accepted it, but it doesn't mean I like it. And having what we have now is all I can take under those circumstances."

He nodded as he rested against the counter nearest to the door. Reading what he was thinking or ready to say was more difficult. His face was an emotionless slate and as stoic as usual.

He started slowly. "Have I not been forthcoming with you? I've made it clear that there are things that I can't tell you, nor will I. Things will not change because we are together. I'm sorry that they won't. It was a mistake for you to think that they would."

Ethan was right. I was fully aware that he had secrets, and he hadn't one time misrepresented himself. He'd said with an odd acceptance that he was a jackass, and he seemed to wear that title with a badge of honor. Of all the variations of gray that were seen in the pack and him, I'd expected some clarity. Perhaps it was naïve of me to think such a thing, but I figured it was subject to change based on our relationship. It hurt that it wasn't. There was the extent of our emotional intimacy, because this was all he was willing to give.

"You have to meet me halfway, Ethan, because I can't do this. It's not fair to me. Or us." I took another breath and let the words spill out quickly because I didn't want to lose the courage to say them. "You have to choose between your secrets and me. You can't have both."

He nodded, taking in my words. He considered them for a long time in tension-filled silence. He approached me, taking my face gently in his hands, but he remained deep in thought, and I figured he was trying to determine where to start. I imagined he had so many. But he didn't say anything more. His lips pressed into a tight line, as if words would escape if he relaxed them for a moment.

Then he kissed me, long and gently. He stopped, went into my bedroom, dressed, and was gone before I could say anything. I didn't know what it meant, although my gut or maybe my heart was telling me I wanted to ignore it. He'd made his choice, and it was the secrets.

I blinked them back, but a few tears streamed down my face.

That day, things went from bad to progressively worse. I stared at the e-mail from my employer. Or rather my ex-employer. My eyes skipped over all the niceties telling me how she'd enjoyed working with me, the BS about my exemplary job performance, and how she would be giving me a good recommendation. I just fixed on the part where she decided to put, if by some chance I hadn't gathered it already, that I was fired.

After Ethan left, I had a lazy day, periodically pulling out a book. I even attempted a few spells. I was distracted, and everything I did was poorly controlled. My magic was a mess and so was I.

Ethan's scent wafting throughout my house was usually comforting; now it just taunted me. Made me feel foolish for my decision and was a reminder of how fragile the seams of our relationship were. I got in my car and drove, speeding down the streets, barely aware of my environment. On autopilot, I figured I'd end up at Winter's home, but instead I pulled into Steven's driveway.

By the time I got to the door, it was open and I just walked in. Giving me one assessing look, he frowned. "Want to talk?"

"No." And I didn't. Not at that moment.

I knew eventually I was going to have to say something to Steven instead of just lying next to him, watching what might have been one of the worst movies we'd ever viewed. It's what we did, watching films that received horrible reviews on Rotten Tomatoes and spending the entire time mocking them. Cheap and lowbrow, but fun nevertheless. I smirked at some of his comments and even laughed at his jokes—empty, hollow, forced laughter. This had spiraled so far out of control that I just didn't know where to begin.

"I got fired today," I finally blurted out. I didn't know why I was surprised. I'd worked as a contractor for a healthcare auditor. It was a job that fit me perfectly. I went into the office occasionally for mandatory meetings. I wasn't in any hospital or facility longer than a week, which allowed me to interact with people, something that at one time I'd craved, but still gave me enough anonymity to maintain my privacy. One week wasn't enough time for most people to feel comfortable probing into my backstory.

Since the pack had come into my life, I'd started taking fewer assignments. After a written warning, I'd made an effort to take more jobs, but between dealing with pack issues and trying to stay alive, I'd missed a couple of assignments. Added to the list of things I needed to do, which included removing a curse that was going to kill most of the were-animals, was searching for a job.

"Is that what's really bothering you?" he asked suspiciously. It seemed like the one thing that I was okay with admitting. People understood being upset about a job, but I wasn't sure my situation with Ethan could be easily understood. I barely understood it, but a heavy weight had been on my chest since Ethan had walked out that morning.

"Yeah."

"You're just really not good at the lying thing at all." He pressed his forehead against mine. "So what are you really upset about?"

He listened as I told him everything, from the spell that went wrong to my magical travel to the past, which was a retelling of an apocalyptic world where were-animals were nothing more than monsters wreaking devastation. I even told him about Cole, his attempt to kiss me, and the exchange between him and Ethan that morning when he'd brought me coffee.

"I told you things were more serious than you wanted to accept with Ethan."

"Probably not anymore." Then I told him about me stopping Ethan from placing a mate marking on me.

When Steven's only response was "oh," I knew things were probably as bad as I suspected. A long, weighted silence followed.

He seemed to carefully choose each of his next words. "Did he tell you it was over?"

"He didn't say anything; he just left."

His full lips drew down into a frown. "Do you think Ethan has ever been rejected?"

Based on his personality, it wasn't unreasonable to believe that if there had been any rejections, they were very few. "Probably not."

"You rejected him as your mate. I can't imagine that feels good. But Ethan's never been one to mince words. If it's over, I don't think he would have a problem saying that. I'm not the one you should be discussing this with. Talk to him."

He was right, and yet it was the last thing I wanted to do. "And if I'm right?"

Ruefully, he cast his eyes down, as if afraid to see how his words would affect me. "Isn't it still better to know? I'm sure it's going to hurt, but not knowing seems to be doing a lot of damage, too," he offered softly.

When I left Steven's home, I had every intention of talking to Ethan when Josh called me to ask me to meet him at the retreat. I was relieved—I'd been given a reprieve from a conversation I needed to have but didn't want to.

CHAPTER 19

*E*than, Josh, and Sebastian were already in the library when I arrived. I busied myself with trying to look at the paper in Josh's hand, and each time my eyes drifted in Ethan's direction, I couldn't tell what he was thinking.

He greeted me, his tone emotionally detached, cool. I ached. It felt like a crushing indictment of where I'd thought our relationship was going. With effort I pulled my eyes from him and looked at Josh, who had a scowl firmly fixed on his face—one he usually reserved for his brother.

"You don't think there is any other way?" Sebastian asked, his face serious and tinged with harsh resignation.

"We've tried everything. We need to get the third book from Samuel." A task that wasn't going to be simple. When dealing with him, it never was.

"I've had someone go to the last three places where his whereabouts were known. He's gone deep into hiding." That was his M.O. He hid from the world, I suspected so that he could hold on to his tenet that magic was bad, all of it, and should be removed from the world. That staunch belief made it hard to see past the rhetoric and realize that there were so many nuances to magic.

He'd reduced his ideology to bare simplicities: magic bad, no magic good. Watching Josh's concerned face, I knew he had to be thinking along the same lines.

"Is there a location spell that we can try?" Sebastian asked.

"Not without his blood," Josh said.

"Senna, she might know," I offered. When doubtful eyes turned in my direction, I frowned at the idea that my younger cousin was consorting with the likes of Samuel. Being acquiescent wasn't in her nature, so I doubted if he could convince her to do anything she didn't want to do. She enjoyed magic, and no matter how attractive she found him, which had been apparent upon them meeting a couple of weeks ago, the fundamentalist wasn't going to convince her that a magicless utopia was the way to go.

"You think she will help?"

I wasn't sure, but of the two, convincing Senna to assist was going to be the easiest of our problems.

I stepped out, pulled out my phone, and called her. I'd saved Senna's life, and remuneration had been made by the pack for unceremoniously taking the Clostra when they'd rescued me from them; I hoped it was enough for all to be forgiven and to persuade her to help.

"Yeah." I could envision the youthful look of defiance that had probably overtaken her face.

"This is Sky."

"All phones have caller ID, I know who it is." *She's just a peach.* "What do you want?"

I guess we aren't going to have any pleasantries. "Do you have a way of getting in touch with Samuel?"

It took the constant skeptic a moment to even entertain the question. "Why?"

"I need him?"

"Is it about the Clostra?" I could imagine the sour look on her round face, which closely resembled mine, although Sebastian was convinced she was adopted. I didn't think so. There seemed to be something familial about her, but maybe I was convinced of this by my desire to have a link to someone else who could read the Clostra. To have that in common with at least one person in the world.

"Yes."

"He's not a library. You don't get to check it out whenever you need it."

I so don't need this.

Dealing with cantankerous, obstinate twenty-year-olds wasn't in my wheelhouse. "I know, but this is very important. Please know that if we need it, the situation is dire." My family had never wanted the books to cause harm, but they'd have taken the money they would have brought them if sold. I wasn't sure why people were willing to risk buying a book of dangerous spells if they didn't have the ability to use it.

"It's very important," I said, filling my voice with urgency. "If it wasn't important, I give you my word, I would not be calling you for this favor."

She sighed heavily. "I'll call you right back."

"Right back" was twenty minutes later. "He wants to know what you need it for."

I knew that was information I couldn't give him. Getting rid of the were-animals was part of his plan, or rather his desire to live in a world without the cursed existence of beasts who presented themselves to the world as men. He wanted the spell that he said was to put the beasts to rest, one that would take away our ability to shift. Sebastian and Ethan were convinced the spell he wanted to use was one to kill them. Either way, the "no magic" cheerleader wasn't likely to remove the veil of his fundamentalism to find sympathy for this situation.

"I need the books, Senna," I said in a stern voice. The moment I said it, I knew it wouldn't work.

"I don't mind helping you, but I'm pretty sure that's not going to work."

"Can you convince him to call me?"

"I'll see what I can do." The light arrogance and confidence of her tone made it apparent that she had a lot more control in regard to that than she was saying. She hung up without saying good-bye. *I swear, she's just sunshine and puppies.*

We waited. And waited even longer. For nearly two hours, we waited for Samuel to call. Sebastian lacked patience when he didn't have control of situations. Free-falling without a plan B and other contingencies obviously made him uncomfortable. We focused on the apex predator who stalked through the room, on a razor's edge. When he took a seat, it was for just a few minutes before he was up again, padding through the large space.

Samuel didn't call me, he called Sebastian.

"You are interested in a trade?" Samuel asked the moment he answered the phone.

"No. I need the third Clostra."

"For?"

"Pack business."

Samuel was silent for a long time as he always was with us. He despised were-animals and entered into agreements with us reluctantly. "Is it true that Marcia is dead and it was your doing?"

Technically, the Wicked Witch of the West was dead because of Josh and her own thirst for vengeance.

"Yes."

Once again, there was a long silence. "Will Josh be taking over as the head of the Creed?"

"No. But there is someone already in place." Sebastian looked as though he was making an attempt to anticipate where the questions were leading.

"The book is yours if I am given Marcia's position. It was rightfully mine before I was exiled, and I want what is mine."

Sebastian was capable of brokering a lot of deals, but getting the witches to sign off on putting the vigilante witch in a position of power was beyond even his control. He didn't even flinch at the request. "Done. Be here tomorrow with the Clostra."

Done? Is Sebastian a wizard? A hypnotist? How in the hell is this "done"?

"Sky, unless you have something you need to say, you might want to close your mouth." My mouth was open in shock, and I had plenty to say—it all started with "how the fuck?" That was all I had.

I looked around the room, waiting for others to show the same concern I had, but it was business as usual. I had seen Sebastian get many impossible things done, but asking the new leader of the Creed to step down so the Midwest Anti-Magic Witch could take her place wasn't just impossible, it was ridiculous.

"Thank you for your help," Sebastian said, and I assumed that was his way of asking us to leave and he couldn't do it like a normal person. Ethan and Josh took the cue, but I had more to say.

Resting back in his chair, he looked at me, the door, and back again. "May I help you with something?"

"How are you going to do this?"

His face didn't falter, unwarranted aplomb worn just as casually as before.

"I'm going to need you to trust me on this."

Trust was one thing—abandoning logic was another. Nothing about this seemed like it was going to work. I didn't care if I had to be the pack's skeptic.

He ushered a smile onto his lips before looking at the door again. "Please close the door behind you, Sky."

"Fine, I'll let you get to your wizardry." And that's what it had to be.

Ethan took me by the arm as soon as I was outside Sebastian's door and led me down the hall to another room. He closed the door and leaned against it. We stood as a protracted quiet consumed the room. What should have been a few seconds ended up being close to five minutes of silence that was meant to indemnify us against the inevitable—addressing the elephant in the room. The raw discord that existed, that didn't seem to have any means of being mended.

Ethan's proclivity for reticence made it inevitable that I was going to have to broach the subject first.

"I love you," Ethan blurted. I swallowed my words, rendered speechless as I just stared at him.

Although he had a wary confidence, when he said it again, it sounded penitent as he looked at me. He'd said it as if he needed to get used to the words. "I love you. It's not what I expected. Definitely not what I wanted, because it only serves to complicate things. But I needed you to know."

"What was your plan, to keep being a jackass until you, me, or both of us died?"

The pensive look on his face made it implicit that it was an option. A viable option. A preferred option. I brushed my hands gingerly over his cheek before I kissed him. I pulled away to look at him, resolved to show feelings he had a hard time expressing and an even harder time succumbing to.

Resting my lips against his, I teased, "Did you think the last part was romantic?"

He laughed.

I kissed him again. "I'm just saying, if you would have left the last part off, we would have had a very kickass moment the first time you confessed your love. Now I'm going to have to take creative license with the story and rework it and take all the 'I don't want to love you, Sky, you're a complicated mess. We are a complicated mess' stuff out. Or no one is going to dote over that story."

He leaned forward and pressed his lips to my forehead, pulling me to him. "You know what I want, but I won't press it. I'm content just being with you, okay?"

I nodded, embracing him tighter.

~

Josh sat at his spot at the desk, his feet kicked up on it, scanning over the translations we'd made for the Clostra when last we'd had all three books. He focused too hard on them, so I knew that there had to be something else going on. We'd gone through them so many times, I knew them by heart. I knew he did as well. Something else was bothering him, and I had a feeling it was the same thing I had been thinking about before Ethan's confession of his feelings not less than two hours earlier. Running his fingers through his hair, he shifted forward in his chair.

"You can stop debating whether to tell me, I already know." He fixed me with a hard stare. "About the challenge."

"He told you?"

"Of course not. Aligning with everything he does when it comes to me, I had to hear from someone else. Kelly told me. Apparently, everyone else was sworn to silence, because I'm a child that needs to be protected at all cost," he said caustically.

I remained quiet because there wasn't anything I could say to make it better. I'd tried to talk Ethan out of challenging Sebastian after he'd been injured and failed. I was doubtful I could do it when he himself was the one being challenged. A challenge to the death—at what point would it stop feeling needless and barbaric? I was pretty sure that wasn't going to happen anytime soon.

"There isn't any shame in choosing a fight to submission rather than death," I commented to myself. Josh had dealt with this longer than I had. Perhaps he'd found some rationale in it.

"To my brother there is." Josh shared my concern and burden. Talking about it didn't make things better, it just ignited a feeling of helplessness, and that wasn't what we needed right then.

Josh returned to looking at the notebook we'd used to translate the Clostra. Finally, in troubled resolve, he said, "If we use any spells from the Clostra for this, you'll have to be used as a conduit. Different than the other spells."

He looked over the notebook with the translations, flipped through a couple of pages, and then started scribbling things on a piece of paper beside him. I really hoped he wasn't trying to mix any of the spells from it together. I was reluctant to use it already. It was like dealing with a wish-granting genie—there were consequences to what you asked for. Not only did we have to deal with the potential consequences, we would have to deal with Samuel.

I shrugged with false bravado, because it wasn't going to help if he was worrying about me, too. We had to use it, and consequences be damned. We'd tried other things because the Clostra was a last-resort option. It was the carpet-bombing approach to magic.

"Do you really understand what it means for you to be a conduit?"

Of course I did, but I tried not to think of complications that could occur. The curse would still happen, but it would happen to me and me alone. Technically, because I existed because of Maya, not my were-animal half, I would be immune. Or so we hoped.

"How dangerous is it?" Ethan asked, walking into the room.

"Not as dangerous as a challenge to the death," Josh shot back, glaring at his brother. "Of all the times to do something so stupid —both of you. Your lives are on the line and you want to have a pissing contest. Good, I guess whoever survives the challenge gets to see if they survive the curse, too."

Ethan sighed his annoyance. "We've agreed to wait until after the curse is lifted."

"How admirable of you two. Good to know, at least you told me that. Why don't you tell me"—he glared and stood—"when exactly you planned on telling me about the challenge? While you were in the middle of the fucking death match?" Josh was yelling, something he didn't do often, and Ethan's dismissive look only fueled his rage, which he clearly didn't have a handle on.

"I didn't tell you because you tend to act like this when I do," Ethan said coolly.

If Josh were a were-animal, I would have expected to see his eyes shift to that of his animal, but instead we were treated to a blast of magic that rolled over us and felt like being near a squall. Both Ethan and I sucked in a sharp breath as it hit.

He tried to leave in silence, but wasn't able to without mumbling that his brother was an ass and some other choice words. When Ethan called his name, he didn't respond. Minutes later I heard the front door slam.

Ethan excused himself and left. I knew he was going after Josh. As much as they argued, they didn't do well with fighting for extended periods of time. Even if they had to punch it out, which happened more often than it should have between grown men, it seemed to end there without lingering animosity.

Counting on Kelly's assurance that Cole was a reasonable person, I visited his hotel. I was clearly not the type of person they catered to in the posh hotel, and since Cole seemed more comfortable in a pair of jeans than a suit, he didn't seem like the type who would feel comfortable there, either. I looked over the hotel before the concierge asked if she could assist me, and with a forced smile she gave my t-shirt and jeans a sweeping look. She delivered the same treatment to my hair, poorly tamed into a bun with masses of wavy locks sprouting from it. Taking the time to bring out my arsenal of straightening agents hadn't been a concern when I'd dressed.

I gave her Cole's name, and she called him to let him know he had a guest. Then she directed me to a sitting area, informing me that he would be down. After a long chunk of time, he came down, dressed in light gray slacks and a light gray shirt; he looked as silver as he had when I'd first met him. His eyes dazzled with amusement when he saw me. I saw him before my gaze landed on the person behind him—Ariel. She waved at me.

He shook her hand, as though it was a friendly business transaction. "I can't thank you enough for meeting with me, and I look forward to more productive meetings in the future."

It was quite apparent that he was laying the groundwork to be an intermediary between the witches and the packs. I remembered Claudia telling me that the strength of the Midwest Pack was that they worked together, whereas most packs destroyed themselves from within because the Alpha always needed to be aware that, if at any point he showed weakness, the Beta was there waiting in the midst, ready to challenge him and take his position. Daily I saw what Sebastian went through. How he had to deal with the fragility of the relationships we had with others, and how easily alliances could be broken or betrayed. I just couldn't figure out what was so broken in him that he would fight for the position.

"Sky, it's good to see you. I was just about to have dinner, will you join me?"

I was starving, but I didn't want to have dinner with him. This wasn't a casual meeting or a date. "I'm pressed for time."

"Of course. I'm starving, so you will have to take a moment for me to eat; you might as well join me. I'm more amicable on a full stomach." There wasn't any doubt that he knew why I was there to speak to him. He extended his hand for me to take; instead I stared at it. The amiable smile remained as he dropped his hand to his side, and I followed him to the hotel's restaurant.

Once we were seated, he ordered a bottle of wine, and when it came and he poured me a glass, I asked, "Are we celebrating something?" My attempt to be sweet and convivial was becoming harder by the second. His ruggedly handsome features were cloaked with the flagrant arrogance and confidence that Alphas possessed. It was their uniform, and there wasn't any mistaking it: I was sitting with the Alpha of the East Coast Pack.

"You tell me. You fixed Ethan, that should be something to celebrate. Or have you already grown tired of your role in his little performance and don't really care?" He took a sip from his glass and leaned in. "You deserve better, you know that?"

Armed with the knowledge of how Ethan really felt about me, I found Cole's attempts to cast doubt about us easier to dismiss. "You've been here all of six days, please don't assume you know anything about us."

"I've been the Alpha of the East as long as Ethan has been the Beta of the Midwest. I am very well aware of Ethan. I'll concede, though, perhaps I don't know. Tell me. Why are you with him?"

"That's none of your business. My biggest concern is why an Alpha would ever be content with taking an inferior role in our pack."

"As you've so astutely pointed out, I've been here six days. A good Alpha understands the dynamics in hours, not days. I don't think it's wise to assume the position of Beta of the Midwest Pack is an inferior role. It's a lateral move. I've seen why they have continued to be a force that's loathed and admired because of their power. I admire it and think I will fit in quite well, don't you?"

Chewing on my bottom lip, I realized that I didn't have an argument that was going to work. I tried it anyway. "If I were you, I'd be reluctant to bet my life on it."

"Well, I guess that is the difference between you and me. And you and Ethan. His arrogance and confidence would never allow you to be here on his behalf. So, I do suspect you are the one who's concerned, not him." He pushed the wineglass in my direction. I took a sip as he studied me, lingering too long over my lips. He moistened his before continuing. "No one's description of you really gave you justice. I'm surprised Ethan controlled himself this long. My understanding is that he usually doesn't possess such control." His easy, languid gaze roved over me several times. "You're not marked. His decision or yours?"

When he leaned into the table, eyes narrowed as he waited for my answer, I knew it would be an exercise in futility to be dishonest. "I didn't come here to discuss my relationship with you."

"Then, Skylar, why are you here?"

I paused, taking too long to choose my words, and he took the opportunity to add, "Ethan is charming, and I definitely see why women are quick to do whatever is necessary to be with him. But when I look at you, I see a woman who isn't as experienced as the other women who have been with him. He doesn't strike me as the type who wouldn't exploit it, and not necessarily out of cruelty but because he can. For whatever nebulous reason, he remains a mystery to me and I suspect to you as well."

Tune him out. I tried, but the confidence I had in Ethan and our relationship was waning. *Tune him out!*

"That's not important to me," I lied. But at this point I didn't care. "But it does seem to be important to you. You are willing to risk your life to find out, and I'm the one you consider naïve?"

Dark amusement coiled around his words as he spoke. "Here you are with me, making a very poor attempt to get me to change my mind. You care about him. It is unfortunate, because he's going to lose." He said it with a cool confidence that made goose bumps run up my arms at the thought. "It will hurt you, and Ethan knows that, yet not once did he consider giving up the position for you, or at least opting for a submission fight. I'm not sure if my ego is that big."

"Are you sure about that? You've been hitting on me since you arrived. You're not the type of man who seems to be easily accepting of rejection. Obviously you thought you had a chance. Should we discuss your ego again?" Indomitable personality, inflated ego, self-assurance, and even shades of arrogance were in the Alpha package and to expect otherwise was foolish. Cole wielded the arrogance like a weapon. His undeniable Alpha hubris could no longer be ignored no matter how much I tried.

With an easy smile he said, "Compromise is hard for Ethan, so he leaves that job for you. When there is a situation that requires concession, is it wrong for me to assume you are the one who does it? I'm getting to you, and I've known you just a matter of days. Are you sure that Ethan wouldn't know what strings to pull, what things to say to you, what displays of affection he must demonstrate to give you enough to feel confident?"

I wasn't sure if Cole was as manipulative as he was painting Ethan to be, but his words rang true, or at least they made me think about my relationship with Ethan. I cursed my meager experience with other men. Dating Ethan was like going from riding a well-trained pony at the fair to wrangling and mounting a free-roaming mustang. Cole had succeeded in making me feel that Ethan's declaration of his feelings was nothing more than a way to manipulate me and the situation.

He scrubbed his hand over the shadow of a beard on his face. He opened his mouth to speak again but took several moments before he spoke. When he did, his voice had dropped, low, silky, and inviting, making me aware of the room, the dimmed lights, and the candles on each table. Waitstaff dressed in pristine white shirts and black slacks spoke in whispers and seldom came to the table to keep from intruding on what I was sure they suspected was a dinner after which we both would end up in his room. There was a miscreant curve to his easy smile that made me think he suspected it, too.

"Do you find me interesting?" he finally asked.

"No."

"That's not the truth."

I remained quiet for a moment, and when I spoke, my intonation was chilled. "Yes, like most people, I find manipulative assholes pretty interesting because they are just one unrestrained act from being sociopaths. There is an odd curiosity in all of us that's drawn to that, not out of interest but solely out of inquisitiveness. I think you might be really close to that act. You're meeting with the new head of the witches as though you are already part of the pack. If by some fluke or accident you do win against Ethan, which is highly unlikely, what do you think happens next? Do you think I will forget him the moment his body is buried and that I come with the position of Beta?"

He chuckled. "From the moment we met, you've been curious. Even if it's born from inexperience, it is there. I see it and I suspect Ethan and others see it, too. I don't think you come with the position, nor would I even consider that an option. Upon his defeat, you will mourn him and your grief is expected. Eventually you'll see your relationship with Ethan as the dalliance that it is. It's trivial, maybe not to you, but to Ethan. I think what you feel for Ethan is real, but you have to question his intentions with you. It's hard to accept it, but if I see it, so does everyone else. You're his little trophy. The odd werewolf with the unique magical abilities that people find simultaneously disturbing and intriguing." His gaze drifted from mine to the window behind me in consideration. I wondered if it was a dubious attempt to get me to contemplate his words.

I knew he was planting the seed of doubt for his purposes, and I just wanted to rebuff him and tell him to go to hell, but most of the things he said were in my head. The seed had been planted long before Cole. He had just come along to water, cultivate, and nurture it to growth. And he was getting to me.

When his attention returned to me, I held his gaze. Kind, soft silver eyes reflected back at me, and I refused the solace they attempted to offer. I refused to be ushered into acceptance of this, coaxed into complacency. Or to be easily seduced by his spurious kindness and concern.

"I'm not as naïve as you would like to believe. You sat here and told me all the things that are wrong with me and Ethan, but obviously you see something in it, because you wouldn't be working so hard to plant the seed of doubt otherwise. Yes, if anything happens to him, I would undoubtedly mourn, and probably not just for a few days. Ethan's an ass, I knew it the first time I met him, but it didn't stop me from falling for him. Most of the pack pretty much feel the same way, but they trust him with their lives. They know in his hands, they're safe. If you think that because you win a fight you will gain their loyalty, you have deluded yourself."

The easy smile fell from his lips, his eyes narrowed, and the mask dropped as it always did, giving me a peek at the predator behind the placid, innocuous smile, gentle, breezy demeanor, and concerned visage.

"This meeting is over," I said as I stood. He got up to walk me out, but I stopped him. "Enjoy your dinner."

"Skylar." He called my name before I could make it to the door. Moving lissomely, he walked toward me, the wine still in his hand; surprisingly he hadn't spilled any from a glass that had been overfilled. The closer he got, the more aware I was of his presence and the confidence that I wished he lacked. Confidence wins fights and emboldens people to do the unachievable. There wasn't concern or fear about this challenge, nothing weighed on him, and I was envious. I wondered if Ethan, too, had the same feelings and Josh and I were the only ones carrying the burden of his impending death.

When Cole finally spoke after several moments of silence, he had a gentle, even tone. "I don't think you despise me as much as you want me to believe." He leaned in. "I'd never pursue an involved woman."

"But you are. That's exactly what you are doing."

He stepped closer, his voice a low whisper. "I guarantee, I'm not."

Then he turned and took a few steps. He stopped midstep and looked over his shoulder. "By your own admission, you didn't like

Ethan very much in the beginning, either, right? Right now you don't like me. I think eventually that, too, will change."

I didn't bother answering. I spun around and headed out the door.

Ethan was waiting in my living room by the time I got home. The drive from Cole's hotel hadn't improved my mood at all. I was divided over what irritated me the most: Cole, Cole's words, the fact that I was letting them bother me, or that maybe there was some truth to what he said, which was why twenty minutes later, I was still thinking about them.

"How did you get in here?" Weary from the many emotions I'd dealt with on the drive home, I sounded tired.

He stood and walked over to me, keys dangling from his fingers. "They're Steven's. It's really not appropriate for him to have a set."

"More rules to make you feel comfortable. It's funny how that works." *Damn.* I tried to shrug off everything that Cole had said, but it was hard.

He placed the keys on the counter. "If you want him to have it, so be it." He leaned in and inhaled. "You smell like Cole."

I couldn't smell anything other than my deodorant and shampoo. He stood back, arms crossed, and waited for me to speak, but I had nothing to say. The truth was probably just as bad as me blankly staring at him, but the latter probably would incite an argument. "Fine. Why do you smell like Cole?"

"Because I met with him earlier."

"About what?" Ethan and Sebastian didn't just want to call you out, they seemed to need an admittance of your transgression and for you to feel the guilt. Sadly, I didn't feel guilt or remorse.

His cool eyes stayed on me and commanded a response: the truth. When I didn't answer he asked the question again.

The longer he watched me with his cool ire, the more irritated

I became. I wasn't wrong, and I refused to be made out to be that way. "Of the two of you, I thought he was the more reasonable."

He let the silence continue until it became uncomfortable for me to bear, and I focused on other things around the room. Eventually I lifted my eyes to his.

"Continue," he said in a tepid voice.

"And he's just as confident and callous about his life." I pushed past him and took a seat on the sofa, shoving the ottoman in front of it out of the way. I moved it with such force it crashed into the wall behind. It surprised me, but not Ethan, cool and impassive. It took everything in me to control my emotions and not overreact. The prevailing uncomfortable silence was too much. "It's not just you anymore," I snapped.

He nodded slowly, taking in my words. "Were you unaware of my position in this pack? Did you think that I wouldn't ever get challenged?"

I could feel tears of anger brimming at the edges of my eyes and I blinked them back. I refused to give him that, no matter how much relief it would have given me. "I thought you would consider others. Me. You're not alone. The decisions you make affect other people, too."

"Sky." He sighed my name in exasperation. He paused, and when he continued, his tone was soft and somber. "No matter how much I want to, I can't prevent you from being affected by pack rules—"

"But it's not pack rules. There aren't any rules that say that a challenge is to the death. That's some arbitrary BS that you and Sebastian hold to just to up the ante to decrease the number of challenges." I referred to what he'd told me the first time we'd met. He'd said that if he didn't make it known that his challenges were to the death, every were-animal trying to make a name for himself would challenge him. But this wasn't some twerp trying to assert his dominance. This was an Alpha of another pack.

"Ethan, it's not the same."

"I do wish I could make this better for you, Sky."

"You condescending prick."

"Sky. *Desculpa por te ter magoado.*" I'm sorry you are hurt.

"*Tu tens o poder de o mudar.*" You have the power to change it.

He stared at me with a blank expression. He might have had the power to do so, but he wasn't interested in exerting it. The more time that passed, the more I knew that Ethan was unwilling to change the rules no matter how barbaric or cruel they appeared to be. He believed the rules were the foundation of a strong pack. It was a blind loyalty and acceptance that I just didn't have. I realized that this was Ethan. He hadn't changed from the first time I'd met him and probably wouldn't. It hurt.

"I don't understand you, Ethan. First you tell me you love me, but not enough to do this for me." *Dammit, I'm spouting the same thing Cole said.* It felt like a betrayal using his words against Ethan, but unfortunately it was how I felt.

"*Já terminaste?*" Are you finished?

I nodded.

Ethan remained quiet for an unusually long time. I wasn't sure if he was actually considering it or attempting to placate me and give me the impression that he was. He moved closer to me until he was within reach. His fingers brushed languidly along the curves of my jaw, to my chin, and then lightly swept over my lips. Then he kissed me gently. "I do love you. If you doubt it, please don't. My stance on the challenge has nothing to do with my feelings for you. I'm sorry you feel that it does. I don't respond to emotional blackmail. It is a tactic I discourage you from using again." He looked away from me. "Do you want me to leave?"

My answer didn't come immediately as I tried to process it all. I was feeling too many things, and sorting them out became so difficult that I just wanted silence, a break from it all, including Ethan.

I nodded.

Without saying another word, he left.

CHAPTER 20

The next day, at Ariel's request, Samuel, Ethan, Josh, Sebastian, and I were the only people in attendance at a meeting. The constant skeptic Samuel didn't have the Clostra with him when he met us at the witches' headquarters and made it very clear that he had no intention of relinquishing it until he had confirmation that Sebastian had brokered the deal. I didn't blame him—I was as doubtful as he was.

We walked into the witches' headquarters, and it looked like the new order had taken over and settled into their roles. No longer were there mirrors on the back wall; instead there was vellum paper with a pledge in Latin to honor their magic and do whatever necessary to protect those in their care. They'd kept the runes on the wall. The table was longer but simple, and to the side were other smaller tables. On the opposite side of the room were shelves filled with books. In another corner was a curio with a lock and sigils running down its dark wood.

As soon as we walked in, Ariel rose from the long table where she was sitting and approached us with the same confidence and ease that she'd had when I'd seen her at the hotel. When she greeted Sebastian with a warm smile, he returned it.

Ariel's genteel smile remained as she greeted Samuel. "I've heard wonderful things about you."

"Then you've been hanging around with liars."

Her light, melodious laughter filled the large room, ebullient enough to even coax a smile out of Samuel. "Well, Marcia hated you, so that means you can't be that bad."

He didn't respond; instead his suspicious gaze narrowed on her.

She continued. "Sebastian informed me of your wishes, and I understand that what happened to you was horrible. You are right, this position is rightfully yours. Unfortunately, you must understand that your reputation will not allow that to happen. The witches had been fractured for some time under Marcia's rule, and there needs to be a show of goodwill and faith. Putting you in any position of power will not do that."

"That was the agreement!" Samuel turned his ire on Sebastian. "You promised."

"I did no such thing. I said bring the book."

Ariel called his name in a soft, soothing timbre one might use when dealing with a fanatic on the edge, and Samuel was there. His unruly ochre hair was longer now and seemed at odds with his intense, sharp cognac-colored eyes. For a person who had magic in his quiver as a means to protect him, his slim build was noticeably lean and fit. Behind the scruffy beard was a faintly handsome man whose appearance was overshadowed by his crazy.

"I understand that was an agreement you feel he made with you; unfortunately, it is something that can't be done at the time. But your goal was to have access to the Aufero to return the magic to those it was taken from. That is something we will help you with. It will be a benevolent act that will improve your standing with others."

"That was something I was going to do anyway."

"Yes, months ago. I suspect that offer from Sebastian is no

longer available. Voided by your inactivity. Not his fault but yours."

Samuel's eyes were fiery, his face flushed with anger—intense accusatory glances of betrayal were shot in Sebastian's direction. "This meeting is over." He started to leave.

Ariel held up her hand to stop him. "That is my first offer to you. My second one is"—she waved her hand toward a corner, and a man came over: dark hair, simple rounded features, and penetrating dark brown eyes—"Eric." Samuel's face blanched, but I had no idea who Eric was.

Ariel paused, assessing the changes in Samuel's expression, which switched from anger to shock and then settled in the uncomfortable place of fear. "I thought you might know him. He rarely needs an introduction as one of the strongest faes on this side of the country. I think we know three or four stronger." Then she made a signal and the witches closed in. "There are eight of us and a fae who can make you tell us anything we want. I don't want to do that. It's distasteful to treat someone that way." She leaned in. "Let's be clear, I find it distasteful but not reprehensible. I will do it. Will my fae friend have to work his magic and make you give us the truth and reveal the whereabouts of the Clostra, or will you do it willingly?"

Samuel looked around the room, evaluating the situation, and for a few moments he thought before revealing the location.

Giving him a smile of appreciation, she directed him to the table, where she'd been seated. Her demeanor was ever so soft, and she wielded her power with a gentleness I had seen only from Claudia. "Please join us while Sebastian retrieves the book. We have things to discuss. I look forward to us working together." Her approach was definitely different than Marcia's, but would it be beneficial? Her invitation was nothing more than giving Sebastian an opportunity to confirm that the location was correct.

When Ariel called Sebastian before he could get out the door, her voice was still cloying, as was her smile. "When you have all

276

three, and you've used them for what you need, I do expect to have two of them given to the witches." Then she shot a look in Josh's direction. "And copies of any translations you may have."

Sebastian stopped. His smile faltered for just a moment, but it quickly reasserted itself, along with the charm that was very often hard to ignore. The cunning dance of the predator that he'd perfected and used often. "That wasn't discussed last night."

When she closed the distance between them, this no longer seemed like a business meeting at all. Now I felt like a voyeur watching two people getting ready to have pillow talk.

"Yes, dinner was nice, and you are ever the charmer. You have a mirror, I don't have to elaborate." She laughed. "I'm sure getting women to swoon over you is a tactic that probably has served you well in the past. I'm not one of them. It was quite an exercise in restraint for me to decline dessert." She stepped back and winked. "I'm not comfortable with you all having them. We split the difference in our favor. We're all friends here. If you need the third at some point, something can always be negotiated, but the Midwest Pack having access to the books and someone who can read and use the spells isn't something I'm comfortable with."

Sebastian's confident grin remained as he took a step closer. He looked her over, giving her a quick assessment before he spoke. "Ariel"—he made her name into a gentle melody—"you know we can be trusted. I can be trusted. These will remain with us."

The curve in her lips didn't shift completely into a smile; it showed more of a subtle challenge than amusement. "Of course, Sebastian, I do believe you can be trusted; however, I guarantee that you will do whatever is necessary to protect your pack. A quality I find admirable," she said as she played with magic, curling it around the tips of her fingers. Her magic could not only be felt, but seen, a smoky-colored ring spreading from her like wings, strong, dangerous magic that was prepared to do damage. Her face was still gentle, the tone of her voice soft, and her demeanor relaxed, which only confirmed why Marcia had wanted her dead. Her magic made Josh's seem like a minor-league performance that should be on a cruise ship. "It's not a matter of trust, but checks and balances. We all need them, which is why I increased the number of people on the Creed. I'm not above requiring checks and balances, either. Tre'ases are unrestricted; vampires are immune to daylight as well as holy water. I understand"—her gaze slipped in my direction and quickly returned to Sebastian—"it is your pack's doing. It's never a bad idea to get a second opinion. I think you can agree with it enough to know there doesn't need to be any more discussion about it."

She smiled and turned her back to him, then tossed a look over her shoulder. "Full disclosure, I was approached by a man who calls himself X this morning. For some reason he is seeking an alliance against your pack. His offer was tempting. If the books aren't returned to us, I don't think it will be a bad idea for me to meet with him again." She gave us a sweeping look. "I'm sure you all can see yourselves out." She spun on her heel and returned to her seat.

Sebastian's gaze, eyes narrowed, lingered on her, and his lips wavered between a smile and a smirk. An implicit appreciation of the tactics of a masterful and skilled opponent. While many people might have balked at the challenge, Sebastian openly welcomed it. She was a worthy opponent, a way to hone his skills.

Dexter was making an effort to form an alliance to seek revenge against the pack, Cole and Ethan were going to have a death match, we sort of had a tenebrous alliance with the witches who would have part of the Clostra, Ariel was decidedly stronger than Josh, and the vampires had been in hiding since they'd attacked me. As we walked deeper into the retreat's woodlands, these thoughts were pushed aside because I was trying to listen to concerned and emphatic brothers: the witch and the werewolf as they went off on the same topic again. And again. It was my fourth time hearing it.

"I know, under no circumstance do I stop the spell. Stay in the sacred circle, and start the spell the moment my blood hits the ground within the sacred circle . . ."

"Because?" Josh quizzed me.

"Santa will put me on the naughty list."

"Sky!" the brothers snapped simultaneously.

I rolled my eyes. "Because my flowing blood is what will be used for the transfer. Once the last drop is spilled, then the offer is sealed," I huffed out. I had gone over it so many times.

"No matter what happens, you can't stop. If you stop, what do you have to do?"

I sighed. "I must do the spell of purity, cleanse the area and myself, and start all over again."

Then Ethan said, "No matter what happens, you can't stop. Even if the world is crumbling around you, the circle is where you will be safe. Do the spell and we'll handle everything else. Okay?" He took my hand in his and looked at my palm and the healing wound from the first time we'd tried it in the house, when I'd stopped because the walls of the room had started to crumble. Watching walls come down and the ceiling cave in had been distracting. The trees outside the house hadn't fared too well, either—reduced to wood chips and scattered bark.

We had no choice but to find a secluded area with sparse trees and very few things that could be destroyed. I was glad we were outside. I had already done heavy damage to the gym and library. I was using magic so strong that it couldn't be contained in a room.

A large open field. The sun was starting to set, providing just streams of light to illuminate the area. Everyone moved out, and my gaze kept skipping over Cole. I wasn't sure why he was there.

Why most of them were there—there were over twenty-five were-animals.

I knelt, placed the knife to my right. *Damn, what I wouldn't do for a spell that only required a strand of hair, even a speck of blood, or a patch of dry, unusable skin.* Blood, a lot of my blood and in essence, Maya's blood, was needed. The Clostra felt heavy. In the past, it hadn't, but it wasn't just the weight of the book; it was the problems, the responsibility, and all the lives that were in my hands.

Ethan knelt down next to me. I was aware of everyone around us staring, but he didn't seem to care. He leaned in, speaking for my ears only. "Be careful."

I nodded and he kissed me gently on my forehead and then on the lips. I could feel his heart race and mine increased in response. Sorrow and desperation consumed the next kiss and he was reluctant to pull away. "Okay. Ready?" he asked.

I nodded. But he didn't move. "I have this," I said confidently. The false bravado hadn't convinced him, but we didn't have other options, so once again, we were doing a spell from the Clostra. I suspected that it would take days to reveal what else we'd done.

"Are you ready?" Josh asked. When I gave him the thumbs-up, he handed me another book and then swiped the knife across his hand and formed the small circle around me while chanting his invocation. His magic ensorcelled me like a gentle, breezy cocoon. The somnolent flow of it moved around me in a lazy beat, became calming, putting me in a tranquil state. The sounds of everyone around me were reduced to white noise. Soothing white noise. It was better being in the open. Here, it was just me, the earth, and my magic.

I rearranged the Clostra, moving them closer so that I could do the spell without any interruption. The book that Josh had given me held the Gem of Levage; I put it to the side so that I could access it. The irony of the situation didn't escape me. We were going to use the very object that had brought the pack into my life.

The vampires had intended to use the Gem of Levage to remove the curse that nullified their aversion to light and holy water, and the only sacrifice they'd needed had been my life. The pack had stepped in to protect me. However, eventually I was indeed the person who'd inadvertently given the vampires what they wanted, years later.

I opened the book to the crimson pages, took the knife and doused it with the liquid that Josh had made to slow my healing. It had been used on me by my cousin when they'd tried to exorcise Maya, and it didn't hurt any less when I did it to myself. I winced at the shooting pain as I sliced my palm—my hand felt like it had been set ablaze.

I let blood trickle onto the ground and started the invocation. Dark smoke swirled around me, engulfing the air and wrapping around the trees, darkening the area, and coolness drifted from the book. A powerful force pushed into the air, leveling the trees closest to us. Bark scattered, and chunks of it blasted in my direction. I shielded my face to protect it, and after the shower of wood stopped, the pages of the book that held the Gem of Levage froze over. When the ice quickly melted away, the Gem lay there on blank beige pages.

I kept saying the spell, and glanced over at Josh. He smiled. *Okay, that part worked. Now for the hard part.* I made another slice in my palm and poured more of the hellfire liquid over it. More blood streamed over my hand; I let it drop over each book of the Clostra. They absorbed it and the words brightened even more, ready to be used. My focus stayed on Josh.

The moment I said the first line from the spell in the Clostra, I could feel her awaken—as she'd used me to initiate the spell, I would use her to end it. I read the first page with ease, a rustling in me as she bucked at my control. I continued, vaguely aware of the changes in the air, different than before, magic similar to what we'd felt at the compound, weak magic that simply nipped at mine. I said the final words, lifted the book, and looked for the source of the unfamiliar magic while continuing the spell. In my peripheral vision, I saw Ethan moving over the area. He took a couple of steps and then was pushed back with a force that hit against my back.

"Keep reading," Josh ordered. I looked up periodically to see what was going on. Dexter was the first one I saw, coming out of a distant thicket. The only indicator that he was doing magic was his open hand and his face, which was flushed with anger. He wouldn't have been much of a threat alone, but with him were nearly twenty others. Diet-witches or not, twenty mages were going to be hard for Josh to contend with on his own. There wasn't significant change in the magic; whatever Dexter had was overshadowed by Josh's and my magic.

Ethan was hit with another weak thrust of magic from two different directions. To my right, Gavin, Steven, and Sebastian shifted, along with several other were-animals. Dexter moved back, allowing the others to continue the fight. Things seemed to settle. I was on the first page of the second book, I just needed to finish. More commotion broke out around me.

"Keep going," Ethan urged, but I heard fighting, aggressive fighting. I kept going until Steven's body crashed to the ground in front of me, nearly breaking the sacred circle. I glanced up—we were dealing with more than just the mages. Michaela and several of her vampires had joined in. *Damn.*

They couldn't break the circle, and I couldn't stop the invocation, but it was getting harder to concentrate. Then I heard a grunt of violence. Michaela headed for me, slamming into the ward erected by the circle. Josh winced, feeling the hit as intensely as if she'd crashed into him. Her fist bashed into the ward again, and Josh cringed but made no move toward her. She whipped around. I looked down at the words and continued reciting the spell. When I looked again, she was behind him and jerking his head to the side. I looked down and gathered more words to continue. Another glance up—Michaela was gone, blood trailed down Josh's neck, and Ethan stood next to him, looking at the puncture wound. I looked down at the words. Another glance— Josh seemed okay, but I didn't have enough time to truly study him.

I was behind a ward, I needed to do this. Refocusing, I blocked out the violence that stirred around me. Another vampire approached the circle. A lynx swiped him, his blood dampened the air, and the vamp fell. Just one more page. The wind whipped around me, and the temperature dropped again. My words were accentuated by frost. Last page. Magic was everywhere, blazing in me as someone fought to break the circle. Maya's rage against being an unwilling accomplice was railing against me. One more page. My lips were cold and my teeth chattered as I spoke.

A stygian gloom fell over the area; the light glow of the words was all I could see. The final words fell from me, and then there was nothing. I was enclosed in silence and magic. It was pleasant, easy, a welcomed relief from the chaos. Agony came at once as I absorbed the curse of a thousand deaths, like someone driving a dagger into me for each life I saved. Cringing at the pain, I looked down at my arm; blood streamed from it. My shirt was covered in it, sodden, matted to my skin. I keeled over, screaming in pain. Finally, it settled. I looked at my arm and my body—everything had faded away.

The darkness lifted and the area warmed to its normal temperature. I looked around, and everyone was on the ground. Dust from fallen vampires peppered the grass and lingered in the air, like pollution. Three mages had been injured and left behind. Josh, Steven, and Ethan looked over the area.

I looked for signs of life among the fallen—not one of them was moving.

"It didn't work," Steven said, wide-eyed, as he looked over the rows of unmoving bodies on the ground. Paralyzed by it, we stood waiting.

And we waited. It might have only been a few minutes, but it felt like hours. I ran over to the books and flipped frantically through the pages looking for something, anything, that would be of use. The words were a blur and nothing made sense. The Gem of Levage had returned to its home in the book. Defeated, I didn't know what to do. "Reverse it!" I yelled at Josh.

"I can't reverse it, Sky."

My pack lay on the ground, unmoving and not breathing. This was a mess. I'd screwed things up somehow and needed to fix it any way I could. Panicked and desperate, I did what most people would do: I searched for an answer and didn't care about the consequences. A possibility flashed—the *rever tempore*. I tried to push that option out of my head. With apprehension, Josh had taught me the forbidden spell that would reverse the last twenty-four hours. It was one of those "in case of emergency spells" for when you had nothing to lose. They were my pack, and seeing them die absolutely qualified as an emergency. I was willing to pay any price to save their lives.

I swiped the knife over my hand, blood eased from it, and I started the spell. The words spilled from my lips. I expected Josh to stop me, but he stepped back, his eyes sympathetic and full of understanding. I was confident that he would have done the same thing. I could feel Ethan's eyes on me, but I kept going with the spell. Conflict over whether to stop me or not was displayed on Ethan's face. His gaze swept over the area, looking over at the bodies of our lifeless pack. He looked away, a tacit acceptance of what I was doing. I squeezed my hand, let more blood fall, and continued. I felt the weight of performing such a dangerous spell. It felt like I was being drawn to the brink of despair. The sky darkened; sound crackled around me. Pressure built and magic wrapped around me like a cocoon. It tightened, restricting my breathing and movements, a warning of its severity and that it was verboten.

"Sky, stop!" Ethan ordered. *It's not the time for that, Ethan. No rules, we have to do this.*

I didn't stop.

"They're moving. . . . They're alive." I looked around. They were. I took a breath, and it felt like something I hadn't done in some time. Ethan was busy checking on everyone. Josh stayed rooted in his spot, and I wondered if he regretted showing me the spell.

Collective gasps for breath rang in the air. Winter was the first to sit up, and I exhaled the breath that I'd been holding. Then everyone started to rise, and I wondered if it was like this for all the were-animals across the world. One day they'd woken up with an indelible mark; some unfamiliar with the curse had sought answers. Days later they'd fallen upon death's sword for a few minutes. It had to be a truly terrifying experience.

"That was not cool," Winter said with a forced smile.

"What?" I asked.

"Wherever you sent us to vacation. That place and . . ." She let her words fade away; she would never admit to being scared. I tried to interpret their faces. Had they been taken to the very place I had been where I'd witnessed the world before we had been changed to what we were today? The shocked looks on their faces made me think so. They began to check themselves for the mark, which was gone from all of them.

I scanned the area. "Is Michaela dead?"

Disappointedly, Winter shook her head. "No, she left when she saw they weren't going to succeed. Leaving her own to die for her cause. She's becoming a pain that I'm really getting sick of having to deal with."

Don't worry, you won't have to for long.

CHAPTER 21

I figured the party would go on until early the next morning—impending death was a heavy burden to carry, and its erasure was worth celebrating. The moment I felt I wouldn't be missed, I slipped out of the house. Looking over at the sword next to me on the seat of my car, I found it pleasantly exhilarating to know that soon it would be slicing through Michaela. My phone rang. I didn't bother to answer it—no sense lying, and the truth was just going to lead to me arguing with or ignoring anyone who tried to talk me out of killing Michaela. She had done so many horrible things that she'd pushed me to the point that I didn't care about the consequences, but none of them could be worse than her vendetta to ally herself with anyone she could to hurt my pack.

Michaela and Demetrius didn't live together although they claimed to be eternally committed to each other. Their polyamorous relationship was something I didn't understand and didn't care to. I drove to the opulent house just a mile from the vampires' communal home. A large fence wrapped around the house but was there for aesthetics and not security. I drove up to the entrance, opened the slightly ajar heavy wrought-iron gate, and followed the black oleander that lined the walkway. How fitting that the Mistress of Death would have such flowers. The oversized Victorian had large, picturesque windows in the front that gave a glimpse of the lavishly expensive furniture that reflected the same arrogance that its owner possessed. Even the manicured lawn and the large trees' lush, willowy leaves that only allowed small streams of light in, leaving the pathway dark, seemed to reek of self-entitlement.

I gripped the sword tighter. Fueled more by anger than logic, I hadn't formulated a plan at all. "Kill Michaela"—that had been my goal from the moment I'd snatched up the sword out of my trunk. The fire of my anger burned so badly that I couldn't manage to subdue it. I was tired of her, annoyed that she did whatever she wanted without considering that she might be subjected to consequences. The otherworld tap-danced around her, forgave her for her indiscretions and terrible acts just to prevent a war with the vampires. She was an overindulged child who wasn't given any boundaries and seemed to be constantly pushing whatever arbitrary limits and lines in the sand that were drawn—for no other reason than that she could.

If she had succeeded, my whole pack would be dead. The more I thought about it, the more the fire blazed in me. Gentle breaths or retreats to my quiet place didn't help. I wanted Michaela dead and needed it as much as oxygen.

My knock at her door went unanswered. I pounded even harder. Peeking through the window, I looked for signs of activity since the lights were on. The vampires used to have thick room-darkening curtains in their homes. Thanks to us lifting their curse, "creature of the night" was now a misnomer, and they no longer needed them. Vampires could walk in the daylight now without consequences. They still could see exceptionally well in the dark, and their graceful strides and movements often made it seem like they floated on air rather than walked on land.

I turned the doorknob—it was locked, which was something I

didn't expect. They didn't usually do that. You wanted to come in their home uninvited, good luck leaving unscathed. I wondered if she was expecting me. Did she have the good sense to be afraid? Probably not. Her arrogance and narcissism would prevent such banal beliefs and feelings.

"The little pup has come to bark at me," taunted the wispy voice behind me. I whipped around to find Michaela just a few inches away. My heart pounded in my chest. She was a predator that moved in silence and was just within striking distance, and I hadn't seen her. A mocking smile slowly moved over her features as she released the arm of whatever "flavor of the month" she had chosen for the evening. I glanced at her new project, toy, victim— whatever he was. He reminded me of Demetrius—a human Demetrius. Instead of black opal eyes that often looked like ominous bottomless wells, these eyes were light brown and lively. He shared many of Demetrius's features, from the dusky olive skin and short dark hair to the tall, svelte physique. I wasn't glancing anymore but staring at Demetrius's human twin. Which only made the relationship between Master and Mistress of the Seethe seem more odd and complex. If Demetrius was what she wanted, why not just be with him?

"He should leave," I said in a low voice.

"Don't worry, I doubt he will be bothered by the Midwest Pack's little bitch yapping and biting at my ankles. Perhaps he will enjoy the performance as well."

"He's awfully young. Has he seen someone killed before? It might traumatize him." My voice was low and dark. His eyes widened as he looked at the sword that I held at my side. I could hear the upbeat of his pounding heart, and if I heard it, I knew she had as well. I noted as well the changes in his respiration and that his blinks per minute had increased from eight to twelve. *Oh, for heaven's sake, don't be a weird were-animal*, I scolded myself. *Damn you, Ethan! Damn you, pack! Now I have to sit at the freak table, too.*

Malice settled over my face. My jaws were clenched so tightly they were starting to ache. "If you want an audience for this—so be it." I raised the sword. She looked at it, her eyes trailing over the length of it before shifting her attention to me.

She turned to the Demetrius look-alike and kissed him lightly on the lips. "We will continue this later." But there wasn't going to be a later for her. As she dismissed me with a roll of her eyes and refocused her attention on her boy toy, I started to care a lot less about having an audience to watch her die.

Demetrius's human twin backed away slowly, and once he was several feet away, his pace quickened until he disappeared around the corner.

Michaela smiled, genteel and demure, one of her often-used weapons of deception. At the moment, she looked kind, unassuming, making it easy for some to forget she was absolutely ruthless. I didn't forget as I kept a careful eye on her as she slowly circled me. I had a sword; she had teeth, which she was quick and efficient at using. I watched her as she looked for vulnerabilities. I'd dealt with her kind—predators—those who knew how to fight and kill effectively and competently. I knew the look and prepared not to fall victim to it.

The delicate smile that overtook her face pulled her lips back enough to expose her teeth. "What is the pack's little bitch here to yap about now?" She closed the distance between us, unmoved by the change in my position to a defensive stance.

Arrogance in full bloom, she simply disregarded me with a roll of her eyes. "Go ahead and just yap away because you will not do anything. Might as well put your toy away, because you aren't going to use it."

I remained in the same position, refusing to satisfy her arrogance.

"Skylar, put it away." Her voice was cooler, angrier. "We can play this little game if you'd like, but I know you will not use that sword. If Sebastian is nothing else, he is strategic, and I think it is safe to say that you are, too. If you kill me there will be a war—my created will seek revenge, and they will get it. I can go out tonight and create thirty more of us. You and your little pack, maybe two, three. We require very little to survive; you'll have a success rate of seventy-five percent at best. Even Sebastian and Ethan have failed at changing someone into a were-animal. The question remains, do you want to take the risk?"

She was right, this would lead to a war. One that we might not win due to sheer numbers. From their initial transition, vampires possessed strength and speed and force to be reckoned with. But Michaela had nearly killed us, and I couldn't let that go unpunished. I kept an eye on her as she slowly circled around me, mirroring her movements. Finally, she stopped and smiled. "Go away." Then she started for her house.

"No." I wanted this to end. I wanted to display some form of diplomacy—if I killed Michaela things would get pretty bad. I realized that, but I knew that things wouldn't change with her. She'd made it her mission to make my life a living hell. I needed to try to change it. Could diplomacy work?

"Michaela, Quell is gone. If you want an apology, I freely give it. You're cruel unnecessarily. You've tried to harm my pack one time too many and I will not stand for it. Either we call a truce now, or . . ." The threat became clipped through my gritted teeth.

Her haughty smile taunted me. "Or nothing. He was mine, you took him. When I feel that you have sufficiently paid for that, I will stop. Until then, I will entertain myself with making your every waking moment a nightmare. You'll bark about it and even nip at my ankles as your kind often do. And that will be it."

Face-to-face, the cool air of her arrogance was the only thing between us. I kept my stance relaxed and prepared to gather the distance I needed to use my sword if necessary.

The night was crisp, gentle breezes of wind stroking against my skin, but it didn't help the anger that was starting to brew in me. I've had to play nice with the likes of her and worse, and my tolerance for it was a small tendril that was being stretched taut. Each day I wondered when it would just break.

Her chuckle floated through the air, soft and melodious at first but quickly devolving into something else. She turned her back to me, dismissing me as being inconsequential, as she headed to her house. Once on the stairs she said, "I've lived over a hundred years and I will live even more. I don't mind taking a few years out of it to make sure you are miserable—just because it entertains me. Run along and tell Sebastian to learn to control his little bi—"

The fragile thread of my controlled anger snapped. I cleared the distance in just a few steps, and the look on her face would forever be imprinted in my mind: the moment she realized she was going to die and that it would be at my hand. I struck, severing her head from her body. I leapt back, but blood and ashes coated the front of my shirt. For a few moments, I stared at the spot where Michaela had once stood and started to back away.

"We underestimated you for so long," Demetrius said softly from behind me. I spun around, assuming my defensive stance, sword angled and ready to strike the moment he was in reach. But he didn't attack; he stilled, carefully watching me, and then his eyes moved over to the spot where Michaela had once stood. They glinted with repressed rage. I remained tensed, in a guarded position.

"You will return Chris to me as repayment for this. If not, your life for hers." Before I could tell him where to go with his request, he was gone.

I started walking to the car, looking back at the spot where Michaela had once stood and would never stand again. My mind no longer clouded by anger, the full impact of what I'd done hit me hard. I waited for guilt and remorse to consume me; they didn't. They didn't surface once I saw Ethan leaning against my car, his platinum eyes holding steady on me. His indomitable presence was as overwhelming as usual. And as usual I didn't know what to expect when I approached. In silence, he moved closer to me, and his thumb swept over my face. When he pulled it back, it was red with Michaela's blood.

"Do you feel better now?" he asked quietly.

I didn't feel better, but I didn't feel bad. I should have felt bad, I knew I should. "I don't feel bad," I admitted.

"Okay."

He backed away and got in his car, and he followed me home.

CHAPTER 22

*T*he sangfroid with which a challenge was handled made it easy to forget that it was a battle between two people until one was beaten so badly he either conceded or, in Ethan and Cole's case, was dead. I was giving Sebastian the same disgusted look I had given Ethan when he'd told me the challenge was deferred until the East's Beta arrived, which he was scheduled to do tomorrow.

Sebastian was relaxed back in his chair, his face unassuming as he drummed his fingers lightly on the armrest.

He waited patiently for me to say something. After a long moment of consideration, I leaned against the door frame and asked, "So why does the Beta have to be here?"

His tone was even and impassive. "In case a transition happens."

"So that Cole can hand over his position to him, if he is the victor, or he can be promoted to Alpha if Cole dies?"

He inclined his head slightly into the nod. I frowned, wishing he'd show more emotion than professional stoicism. I needed him to be bothered by this and not handle it with the same cool indifference of someone changing staff at the local bakery. In fact, they might have shown more emotions about the change.

"Is this why you asked for a meeting?" he asked casually once I had settled in the chair in front of his large mahogany desk. I wasn't sure what he'd told the interior designer: "This is only business" chic or "talk and then get out" contemporary. On the large shelves were rows of books, most historical in subject matter. Then there was the large leather-bound Charter, the book with the history and rules of the were-animals. On a bottom shelf were first editions of poets and a few other books. Like the rest of the house, there were canvases of wildlife decorating the tan walls. The wolves in the pictures on each side of me were wild, baring their teeth and assuming an attack pose. In the corner was a table with a small waterfall that filled the room with the sound of trickling water. He probably wouldn't need the waterfall if the wolves in the picture were frolicking in a meadow as opposed to ready for an attack. Who could relax with those pictures? The Alpha wolf in front of me pretending to be gentle and innocuous wasn't helping.

"You know why I'm here, don't you?"

He nodded. "Sky, if there was anything I could do, I would."

"There is—you can make a rule against all fights to the death. Decree that all fights are to submission."

"Decree. I'm not a king, Sky. I don't have omnipotent power. There are rules, and without them, there will be anarchy, a decline in trust, and a breakdown in structure. Some unspoken rules are necessary. I stand by Ethan's belief as well. I don't do challenges to submission. If I felt I couldn't perform my job, I would step down. Until then, I know I can handle things, and if someone dares to challenge me, there are consequences. Joan has been challenged nine times since taking her position. She has now adopted the same rule. It gets tiring when every snot-nosed newbie who wants to make a name for himself asks for a challenge even if only to prove they can somewhat hold their own, or to say they landed a punch during it. No one does that with me."

"But Cole isn't some snot-nosed newbie trying to make a name for himself. He's an Alpha, and you've seen him fight." I tried to hold my voice level, but it was starting to shake. Cole was an animal, wild, aggressive, and ravaging like a multivortex tornado destroying everything in sight until his thirst for destruction and violence had been sated.

"I realize that."

I considered the situation. The strength of the pack was the most important thing to Sebastian, and I was pretty sure this was Ethan's position as well. Although he denied it, he had despotic power even if he used it sparingly.

"Cole is a viper waiting to strike. Are you sure you want him as your Beta? Claudia once said the strength of this pack is that, unlike the others, here the Beta isn't lying in wait for you to show a moment of weakness to issue a challenge. When you were hurt, Ethan thought long and hard before he considering challenging you. He declined because he felt you were still able to do your job. Are you sure that Cole would do that?"

Amusement curved his lips, and he evaluated me with interest. Approval placed a lively glow over his face. It was doubtful he didn't see what I was trying to do. "Then I would accept the challenge and it would determine if I am," he admitted confidently.

"He met with Ariel," I blurted.

He nodded in assent. "She told me this morning."

Now I was the observer. It was obvious he was attracted to her, because a woman with the power to rip out his innards with a wave of her hand seemed like someone he'd find interesting. It was a special type of abstruse attraction: often those who dominated found an allure in someone who wasn't easily subjugated. They became a worthy adversary, but in the end, it turned into a stalemate when one wasn't willing to take on the submissive role and concede when necessary. If he pursued anything with her, if nothing else, it would be interesting.

I was searching for more to offer despite knowing it was a fruitless endeavor. I wasn't ready to give up. Before I could continue my case, there was a knock on the door. Sebastian invited them in, and Steven entered.

He gave me a sympathetic half-grin, and it was obvious he knew why I was meeting with Sebastian. Then he directed his attention to our Alpha. "I checked out the new pack that moved in. There is something strange about them suddenly uprooting from the East to come here." He made a face as he was drawn into his thoughts. "They don't really seem concerned about money, which leads me to believe they were paid to come here. They left a larger pack, and there are only twelve of them."

"What do you think of them?"

"You were right to be concerned. Either they are here to start trouble, or they've been hired to."

Sebastian made an irritated sound. "Do they know we no longer allow smaller packs in the Midwest?"

Steven nodded. "Yes, and they don't seem to think the rules apply to them. I explained that was a rule that applied to all packs and gave them the option of disbanding and considering themselves lone wolves. They also know that if lone wolf is the route they choose, it can't be in name only—we would check."

Sebastian seemed impressed with Steven, as he always was. Coming into the pack at a young age after being changed, Steven had had Sebastian as his mentor, and we were constantly seeing the results of it. But Steven also had something that was the result of living with Joan. He'd acquired the delicate art of negotiation and handled distasteful things in the most palatable way. He was a skilled negotiator and his placid look and angelic features often belied his ability to be ruthless when necessary, which worked to his advantage. People wrongly—to their peril—underestimated him.

"What's the next step?" Steven asked.

"You've warned them. Follow up in a couple of days. If they are still a pack, give them the option to join this one or leave."

Steven nodded and started out the door, but before he could exit, Sebastian asked, "Do you know who hired them?"

"They weren't forthcoming, but I asked Dan, the new computer guy, and once he had their names, he was able to find out by getting into their accounts."

I'll just ignore that violation of federal law.

"Bolten Corporation gave them a very impressive check, close to seven figures, about a week ago. It's owned by Dexter Seagal," Steven said, and then he made an annoyed face similar to the one Sebastian had displayed at the mention of the name. Mr. Annoying X was quickly becoming a pain in the ass.

Sebastian started to stroke his chin, his brows drawing closer together and his lips twisting to the side, I suspected considering why Dexter was hiring were-animals and bringing them in. Was he trying to do his experiment again, or have them recruit?

He nodded, dismissing Steven.

As soon as Steven closed the door, I said, "You made it a rule that no other pack could live in the Midwest. Why can't you do the same with challenges?"

"Because it's not the same thing, and I'm sure you know that. You are testing things, Sky. I really do wish I could help you. Ethan can always step down—"

"You know he will never do that."

"Then you have your answer as to what will happen. Please close the door behind you."

I wasn't sure what I would do if Sebastian actually asked a person to leave. Maybe he would be treated to my happy dance.

"Is there more?" he asked when I didn't immediately exit. I hated the emerging hopelessness that I felt. As soon as I thought I had a handle on being in the pack, the ins and outs, the mercurial dynamics and myriad of rules, customs, and tenets, I was faced with something else that I had to deal with.

I stood slowly and had almost made it to the door when I turned and asked, "Do you think he's going to win?"

I appreciated that he considered the question for a long time, and when he spoke, his tone was so genial that it was as if he was easing me into bad news. "What do you need to hear?"

"The truth."

He nodded. "Usually, I'm good at determining who will lose. I've been surprised sometimes, maybe six percent of the times that I've been mediating them and . . . I honestly don't know." He wore the unease with a frown that fanned across his face. This might be harder than Sebastian would ever admit, and I doubted if I or anyone else would ever know.

I nodded because my mouth was too dry to speak. I'd gotten the truth, and it wasn't what I'd wanted or needed to hear.

I tossed and turned and couldn't believe that Ethan was sleeping so soundly next to me, as if tomorrow couldn't very well be his last day. Whatever had happened over the past days, and no matter how many times the pack had been there for me, today I despised them with all my heart. I hated the rules and the challenges and everyone's rigid adherence to them. I despised Ethan for his arrogance and pride and Cole for being just as unreasonable.

Settling closer to Ethan, I tried to put it all aside and adopt the same unwavering confidence he had. But at what point was confidence foolish? No one went into a challenge thinking they were going to lose, especially one that had such dire consequences. The harder I tried to avoid thinking about it, the more I thought about it. Images of Cole fighting dominated my mind. He was a skilled and vicious combatant, as was Ethan, and on any given day, a challenge between equally skilled fighters boiled down to who was having a good day.

"Sky." He pulled me closer, until there wasn't any space between us. Then he wrapped his arms around me. I tried not to, but the more I blinked the tears back the more they threatened to stream down my face.

He nudged me until I turned to look at him. His thumb ran over my cheek wiping the moisture away, and I kept blinking. "I'm never going to get used to this," I admitted.

"I don't get challenged a lot. I've had five, and one person stepped down when I challenged him." Ethan had challenged someone for the Beta position, but instead of accepting, that person had stepped down and transferred. He'd lived with anger for years and had betrayed the pack just to get back at Ethan.

Well, since only five people have tried to kill you for your position, maybe I should relax.

It only took five minutes for Ethan to find sleep again. I knew I wasn't going to sleep, so I got up and went to the living room, where I'd been for several minutes, trying to read a book I couldn't focus on.

"There isn't a way to counter a fae truth spell," Ethan said, coming out of the bedroom. He took a seat next to me, turned until his back was against the armrest, and then pulled me over until my back rested against his chest.

"It's not easy to fight it, but it can be done." His lips brushed against my ear as he spoke, his tone gentle and rhythmic. I closed my eyes and rested back against him as he continued. "It hurts like hell. Like a small explosion in your chest, acid on the skin. But it never lasts."

I wasn't sure why he was telling me this, but I listened. "If you clear your mind and only focus on what's happening, it makes it easier. No matter how strong they are, you can do it. I know you can do it. Don't even think about your animal half, it doesn't work. I tell you this from experience."

He paused for a long time. I stilled against him, listening to his heart and the ragged breaths that came from him. He wrapped his arms around me, holding me closer. It was the first time I seemed to have more control than he did. The rapid beats of his heart made mine increase, matching his. I touched his hand; he calmed and pulled me in even closer. "We should practice sometime. Perhaps Ariel can help."

Another long pause stretched for minutes. "You've been able to use the Clostra, not because of the magic you may have from your mother, but from Maya." He started slowly. "Some spells require stronger magic; the Vitae was one of them. We didn't have the convenience of asking another witch because they all knew of the curse placed on Josh. It would have made things simpler." He took a moment to gather his thoughts, and for once I didn't feel like he was doing it to get me to see the reality in which he wanted me to believe. It was the truth, probably spoken one other time, to Sebastian.

"My mother thought he was a powerful witch, one strong enough to use the Vitae to keep Josh alive. It wasn't until we used his magic that we knew differently. It was different than anything I'd felt, not like Josh's magic. Not like mine."

I knew that feeling, very well. I'd experienced it and had an intimate relationship with it, but Ethan wasn't like me when it came to mastering it.

I remained silent and his apprehension melted away. When he spoke again it was without hesitation. "Then we met you, and the first time I was around you, I felt the odd magic again. I'd known about spirit shades, but at the time it was a limited knowledge. I knew witches had usually done it as a way to obtain immortality."

I started to ask why they didn't just allow a vampire to turn them, but he was giving information freely, and I didn't want to interrupt. I assumed that if they were able to be changed and maintain their magical ability, Demetrius's seethe would be filled with them.

He paused again, pulling me even closer, holding me tighter as if he feared I would leave. "Finding the host of the spirit shade was easy. Switching hosts was harder because he was reluctant. You can imagine that the host didn't want to be divested of the power." He took another break, and my thoughts spiraled. How had they taken the shade from the host? Had they exorcised it? Or had they killed him?

I was sure he felt me tense, or perhaps he knew me so well he could imagine my thoughts. His dark chuckle lacked mirth. "He woke up, no longer a host. He was human; he couldn't even use his magic. I have no idea why he was so attached to the shade. But, I'm sure he's still trying to figure out what happened. But it needed to be done. I was going to do whatever was necessary to protect Josh. Then we met you and everyone predicted you would hurt the pack. I'd always figured it would be through me, or Josh. Your magic was so similar to what I had—I knew there was a connection."

"When did you find out the spirit shade was a Faerie?"

"When we first encountered the books I gave you. When Logan told me how they could be killed, Claudia and I had to find the Tre'ase who'd created him. We knew it would be too dangerous not to have him secured where no one could find him. Now the Tre'ase is secured and can never be found." His voice was tight and I knew there was more to the story—a lot more.

"Who are you hosting? Ravyn or Leonel?" I asked.

Again the room was plagued with silence. "The one that they all deemed too dangerous. Instead of killing him, they forced him to live hosted by a body he couldn't use. And that's why it is so important for it to never be known that I'm the host. Too many people want him dead, and the ones that don't will want the power he possesses."

Not overreacting to that information was hard. I'd skimmed the books and knew how horrible the Faeries were, and Ethan had the one that everyone else thought was too horrible to live.

I turned to him, cradling his face in my hands. A light smile feathered across his lips, removing the look of remorse.

"Thank you." I kissed him.

He returned it and then pulled away to look at me. His thumb stroked against my cheek. He kissed me again, first on the lips, then light kisses along my jaw. His lips drifted down lower along the curve of my neck. His teeth nipped at my skin, and I shivered at his touch, leaning into him more. Wanting more. Needing more. My fingers laced through his hair, drawing him closer to me. His teeth grazed against my skin. I shivered from his touch. I moaned as he traveled to my shoulder. Cool air mixed with the warm trails he left in his wake. More pressure against my skin, a gentle entreaty. He pulled away and looked at me. I nodded in assent.

His lips crushed against mine, his tongue explored my mouth, and his fingers moved along the curves of my body until he came to my underwear. One hard tug, and he'd yanked away the barrier between us. I slid onto him, yielding to his invasion. Relishing my erotic connection with him as he continued to kiss me, hungrier, quenching a need that only I could sate. I reveled in the feeling, the knowledge that it was something solely for me. As we moved in our passionate joining, my fingers pressed into his back, gripping tighter. It was as if we were ravishing each other, trying to satisfy a hunger that had erupted in us. Calm a fire that burned deep in us, ravaging our bodies. Kindling a lust that couldn't be easily satisfied. I thrust harder against him, seeking out pleasure.

His breath beat lightly against my lips before moving to my shoulder. The heat of his body ensorcelled me. I was drawn to it as the overwhelming desire to become one with it took me over. At the height of connection, the wave wasn't gentle but a strong, powerful, rampaging storm, and I desperately succumbed to it. Groaning as his teeth sank into my skin, he laved his tongue over the bite. Pain. Fire burned over it and slowly diminished into a comforting warmth. His lips covered mine.

I was his and he was mine.

~

I descended the stairs as Winter led me to a part of the house that I hadn't known existed. We walked past the game room, down a corridor where the halls narrowed; it was clearly an addition to the house that they hadn't bothered to invest a great deal of time or money in. We turned the corner, and I saw the area where challenges occurred. I supposed it wasn't good to have people fighting to death or even submission in the main house or outside.

When I walked through the door, I looked around the room, and the ranked members were there. My gaze roved slowly over their faces. I didn't see the thrill of the fight, the confidence in victory. I saw concern so deep they were unable to mask it. Fear reasserted itself and settled in my belly. I still couldn't believe it was happening.

Josh was sunk into the corner on the very opposite side of the room trying his hardest to keep whatever he was feeling from showing on his face. He was failing miserably. I could feel Cole's intense gaze on me but couldn't bring myself to look at him—instead I looked around the sparse room. It reminded me of the gym where Winter and I went to practice, particularly the section where we sparred, called the dungeon. A large room, plaster on the walls that hadn't been painted, and a concrete floor with stains on it where harsh chemicals had been used to clean even worse substances from it.

Sebastian approached Ethan with an iridium cuff, placing it on his ankle so that he couldn't use magic during the challenge. My heart dropped to my stomach. Even if he wanted to, using magic wasn't going to be an option. I didn't know it was considered cheating to use it when you were fighting for your life. Didn't you have the right to use everything you had at your disposal?

When Sebastian turned away from Ethan, his eyes landed on

me, his brows rose, and he glanced over at Ethan again. He leaned in and inhaled, his brow furrowed.

"Sky, you'll have to step out," he informed me gently.

"What? I'm not going anywhere."

"Mates aren't allowed to stay during a challenge."

What? How the hell did it get out so fast? I quickly remembered Cole noticing that I didn't have Ethan's mark. I looked back at Ethan and glared at him. He looked away, and I tried not to get my suspicions up, but the thought crossed my mind that he could have waited for us to be mated after. Instead, he chose to do it before. Was this the reason, so I would be forced out?

Sebastian inclined his head in the direction of the door. Did he think I was going to leave? I wasn't going to leave and didn't care about the rules.

Ethan just stared at me, waiting for me to leave. He was going to adhere to the rules like he always did. I was sure he was happy with that rule being in place. I narrowed my eyes on him and started toward him, ignoring Sebastian calling my name. Inches from him, I didn't want dramatic displays of emotions. He seemed so confident; I wanted desperately for me to have it as well.

"You have fifteen minutes and then I'm coming back in."

His lips kinked into a half-smile as he leaned in. "I only need ten."

Ethan looked in his brother's direction and then in Sebastian's. "Josh, too," he said. If looks could kill Ethan would have died a thousand deaths with just one of Josh's sharp glares. Josh's lips drew back into a snarl that would have made any were-animal proud, but he was more compliant than I was. I was still meandering, stupidly thinking they might not push the issue if it seemed too difficult of a task. But there weren't too many tasks they deemed too difficult to achieve.

"Is this your first time?" I asked Josh as the heavy metal door closed behind me. I leaned into it and tried to listen, but no sound came through it. Like so many of the rooms in the house, it was soundproof.

"No, but I always seem to end up on this side of it when it's Ethan."

As soon as ten minutes passed, I grabbed the handle and yanked at it, only to find that I was locked out. I started banging on the door, but I wondered if they could even hear me through its thickness. After a few minutes of drilling on it with my fists, I conceded.

Minutes later Cole walked out, his face covered in bruises and his lip split. His nose might have been broken—it had definitely taken some hits. He limped a little farther out, and the ache in my chest didn't stop. It pounded harder and the room started to spin. I heard Sebastian calling my name, but I couldn't respond or focus on it. His sharp growl as he called my name snapped me into a response. This felt wrong, surreal, and the anger hit me harder than anything I could imagine. I didn't know who to direct it toward. Sebastian, for not making it a submission fight. He could have done it. It was in his power. Josh, for not trying harder to talk Ethan out of it. Or Ethan, with his stupid, ridiculous, and insufferable arrogance, taking his position so seriously he compromised his life.

When I didn't move from the spot, Sebastian grabbed me by the arm and grumbled, "Come in." How cruel was this—how callous could one be about this death, my loss?

He pulled me in and I was ready to tell him and anyone who would listen what they could do with the pack and their ridiculous primitive, barbaric, and antiquated rules. I was leaving the pack. This wasn't the life or the world for me.

I closed my eyes for a moment, preparing for it. I just needed a moment, but I knew all the time in the world wasn't going to prepare me.

"Why are your eyes closed?" Ethan's voice asked. I looked around the room, which had blood splashed everywhere.

Ethan was stretched out on the floor, propped up on his elbows. Dr. Jeremy frowned at his ankle as he assessed it. Confused, I directed my attention to Sebastian for more information, but he was preoccupied with his conversation with Winter.

Okay . . . I figured the fight had been stopped, but looking at Ethan, I had no idea who had won.

I knelt next to him. "Did someone stop it?" I asked as I looked at his ankle, which was swollen and angled in an odd position. There wasn't any doubt: it was broken, badly.

"Ethan won, and Cole is in a little hiss. He decided to leave without me looking at his injuries. Pride." Jeremy cast a derisive look in the door's direction and then gave Ethan the same look. "The same pride that led him to continue when he shouldn't have." He gave Ethan a stern look. "This isn't going to heal right away, you know this?"

Ethan shrugged; it would heal.

"It was a submission fight?" I asked.

Ethan nodded.

"Why didn't you tell me?" I pushed the words through gritted teeth, trying to master my anger, but it was getting difficult. For thirty minutes, I'd stood on the other side of the door wondering, scared, when I had had nothing to worry about.

"I decided at the last minute," he admitted softly. "Actually during it, when I knew I was going to win." I smiled inwardly. He'd done it for me, but I had a feeling this was going to be on the short list of compromises he would make.

Dr. Jeremy wiggled in between us and grumbled, "All he had to do was win a damn fight. I have to come in and work a miracle and make his ankle new again."

Ethan smirked and gave me the look we all gave one another when Dr. Jeremy started with his "woe is me" speeches about how underappreciated he was and how excellence was always expected. We'd have to appease his ego and tell him how wonderful he was. It didn't take much, and it had become something we'd grown to expect.

I leaned in and affectionately nudged my nose against his cheek. "You're are the best, and if anyone can make him as good as new, it's you."

~

I didn't expect Cole to make a big issue out of leaving, but I definitely didn't expect him to leave in the middle of the night the day after the challenge. The bruises to his ego were just as bad as those to his body. He'd waited the day it took to heal but had refused to do it in the pack's infirmary. Instead Dr. Jeremy had done a hotel visit. While Ethan had a broken ankle, Cole had several minor breaks: ribs and nose, and small fractures to his cheek. Injuries that would have taken humans weeks to heal from.

Being mated made Ethan more acquiescent. By more acquiescent, he was less of an ass. Less of an ass meaning he continued to ignore most of the things I said, but at least he listened quietly while smirking. Which is what he did each time I reminded him he had to stay off his feet for three days.

On the morning after Cole left, Ethan limped into the kitchen. I looked at his ankle, which had started to swell more. "Most people would have pins in their ankle and not be able to walk on the foot at all and would be reduced to getting around using a leg scooter. Dr. Jeremy recommended three days. But if you are okay with dealing with him, good luck."

CHAPTER 23

Two days after the challenge, I slipped into the passenger side of Sebastian's car and glanced back at Josh, who had moved to the backseat. I tried to remain calm, but seeing Josh made the situation seem worse. Ariel wanted to meet with me, and I had a feeling it wasn't just to get to know the weird wolf with the magical ability. I was foolish to think I could start a spell like the rever tempore and it would go unnoticed. It wasn't the type of spell that could be done without consequences—major consequences. It often resulted in a punishment that made the person who'd performed it regret that they had done it and deterred others from even considering doing it.

"She just wants to talk," Sebastian asserted in a gentle voice. Of course she was going to say she just wanted to talk. She certainly couldn't expect Sebastian to bring me to a meeting with an agenda of inflicting merciless pain upon me. With Sebastian's calming reassurance, and Josh's relaxed state, I was able to let go of some of my apprehension. But there was still a remnant of it, an ever-present nagging feeling, a reminder of what I had done and that it had consequences. It was a repeating theme with magic —it had consequences.

"How is Ethan?" Josh asked. I figured it was a distraction. He knew how his brother was, he'd seen his behavior the day before. He was being Ethan—caustic, dogmatic, and stubborn. Dr. Jeremy had told him to stay off his ankle for a couple of days and it should be good in no time. Ethan cared to hear only the last part. For a person who was a stickler for pack rules, he had a rather casual relationship with medical ones.

"You know how he is. I guess he's decided he really doesn't need that leg, so he's going to go against all medical advice and do whatever the hell he wants. I guess he obtained a medical as well as a law degree," I retorted, having difficulty keeping the irritation out of my voice. Josh flashed me a grin. Why the hell was he so relaxed? I hoped he was high—that would explain why he wasn't overly concerned about this meeting with Ariel and the new Creed, or his brother, who was the most annoying patient ever. Maybe London had given him information that had reassured him.

The apprehension revved back up the moment we got out of the car and went into the metaphysical store, which was a front for the witches' headquarters. I meandered, looking at the various things on the shelves. Fidgeting with candles, perusing the small library of books of spells, and focusing on the alchemist's and Wiccan protection stones that were near the entrance. Even the woman at the counter seemed to be irritated that I was wasting time. I didn't recognize her as being one of the new members of the Creed.

After several more minutes of me meandering, we walked back into the main room. Ariel sat at a desk and smiled at our approach. First at Sebastian, and then she extended it in our direction.

"I'm so glad you agreed to this meeting. I will try not to take up much of your time."

Did we really have a choice? That request had subtle undertones of "if you don't comply, we will rain hell on your pack until you do." I had to give it to Ariel; she was working overtime to be the new, nonthreatening face of the Creed, which made me more concerned about the amount of power we were dealing with. Once we were directly in front of the usher, she stood and came around to the front of the desk, standing before us, relaxed and personable. When she spoke, her tone and genteel manner were obviously intended to make things seem less scary. I wasn't buying it.

I kept a cautious eye on the other witches, who came from the corner where they were working to take up positions on each side of her. "Witches were once considered the protectors of this world. Before the infighting, the power-lust, and Marcia's replacing the witches who wanted to maintain that role with sycophants who allowed her to abandon our values, we took pride in doing that job and doing it well. It's been so long since we've been held to that esteemed role. I would like to restore the witches to it."

She flashed a wry smile. "This"—she waved her hand toward the witches who surrounded her, and a breeze of magic hummed in the room—"was a long time in the making. When my mother was removed from the Creed and Marcia continued with her numerous attacks on me, I vowed to take over. It's fortuitous that things happened the way that they did." Her gaze shifted in Josh's direction and she gave him an appreciative smile. "We've worked behind the scenes, but we're no longer forced to do that."

London came to mind, how she had reluctantly assisted us and maintained her distance from the Creed—Marcia's regime. Josh and I looked in her direction.

Ariel continued. "Magic is powerful. I'd even go as far as to say sacred. And it hasn't been given the respect that it deserves." Her tone was still gentle but had become firm. "As I said, my goal is to succeed where Marcia failed. I am not driven by lust for power, but by the obligation to maintain the same path of those who came before me. Magic is a gift, and the significance of it needs to be appreciated. Not to exert force or to display power, but as a tribute to the great impact that it has. All magic has consequences, often so minor they are negligible and can be dismissed when magic has been used frivolously. I understand my role. I was born into it, burdened with the knowledge that I am strong and would be expected to lead—something that Marcia didn't want, but I accepted it as my calling—my obligation to the witches. In doing so, I will enforce regulations not because I am trying to show a display of power, but because it is right. As you uphold your pack rules, I uphold our laws. Although Marcia and the others upheld them at their discretion, I will not."

"I respect that," Sebastian offered, and I could tell he was getting impatient but was being his typical curt self. With anyone else, he would have quickly expressed his boredom and directed them to get to the point.

"I'm glad you do. Skylar almost performed the *rever tempore*, and the penalties for doing such a thing are severe. That is not acceptable. She doesn't respect magic. It's not her fault, but it is her burden." Then she directed her attention to me. "As a show of good faith, we require that you submit to *interdico*."

"That's as bad as her wearing an iridium brace. And the amount of magic required—"

"Yes, we are aware of the amount of magic we will be sacrificing to do this. You now understand the severity of this." She looked over at the new Creed; they stood from their desks in solidarity. A powerful display, and whether it was intentional or not, magic moved through the air, pricked at my skin before thrumming at me with a hint of force. "We will stand weakened, but you must understand how important this new order is to us."

"She made a mistake. Sky is mine to punish, not yours."

"She is *your* wolf, but magic is *our* responsibility."

Sebastian looked in my direction, waiting for my response,

which came quickly without hesitation. "I'm not going to agree to it," I asserted forcibly.

Magic feathered out behind Ariel, no longer a gentle wave but a violent sandstorm pounding against us. Sebastian hissed at the sharp pain. The door closed behind us. "I didn't ask for your consent. I simply informed you what will be done." Her voice was so cloying and sweet it was easy to dismiss her command. "Sebastian, my goal is to have a harmonious relationship with you. Don't let this be the incident that destroys it. I can assure you it will not end well for either one of us."

"She said no." Sebastian would stand his ground on principle, a display that we would not be controlled by the witches. But I wasn't ready to toss aside a potential alliance, an entente cordiale that we desperately needed. I would not be responsible for discord between us. But I wondered if it would even work. She was under the assumption that I possessed witch magic. Could Maya's magic be so easily contained? Part of me found comfort in the prospect that it could.

I nodded in assent.

Ariel kept a cautious eye on Josh and Sebastian as she made her way to a dark wooden cabinet. Sigils ran along the side and hints of magic radiated off it. She whispered an incantation and the doors opened, revealing a medium-sized box. She might have been kinder and less power-driven than Marcia, but I had the impression that she was far more cynical and cautious.

She pulled the box out, handling it with reverence as the others looked at it with the same respect. Sebastian and I looked to Josh for cues, but he didn't offer anything of use. Whetted curiosity caused his brow to furrow as he watched her carefully. He stepped closer when she pulled out a small glowing band. Magic more powerful and potent than I had felt on Josh or Ariel fanned over the room. I leaned in; the band had markings similar to those I'd seen on Logan. *What the hell did I agree to?*

"What's that?" Josh asked, stepping closer and inspecting it, and again his lust for magic was evident. It was neither natural nor dark magic, finding an idiosyncratic place between the two. Intrigued, Josh stepped even closer, looking mesmerized by it. I understood the allure of it, magic that was elusive and neither dark, natural, Faerie, fae, nor mage. It was magic that worked on a frequency that none of the other types did, which meant it was its own source. With a faint smile, she offered, "It's a Lar." The name alone evoked the same sense of reverence that the other witches displayed.

"You know what it is?" she asked.

He nodded. "You did the spell on Logan?"

"No, my mother and her contemporaries did. It uses the magic from us to create its own. But—"

She waved her hand over the room at the other seven witches. "It will take all of us to do one spell. Not one of us is strong enough to use a spell from it. It will not be able to be lifted without the Lar and enough magic."

"I don't think it is necessary. Sky won't do it again."

"Of course she won't, and we will make certain of it."

The other witches closed in, moving around me, until I was encircled by them and the overwhelming gust of magic that moved with them.

She picked up the ring and joined the others, completing the circle that formed around me. I tried to calm down, but magic was roaring in me. Burning, fighting to be released. Maya was railing against being subdued in any manner. Did I want something that could counter even Faerie magic on me? Ariel dropped the ring in front of me. I watched each of the witches take out a small knife and slash it over their palm, giving their blood sacrifice. They linked hands. I had agreed to it. Fear sparked in me, unnatural fear. It wasn't mine, but it drove me into fight mode nonetheless. *Protect or die trying.*

"Sky, are you okay?" Sebastian asked in a gentle voice. I wasn't.

I kept taking breaths to ease it, but I was too far gone. *Protect or die trying. Just survive this.* That's what happened.

Magic burst from me, sending Ariel crashing into the wall. Blustering flows of it came from me. I'd lost control of it and the storm that took over the room. *Protect or die trying.* But the impulse was no longer to save my life but to take the lives of those who were trying to do me harm. Logic had left, and I tried everything to rein it in. Maya was fighting for survival, and it felt like she was ready to leave a trail of bodies in her wake. I did the only thing I could to stop her. I dropped to my knees and forced a change.

The humbling pain tore through me as my clothes were ripped from my body. I gasped for a breath during that torturous moment when my bones broke. Ligaments stretched taut, organs shut down for moments to accommodate the transition, and my body gave way to its new form. My bloodcurdling screams rang through the room.

Sebastian's hands rested against my back, helping with the change. Maya was fighting tooth and nail to prevent it. Finally, in wolf form, I collapsed on the ground. Sweat matted my fur. Exhausted, I closed my eyes. The storm had stopped, and the pain subsided. The desire to destroy everything in sight lingered, but I was too exhausted to act on it.

"Give her a minute," Sebastian said, his tone low and soothing, but there was an undercurrent of anger. I wasn't sure who it was directed at.

After a few moments, the fatigue had lifted—the desire to protect myself hadn't. I rose, growling at Sebastian, who attempted to keep me on the ground.

"Sky"—he said, his voice latent with command—"stop."

Paranoia took over; if he wasn't going to protect me, he was against me. I lunged at him. He moved. His hands slammed into my side, and I soared back and crashed into one of the witches. I rolled to my feet and clamped down on her arm. She wailed, pounding her fist against me. A sharp pain hit me in my side. I whipped around, not caring to be gentle with the witch as I tore myself from her arm. I bared my teeth at the witch who had hit me, and jumped at her. Sebastian's solid-muscled form slammed into me midleap, and I crashed to the floor.

When I attempted to roll onto my legs, he held me down. "You all need to move fast. I am about to change her."

He pressed his hands against me as I clawed and bit at him. Soon, the inevitable prick of my body easing back into its human form came.

I lay on the floor naked. Words filled the air but became nothing but a string of rhythmic prose, a harmony that I allowed to overtake my thoughts. Warmth wrapped around me, and I opened my eyes only for a second as black marks appeared on my body. I only briefly wondered whether they would be permanent. I closed my eyes, caring far less than I should.

I awoke covered by a blanket. I sat up and looked over my naked body: my marks weren't like Logan's, but I had two small ones on the insides of my wrists, easily hidden, but marks none-theless. No matter how eloquently they'd said it, I had been cursed by the witches. Like Logan, forced to bear marks as some form of punishment. He was restricted from forming deals without the indebted party knowing; I was prohibited from doing magic.

I looked around the room. There were small pools and trails of blood. Papers littered the room, and several chairs were flipped over. I wondered if it was from me, the wolf revolt, or the curse that they had just cast.

"How do you feel?" Ariel asked. There was a lingering feeling of anger and hate, and I tried to subdue it. It wasn't warranted, I had agreed. I was going to need a moment to reconcile myself to it.

"Fine," I whispered.

She nodded. "I do appreciate your offering." It was said with such a level of sincerity it was difficult to be angry. Difficult . . .

not impossible—Maya held on to it for all that it was worth. Despite parts of me feeling a level of peace, there was that little part where Maya had taken up space that held on to the umbrage.

After several minutes, I stood. I made an attempt to catch the attention of the witch whom I'd bitten, but as she glared at me from across the room, it was obvious I wouldn't receive forgiveness from her anytime soon.

Dressed in the clothes that the witches had put on me and my shoes, the only things that had somewhat survived my transition, we headed out.

Before we could leave, Ariel called Josh's name. He stopped; his icy eyes didn't welcome her, and she approached him cautiously. She fished in her pocket and then extended an oddly shaped medallion similar to the one he'd tossed to the floor in front of Marcia. He looked at the silver peace offering and back at her. His gaze slowly swept over the room before he returned to looking at it. His gaze was steely and cold, but when he spoke, his tone was even and tepid. "I'm not ready to accept that. Respect and allegiance have to be earned. You've not done that yet."

Before he left, he took another look at London and they held each other's gaze for a long time; the weighted silence spoke louder than any words could. This was yet another thing that had strained their relationship.

We dropped Josh off first, and Sebastian immediately took me to a restaurant drive-through. I was starving, as was apparent when I started on the second burger mere seconds after I'd devoured the first. I'd attacked the food that Sebastian had handed me the moment we'd left the drive-through like a rabid animal. He'd ordered four burgers, a shake, and two large fries; I should have asked if he had ordered any for himself.

"Did you want one?" I asked, stuffing a handful of fries into my mouth and holding up one of the two burgers left.

He made a face. "No, thank you. I have a feeling if I reach for it, my hand might be in danger of being devoured."

"I'm hungry," I admitted, wiping crumbs from my lips.

"Wouldn't have guessed that by the way you accosted the burgers," he said as he handed me several napkins out of the glove compartment. I think he was more concerned about his shirt, which was covered in ketchup because I'd used it and his seats to wipe off my hands. Watching him wince each time my hands touched the soft leather, I couldn't help but smile. I thought he kept looking in my direction because of my appalling eating habits, but he seemed to be troubled for other reasons.

"I'm sorry," he finally said after several long moments of quiet, which seemed to work between us. Sebastian and I had a unique silence. Not comfortable but not uncomfortable. A neutral lull.

"For what?"

"I feel like I didn't protect you."

"From what, me making a big mistake that deserved to be addressed? I screwed up, you weren't going to be able to get me out of that without consequences."

He inhaled a ragged breath, and I knew that it came from a place where he lived—a person who protected his pack, consequences be damned.

I looked at him for a long time, trying to find the right words when it was obvious that the truth would suffice. "I'm kind of happy to have this." I looked at the markings on my wrist and felt a sense of relief. "I like magic, but it's hard to control. Each day I live with the struggle of controlling Maya. I'm sure it would get easier, but honestly, there is some comfort in knowing I don't have to. No apologies needed."

A small, relieved smile feathered along his lips.

"And I won't be angry if you continue to pursue Ariel, I definitely see why."

"It's business."

"Yeah, Ethan gives me that 'business' look all the time, too. Usually while he's disrobing me," I teased.

Sebastian still had a smile on his face when he pulled up to my home; I'd been sure it would have dropped from fatigue by now. His smile muscles had never been used that long. But his scorn, scowl, frown, and grimace muscles were probably made of steel by now.

Before I got out, he said, "Sky Brooks you are . . ." He smiled, lost for words. I just leaned in to let him pet me on the head, I figured that was going to be our thing. He grinned and placed his hand lightly on my head before removing it.

I walked into the house, and Ethan was sitting on the sofa waiting for me, a small plaintive smile on his face. I took a seat next to him, and for a long moment, he didn't say anything, just sat, allowing the things we wanted to say to go unspoken. When we finally looked at each other, I knew my face reflected the same expression as his: the cruel irony of things. I no longer had access to magic because I'd attempted to do the rever tempore, Josh was sentenced to death because of it, and Ethan hosted a dangerous and reviled spirit shade because of it. He traced his fingers along my marks before he kissed them with admiration and sorrow. He understood that I wore the marks of doing whatever was necessary to save the pack.

CHAPTER 24

he next evening, I decided I needed a reprieve from thinking about what had happened to me with the witches, the challenge, Michaela's death, and even Ethan, who was consistently disobeying Dr. Jeremy's orders. When I came out of the bedroom, it was one of the few times Ethan was adhering to medical advice and staying off the ankle. He was seated on the sofa with his legs elevated. He gave me a look—my hair was pulled back into a straight ponytail, and I wore a fitted lilac shirt, jeans, and short heels.

"You're going out with Steven?" He raised a brow. I knew he wasn't jealous of Steven, but I usually didn't put a lot of effort into dressing up when he and I went out.

I made a face. "And David." Although David was too polite to make disparaging comments, he was a man who considered cashmere, linen, and button-down shirts casual wear. I didn't want to spend the evening with him telling me which of my outfits he liked, a roundabout critique of the one that I actually was wearing.

Driving to Steven's home with David next to me made me realize how much I needed both him and Steven. Despite everything David had been through, he was still himself. Human, normal, refined normalcy, something I desperately needed. Steven knew how to shut off the pack and conform to it. I was looking forward to a night without magic, shifting animals, vampires, and chaos.

"I see that our tasty boyfriend has moved in. I want your life," David said. He held on to the comment as long as he could, and I watched the struggle. Ethan unfortunately lived a clothing-optional lifestyle, and David had seen more of him than any neighbor should have.

I laughed. "You can have it. And the way I feel about 'the boyfriend,' you can have him, too."

"Are you two having spats already? He is an intense one, isn't he? But damn." He made a overexaggerted gesticulation that reminded me of a swoon executed by an actress in an old movie.

"Oh stop. Trent's the best," I said.

"He is indeed. But our lovely Dark Swan has taken to showing him how to fight vampires. I suspect he will be quitting his job soon and assuming his position as Buffy the Vampire Slayer." He rolled his eyes, but he wasn't fooling me. If Winter was teaching Trent how to protect himself and them, it was a good thing. It lifted a burden off me.

"How long will we have guards? I think we are going to die of liver damage before another vampire attack."

"I already told you, there is no way you are going to be able to hold your own drinking with us. Stop it, because I'm not sharing my liver with you," I teased.

"Can that be done?" He seemed genuinely curious, and I didn't answer. After what had happened with Dexter, I really hoped not. I wouldn't put it past him to create were-animals for parts and black-market organ trafficking.

I shrugged and pushed the thought out of my mind. I planned to drink and be merry with the two best people to do it with.

"I get to see where you tucked away the old boyfriend."

"Once again, he wasn't my boyfriend. He was my housemate."

He made a face. "You have limitless control, cupcake."

Of course. Because we can't have one night without me being a sweet carbohydrate.

"So, Ethan has moved in?"

"No, he's just staying with me until his ankle heals."

"How did he hurt his ankle?"

A million excuses went through my mind. The guilt that I had about plunging David into a world where he didn't belong still bothered me, and I knew he worked effortlessly to try not to behave like it was disturbing to him. I wasn't about to tell him we periodically had death matches to determine rank. "He broke it."

Surprise. "Really? I thought you all were indestructible."

"We break just like everyone else, but we heal faster."

As I turned down Steven's street, I tried to get past a crowd of cars that had stopped or pulled over to look at something. A knot of people had gathered around Steven's home. The flashing lights of four police cars lit up the street. A sharp breath caught in my throat and my heart raced erratically. Had something happened to Steven? I stopped the car and jumped out with David right behind me.

Most of his neighbors were out being smartphone journalists as they filmed Steven walking out of the house, his head down, his hands held up in surrender. He dropped to his knees. The police descended on him, uniformed in body armor with their guns trained on him. The cameras flashed, and the neighbors whispered in ardent fascination as the officers cuffed him and pulled him to his feet. Frightened olive-green eyes found mine amid the crowd. With his hair short again and the beard removed, he looked younger than his twenty-one years, docile and innocuous.

The news cameras arrived in time to record the solemn Steven as a police officer put him in the back of a patrol car. The cherubic face and supple ruby lips automatically tugged at your instincts that he was innocent of whatever he was accused of. If he was playing it up for the cameras, then he was winning, because he looked out of place shackled in handcuffs. The various looks on his neighbors' faces supported my thoughts. Their concerned stares were directed at him—an assumption that he was a victim of circumstance or wrongly accused.

"What happened?" I asked a neighbor.

She shrugged. "I don't know, we just saw a bunch of police cars driving down our street and were surprised they stopped here. He's so nice. I can't imagine he'd done anything that would warrant this." Her hand swept over the spectacle. I wanted to believe that.

I backed away toward my car, keeping an eye on the patrol car as it drove away. Once I was in my car, I saw a familiar face several feet away. Dexter. He turned, making sure I got a good look at him, then he smiled, nodding his head in my direction. He dropped into his car.

David scrolled through his phone.

"I wonder what happened?" I said out loud to myself.

"This," he said, and he turned his phone to me. There was a video of Steven in front of four men that I didn't recognize. He was talking but kept his eyes on the one who was creeping to the side. One of the men took a swing at Steven. He blocked it, returned it, and spun around in time to block the other. The third guy took an elbow to his throat. He dropped down to the ground. To a casual observer, it looked like a man heaving for a breath, but he was actually readying himself to change into his animal form. Steven lunged, kicking him over, slinking around him until he had him in a hold. A rough jerk and a were-animal with a human head was twisted to the side.

I closed my eyes for a moment, imagining other people seeing this without knowing anything about us, the pack, and the dynamics. It was hard to look at the rest of the fight, but it ended with two deceased bodies and one severely injured and looking off to the side. The camera footage faded to black for a moment, and then the final shot was of Steven standing over what looked like a big dog but I was sure with closer examination one could make out either a coyote or a small wolf. The video faded to black again, cutting off the part where the animal shifted back to human form, which happened to were-animals upon death.

My phone buzzed; I picked it up to hear Ethan. He sounded the way I felt. "We are about to be outed," he said.

MESSAGE TO THE READER

∼

Thank you for choosing *Moon Cursed* from the many titles available to you. My goal is to create an engaging world, compelling characters, and an interesting experience for you. I hope I've accomplished that. Reviews are very important to authors and help other readers discover our books. Please take a moment to leave a review. I'd love to know your thoughts about the book.

For notifications about new releases, *exclusive* contests and giveaways, and cover reveals, please sign up for my newsletter at www.mckenziehunter.com

www.McKenzieHunter.com
MckenzieHunter@MckenzieHunter.com

Made in the USA
Middletown, DE
12 August 2018